"*Facing the Music* might not be easy, but it's great reading."

—Bob Moyer

"Larry Brown has an unerring comic sense, a sensitive ear for talk, an unsentimental commitment to his characters and, above all, the intimate, ruthless loving connections with the world he writes about that is the hallmark of a good and honest writer." —Ellen Douglas

"Larry Brown has the ear, the eye, and the hand. The fellow can write a blue streak. He doesn't write characters, he writes live people, and he knows things about them you didn't think would get found out until Judgment Day." —Jack Butler

"Brown, along with other minimalist masters like Ernest Hemingway, Joan Didion, and Raymond Carver, uses the discipline as it was intended to be used: to treat raw, powerful emotions without resorting to melodrama." —Joyce Slater, *Cleveland Plain-Dealer*

"What makes these stories exceptional is Brown's flair for the nuances of brutality." —Barry Walters, *Village Voice*

"Larry Brown is a choir of Southern voices, all by himself. . . . In both the experimental and straightforward pieces, Brown can conjure up a character with a single down-home image or put the reader right smack inside a place with a word."

—Jay Jennings, *Dallas Morning News*

"It's hard to put a finger on what makes these stories so good, not merely gritty or bleak. Often it's that the narrators are, though down and out, surprisingly powerful and sympathetic people."

—Miriam Marty Clark, *St. Louis Post Dispatch*

". . . what makes *Facing the Music* so interesting is the arc between Brown's sometimes funny, always cool narrative and the stories' explosive action." —Melinda Ruley, *The Independent*

"There are small, private moments here which Brown dissects with the precision of a neurosurgeon, peeling back layers to expose the heart of darkness within. The humor is grounded in tragedy, the tragedy often a perverse heroism." —William Starr, *The State*

"Brown's characters struggle; they are often abused by their time, place and situation. There is an element in them, however, their common problems and uncommon fortitude, that makes it essential their stories be heard." —Dan Ahlport, *Greensboro News & Record*

FACING TH

E MUSIC

STORIES

BY

Larry Brown

PERENNIAL LIBRARY

HARPER & ROW, PUBLISHERS, New York
Grand Rapids, Philadelphia, St. Louis, San Francisco
London, Singapore, Sydney, Tokyo

for Mary Annie

Several stories in this book have appeared previously: "Boy and Dog" in *Fiction International*; "Facing the Music" and "The Rich" in *Mississippi Review*; "Kubuku Rides (This Is It)" in *The Greensboro Review*; "Samaritans" in *St. Andrews Review*.

A hardcover edition of this book was published in 1988 by Algonquin Books of Chapel Hill. It is here reprinted by arrangement with Algonquin Books of Chapel Hill.

First PERENNIAL LIBRARY edition published 1989.

Library of Congress Cataloging-in-Publication Data

Brown, Larry, 1951 July 9–
    Facing the music: stories/by Larry Brown.—1st Perennial library ed.
      p.   cm.
    Reprint. Originally published: Chapel Hill, N.C.: Algonquin Books, 1988.
    ISBN 0-06-097255-6
    I. Title.
PS3552.R6927F3   1989
813′.54—dc20
                                          89-45120

93 94 95 96 97 RRD 10 9 8 7 6 5 4 3 2

CONTENTS

FACING THE MUSIC

For Richard Howorth

I cut my eyes sideways because I know what's coming. "You want the light off, honey?" she says. Very quietly.

I can see as well with it as without it. It's an old movie I'm watching, Ray Milland in *The Lost Weekend*. This character he's playing, this guy will do anything to get a drink. He'd sell children, probably, to get a drink. That's the kind of person Ray's playing.

Sometimes I have trouble resting at night, so I watch the movies until I get sleepy. They show them—all-night movies—on these stations from Memphis and Tupelo. There are probably a lot of people like me, unable to sleep, lying around watching them with me. I've got remote control so I can turn it on or off and change channels. She's stirring around the bedroom, doing things, doing something—I don't know what. She has to stay busy. Our children moved away and we don't have any pets.

We used to have a dog, a little brown one, but I accidentally killed it. Backed over its head with the station wagon one morning. She used to feed it in the kitchen, right after she came home from the hospital. But I told her, no more. It hurts too much to lose one.

"It doesn't matter," I say, finally, which is not what I'm thinking.

"That's Ray Milland," she says. "Wasn't he young then." Wistful like.

So he was. I was too once. So was she. So was everybody. But this movie is forty years old.

"You going to finish watching this?" she says. She sits on the bed right beside me. I'm propped up on the TV pillow. It's blue corduroy and I got it for Christmas last year. She said I was spending so much time in the bed, I might as well be comfortable. She also said it could be used for other things, too. I said what things?

I don't know why I have to be so mean to her, like it's her fault. She asks me if I want some more ice. I'm drinking whiskey. She knows it helps me. I'm not so much of a bastard that I don't know she loves me.

Actually, it's worse than that. I don't mean anything against God by saying this, but sometimes I think she worships me.

"I'm okay," I say. Ray has his booze hanging out the window on a string—hiding it from these booze-thieves he's trying to get away from—and before long he'll have to face the music. Ray can never find a good place to hide his booze. He gets so drunk he can't remember where he hid it when he sobers up.

Later on, he's going to try to write a novel, pecking the title and his name out with two fingers. But he's going to have a hard time. Ray is crazy about that booze, and doesn't even know how to type.

She may start rubbing on me. That's what I have to watch out for. That's what she does. She gets in bed with me when I'm watching a movie and she starts rubbing on me. I can't stand it. I especially can't stand for the light to be on when she does it. If the light's on when she does it, she winds up crying in the bathroom. That's the kind of husband I am.

But everything's okay, so far. She's not rubbing on me yet. I go ahead and mix myself another drink. I've got a whole bottle beside the bed. We had our Christmas party at the fire station the other night and everybody got a fifth. My wife didn't attend. She said every person in there would look at her. I told her they wouldn't, but I didn't argue much. I was on duty anyway and couldn't drink anything. All I could do was eat my steak and look around, go get another cup of coffee.

"I could do something for you," she says. She's teasing but she means it. I have to smile. One of those frozen ones. I feel like shooting both of us because she's fixed her hair up nice and she's got on a new nightgown.

"I could turn the lamp off," she says.

I have to be very careful. If I say the wrong thing, she'll take it the wrong way. She'll wind up crying in the bathroom if I say the wrong thing. I don't know what to say. Ray's just met this good-looking chick—Jane Wyman?—and I know he's going to steal a lady's purse later on; I don't want to miss it.

I could do the things Ray Milland is doing in this movie and worse. Boy. Could I. But she's right over here beside my face wanting an answer. Now. She's smiling at me. She's licking her lips. I don't want to give in. Giving in leads to other things, other givings.

I have to say something. But I don't say anything.

She gets up and goes back over to her dressing table. She picks up her brush. I can hear her raking and tearing it through her hair. It sounds like she's ripping it out by the roots. I have to stay here and listen to it. I can understand why people jump off bridges.

"You want a drink?" I say. "I can mix you up a little bourbon and Coke."

"I've got some," she says, and she lifts her can to show me. Diet Coke. At least a six-pack a day. The refrigerator's crammed full of them. I can hardly get to my beer for them. I think they're only one calorie or something. She thinks she's fat and that's the reason I don't pay enough attention to her, but it isn't.

She's been hurt. I know she has. You can lie around the house all your life and think you're safe. But you're not. Something from outside or inside can reach out and get you. You can get sick and have to go to the hospital. Some nut could walk into the station one night and kill us all in our beds. You can read about things like that in the paper any morning you want to. I try not to think about it. I just do my job and then come home and try to stay in the house with her. But sometimes I can't.

Last week, I was in this bar in town. I'd gone down there with some of these boys we're breaking in, rookies. Just young boys, nineteen or twenty. They'd passed probation and wanted to celebrate, so a few of us older guys went with them. We drank a few pitchers and listened to the band. It was a pretty good band. They did a lot of Willie and Waylon stuff. I'm thinking about all this while she's getting up and moving around the room, looking out the windows.

I don't go looking for things—I don't—but later on, well, there was this woman in there. Not a young woman. Younger than me. About forty. She was sitting by herself. I was in no hurry to go home. All the boys had gone, Bradshaw, too. I was the only one of the group left. So I said what the hell. I went up to the bar and bought two drinks and carried them over to her table. I sat down with them and I smiled at her. And she smiled back. In an hour we were over at her house.

I don't know why I did it. I'd never done anything like that before. She had some money. You could tell it from her house and things. I was a little drunk, but I know that's no excuse. She took me into her bedroom and she put a record on, some nice slow orchestra or something. I was lying on the bed the whole time, knowing my wife was at home waiting up on me. This woman stood up in the middle of the room and started turning. She had her arms over her head. She had white hair piled up high. When she took off her jacket, I could tell she had something nice underneath. She took off her shirt, and her breasts were like something you'd see in a movie, deep long things you might only glimpse in a swimming suit. Before I knew it, she was on the bed with me, putting one of them in my mouth.

"You sure you don't want a drink?" I say.

"I want you," she says, and I don't know what to say. She's not looking at me. She's looking out the window. Ray's coming out of the bathroom now with the lady's purse under his arm. But I know they're all going to be waiting for him, the whole club. I know what he's going to feel. Everybody's going to be looking at him.

When this woman got on top of me, the only thing I could think was: God.

"What are we going to do?" my wife says.

"Nothing," I say. But I don't know what I'm saying. I've got these big soft nipples in my mouth and I can't think of anything else. I'm trying to remember exactly how it was.

I thought I'd be different somehow, changed. I thought she'd know what I'd done just by looking at me. But she didn't. She didn't even notice.

I look at her and her shoulders are jerking under the little green gown. I'm always making her cry and I don't mean to. Here's the kind of bastard I am: my wife's crying because she wants me, and I'm lying here watching Ray Milland, and drinking whiskey, and thinking about putting another woman's breasts in my mouth. She was on top of me and they were hanging right over my face. It was so wonderful, but now it seems so awful I can hardly stand to think about it.

"I understand how you feel," she says. "But how do you think I feel?"

She's not talking to me; she's talking to the window and Ray is staggering down the street in the hot sunshine, looking for a pawnshop so he can hock the typewriter he was going to use to write his novel.

A commercial comes on, a man selling dog food. I can't just sit here and not say anything. I have to say something. But, God, it hurts to.

"I know," I say. It's almost the same as saying nothing. It doesn't mean anything.

We've been married for twenty-three years.

"You don't know," she says. "You don't know the things that go through my mind."

I know what she's going to say. I know the things going through her mind. She's seeing me on top of her with her legs over my shoulders, her legs locked around my back. But she won't take her gown off anymore. She'll just push it up. She never takes her gown off, doesn't want me to see. I know what will happen. I can't do anything about it. Before long she'll be over here rubbing on me, and if I don't start, she'll stop and wind up crying in the bathroom.

"Why don't you have a drink?" I say. I wish she'd have a drink. Or go to sleep. Or just watch the movie with me. Why can't she just watch the movie with me?

"I should have just died," she says. "Then you could have gotten you somebody else."

I guess maybe she means somebody like the friendly woman with the nice house and the nice nipples.

I don't know. I can't find a comfortable place for my neck.

"You shouldn't say that."

"Well it's true. I'm not a whole woman anymore. I'm just a burden on you."

"You're not."

"Well you don't want me since the operation."

She's always saying that. She wants me to admit it. And I don't want to lie anymore, I don't want to spare her feelings anymore, I want her to know I've got feelings too and it's hurt me almost as bad as it has her. But that's not what I say. I can't say that.

"I do want you," I say. I have to say it. She makes me say it.

"Then prove it," she says. She comes close to the bed and she leans over me. She's painted her brows with black stuff and her face is made up to where I can hardly believe it.

"You've got too much makeup on," I whisper.

She leaves. She's in the bathroom scrubbing. I can hear the water running. Ray's got the blind staggers. Everybody's hiding his whiskey from him and he can't get a drink. He's got it bad. He's on his way to the nuthouse.

Don't feel like a lone ranger, Ray.

The water stops running. She cuts the light off in there and then she steps out. I don't look around. I'm watching a hardware store commercial. Hammers and Skilsaws are on the wall. They always have this pretty girl with large breasts selling their hardware. The big special this week is garden hose. You can buy a hundred feet, she says, for less than four dollars.

The TV is just a dim gray spot between my socks. She's getting on the bed, setting one knee down and pulling up the hem of her gown. She can't wait. I'm thinking of it again, how the woman's breasts looked, how she looked in her shirt before she took it off, how I could tell she had something nice underneath, and how wonderful it was to be drunk in that moment when I knew what she was going to do.

It's time now. She's touching me. Her hands are moving, sliding all over me. Everywhere. Ray is typing with two fingers somewhere, just the title and his name. I can hear the pecking of his keys. That old boy, he's trying to do what he knows he should. He has responsibilities to people who love him and need him; he can't let them down. But he's scared to death. He doesn't know where to start.

"You going to keep watching this?" she says, but dreamy-like, kissing me, as if she doesn't care one way or the other.

I don't say anything when I cut the TV off. I can't speak. I'm thinking of how it was on our honeymoon, in that little room at Hattiesburg, when she bent her arms behind her back and slumped her shoulders forward, how the cups loosened and fell as the straps slid off her arms. I'm thinking that your first love is your best love, that you'll never find any better. The way she did it was like she was saying, here I am, I'm all yours, all of me, forever. Nothing's changed. She turns the light off, and we reach to find each other in the darkness like people who are blind.

KUBUKU RIDES

(This Is It)

Angel hear the back door slam. It Alan, in from work. She start to hide the glass and then she don't hide the glass, he got a nose like a bloodhound and gonna smell it anyway, so she just keep sitting on the couch. She gonna act like nothing happening, like everything cool. Little boy in the yard playing, he don't know nothing. He think Mama in here watching Andy Griffith. Cooking supper. She better now anyway. Just wine, beer, no whiskey, no vodka. No gin. She getting well, she gonna make it. He have to be patient with her. She trying. He no rose garden himself anyway.

She start to get up and then she don't, it better if she stay down like nothing going on. She nervous, though. She know he looking, trying to catch her messing up. He watch her like a hawk, like somebody with eyes in the back of they head. He don't miss much. He come into the room and he see her. She smile, try to, but it wrong, she know it wrong, she guilty. He see it. He been out loading lumber or something all day long, he tired and ready for supper. But ain't no supper yet. She know all this and ain't said nothing. She scared to speak because she so guilty. But she mad over having to *feel* guilty, because some of this guilt *his* fault. Not all his fault. But some of it. Maybe half. Maybe less. This thing been going on a while. This thing nothing new.

"Hey honey," she say.

"I done unloaded two tons of two-by-fours today," he say.

"You poor baby," she say. "Come on and have a little drink with Mama." That the wrong thing to say.

"What?" he say. "You drinkin again? I done told you and told you and told you."

"It's just wine," she say.

"Well woman how many you done had?"

"This just my first one," she say, but she lying. She done had five and ain't even took nothing out the deep freeze. Wind up having a turkey pot pie or something. Something don't nobody want. She can't cook while she trying to figure out what to do. Don't know what to do. Ain't gonna drink nothing at all when she get up. Worries all day about drinking, then in the evening she done worried so much over *not* drinking she starts *in* drinking. She in one of them vicious circles. She done even thought about doing away with herself, but she hate to leave her husband and her little boy alone in the world. Probably mess her little boy up for the rest of his life. She don't want to die anyway. Angel ain't but about thirty years old. She still good-looking, too. And love her husband like God love Jesus. Ain't no answer, that's it.

"Where that bottle?" he say.

Now she gonna act like she don't know what he talking about. "What bottle?" she say.

"Hell, woman. Bottle you drinkin from. What you mean what bottle?"

She scared now, frightened of his wrath. He don't usually go off. But he go off on her drinking in a minute. He put up with anything but her drinking.

"It's in the fridge," she say.

He run in there. She hear him open the door. He going to bust it in a million pieces. She get up and go after him, wobbly. She grabbing for doors and stuff, trying to get in there. He done took her money away, she can't have no more. He don't let her write no checks. He holding the bottle up where she can see it good. The contents of that bottle done trashed.

He say, "First glass my ass."

"Oh, Alan," she say. "That a old bottle."

"Old bottle? That what you say, old bottle?"

"I found it," she say.

"Lyin!" he say.

She shake her head no no no no no. She wanting that last drink because everything else hid.

"What you mean goin out buying some more?" he say. He got veins standing up in his neck. He mad, he madder than she ever seen him.

"Oh, Alan, please," she say. She hate herself begging like

this. She ready to get down on her knees if she have to, though.

"I found it," she say.

"You been to the liquor store. Come on, now," he say. "You been to the liquor store, ain't you?"

Angel start to say something, start to scream something, but she see Randy come in from the front yard. He stop behind his daddy. Mama fixing to get down in the floor for that bottle. Daddy yelling stuff. Ain't no good time to come in. He eight year old but he know what going on. He tiptoe back out.

"Don't pour it out," she say. "Just let me finish it and I'll quit. Start supper," she say.

"Lie to me," he say. "Lie to me and take money and promise. How many times you promised?"

She go to him. He put the bottle behind his back, saying, "Don't, now, baby." He moaning, like.

"Alan *please*," she say. She put one arm around his waist and try for that bottle. He stronger than her. It ain't fair! They stumble around in the kitchen. She trying for the bottle, he heading for the sink, she trying to get it. Done done this before. Ain't no fun no more.

He say, "I done told you what I'm goin to do."

She say, "Just let me finish it, Alan. Don't make me beg," she say. Ain't no way she hold him, he too strong. Lift weights three days a week. Runs. Got muscles like concrete. Know how to box but don't never hit her. She done hit him plenty with her little drunk fists, ain't hurt him, though. He turn away and start taking the cap off the bottle. She grab for it. She got both hands on it. He trying to pull it away. She panting. He pulling the bottle away, down in the sink so he can pour it out. They going to break it. Somebody going to get cut. May be him, may be her. Don't matter who. They tugging, back and forth, up and down. Ain't nobody in they right mind.

"Let go!" she say. She know Randy hearing it. He done run away once. Ain't enough for her. Ought to be but ain't.

He jerk it away and it hit the side of the sink and break. Blood gushing out of his hand. Mixing with the wine. Blood and wine all over the sink. Don't look good. Look bad. Look like maybe somebody have to kill theirself before it all get over with. Can't keep on like this. Done gone on too long.

"Godomightydamn," he say. Done sliced his hand wide open. It bad, she don't know how bad. Angel don't want to see. She run back to the living room for the rest of that glass. She don't drink it, he'll get it. She grab it. Pour it down. Two inches of wine. Then it all gone. She throw the glass into the mirror and everything break. Alan yell something in the kitchen and she run back in there and look. He got a bloody towel wrap around his hand. Done unloaded two tons of wood today and hospital bill gonna be more than he made. Won't take fifteen minutes. Emergency room robbery take longer than plain robbery but don't require no gun.

He shout, "This is it!" He crying and he don't cry. "Can't stand it! Sick of it!"

She sick too. He won't leave her alone. He love her. He done cut his hand wide open because of this love. He crying, little boy terrified. He run off again, somebody liable to snatch him up and they never see him again. Ought to be enough but ain't. Ain't never enough.

She flashing back now. She done had a wreck a few weeks ago. She done went out with some friends of hern, Betty and Glynnis and Sue. She done bought clothes for Randy and towels for her mama and cowboy boots for Alan. Pretty ones. Rhino's hide and hippo's toes. She working then, she still have a job then. It a Saturday. Randy and Alan at Randy's Little League game. She think she going over later, but she never make it. She get drunk instead.

They gone have just one little drink, her and Betty and Sue and them. One little drink ain't gone hurt nothing or nobody. Betty telling about her divorce and new men she checking out. She don't give no details, though. They drinking a light white wine but Angel having a double One Fifty-One and Coke. She ain't messing around. This a few weeks ago, she ain't got time for no wine. And she drink hers off real quick and order and get another one before they even get they wines down. She think maybe they won't even notice she done had two, they all so busy listening to Betty telling about these wimps she messing with. But it ain't even interesting and they notice right away. Angel going to the game, though. She definitely going to the game. She done promised everybody in the country. Time done come where she have to be straight. She got to quit breaking these promises. She got to quit all this lying and conniving.

Then before long they start talking about leaving. She ask them to stay, say Please, ya'll just stay and have one more. But naw, they got to go. Glynnis, she claim she got this hot date tonight. She talk like she got a hot date every night. Betty got this new man she going out with and she got to roll her hair and stuff. But Sue now is true. Angel done went to high school with her. They was in school together back when they was wearing hot pants and stuff. This like a old relationship. But Sue know what going on. She just hate to say anything. She just hate to bring it out in the wide open. She got to say something, though. She wait till the rest of them go and then she speak up.

She say, "I thought you goin to the ball game, girl." She look at her watch.

"Yeah," Angel say. "Honey, I'm goin. I wouldn't miss it for the world. But first I got to have me some more One Fifty-One and Coke."

Sue know she lying. She done lied to everybody about everything. This thing a problem can't keep quiet. She done had troubles at work. She done called in late, and sick, done called in and lied like a dog about her physical condition with these hungovers.

Now Angel hurting. She know Sue know the truth but too good to nag. She know Sue one good person she can depend on the rest of her life, but she know too Sue ain't putting up with her killing herself in her midst. She know Sue gone say something, but Sue don't say nothing until she finish her second wine. This after Angel ask her to have a third wine. Somebody got to stop her. She keep on, she be asking to stay for a eighth and a ninth wine. She be asking to stay till the place close down.

So Sue say, "You gone miss that ball game, girl."

She say she already late. She motion for another drink. Sue reach over and put her hand over Angel's glass and say, "Don't do that, girl."

"Late already," she say. "One more won't make no difference."

She know her speech and stuff messed up. It embarrassing, but the barmaid, she bring the drink. And Sue reach out, put her hand over the glass and say, "Don't you give her that shit, woman."

Girl back up and say, "*Ma'am?*" Real nice like.

"Don't you give her that," say Sue.

Girl say, "Yes'm, but ma'am, she order it, ma'am."

Girl look at Angel.

"Thank you, hon," she say. She reach and take the drink and give the girl some money. Then she tip her a dollar and the girl walk away. Angel grab this drink and slosh some of it out on her. She know it but she can't help it. She don't know what went wrong. She shopping and going to the ball game and now this done happened again. She ain't making no ball game. Ball game done shot to hell. She be in perhaps two three in the morning.

Sue now, she tired of this.

"When you goin to admit it?" she say.

"Admit what?"

"Girl, *you* know. Layin drunk. Runnin around here drinkin every night. Stayin out."

She say, "I don't know what you talkin about," like she huffy. She drinking every day. Even Sunday. Especially Sunday. Sunday the worst because ain't nothing open. She don't hit the liquor store Saturday night she climbing the walls Sunday afternoon. She done even got drunk and listened to the services on TV Sunday morning and got all depressed and passed out before dinnertime. Then Alan and Randy have to eat them turkey pot pies again.

"Alan and Randy don't understand me," she say.

"They love you," Sue say.

"And I love them," she say.

"Listen now," Sue tell her, "you gonna lose that baby and that man if you don't stop this messin around."

"Ain't gonna do that no such of a thing," she say, but she know Sue right. She still pouring that rum down, she ain't slacked off. She just have to deny the truth because old truth hurt too much to face.

Sue get up, she got tears in her eye and stuff, she dabbing with Kleenexes. Can't nobody talk sense to this fool.

"Yes you will," she say, and she leave. She ain't gone hang around and watch this self-destruction. Woman done turned into a time bomb ticking. She got to get away from here, so she run out the door. She booking home. Everybody looking.

Angel all alone now. She order two more singles and drink both of them. But she shitfaced time she drink that last one, she done been in the booth a hour and a half. Which has done caused some men to think about hitting on her, they done seen them thin legs and stuff she got. This one wimp done even come over to the table, he just assume she lonesome and want some male company, he think he gonna come over like he Robert Goulet or somebody and just invite himself to sit down. He done seen her wedding ring, but he thinking, Man, this woman horny or something, she wouldn't be sitting here all by her lonesome. And this fool almost sit down in the booth with her, he gonna buy her a drink, talk some trash to her, when he really thinking is he gonna get her in some motel room and take her panties off. But she done recognized his act, she ain't having nothing to do with this fool. She tell him off right quick. Of course he get huffy and leave. That's fine. Ain't asked that fool to sit down with her anyway.

Now she done decided she don't want to have another drink in this place. Old depression setting in. People coming in now to eat seafood with they families, little kids and stuff, grandmamas, she don't need to be hanging around in here no more. Waiters looking at her. She know they wanting her to leave before she give their place a bad name. Plus she taking up room in this booth where some family wanting to eat some filet catfish. She know all this stuff. She know she better leave before they ask her to. She done had embarrassment enough, don't need no more.

Ain't eat nothing yet. Don't want nothing to eat. Don't even eat at home much. Done lost weight, breasts done come down, was fine and full, legs even done got skinny. She know Alan notice it when she undress. She don't even weigh what she weigh on they wedding night when she give herself to Alan. She know he worried sick about her. He get her in the bed and squeeze her so tight he hurt her, but she don't say Let go.

She trying to walk straight when she go out to her car, but she look like somebody afflicted. Bumping into hoods and stuff. She done late already. Ball game over. It after six and Randy and Alan already home by now. Ain't no way she going home right now. She ain't gonna face them crying faces. And, too, she go home, Alan ain't letting her drink another drop. So she decide to get her a bottle and just ride around a while. She gonna ride around and sober up, then she gonna go home. And she need to do this anyway because this give her time to think something up like say the car tore up or something, why she late.

Only thing, she done gone in the liquor store so many times she ashamed to. She see these same people and she know they thinking: Damn, this woman done been in here four times this week. Drinking like a fish. She don't like to look in they eyes. So she hunt her up another store on the other side of town. She don't want to get too drunk, so she just get a sixer of beers and some schnapps. She going to ride around, cruise a little and sober up. That what she thinking.

She driving okay. Hitting them beers occasionally, hitting that peach schnapps every few minutes because it so good and ain't but forty-eight proof. It so weak it ain't gonna make her drunk. Not no half pint. She ain't gonna ride around but a hour. Then she gonna go home.

She afraid to take a drink when anybody behind her. She

thinking the police gonna see her and throw them blue lights on her. Then she be in jail calling Alan to come bail her out. Which he already done twice before. She don't want to stay in town. She gonna drive out on the lake road. They not as much traffic out there. So she go off out there, on this blacktop road. She gonna ride out to the boat landing. Ain't nobody out there, it too cold to fish. She curve around through the woods three or four miles. She done finished one of them beers and throwed the bottle out the window. She get her another one and drink some more of that schnapps. That stuff go down so easy and so hard to stop on. Usually when she open a half pint, she throw the cap far as she can.

Angel weaving a little, but she ain't drunk. She just a little tired. She wishing she home in the bed right now. She know they gonna have a big argument when she get home. She dreading that. Alan, he have to fix supper for Randy and his mama ain't taught him nothing about cooking. Only thing he know how to do is warm up a TV dinner, and Randy just sull up when he have to eat one of them. She wishing now she'd just gone on home. Wouldn't have been so bad then. Going to be worse now, much worser than if she'd just gone on home after them double One Fifty-Ones. Way it is, though. Get started, can't stop. Take that first drink, she ain't gonna stop till she pass out or run out. She don't know what it is. She ain't even understand it herself. Didn't start out like this. Didn't use to be this way. Use to be a beer once in a while, little wine at New Year's. Things just get out of hand. Don't mean to be this way. Just can't help it. Alan used to would drink a little beer on weekends and it done turned him flat against it. He don't even want to be around nobody drinking now. Somebody offer him a drink now he tell em to get it out of his face. He done even lost some of his friends over this thing.

Angel get down to the boat ramp, ain't a soul there. Windy out there, water dark, scare her to death just to see it. What would it be to be out in them waves, them black waves closing over your head, ain't nobody around to hear you screaming. Coat be waterlogged and pulling you down. Hurt just a little and that's all. Just a brief pain. Be dead then, won't know nothing. Won't have no hurts. Easy way out. They get over it eventually. Could make it look like an accident. Drive her car right off in the water, everybody think it a mistake. Just a tragedy, that's all, a unfortunate thing. Don't want to hurt nobody. What so wrong with her life she do the things she do? Killing her baby and her man little at a time. And her ownself. But have to have it. Thinking things when she drinking she wouldn't think at all when she not drinking. But now she drinking all the time, and she thinking same way all the time.

She drink some more beer and schnapps, and then she pass out or go to sleep, she don't know which. Same thing. Sleeping she don't have to think no more. Ain't no hurting when she sleeping. Sleeping good, but can't sleep forever. Somebody done woke her up, knocking on the glass. Some boy out there. High school boy. Truck parked beside, some more kids in it. She scared at first, think something bad. But they look all right.

Don't look mean or nothing. Just look worried. She get up and roll her window down just a little, just crack it.

"Ma'am?" this boy say. "You all right, ma'am?"

"Yes," she say. "Fine, thank you."

"Seen you settin here," he say. "Thought your car tore up maybe."

"No," Angel say. "Just sleepy," she say. "Leavin now," she say, and she roll the window up. She turn the lights on, car still running, ain't even shut it off. Out in the middle of nowhere asleep, ain't locked the door. Somebody walk up and slit her throat, she not even know it. She crazy. She got to get home. She done been asleep no telling how long.

She afraid they gonna follow her out. They do. She can't stand for nobody to get behind her like that. Make her nervous. She decide she gonna speed up and leave them behind. She get up to about sixty-five. She start to pull away. She sobered up a little while she asleep. Be okay to get another one of them beers out the sack now. Beer sack down in the floor. Have to lean over and take her eyes off the road just a second to get that beer, no problem.

Her face hit the windshield, the seat slam her up. Too quick. Lights shining up against a tree. Don't even know what happened. Windshield broke all to pieces. Smoke coming out the hood. She wiping her face. Interior light on, she got blood all over her hands. Face bleeding. She look in the rearview mirror, she don't know her own self. Look like something in a monster movie. She screaming now. Face cut all to pieces. She black out again. She come to, she out on the ground. People helping her up. She screaming I'm ruint I'm ruint. Lights in her eyes, legs moving in front of her. Kids talking. One of them say she just drive right off the road into that tree. She don't believe it. Road move or something. Tree jump out in front of her. She a good driver. She drive too good for something like this.

Cost three thousand dollars to fix the car this time. Don't even drive right no more. Alan say the frame bent. Alan say it won't never drive right no more. And ain't even paid for. She don't know about no frame. She just know it jerk going down the road.

She in the hospital a while. She don't remember exactly, three or four days. They done had to sew her face up. People see them scars even through thick makeup the rest of her life. She bruised so bad she don't get out the bed for a week. Alan keep saying they lucky she ain't dead. He keep praising God his wife ain't dead. She know she just gonna have to go through it again now sometime, till a worse one happen. Police done come and talked to her. She lie her way out of it, though. Can't prove nothing. Alan keep saying we lucky.

Ain't lucky. Boss call, want to know when she coming back to work. She hem and haw. Done missed all them Mondays. She can't give no definite answer. He clear his throat. Maybe he should find somebody else for her position since she so vague. Well yessir, she say, yessir, if you think that the best thing.

Alan awful quiet after this happen. He just sit and stare. She touch him out on the porch, he just draw away. Like her hand a bad thing to feel on him. This go on about a week. Then he come home from work one evening and she sitting in the living room with a glass of wine in her hand.

He back now from having his hand sewed up. He sitting in the kitchen drinking coffee, he done bought some cigarettes and he smoking one after another. Done been quit two years, say it the hardest thing he ever done. He say he never stop wanting one, that he have to brace himself every day. Now he done started back. She know: This what she done to him.

Angel not drinking anything. Don't mean she don't have nothing. Just can't have it right now. He awake now. Later he be asleep. He think the house clean. House ain't clean. Lots of places to hide things, you want to hide them bad enough. Ain't like Easter eggs, like Christmas presents. Like life and death.

Wouldn't never think on her wedding night it ever be like this. She in the living room by herself, he in the kitchen by himself. TV on, she ain't watching it, some fool on Johnny Carson telling stuff ain't even funny. She ain't got the sound on. Ain't hear nothing, ain't see nothing. She hear him like choke in there once in a while. Randy in the bed asleep. Want so bad to get up and go in there and tell Alan, Baby I promise I will quit. Again. But ain't no use in saying it, she don't mean it. Just words. Don't mean nothing. Done lost trust anyway. Lose trust, a man and wife, done lost everything. Even if she quit now, stay quit, he always be looking over that shoulder, he always be smelling her breath. Lost his trust she won't never get it back.

He come in there where she at finally. He been crying, she

tell it by looking at him. He not hurting for himself, he not hurting for his hand. He cut off his hand and throw it away she ask him to. He hurting for her. She know all this, don't nobody have to tell her. Why it don't do no good to talk to her. She know it all already.

"Baby," he say. "I goin to bed. Had a long day today."

His face look like he about sixty years old. He thirty-one. Weigh one sixty-five and bench press two-ninety. "You comin?" he say.

She want to. Morning be soon enough to drink something else. He be gone to work, Randy be gone to school. House be quiet by seven-thirty. She do what she want to then. Whole day be hers to do what she want to. Things be better tomorrow maybe. She cook them something good for supper, she make them a good old pie and have ice cream. She get better. They know she trying. She just weak, she just need some time. This thing not something you throw off like a cold. This thing deep, this thing beat more good people than her.

Angel say, "Not just yet, baby. I going to sit in here in the livin room a while. I so sorry you cut your hand," she say.

"You want to move?" he say. "Another state? Another country? You say the word I quit my job tomorrow. Don't matter. Just a job," he say.

"Don't want to move," she say. She trembling.

"Don't matter what people thinks," he say.

She think he gonna come over and get down on the floor and hug her knees and cry, but he don't. He look like he holding back to keep from doing that. And she glad he don't. He do that, she make them promises again. She promise anything if he just stop.

"Okay," he say. "I goin to bed now." He look beat.

He go. She by herself. It real quiet now. Hear anything. Hear walls pop, hear mice move. They eating something in the cabinet, she need to set some traps.

Time go by so slow. She know he in there listening. He listen for any step she make, which room she move into, which furniture she reach for. She have to wait. It risky now. He think she in here drinking, they gonna have it all over again. One time a night enough. Smart thing is go to bed. Get next to him. That what he want. Ought to be what she want. Use to be she did.

Thirty minutes a long time like this. She holding her breath when she go in there to look at him. He just a lump in the dark. Can't tell if he sleeping or not. Could be laying there looking at her. Too dark to tell. He probably asleep, though. He tired, he give out. He work so hard for them.

Tomorrow be better. Tomorrow she have to try harder. She know she can do it, she got will power. Just need a little time. They have to be patient with her. Ain't built Rome in a day. And she gonna be so good in the future, it ain't gonna hurt nothing to have a few cold beers tonight. Ain't drinking no whiskey now. Liquor store done closed anyway. Big Star still open. She just run down get some beer and then run right back. Don't need to drink what she got hid anyway. Probably won't need none later, she gonna quit anyway, but just in case.

She know where the checkbook laying. She ain't making

no noise. If he awake he ain't saying nothing. If he awake he'd be done said something. He won't know she ever been gone. Won't miss no three dollar check no way. Put it in with groceries sometime.

Side door squeak every time. Don't never notice it in daytime. Squeak like hell at night. Porch light on. He always leave it on if she going to be out. Ain't no need to turn it off. She be back in ten minutes. He never know she gone. Car in the driveway. It raining. A little.

Ain't cold. Don't need no coat.

She get in, ease the door to. Trying to be quiet. He so tired, he need his rest. She look at the bedroom window when she turn the key. And the light come on in there.

Caught now. Wasn't even asleep. Trying to just catch her on purpose. Laying in there in the dark just making out like he asleep. Don't trust her. Won't never trust her. It like he making her slip around. Damn him anyway.

Ain't nothing to do but talk to him. He standing on the step in his underwear. She put it in reverse and back on up. She stop beside him and roll down the window. She hate to. Neighbors gonna see him out here in his underwear. What he think he doing anyway, can't leave her alone. Treat her like some baby he can't take his eye off of for five minutes.

"I just goin to the store," she say. "I be right back."

"Don't care for you goin to the store," he say. "Long as you come back. You comin back?"

He got his arms wrapped around him, he shivering in the night air. He look like he been asleep.

"I just goin after some cigarettes," she say. "I be back in ten minutes. Go on back to bed. I be right back. I promise."

He step off the porch and come next the car. He hugging himself and shaking, barefooted. Standing in the driveway getting wet.

"I won't say nothin about you drinkin if you just do it at home," he say. "Go git you somethin to drink. But come back home," he say. "Please," he say.

It hit her now, this enough. This enough to stop anything, anybody, everything. He done give up.

"Baby," he say, "know you ain't gone stop. Done said all I can say. Just don't get out on the road drinkin. Don't care about the car. Just don't hurt yourself."

"I done told you I be back in ten minutes," she say. "I be *back* in ten minutes."

Something cross his face. Can't tell rain from tears in this. But what he shivering from she don't think is cold.

"Okay, baby," he say, "okay," and he turn away. She relieved. Now maybe won't be no argument. Now maybe won't be no dread. She telling the truth anyway. Ain't going nowhere but Big Star. Be back in ten minutes. All this fussing for nothing. Neighbors probably looking out the windows.

He go up on the porch and put his hand on the door. He watching her back out the driveway, she watching him standing there half naked. All this foolishness over a little trip to Big Star. She shake her head while she backing out the driveway. It almost like he ain't even expecting her to come back. She almost laugh at this. Ain't nothing even open this late but bars, and she *ain't* going to none of them, no ma'am. She see him watch her again, and then she see him step inside. What he need to do. Go on back to bed, get him some rest. He got to go to work in the morning. All she got to do is sleep.

She turn the wipers on to see better. The porch light shining out there, yellow light showing rain, it slanting down hard. It shine on the driveway and on Randy's bicycle and on they barbecue grill setting there getting wet. It make her feel good to know this all hers, that she always got this to come back to. This light show her home, this warm place she own that mean everything to her. This light, it always on for her. That what she thinking when it go out.

THE RICH

Mr. Pellisher works at the travel agency, and he associates with the rich. Sometimes the rich stop by in the afternoon hours when the working citizens have fled the streets to punch their clocks. The rich are strangers to TUE IN 6:57 OUT 12:01 IN 12:29 OUT 3:30. Mr. Pellisher keeps his punch clock carefully hidden behind stacks of travel folders, as if he's on straight salary. As if he's like the rich, free of the earthly shackles of timekeepers. He keeps a pot of coffee on hot for the rich, in case the rich deign to share a cup with him, even though Mr. Pellisher pays for the coffee himself.

But the rich don't drink coffee in the afternoons. The rich favor Campari and soda, Perrier, and old, old bottles of wine. The rich are impertinent. The rich are impatient. The rich are rich.

Mr. Pellisher can see the rich coming from his office window, where he pores over folders of sunny beaches and waving palms, of cliff divers and oyster divers. The rich arrive in Lincolns white and shimmering, hubcaps glittering like diamonds. They are long and sleek, these cars the rich drive, and clean. No one has ever puked on the floormats of a car belonging to the rich. Empty potato chip bags and candy wrappers are not to be found—along with Coke cans and plastic straws—on the car seats of the rich. If they are, they were dropped there by the rich.

He straightens his tie when he sees the rich coming, and sets out styrofoam cups and sugar cubes. He straightens his desk and pulls out chairs, waiting for the rich. And when the rich push the door open, he springs from his desk, hand offered in offertory handshake. But the handshakes of the rich are limp, without feeling, devoid of emotion. Mr. Pellisher pumps the hands of the rich as if he'd milk the money from their fingers. The fingers of the rich are fat and white, like overgrown grubs. Mr. Pellisher offers the rich a seat. He offers coffee. The rich decline both with one fat wave of their puffy white hands. The rich often wear gold chains around their necks. Most of the rich wear diamond rings. Some of the rich wear gold bones in their noses. A lot of the rich, especially the older rich, have been surgically renovated. The rich can afford tucks and snips. With their rich clothes off, most of the rich are all wrinkles below their chins.

The rich live too richly. The rich are pampered. The rich are spoiled by the poor, who want to be rich. To Mr. Pellisher, who is poor, the rich are symbols to look up to, standards of excellence which must be strived for. The rich, for instance, are always taking vacations.

Mr. Pellisher turns the air-conditioning up a notch in his office, as the rich begin to sweat. He offers coffee again. The rich refuse. The rich have only two minutes to spare. They must lay their plans in the capable hands of Mr. Pellisher and depart to whatever richening schemes the rich pursue. Just one time Mr. Pellisher would like to take a vacation like the rich do, and see the things the rich see, and have sex with the women the rich have sex with. He often wonders about the sex lives of the rich. He speculates upon how the rich procure women. Do the rich advertise? Do the rich seek out the haunts of other rich, in the hope of ferreting out rich nymphomaniacs? Or do the rich hire people to arrange their sex? Just how do the rich make small talk in bars where only strangers abound? Do the rich say, "I'm rich," and let it go at that? Or do the rich glide skillfully into a conversation with talk of stocks and bonds? Are the rich perverted? Do the rich perform unnatural sex acts? Can the rich ever be horny? Do the rich have sex every night? Watch kung-fu quickies? Eat TV dinners? Buy their own beer? Wash their own dishes? Are the rich so different from himself?

He thinks they are not. He knows they are only rich. And if some way, somehow, he could be rich, too, he knows he would be exactly like them. He knows he would be invited to their parties. Summoned to their art exhibits. Called from the dark confines of his own huge monstrous cool castle to sit at the tables of other rich and tell witty anecdotes, of which he has many in great supply. He knows the rich are not different from himself. They are not of another race, another creed, another skin. They do not worship a different God.

Mr. Pellisher has many travel folders. He spreads them before the rich, as a man would fan a deck of cards. He has all the points of the globe at his fingertips, like the rich, and he can make arrangements through a small tan telephone that sits on his desk. He is urgent, ready. He has a Xeroxed copy of international numbers taped beneath the Plexiglas that covers his desk. He can send the rich to any remote or unremote corner of the world with expert flicks of his fingers. He can line up hotels, vistas, visas, Visacards, passports, make reservations, secure hunting licenses, hire guides, Sherpas, serfs, peasants, waiters, cocktail waitresses, gardeners, veterinarians, prostitutes, bookies, make bets, cover point-spreads, confirm weather conditions, reserve yachts, captains, second mates, rods, reels, secure theater tickets, perform transactions, check hostile environments in third-world countries, wire money, locate cocaine, buy condos, close down factories, watch the stock market, buy, sell, trade, steal. With his phone, with the blessing of the rich, he is as the rich. He is their servant, their confidant, their messenger. He is everything anybody rich wants him to be.

But he wonders sometimes if maybe the rich look down on him. He wonders sometimes if maybe the rich think that just possibly they're a little bit *better* than him. The rich are always going to dinner parties and sneak previews. The rich have daughters at Princeton and sons in L.A. He knows the rich have swimming pools and security systems. He wonders what the rich would do if he and Velma knocked on their door one night. Would the rich let them in? Would they open the door wide and invite them in for crab? Or would they sic a slobbering Doberman on them? The rich are unpredictable.

The rich do not compare prices in the grocery stores or cut out coupons. The rich are rich enough to afford someone to do this for them, who, by working for the rich, does not feel at all compelled to check prices. No, the rich have their groceries bought for them by persons whose instructions do not include checking prices.

Mr. Pellisher, poor, lives with the constant thought that leg quarters at forty-nine cents per pound are cheaper than whole chickens at seventy-nine cents per pound, and even though he does not like dark meat, Mr. Pellisher must eat dark meat because he is not like the rich. That is to say that he is not rich. He figures the rich eat only breasts and pulley bones. The rich do not know the price of a can of Campbell's chicken noodle soup. The rich have no use for such knowledge.

How great Mr. Pellisher thinks this must be, to live in a world so high above the everyday human struggles of the race. The rich, for instance, never have to install spark plugs. The rich have never been stranded on the side of the road. The rich have never driven a wheezing '71 Ford Fairlane with a vibrating universal joint. Or put on brake shoes, tried to set points, suffered a burst radiator hose. They have never moaned and cursed on gravel flat on their collective rich backs with large rocks digging into their skin as they twisted greasy bolts into a greasy starter. The rich have it so easy.

The rich are saying something now. The rich are going on

vacation again. South of France? Wales? The rich have no conception of money. They have never bought a television or stereo on credit. They owe nothing to Sears. Their debutante daughters' braces were paid for with cash. The rich have unlimited credit which they do not need. In addition, the rich have never dug up septic tanks and seen with their own eyes the horrors contained there.

It appears that the rich are meeting other rich in June at Naples. From there they will fly to Angola. The ducks will darken the sky in late evening. The rich will doubtless shoot them with gold-plated Winchesters. The rich have never fired a Savage single-shot. The rich will go on to Ridder Creek in Alaska, where the salmon turn the water blood-red with their bodies. The rich have never seined minnows to impale upon hooks for pond bass. The rich do not camp out. The rich have never been inside a mobile home.

Mr. Pellisher has dreams of being rich. He plays Super Bingo at Kroger's. He goes inside and makes the minimum purchase twice a week, and gets the tickets. Each one could be the one. This is not the only thing he does. He also buys sweepstakes tickets and enters publishers' clearing house contests. But he never orders the magazines from the publishers. He does not affix the stamps. He has an uneasy feeling that the coupons from people who do not buy the magazines wind up at the bottom of the drawing barrel, but he has no way to prove this. He has no basis for this fear. It is unreasonable for him to think this. It is a phobia that has not yet been named.

The rich wish to have their matters taken care of immediately. They have their priorities in order. The rich have mixed-doubles sets to play. The rich have eighteen holes at two o'clock. Mr. Pellisher has taken to putting on the weekends and acquiring some of the equipment necessary for golfing. He watches the Masters' Classic and studies their pars and handicaps.

The rich are saying something else now. The rich wish to know which card Mr. Pellisher requires. The rich can produce MasterCharge, etc., upon request. The rich are logged and registered in computers all over the world. The wealth of the rich can be verified in an instant.

Mr. Pellisher has filled out all the needed forms. He has written down all the pertinent information. He has been helpful, courteous, polite, professional, warm, efficient, jovial, indulgent, cordial, ingratiating, familiar, benevolent. He has served the rich in the manner they are accustomed to. There is no outward indication of malice or loathing. But inside, in the deep gray portions of his mind where his secret thoughts lie, he hates the rich. What he'd really like to do is machine-gun the rich. Throttle the rich. He would like to see the great mansions of the rich burned down, their children limned in flame from the high windows. He would like to see the rich downtrodden, humbled, brought to their knees. He'd like to see the rich in rags. He'd like to see the rich on relief, or in prison. Arrested for smuggling cocaine. Fined for driving drunk. He'd like to see the rich suffer everything he ever suffered that all their money could heal.

But he knows it can never be so. He knows that the rich

can never be poor, that the poor can never be rich. He hates himself for being so nice to the rich. He knows the rich do not appreciate it. The rich merely expect it. The rich have become accustomed to it. He doubts the rich ever even think about it.

He tells none of this to the rich. He would like to, but he cannot. The rich might become offended. The rich might feel insulted. The rich might stop doing their business with him. Mr. Pellisher feeds off the rich. He sucks their blood, drawing it, little by little unto himself, a few dollars at a time, with never enough to satisfy his lust, slake his thirst.

The rich are leaving now. They are sliding onto their smooth leather seats, turning the keys in ignitions all over the world that set high-compression motors humming like well-fed cats. Their boats are docked and hosed down with fresh water. Their airplanes are getting refueled and restocked with liquor. Their accountants are preparing loopholes. Their lobsters are drowning in hot water, their caviar being chilled on beds of ice.

Mr. Pellisher waves to the rich as they pull away from the curb. But the rich don't look back.

OLD FRANK AND JESUS

Mr. Parker's on the couch, reclining. He's been there all morning, almost, trying to decide what to do.

Things haven't gone like he's planned. They never do.

The picture of his great-grandpa's on the mantel looking down at him, a framed old dead gentleman with a hat and a long beard who just missed the Civil War. The picture's fuzzy and faded, with this thing like a cloud coming up around his neck.

They didn't have good photography back then, Mr. P. thinks. That's why the picture looks like it does.

Out in the yard, his kids are screaming. They're just playing, but to Mr. P. it sounds like somebody's killing them. His wife's gone to the beauty parlor to get her hair fixed. There's a sick cow in his barn, but he hasn't been down to see about her this morning. He was up all night with her, just about. She's got something white and sticky running out from under her tail, and the vet's already been out three times without doing her any good. He charges for his visits anyway, though, twenty-five smacks a whack.

That's . . . seventy-five bucks, he thinks, and the old white stuff's just pouring out.

Mr. P. clamps his eyes shut and rolls over on the couch, feels it up. He had cold toast four hours ago. He needs to be up and out in the cotton patch, trying to pull the last bolls off the stalks, but the bottom's dropped out because foreign rayon's ruined the market. He guesses that somewhere across the big pond, little Japanese girls are sewing pants together and getting off from their jobs and meeting boyfriends for drinks and movies after work, talking about their supervisors. Maybe they're eating raw fish. They did that on Okinawa after they captured the place and everything settled down. He was on Okinawa. Mr. P. got shot on Okinawa.

He reaches down and touches the place, just above his knee. They were full of shit as a Christmas turkey. Eight hundred yards from the beach under heavy machine-gun fire. No cover. Wide open. They could have gotten some sun if they'd just been taking a vacation. They had palm trees. Sandy beaches. No lotion. No towels, no jamboxes, no frosty cool brewskies. They waded through water up to their necks and bullets zipped in the surf around them killing men and fish. Nobody had any dry cigarettes. Some of their men got run over by their own carriers and some of the boys behind shot the boys in front. Mr. P. couldn't tell who was shooting whom. He just shot. He stayed behind a concrete barrier for a while and saw some

Japanese symbols molded into the cement, but he couldn't read them. Every once in a while he'd stick his head out from behind the thing and just shoot.

He hasn't fired a shot in anger in years now, though. But he's thinking seriously about shooting a hole in the screen door with a pistol. Just a little hole.

He knows he needs to get up and go down to the barn and see about that cow, but he just can't face it today. He knows she won't be any better. She'll be just like she was last night, not touching the water he's drawn up in a barrel for her, not eating the hay he's put next to her. That's how it is with a cow when they get down, though. They just stay down. Even the vet knows that. The vet knows no shot he can give her will make her get up, go back on her feed. The vet's been to school. He's studied anatomy, biology. Other things, too. He knows all about animal husbandry and all.

But Mr. P. thinks him not much of a vet. The reason is, last year, Mr. P. had a stud colt he wanted cut, and he had him tied and thrown with a blanket over his head when the vet came out, and Mr. P. did most of the cutting, but the only thing the vet did was dance in and out with advice because he was scared of getting kicked.

The phone rings and Mr. P. stays on the couch and listens to it ring. It's probably somebody calling with bad news. That's about the only thing a phone's good for anyway, Mr. P. thinks, to let somebody get ahold of you with some bad news. He knows people just can't wait to tell bad news. Like if somebody dies, or if a man's cows are out in the road, somebody'll be sure to pick up the nearest phone and call somebody else and tell him or her all about it. And they'll tell other things, too. Personal things. Mr. P. thinks it'd probably be better to just not have a phone. If you didn't have a phone, they'd have to come over to your house personally to give you bad news, either drive over or walk. But with a phone, it's easy to give it to you. All they have to do's just pick it up and call, and there you are.

But on second thought, he thinks, if your house caught on fire and you needed to call up the fire department and report it, and you didn't have a phone, there you'd be again.

Or the vet.

The phone's still ringing. It rings eight or nine times. Just ringing ringing ringing. There's no telling who it is. It could be the FHA. They hold the mortgage on his place. Or, it could be the bank. They could be calling again to get real shitty about the note. He's borrowed money from them for seed and fertilizer and things and they've got a lien. And, it could be the county forester calling to tell him, Yes, Mr. Parker, it's just as we feared: your whole 160-acre tract of pine timber is heavily infested with the Southern pine beetle and you'll have to sell all your wood for stumpage and lose your shirt on the whole deal. It rings again. Mr. P. finally gets up from the couch and goes over to it. He picks it up. "Hello," he says.

"Hello?"

"Yes," Mr. P. says.

"Mr. Marvin Parker," the phone says.

"Speaking," says Mr. P.

"Jim Lyle calling, Mr. Parker. Amalgamated Pulpwood and

Benevolent Society? Just checking our records here and see
you're a month behind on your premium. Just calling to check
on the problem, Marv."

They always want their money, Mr. P. thinks. They don't
care about you. They wouldn't give a damn if you got run over
by a bush hog. They just want your money. Want you to pay
that old premium.

"I paid," Mr. P. says. He can't understand it. "I pay by
bank draft every month."

A little cough comes from the phone.

"Well yes," the voice says. "But our draft went through on
a day when you were overdrawn, Mr. Parker."

Well kiss my ass, Mr. P. thinks.

Mr. P. can't say anything to this man. He knows what it is.
His wife's been writing checks at the Fabric Center again. For
material. What happened was, the girls needed dresses for the
program at church, capes and wings and things. Plus, they had
to spend $146.73 on a new clutch and pressure plate for the
tractor. Mr. P. had to do all the mechanical stuff, pull the motor
and all. Sometimes he couldn't find the right wrenches and had
to hunt around in the dirt for this and that. There was also an
unfortunate incident with a throw-out bearing.

Mr. P. closes his eyes and leans against the wall and wants
to get back on the couch. Today, he just can't get enough of
that couch.

"Can I borrow from the fund?" says Mr. P. He's never
borrowed from the fund before.

"Borrow? Why. . . ."

"Would it be all right?" Mr. P. says.

"All right?"

"I mean would everything be fixed up?"

"Fixed up? You mean paid?" says the voice over the phone.

"Yes," says Mr. P. "Paid."

"Paid. Why, I suppose. . . ."

"Don't suppose," says Mr. P. He's not usually this ill with people like Jim Lyle of APABS. But he's sick of staying up with that cow every night. He's sick of his wife writing checks at the Fabric Center. He's sick of a vet who's scared of animals he's sworn to heal. He doesn't want Jim Lyle of APABS to suppose. He wants him to know.

"Well, yes sir, if that's the way. . . ."

"All right, then," Mr. P. says, and he hangs up the phone.

"Goodbye," he says, after he hangs it up. He goes back to the couch and stretches out quick, lets out this little groan. He puts one forearm over his eyes.

The kids are still screaming at the top of their lungs in the yard. He's worried about them being outside. There's been a rabies epidemic: foaming foxes and rabid raccoons running amuck. Even flying squirrels have attacked innocent people. And just last week, Mr. P. had to take his squirrel dog off, a little feist he had named Frank that was white with black spots over both eyes. He got him from a family of black folks down the road and they all swore up and down that his mama was a good one, had treed as many as sixteen in one morning. Mr. P. raised that dog from a puppy, played with him, fed him, let him sleep on his stomach and in front of the fire, and took him out in the summer with a dried squirrel skin and let him trail it all over the yard before he hung it up in a tree and let him tree it. He waited for old Frank to get a little older and then took him out the first frosty morning and shot a squirrel in front of him, didn't kill it on purpose, just wounded it, and let old Frank get ahold of it and get bitten in the nose because he'd heard all his life that doing that would make a squirrel dog every time if the dog had it in him. And old Frank did. He caught that squirrel and fought it all over the ground, squalling, with the squirrel balled up on his nose, bleeding, and finally killed it. After that he hated squirrels so bad he'd tree every squirrel he smelled. They killed nine opening day, one over the limit. Mr. P. was proud of old Frank.

But last week he took old Frank out in the pasture and shot him in the head with a .22 rifle because his wife said the rabies were getting too close to home.

Now why did I do that? Mr. P. wonders. Why did I let her talk me into shooting old Frank? I remember he used to come in here and lay down on my legs while I was watching "Dragnet." I'd pat him on the head and he'd close his eyes and curl up and just seem happy as anything. He'd even go to sleep sometimes, just sleep and sleep. And he wouldn't mess in the house either. Never did. He'd scratch on the door till somebody let him out. Then he'd come back in and hop up here and go to sleep.

Mr. P. feels around under the couch to see if it's still there. It is. He just borrowed it a few days ago, from his neighbor,

Hulet Steele. He doesn't even know if it'll work. But he figures it will. He told Hulet he wanted it for rats. He told Hulet he had some rats in his corncrib.

Next thing he knows, somebody's knocking on the front door. Knocking hard, like he can't even see the kids out in the yard and send them in to call him out. He knows who it probably is, though. He knows it's probably Hereford Mullins, another neighbor, about that break in the fence, where his cows are out in the road. Mr. P. knows the fence is down. He knows his cows are out in the road, too. But he just can't seem to face it today. It seems like people just won't leave him alone.

He doesn't much like Hereford Mullins anyway. Never has. Not since that night at the high school basketball game when their team won and Hereford Mullins tried to vault over the railing in front of the seats and landed on both knees on the court, five feet straight down, trying to grin like it didn't hurt.

Mr. P. thinks he might just get up and go out on the front porch and slap the shit out of Hereford Mullins. He gets up and goes out there.

It's Hereford, all right. Mr. P. stops inside the screen door. The kids are still screaming in the yard, getting their school clothes dirty. Any other time they'd be playing with old Frank. But old Frank can't play with them now. Old Frank's busy getting his eyeballs picked out right now probably by some buzzards down in the pasture.

"Ye cows out in the road again," says Hereford Mullins. "Thought I'd come up here and tell ye."

"All right," says Mr. P. "You told me."

"Like to hit em while ago," says Hereford Mullins. "I'd git em outa the road if they's mine."

"I heard you the first time," says Mr. P.

"Feller come along and hit a cow in the road," goes on Hereford Mullins, "he ain't responsible. Cows ain't sposed to be in the road. Sposed to be behind a fence."

"Get off my porch," says Mr. P.

"What?"

"I said get your stupid ass off my porch," Mr. P. says.

Hereford kind of draws up, starts to say something, but leaves the porch huffy. Mr. P. knows he'll be the owner of a dead cow within two minutes. That'll make two dead cows, counting the one in the barn not quite dead yet that he's already out seventy-five simoleans on.

He goes back to the couch.

Now there'll be a lawsuit, probably. Herf'll say his neck's hurt, or his pickup's hurt, or something else. Mr. P. reaches under the couch again and feels it again. It's cold and hard, feels scary.

Mr. P.'s never been much of a drinking man, but he knows there's some whiskey in the kitchen cabinet. Sometimes when the kids get colds or the sore throat, he mixes up a little whiskey and lemon juice and honey and gives it to them in a teaspoon. That and a peppermint stick always helps their throats.

He gets the whiskey, gets a little drink, and then gets another pretty good drink. It's only ten o'clock. He should have had a lot of work done by now. Any other time he'd be out on the tractor or down in the field or up in the woods cutting firewood.

Unless it was summer. If it was summer he'd be out in the garden picking butter beans or sticking tomatoes or cutting hay or fixing fences or working on the barn roof or digging up the septic tank or swinging a joe-blade along the driveway or cultivating the cotton or spraying or trying to borrow some more money to buy some more poison or painting the house or cutting the grass or doing a whole bunch of other things he doesn't want to do anymore at all. All he wants to do now's stay on the couch.

Mr. P. turns over on the couch and sees the picture of Jesus on the wall. It's been hanging up there for years. Old Jesus, he thinks. Mr. P. used to know Jesus. He used to talk to Jesus all the time. There was a time when he could have a little talk with Jesus and everything'd be all right. Four or five years ago he could. Things were better then, though. You could raise cotton and hire people to pick it. They even used to let the kids out of school to pick it. Not no more, though. Only thing kids wanted to do now was grow long hair and listen to the damn Beatles.

Mr. P. knows about hair because he cuts it in his house. People come in at night and sit around the fire in his living room and spit tobacco juice on the hearth and Mr. P. cuts their hair. He talks to them about cotton and cows and shuffles, clockwise and counterclockwise around the chair they're sitting in, in his house shoes and undershirt and overalls and snips here and there.

Most of the time they watch TV, "Gunsmoke" or "Perry Mason." Sometimes they watch Perry Como. And *some*times, they'll get all involved and interested in a show and stay till the show's over.

One of Mr. P.'s customers—this man who lives down the road and doesn't have a TV—comes every Wednesday night to get his haircut. But Mr. P. can't cut much of his hair, having to cut it every week like that. He has to just snip the scissors around on his head some and make out like he's cutting it, comb it a little, walk around his head a few times, to make him think he's getting a real haircut. This man always comes in at 6:45 P.M., just as Mr. P. and his family are getting up from the supper table.

This man always walks up, and old Frank used to bark at him when he'd come up in the yard. It was kind of like a signal that old Frank and Mr. P. had, just between them. But it wasn't a secret code or anything. Mr. P. would be at the supper table, and he'd hear old Frank start barking, and if it was Wednesday night, he'd know to get up from the table and get his scissors. The Hillbillies always come on that night at seven, and it takes Mr. P. about fifteen minutes to cut somebody's hair.

This man starts laughing at the opening credits of the Hillbillies, and shaking his head when it shows old Jed finding his black gold, his Texas tea, just as Mr. P.'s getting through with his head. So by the time he's finished, the Hillbillies have already been on for one or two minutes. And then, when Mr. P. unpins the bedsheet around this man's neck, if there's nobody else sitting in his living room watching TV or waiting for a haircut, this man just stays in the chair, doesn't get up, and says, "I bleve I'll jest set here and watch the Hillbillies with ya'll since they already started if ya'll don't care."

It's every Wednesday night's business.

Mr. P. doesn't have a license or anything, but he actually does more than a regular barber would do. For one thing, he's got some little teenincy scissors he uses to clip hairs out of folks' noses and ears. Plus, Mr. P.'s cheaper than the barbers in town. Mr. P.'ll lower your ears for fifty cents. He doesn't do shaves, though. He's got shaky hands. He couldn't shave a balloon or anything. He could flat shave the damn Beatles though.

Mr. P.'s wondering when the school bus will come along. It's late today. What happened was, Johnny Crawford got it stuck in a ditch about a mile down the road trying to dodge one of Mr. P.'s cows. They've called for the wrecker, though, on Mr. P.'s phone. They gave out that little piece of bad news over his phone, and he thinks he heard the wrecker go down the road a while ago. He knows he needs to get up and go down there and fix that fence, get those cows up, but he doesn't think he will. He thinks he'll just stay right here on the couch and drink a little more of this whiskey.

Mr. P. would rather somebody get him down on the ground and beat his ass like a drum than to have to fix that fence. The main thing is, he doesn't have anybody to help him. His wife has ruined those kids of his, spoiled them, until the oldest boy, fourteen, can't even tie his own shoelaces. Mr. P. can say something to him, tell him to come on and help him go do something for a minute, and he'll act like he's deaf and dumb. And if he does go, he whines and moans and groans and carries on about it until Mr. P. just sends him on back to the house so he won't have to listen to it. Mr. P. can see now that he messed up with his kids a long time ago. He's been too soft on them. They don't even know what work is. It just amazes Mr. P. He wasn't raised like that. He had to work when he was little. And it was rough as an old cob back then. Back then you couldn't sit around on your ass all day long and listen to a bunch of long-haired hippies singing a bunch of rock and roll on the radio.

Mr. P.'s even tried paying his kids to get out and help him work, but they won't do it. They say he doesn't pay enough. Mr. P.'s raised such a rebellious bunch of youngsters with smart mouths that they'll even tell him what the minimum wage is.

Even if his oldest boy would help him with the fence, it'd still be an awful job. First off they'd have to move all the cows to another pasture so they could tear the whole fence down and do it right. And the only other pasture Mr. P.'s got available is forty acres right next to his corn patch. They'd probably push the fence down and eat his corn up while he's across the road putting up the new fence, because his wife won't run cows. Mr. P.'s run cows and run cows and tried to get his wife out there to help him run cows and she won't hardly run cows at all. She's not fast enough to head one off or anything. Plus, she's scared of cows. She's always afraid she's going to stampede them and get run over by a crazed cow. About the only thing Mr. P.'s wife is good for when it comes to running cows is just sort of jumping around, two or three feet in any direction, waving her arms, and hollering, "Shoo!"

Mr. P. can't really think of a whole lot his wife *is* good for except setting his kids against him. It seems like they've fought him at every turn, wanting to buy new cars and drive up to Memphis to shop and getting charge accounts at one place and another and wanting him to loan money to her old drunk brother. Mr. P. doesn't know what the world's coming to. They've got another damn war started now and they'll probably be wanting his boys to go over there in a few more years and get killed or at the very least get their legs blown off. Mr. P. worries about that a good bit. But Mr. P. just worries about everything, really. Just worries all the time. There's probably not a minute that goes by when he's awake that he's not worrying about something. It's kind of like a weight he's carrying around with him that won't get off and can't get off because there's no way for it *to* get off.

The whiskey hasn't done him any good. He hoped it would, but he really knew that it wouldn't. Mr. P. thinks he knows the only thing that'll do him any good, and it won't be good.

He wonders what his wife'll say when she comes in and sees him still on the couch. Just him and Jesus, and grandpa. She's always got something to say about everything. About the only thing she doesn't say too much about is that guy who sells the siding. Mr. P.'s come up out of the pasture on the tractor four or five times and seen that guy coming out of the house after trying to sell some siding to his wife. She won't say much about him, though. She just says he's asking for directions.

Well, there the bus is to get his kids. Mr. P. can hear it pull up and he can hear the doors open. He guesses they got it out of the ditch all right. He could have taken his tractor down there and maybe pulled it out, but he might not have. A man has to be careful on a tractor. Light in the front end like they are, a man has to be careful how he hooks onto something.

Especially something heavy like a school bus. But the school bus is leaving now. Mr. P. can hear it going down the road.

It's quiet in the house now.

Yard's quiet, too.

If old Frank was in here now he'd be wanting out. Old Frank. Good little old dog. Just the happiest little thing you'd ever seen. He'd jump clean off the ground to get a biscuit out of your hand. He'd jump about three feet high. And just wag that stubby tail hard as he could.

Old Frank.

Mr. P. thinks now maybe he should have just shot his wife instead of old Frank when she first started talking about shooting old Frank. Too late now.

Mr. P. gets another drink of the whiskey and sees Jesus looking down at him. He feels sorry for Jesus. Jesus went through a lot to save sinners like him. Mr. P. thinks, Jesus died to save me and sinners like me.

Mr. P. can see how it was that day. He figures it was hot. In a country over there like that, it was probably always hot. And that cross He had to carry was heavy. He wonders if Jesus cried from all the pain they put Him through. Just thinking about anybody being so mean to Jesus that He'd cry is enough to make Mr. P. want to cry. He wishes he could have been there to help Jesus that day. He'd have helped Him, too. If he could have known what he knows now, and could have been there that day, he'd have tried to rescue Jesus. He could have fought some of the soldiers off. But there were probably so many of them, he wouldn't have had a chance. He'd have fought for Him, though. He'd have fought for Jesus harder than he'd ever fought for anything in his life, harder than he fought on the beach at Okinawa. Given his own blood. Maybe he could have gotten his hands on a sword, and kept them away from Jesus long enough for tHem to get away. But those guys were probably good sword-fighters back then. Back then they probably practiced a lot. It wouldn't have mattered to him, though. He'd have given his blood, all of it, and gladly to help Jesus.

The kids are all gone now. Old Frank's gone. His wife's still at the beauty parlor. She won't be in for a while. He gets another drink of the whiskey. It's awful good. He hates to stop drinking it, but he hates to keep on. With Jesus watching him and all.

The clock's ticking on the mantel. The hair needs sweeping off the hearth. He knows that cow's still got that white stuff running out from under her tail. But somebody else'll just have to see about it. Maybe the guy who sells the siding can see about it.

Mr. P. figures he ought to make sure it'll work first, so he pulls it out from under the couch and points it at the screen door in back. Right through the kitchen.

He figures maybe they won't be able to understand that. It'll be a big mystery that they'll never figure out. Some'll say Well he was making sure it'd work. Others'll say Aw it might have been there for years. They'll say What was he doing on the couch? And, I guess we'll have to go to town for a haircut now.

They'll even talk about how he borrowed it from Hulet for rats.

Old Frank has already gone through this. He didn't understand it. He trusted Mr. P. and knew he'd never hurt him. Maybe Mr. P. was a father to him. Maybe Mr. P. was God to him. What could he have been thinking of when he shot his best friend?

What in God's name can he be thinking of now?

Mr. Parker, fifty-eight, is reclining on his couch.

BOY AND DOG

The dog was already dead.
He was in the road.
A kid watched behind trees.
Tears shone on his face.
He dashed into the road.
Then a car came along.
He retreated to the sidewalk.
He heard his mother calling.
More cars were coming now.
The dog was really dead.
Blood was on the asphalt.
He could see it puddling.
The hubcap was bloody too.
It was also badly dented.
It came off a Mustang.

He ran to the dog.
A car drove up fast.
He caught up the tail.
He pulled on the dog.
It slid in slick blood.
The car got even closer.
He dropped it and ran.
His mother called to him.
She was on the porch.
Johnny what are you doing?
She couldn't see him crying.
His Spam was getting cold.
Bozo was the dog's name.
Bozo was an old dog.
The boy was only eight.
Bozo would be eleven forever.
He ran back to Bozo.
Then he pulled Bozo closer.
But another car came along.
It was the killer Mustang.
It was hunting its hubcap.
The boy had seen it.
He picked up a brick.
The driver was going slow.
He looked out the window.
He really wanted that hubcap.
It was a '65 fastback.
It was worth some money.

It had bad main seals.
Black oil leaked each night.
The dipstick was always low.
It had clobbered the dog.
The wheel hit him hard.
The shiny hubcap said BONG!
The kid held his brick.
He was hiding behind trees.
The driver was slowing down.
It was around here somewhere.
The brick was antique lemon.
It had three round holes.
But it was still heavy.
The car got awful close.
The kid held his brick.
The guy turned his head.
He didn't see the kid.
The kid threw the brick.
It landed on his head.
The driver fell over unconscious.
He jammed the gas down.
The Mustang burned some rubber.
It also burned some oil.
A big tree stopped it.
The tree shook pretty hard.
The windshield shattered in spiderwebs.
The horn started blowing loud.
The guy's head was down.

The horn blew and blew.
The kid got really panicky.
He ran out to help.
He had always loved dogs.
He grabbed the tail again.
The dog was pretty heavy.
The blood made him slide.
The kid kept looking around.
Something popped under the hood.
A little smoke rolled up.
The horn was still blowing.
Wires popped and something crackled.
Then the smoke turned black.
The kid got his dog.
The dog was messed up.
One of his eyes protruded.
Tire tracks were on him.
He was starting to stiffen.
All right then young man.
I'll put these Doritos up.
She didn't hear him yelling.
He couldn't yell very loud.
She went back to lunch.
The smoke wasn't bad yet.
The kid ran back across.
The horn was still blowing.
It was weaker than before.
The battery was getting tired.

Flames leaped under the car.
The guy blew the horn.
He looked sort of dead.
He had this big hole.
It was in his head.
The yellow flames went WHOOSH!
Then the paint started burning.
It was really getting hot.
Nobody would want it now.
The guy's hair was curling.
Fire was coming out everywhere.
The gas tank blew up.
There was this big explosion.
It knocked the kid down.
The car rocked with it.
Two of the tires blew.
The car sat lower then.
The kid said oh shit.
He regretted throwing the brick.
He touched the door handle.
Some of his skin melted.
His fingerprints were instantly gone.
It didn't hurt a bit.
He knew it should have.
It scared him pretty bad.
He could hear music playing.
He rubbed his melted hand.
The guy's hair was gone.

Smoke was thick and black.
It choked him something awful.
He coughed and gagged some.
He ran across the road.
He was needing the telephone.
The emergency number was 911.
He learned it in school.
His class visited the firemen.
They mentioned playing with matches.
They didn't mention throwing bricks.
He ran fast toward home.
But halfway there he stopped.
He didn't have enough time.
He had to go back.
The Mustang had turned black.
The tires were burning off.
Coils of wire fell away.
It wasn't worth much now.
The guy's shirt was burning.
The kid could smell it.
It looked like an Izod.
People were pulled over gawking.
One man came running up.
He was evidently a hero.
A shirt swaddled his hands.
The man grabbed the door.
The hero screamed a little.
The door handle had him.

It wouldn't turn him loose.
The fire rolled around him.
It started curling his hair.
He tried rescuing the driver.
The driver was buckled up.
He was also shoulder-harnessed.
The hero finally got loose.
But he screamed a lot.
His clothes were smoking bad.
He fell and rolled over.
The grass was scorched black.
He was beating himself silly.
His arm had turned black.
The kid watched all this.
The hero flailed the grass.
Somebody needed to get help.
But of course nobody did.
Some people won't get involved.
The car was fully involved.
It wasn't worth twenty bucks.
The motor was probably okay.
The aluminum transmission had melted.
The hero was still screaming.
Suddenly they heard an airhorn.
A big red truck arrived.
Firemen jumped off the truck.
They started hollering Jesus Christ.
One fireman hollered holy shit!

The driver was pretty nervous.
It was his first run.
He didn't set the brake.
The nozzlemen pulled the hose.
They were ready for water.
They were holding it tight.
The driver engaged the pump.
This disengaged the rear wheels.
Nozzlemen were screaming for water.
The hose was pulled away.
The truck was rolling backwards.
The firemen were chasing it.
They were really yelling loud.
It rolled into a ditch.
It was a deep ditch.
It was really a canal.
The canal held deep water.
The truck was pointing up.
The motor had already quit.
They couldn't pump any water.
The hoses wouldn't work now.
The Mustang driver got smaller.
The kid took it in.
He looked for the brick.
It was under the Mustang.
He tried to get it.
He thought about his fingerprints.
But he didn't have any.

So he let it go.
The firemen were screaming loud.
One had sense and radioed.
A crowd of spectators gathered.
A van with newsmen arrived.
There was an anchorman inside.
They started setting up cameras.
The announcer straightened his tie.
The Mustang was solid black.
The fire department came running.
They carried some powdered extinguishers.
They weighed almost twenty pounds.
They started mashing the handles.
White clouds of chemicals rolled.
Fire flashed here and there.
People coughed and almost gagged.
The gas tank kept burning.
They couldn't put it out.
They ran out of powder.
It was only baking soda.
Most people don't know that.
Firemen make money servicing them.
These had steak suppers sometimes.
They played bingo and drank.
Once they had a party.
Some of them got drunk.
Then they had a run.
Their food was barbecued goat.

But the goat burned up.

So did the Mustang driver.

The other truck came then.

A captain of firemen arrived.

He issued orders and radioed.

They stretched lines and attacked.

Only one tire was burning.

Bystanders muttered about their incompetence.

The firemen were pretty embarrassed.

An ambulance pulled up next.

The firemen acted very important.

They bullied the ambulance attendants.

They pried open the door.

One joked about Crispy Critters.

This is a breakfast cereal.

The captain's face turned red.

He began questioning some witnesses.

The kid sidled off unobtrusively.

His Spam was still waiting.

He went to the dog.

The dog was getting stiff.

He picked up one leg.

It stayed up like that.

He looked at the car.

A wrecker was driving up.

He'd never seen a wrecker.

He stuck around to watch.

The anchorman made eyewitness reports.

Several people were interrogated live.
They rushed home to brag.
They were almost real celebrities.
They would phone their neighbors.
They would phone their friends.
Neighbors and friends would watch.
The almost-celebrities would celebrate.
The parties would be gay.
The kid would see them.
He would recognize them all.
It would all be over.
Johnny Carson would come on.
He would be safe forever.
He would request a puppy.
His father would deny him.
He would make different promises.
His daddy would say no.
There were licenses and fees.
Puppies always grew into dogs.
And dogs sometimes chased cars.
And cars sometimes killed dogs.
And bricks sometimes got thrown.
Boys still go to woodsheds.
But fathers must be cautious.
Kids are violent these days.
Especially where pets are concerned.

JULIE: A MEMORY

It was muddy where we parked and I had to be careful not to get on soft ground. That's just a blank space. When I tried to touch her, she slapped my hands away. I heard him slip the safety off. "I don't want you to if you don't want to," she said. Then we went inside. I don't know why I drove all the way through. She didn't say. And then Julie came in. I figured that would make her happy. She had some kind of a fit all of a sudden. "Lock the doors," she said. He had the wrench up in one hand and his fingers were greasy and black and trembling. I didn't want to tell her. We got inside and we sat down. The blood had scabbed on my face. "Don't," she said. I crawled on my hands and knees to the first one just as he picked up the rifle. She wanted popcorn. You see all this stuff on TV now about abortions, and once I saw a doctor holding a fetus in his fingers. She'd left me some sandwich stuff in the refrigerator. I got dressed and turned off all the lights and locked the door. I don't know how many times he hit me. She didn't want to. She said that everything was a mistake, that she didn't love me. He begged hard for his life. And for no reason then, he just slapped her. When I thought of all that, I started feeling good. He looked like he was half asleep. The first boy pulled her panties down around her knees and she whimpered. They say they don't cook their hamburgers ahead of time, but they do. There was a little road that ran back behind, where all the black people were buried. I'd have to hunt under the seat for my socks. "Don't open it," she said. I wiped it with my hand and looked at it. But I wasn't really sure. Then he grabbed her legs, panting, and spread them apart. We lost track of time. I could have reached out and grabbed it. I recognized the second boy. He slapped her so hard her face leaped around sideways. Everybody has to have love. And it seemed like it ruined everything. But that car was there again. It happened quickly. What Julie and I were doing was no different. It was an adventure story. I think I said please to him that night. You can't ask things like that. I didn't even know if we could live together. But I knew she'd be on my side anyway. I worried about it for a long time, that I'd get caught. But I knew we had to try. I didn't want to turn his soul loose if he wasn't ready, so I told him to pray. It's a big step. He had a motor jack set up in front of the grill. One of them said that he didn't have any matches. Houses were all around. I had to keep my shirt on in front of my mother so she wouldn't see the scratches on my back. I stopped outside the city limits and got us a beer from the trunk.

She wasn't showing yet. I was trying to get up but I felt like I was drunk. I didn't figure he was ready. "Open that door, " he said. I got up on my knees. I'd been planning on staying overnight with some friends at the spillway, but it started raining hard about ten o'clock and we didn't want to sleep in our cars, so we just went home. When we'd first started doing it, we'd always used rubbers. I'd put off telling Mother. And it was driving him nuts. He jammed the rifle against my head. I wanted to go for pizza. Just his feet were sticking out from under the car. She said he was always buying her coffee and eating his lunch with her. I didn't say too much. We were quiet for a while then. I was wet with mud and it was cold on my legs. None of that mattered. And then she got pregnant. Trying to get her hot. So I just kept my mouth shut. I thought they were going to kill us. I listened. But she didn't even say anything about it. I thought we were going to talk. "Somebody with car trouble, I guess," I said. I think my mother wanted to ask me why I wasn't going with Julie anymore, but she didn't. We finally got out there, and the woods were dark and wet. She had her hands up in front of her face. I've even seen her in bars. It was so clear when it was happening. It didn't change anything. "I don't want no part of it," he said. Once we did it right there on the couch with her mother in the next room. I knew I had done the right thing. The first one handed the rifle to the second one and pushed her dress up. I could never go over there without thinking about all those dead people under the stones. Finally it was over. I didn't know if it would work. I put my face between her breasts and closed my eyes and just laid there. If we weren't doing it we were talking about doing it. I finished my beer and then got back in the car. He wanted to know who it was but I didn't say anything. "Thanks," she said. I didn't want to marry her. The road was wet so I drove carefully. It's not something you should do without thinking about it. She said he loved to dance. I cranked it and we sat hugging each other until it warmed up. Before she got out of the car, I made her tell me where he lived. She chain-smoked cigarettes and had brown stains on her fingertips. I wondered if maybe she'd had a child born out of wedlock herself. "Don't," she said. "Please don't." I thought, If you were married to her, you could do this all the time. Mother had offered to buy some for me, but I told her I wanted to take care of things like that by myself. I didn't want to embarrass her. She was talking about baby showers and baby clothes. I could see the rifle lying there, pointing toward the road. Her mother was strange to me. We started dressing. "Hurry up," she'd say. "Hurry up and get it in me." There was something about it on the news. He had his finger on the trigger. His soul was what I thought about, and mine, too. Her mother looked up when I went in, but then she turned away, back to the television. She had mud all over her face and she didn't want me to look at her. There was another boy standing in the rain, watching me. "I love you, " she said. They had her tied when I came to. I had to go home finally. He didn't hear me walk up to the car. The porch light was on when we pulled in and neither of us said anything. I figured she'd probably scream. I wiped my forearm across my eyes. He was probably about twenty. Maybe it wasn't even my baby. "When you going to tell your mother?" she said. I didn't know what I was going to tell my mother. You could hear that rain drumming on the roof while you were taking your clothes off and then when you were naked together on the backseat, with the doors locked, it was just the best thing you could want. Down behind the fence there were squirrels and deer. They used to live beside her. I didn't know what to do. Give up my whole life for her and the baby? I walked up on the porch and knocked on the door and heard her mother tell me to come in. I got her in my car and the first thing she did was pull my hand up her dress. She wasn't rude, but I could see that she just didn't want to talk. By then I couldn't do anything. He must have brought the whiskey because she never kept liquor in the house. "You bout two seconds away from gettin a bullet through your head," he said. But I wasn't ready to marry her. Then she squatted down, like she was going to pee on the ground. It was where we always went. She said she didn't want to get married. We held hands. "Ya'll done lost your fuckin minds," he said. "I want to," I said. It was cold outside. I parked my car in the woods and walked back down the road quickly, then went over a barbed-wire fence and down through a pasture. I know he was thinking about that night and what he'd done to us. She had her hand on my dick. I looked at Julie. "Don't," she said. That woman always seemed so hurt. I didn't know what to say. "Hell, she wants it," he said. We'd rest for ten minutes, kissing, and then we'd start again. I wanted to tell my mother and ask her what I should do. We pulled out finally and headed out of town. This night was a night we were going to talk. I thought I was going to wreck the car. You can't do without it. I couldn't see anything. We talked some more. She'd take her nails and scrape me so hard I'd almost tell her to stop. The rifle fell into the mud. "What are you waiting on?" she said. I got to be an expert at getting fully dressed sitting down. I was afraid she'd get up and walk in there and see us on the couch, but it didn't stop us. The first boy had her by the arms and he was dragging her toward a tree. "Tell her to open the door," he said. I'd always thought that having kids was something you should give some thought to. There's nothing blacker than woods at night. You could have her whenever you wanted her. There were a lot of people on the square when I cut through. She unbuckled my belt and unzipped my pants. We ate in the parking lot. We had to hurry because the movie was about to start. And then we said we didn't care what it was as long as it was healthy. When I went to bed, I pulled the covers all the way up over my head and saw it all again, every word and every sound and every raindrop. I didn't want her to have an abortion. I guess it was kind of like when you're little, and you've done something your mother or your father is going to whip you for, but you're hoping that if you beg hard enough they won't. I rolled the window down. He ran off into the woods with a crazy little cry. I got up quickly and went to meet her. "You get out of that car," the boy with the rifle said. He sounded drunk. I took a drink of it. I like adventure. It surprised me when she said she did. I think she felt guilty about the night we got rained out on our fishing trip. She slid up on the console next to me and we left. The second one turned around and looked at me with his dick sticking out of his pants. She laid her head back down. I couldn't understand why they were doing what they were doing. She pushed her dress up and pulled my hand in between her legs. I tried to talk to her for a while, but it was never any use. She got to telling me all about her job, and how this man who worked there was always trying to sweet-talk her on break. I had an old pistol that had belonged to my father. She said leave it alone. I had some beer iced down in my car and I asked her if she wanted one. Or three. "Get out," the one with the rifle said. She did say that Julie would be ready in a few minutes. I sat in the driveway for a long time just looking at the house. The one I hit got up off the ground. People were watching television within sight of us. I was running late when I got home, but she had my clothes ironed and laid out for me. It couldn't have been easy for her. I'd thought he was hurting her because of the way she was moaning. I went inside quietly and washed the blood off my face with a wet towel. They had a nice home there, but he was a long way from the house. I romped on it a little and the back end slid. She said if I wanted to take care of her, take her home. Something cold touched the side of my head. "Please, God," he said. I asked her what she would do about her clothes. When it was dry we'd take a blanket out of the trunk and spread it on the ground. The first thing she did was go over to the boy and spit on him. I knew we'd have a good time. She always made me lock the doors. I couldn't understand why nobody was coming to help us. "Listen," I said, "I don't know what you guys want." I could tell that she was happy. But one night we ran out or I forgot to buy some, or something. It didn't have a jack under it anywhere. The dates were so faded, and the names, too, that you couldn't read them. She didn't know the third one. Sometimes we'd tear each other's clothes getting them off. She told me on the way home. I knew the leaves were wet and cold and I knew how they felt on her skin. She raised up and looked at me. The tires were spinning in the mud. But then I thought that maybe she was just lonely. "You want to do it up here?" I said. "Or you want to get in the back?" But we were running late. She was on her knees and I could see him lunging at her face. I asked her if we were finished and she said yes. We'd have to find a place to live. I didn't want it growing up with just its mother's name, either. She had enough on her already. She was like me. I could have let him live. There were cars passing on the road and I kept thinking that one would surely pull in. I didn't even know where Julie's daddy was. There was a fifth of Wild Turkey on the kitchen table. I used to hunt there. He put his hands up in front of his face and closed his eyes and said, "Jesus, Jesus, oh please Jesus." The night I came in from fishing, I went to bed quietly and tried to go to sleep, but I could hear them moving in her bed, and once in a while, her moaning. But she got up that night and put on a robe and told me it was all right. I was afraid it would hurt her too much. I could do it, too. I just wanted her to be happy. The only thing we could think about was getting it into her as quickly as possible. I loved that rain. She said, "If I could dance, I'd marry that man." I was hungry and wanted to fix myself some breakfast. Some were killed in the Civil War. Blood was in my eyes. You could see the ruts deep in the mud where the tires had gone before us. That night was no different. I took her blouse and bra off and she got on top of me. I told her that I wanted to take care of her. He was gone the next morning and we didn't talk about it. I said I hoped it was a boy. "You just shut your mouth," he said. I thought about it. His eyes didn't close. Give me a good old love story anytime. It was one of those space movies. The foot of the fetus was smaller than his thumb. It was just like shooting a dog. I yelled for him as loud as I could. The first boy went around and tried to open the door. I made a decision right there on that backseat, naked, holding her. Julie drew up and leaned against her side of the car. I didn't say anything. My mother would be a grandmother. "You can't hide it forever," I said. But sometimes when you do things, you have to pay for them. She had on a red dress and white shoes. She had already gone somewhere, on a date, I guess. Almost all of her friends were married and she wasn't used to dating and she probably worried over what I thought about it. I went into her room and I woke her up. I thought about it. I don't know how long we did it that night. It seemed like that broke the ice. There was blood dripping off my face. It made everything seem so nice. "What do you think?" she said. You can't place your order and pull on around and have it ready within thirty seconds without having it cooked ahead of time. She was two months pregnant. So I went out there and got her one. His hands relaxed and one of his feet kicked. They have to. But it was only a matter of time. "We don't want any trouble," I said. On that backseat with her I felt I had all the happiness I'd ever need. They had her tied on the ground with her arms around a tree. In Memphis. All this is fuzzy. I had to keep wiping the blood out of my eyes. Mother stays gone all the time. I couldn't tell her. It had already been in all the papers about the boy they found. Maybe even me. He stomped on my head. The third boy was still standing in the road. I remember he just rolled over and pulled the covers up over him. We'd taken all kinds of crazy chances. She said what was done was done. His face was down in the mud. I'm for life. There weren't any napkins and they didn't give us enough ketchup. "You told her?" I said. She said think about it. She hadn't come right out and said it. Nobody wants to. I eased it up into park and got out with my hands up. It had taken her a long time to get over Daddy leaving her, but she was beginning to make the most of it. It was sharp. They must have known I was there. "You kids have a good time," her mother said. I asked her if she wanted to go to the police or the hospital or what. I don't know how we got over in the woods. Julie wasn't anywhere around. She told it like she was in a trance. There were junked cars all over the pasture. "Just tell me what you want me to do," I said. "If you want this car you can have it." We'd get so hot we just wouldn't think clearly. He'd laid the rifle down. I just unlocked the door and went on into the kitchen. I knew he'd hurt her. "Please," I said, "don't hurt her." He was trying to pull the motor out of a '68 Camaro down in the pasture. I think my mind has tried to cover it up some way. "Please," he said. "Please please please." It wasn't that bad. I didn't think anything about it. "What's wrong?" she said. They had homemade tombstones, carved out of sandrock. I didn't want to hurt her. The first one was doing something to her. The glass was fogged over with our breathing. My car was over there. I didn't want to get up. I couldn't see her getting an abortion. It was pretty good. The first one was puking against a tree. It's a hell of a thing, to see your mother doing that. "Would you just hold me for a little while?" I said. The gun went off. "What?" I said. The one who kicked me put a knife against my throat and I didn't do anything else. "Then we'll tell yours," she said. But I probably wasn't the only kid who'd ever seen something like that. I just had gotten my car paid for, but it needed new tires. It squealed once in the road and was gone. He didn't want to die. I got out to take a leak and the ground was soft. When I grabbed for it, the other one kicked me. The vinyl top was rotted. He screamed when he came. And I wondered what she'd say. They must have heard my car pull up. She wouldn't even look up from the TV when I said something. "Are you sure?" she said. I cared about her. "I'm sure," I said. He rolled out from under it with a wrench in his hand and a pissed-off look on his face, and he knew me then. It was a green '72 Camaro with a black top. He slammed me against the fender. He dropped the wrench. "Don't ask me any questions, " I said. "Just hold me." I didn't know if I loved her. "You having trouble?" I said. I thought my nose was running. She was watching "Knot's Landing" and I watched it with her for a while. Randy Hillhouse lived not an eighth of a mile away. I missed Daddy, sure. "Remember me?" I said. I wound up getting about half fucked-up in the kitchen before I got my sausage and eggs fried. "We won't be out late," she

said. It was the muzzle of a .22 rifle. I knew she wanted me
to marry her. "I wonder what that's doing there," she said. I
thought I'd seen the boy somewhere before. Julie was quiet.
I went down like I'd been shot. "Oh, man, no," he said. It
was raining, not hard, just enough to where you had to keep
the wipers going to see. The movie wasn't that great. I could
have let it go, I guess. We never did it less than twice. I've
seen hogs do like that. I stuck it in his face. After it was over,
we held each other for a long time. Later on I remembered it
like a nightmare. It seems like I cried. Every night. I wanted a
cigarette and couldn't smoke in there. She won't even talk to me
now, doesn't act like she remembers who I am. "You told her?"
I said. I didn't love her. Pow! I think now that I must have been
trying to choke him. We'd talked about telling her. But I loved
my mother. The first one and the second one were brothers.
About the same age as me. I turned and looked at it. "It's okay
to cry sometimes," she said. The car was parked at the end
of the turnaround. I could see this kid in my mind, running
around on a softball field. "You want to tell her?" I said. When
I pulled the door shut, I thought about it and unlocked it and
stepped inside the living room and turned on the lamp. It's
more like a dream now that never really happened. She was
screaming for me to help her. She hadn't held me like that in
a long time. I waited a week. Her mouth tasted like chewing
gum. I think I cried some. It got hard again. I'd already put it
up in reverse when the first one knocked on the window. We
kissed. I was late when I got over there. I must have passed
out. She kissed me, and then she looked at her mother. "For

God's sake," I said. I only put one shell in it. I always felt like
her mother knew what we were doing. We'd have clothes lying
everywhere. I remember one time I walked in on them when
they were in bed. I made sure it was him. "You can talk to me
anytime you want to," she said. I can't forget how he looked
lying there. She said take her home. There was a strange car
in the driveway when I pulled up. It was about fifteen miles
from town. I stopped and watched for a long time before I went
up. They were waiting for us. I thought I was going to vomit,
but I didn't. I smashed his head into the fender and caught his
hair in both my hands and kneed him in the nose. I'd never
done anything to him. We heard their car leave. I kissed her
and opened her blouse. I shot him and he fell. "You can get
me so damn hot," she said. Then I got myself some Coke out
of the icebox and mixed a drink. One was all I needed. She
told me how this man had three kids and a wife who didn't
like to dance. I didn't move. I could just touch her between
her legs and she'd be ready to come. I guess we were both
surprised. We were both quiet. "Let's get up and go home, and
we'll tell your mother first," I said. I didn't know whether to
just go on in or knock on the door. The one on Julie's side said
something to the one with the rifle. His pants were down around
his knees and she sounded like she was choking. "No," he said,
"I don't know you." It seemed that she was what I had been
wanting my whole life. I turned around and grabbed his head.
They didn't look like people who would raise a son like that.
"We've got a flat," he said, but the car looked level. The second
one went over to her. I didn't know what they were doing.

"Yes, you do," I said. Another, third boy stood in the rain with his hands in his pockets. I was lying on the ground in front of the car. Her body was the temple where I worshipped. They hit me in the head with the gun and then I couldn't see what they were doing with her. I blame that on him. He might have been their cousin. I'd seen his parents before. I eased through town. "Let's get married," I said. The rain was falling in front of the headlights. I had to pull over and stop. It was the best thing I'd ever done. I didn't have an inspection sticker and I was trying to stay away from the law. She'd never mentioned him. But they do. He'd been to the funeral of his brother. I didn't know what to do. "I'll do anything if you don't," she said. I thought she was full of bullshit. Sideways. I didn't like them anyway. I pulled the trigger. I saw then what they'd done. We pulled up into the graveyard and the tires slid in the mud. "He's got a gun," she said. I don't remember driving there. They were both naked and he was between her legs. He was dead, just like that. But the fetus was alive. We hadn't talked about telling anybody. I watched it, but I couldn't concentrate on it for thinking about what we were going to do later. She was still getting ready. He had it out and was holding it in his hand. There were a lot of things I could have said to him, I guess. She said she hoped it was a girl. I know I was scared. I cranked the car and let it warm up. The third one looked like he was puking in the ditch. It made a little red hole between his eyes. She had an abortion. What's bad is that he may be burning for an eternity because of me. She couldn't stop kissing me. I could remember, faintly, seeing them doing it when I was little.

When I grabbed the barrel, he turned loose and ran. When it was raining, it was wonderful to park with her. We'd have to get married soon. I know she was thinking about doing it just like me. I kicked the bottoms of his feet. But it's all posted now and you can't hunt on it. I helped her into the car and we looked for the third boy but we didn't see him. There was so much I had to tell her and so much I needed to tell her and in the end I told her nothing. And maybe we wouldn't even be able to make it. I couldn't feel her with one on. I took a shower and shaved, walking around naked in the house. I didn't want to see her hurt. She knew them. "Hey," I said. Jeans and a striped shirt. I didn't know what in the hell to do. I didn't mind killing him so much, after what he'd done. It was my child. I guess he was loosening the transmission bolts. So safe and warm. "Whenever you tell yours," I said. I turned on the defroster when it warmed up. I kept messing around with her. They used to come over and talk to her. The grass was high and there was an old dog pen or hog pen in the pasture with rotten posts and rusted wire. I'd always come right away the first time. We'd been going at each other for the last five months. He was crying and begging me not to do it. I begged him not to hurt her and he kicked me in the face. It hurt.

SAMARITANS

I was smoking my last cigarette in a bar one day, around the middle of the afternoon. I was drinking heavy, too, for several reasons. It was hot and bright outside, and cool and dark inside the bar, so that's one reason I was in there. But the main reason I was in there was because my wife had left me to go live with somebody else.

A kid came in there unexpectedly, a young, young kid. And of course that's not allowed. You can't have kids coming in bars. People won't put up with that. I was just on the verge of going out to my truck for another pack of smokes when he walked in. I don't remember who all was in there. Some old guys, I guess, and probably, some drunks. I know there was one old man, a golfer, who came in there every afternoon with shaky hands, drank exactly three draft beers, and told these crummy dirty jokes that would make you just close your eyes and shake your head without smiling if you weren't in a real good mood. And back then, I was never in much of a good mood. I knew they'd tell that kid to leave.

But I don't think anybody much wanted to. The kid didn't look good. I thought there was something wrong the minute he stepped in. He had these panicky eyes.

The bartender, Harry, was a big muscled-up guy with a beard. He was washing beer glasses at the time, and he looked up and saw him standing there. The only thing the kid had on was a pair of green gym shorts that were way too big for him. He looked like maybe he'd been walking down the side of a road for a long time, or something similar to that.

Harry, he raised up a little and said, "What you want, kid?" I could see that the kid had some change in his hand. He was standing on the rail and he had his elbows hooked over the bar to hold himself up.

I'm not trying to make this sound any worse than it was, but to me the kid just looked like maybe he hadn't always had enough to eat. He was two or three months overdue for a haircut, too.

"I need a pack a cigrets," he said. I looked at Harry to see what he'd say. He was already shaking his head.

"Can't sell em to you, son," he said. "Minor."

I thought the kid might give Harry some lip. He didn't. He said, "Oh," but he stayed where he was. He looked at me. I knew then that something was going on. But I tried not to think about it. I had troubles enough of my own.

Harry went back to washing his dishes, and I took another drink of my beer. I was trying to cut down, but it was so damn hot outside, and I had a bunch of self-pity loading up on me at that time. The way I had it figured, if I could just stay where I was until the sun went down, and then make my way home without getting thrown in jail, I'd be okay. I had some catfish I was going to thaw out later.

Nobody paid any attention to the kid after that. He wasn't making any noise, wasn't doing anything to cause people to look at him. He turned loose of the bar and stepped down off the rail, and I saw his head going along the far end toward the door.

But then he stuck his face back around the corner, and motioned me toward him with his finger. I didn't say a word, I just looked at him. I couldn't see anything but his eyes sticking up, and that one finger, crooked at me, moving.

I could have looked down at my beer and waited until he went away. I could have turned my back. I knew he couldn't stay in there with us. He wasn't old enough. You don't have to get yourself involved in things like that. But I had to go out for my cigarettes, eventually. Right past him.

I got up and went around there. He'd backed up into the dark part of the lounge.

"Mister," he said. "Will you loan me a dollar?"

He already had money for cigarettes. I knew somebody outside had sent him inside.

I said, "What do you need a dollar for?"

He kind of looked around and fidgeted his feet in the shadows while he thought of what he was going to say.

"I just need it," he said. "I need to git me somethin."

He looked pretty bad. I pulled out a dollar and gave it to him. He didn't say thanks or anything. He just turned and pushed open the door and went outside. I started not to follow him just then. But after a minute I did.

The way the bar's made, there's a little enclosed porch you come into before you get into the lounge. There's a glass door where you can stand inside and look outside. God, it was hot out there. There wasn't even a dog walking around. The sun was burning down on the parking lot, and the car the kid was crawling into was about what I'd expected. A junky-ass old Rambler, wrecked on the right front end, with the paint almost faded off, and slick tires, and a rag hanging out of the grill. It was parked beside my truck and it was full of people. It looked like about four kids in the backseat. The woman who was driving put her arm over the seat, said something to the kid, and then reached out and whacked the hell out of him.

I started to go back inside so I wouldn't risk getting involved. But Harry didn't have my brand and there was a pack on the dash. I could see them from where I was, sitting there in the sun, almost close enough for the woman to reach out and touch.

I'd run over a dog with my truck that morning and I wasn't feeling real good about it. The dog had actually been sleeping in the road. I thought he was already dead and was just going to straddle him until I got almost on top of him, when he raised up suddenly and saw me, and tried to run. Of course I didn't have time to stop by then. If he'd just stayed down, he'd have been all right. The muffler wouldn't have even hit him. It was just a small dog. But, boy, I heard it when it hit the bottom of my truck. It went *WHOP!* and the dog—it was a white dog—came rolling out from under my back bumper with all four legs stiff, yelping. White hair was flying everywhere. The air was full of it. I could see it in my rearview mirror. And I don't know why I was thinking about that dog I'd killed while I was watching those people, but I was. It didn't make me feel any better.

They were having some kind of terrible argument out there in that suffocating hot car. There were quilts and pillows piled up in there, like they'd been camping out. There was an old woman on the front seat with the woman driving, the one who'd whacked hell out of her kid for coming back empty-handed.

I thought maybe they'd leave if I waited for a while. I thought maybe they'd try to get their cigarettes somewhere else. And then I thought maybe their car wouldn't crank. Maybe, I thought, they're waiting for somebody to come along with some jumper cables and jump them off. But I didn't have any jumper cables. I pushed open the door and went down the steps.

There was about three feet of space between my truck and their car. They were all watching me. I went up to the window of my truck and got my cigarettes off the dash. The woman driving turned all the way around in the seat. You couldn't tell how old she was. She was one of those women that you can't tell about. But probably somewhere between thirty and fifty. She didn't have liver spots. I noticed that.

I couldn't see all of the old woman from where I was standing. I could just see her old wrinkled knees, and this dirty slip she had sticking out from under the edge of her housecoat. And her daughter—I knew that was who she was—didn't look much better. She had a couple of long black hairs growing out of this mole on her chin that was the size of a butter bean. Her hair kind of looked like a mophead after you've used it for a long time. One of the kids didn't even have any pants on.

She said, "Have they got some cold beer in yonder?" She shaded her eyes with one hand while she looked up at me.

I said, "Well, yeah. They do. But they won't sell cigarettes to a kid that little."

"It just depends on where they know ye or not," she said. "If they don't know ye then most times they won't sell em to you. Is that not right?"

I knew I was already into something. You can get into something like that before you know it. In a minute.

"I guess so," I said.

"Have you got—why you got some, ain't you? Can I git one of them off you?" She was pointing to the cigarettes in my hand. I opened the pack and gave her one. The kid leaned out and wanted to know if he could have one, too.

"Do you let him smoke?"

"Why, he just does like he wants to," she said. "Have you not got a light?"

The kid was looking at me. I had one of those Bics, a red one, and when I held it out to her smoke, she touched my hand for a second and held it steady with hers. She looked up at me and tried to smile. I knew I needed to get back inside right away, before it got any worse. I turned to go and what she came out with stopped me dead in my tracks.

"You wouldn't buy a lady a nice cold beer, would you?" she said. I turned around. There was this sudden silence, and I knew that everybody in the car was straining to hear what I would say. It was serious. Hot, too. I'd already had about five and I was feeling them a little in the heat. I took a step back without meaning to and she opened her door.

"I'll be back in a little bit, Mama," she said.

I looked at those kids. Their hair was ratty and their legs were skinny. It was so damn hot you couldn't stand to stay out in it. I said, "You gonna leave these kids out here in the sun?"

"Aw, they'll be all right," she said. But she looked around kind of uncertainly. I was watching those kids. They were as quiet as dead people.

I didn't want to buy her a beer. But I didn't want to make a big deal out of it, either. I didn't want to keep looking at those kids. I just wanted to be done with it.

"Lady," I said, "I'll buy you a beer. But those kids are burning up in that car. Why don't you move it around there in the shade?"

"Well." She hesitated. "I reckon I could," she said. She got back in and it cranked right up. The fan belt was squealing, and some smoke farted out from the back end. But she limped it around to the side and left it under a tree. Then we went inside together.

The first Bud she got didn't last two minutes. She sucked the can dry. She had on some kind of military pants and a man's long-sleeved work shirt, and house shoes. Blue ones, with a little fuzzy white ball on each. She had the longest toes I'd ever seen.

Finally I asked her if she wanted another beer. I knew she did.

"Lord yes. And I need some cigrets too if you don't care. Marlboro Lights. Not the menthol. Just reglar lights."

I didn't know what to say to her. I thought about telling her I was going to the bathroom, and then slipping out the door. But I really wasn't ready to leave just yet. I bought her another beer and got her some cigarettes.

"I'm plumb give out," she said. "Been drivin all day."

I didn't say anything. I didn't want anybody to think I was going with her.

"We tryin to git to Morgan City Loozeanner. M'husband's sposed to've got a job down there and we's agoin to him. But I don't know," she said. "That old car's about had it."

I looked around in the bar and looked at my face in the mirror behind the rows of bottles. The balls were clicking softly on the pool tables.

"We left from Tuscalooser Alabama," she said. "But them younguns has been yellin and fightin till they've give me a sick headache. It shore is nice to set down fer a minute. Ain't it good and cool in here?"

I watched her for a moment. She had her legs crossed on the bar stool and about two inches of ash hanging off her cigarette. I got up and went out the door, back to the little enclosed porch. By looking sideways I could see the Rambler parked under the shade. One of the kids was squatted down behind it, using the bathroom. I thought about things for a while and then went back in and sat down beside her.

"Ain't many men'll hep out a woman in trouble," she said. "Specially when she's got a buncha kids."

I ordered myself another beer. The old one was hot. I set it up on the bar and she said, "You not goin to drank that?"

"It's hot," I said.

"I'll drank it," she said, and she pulled it over next to her. I didn't want to look at her anymore. But she had her eyes locked on me and she wouldn't take them off. She put her hand on my wrist. Her fingers were cold.

"It's some people in this world has got thangs and some that ain't," she said. "My deddy used to have money. Owned three service stations and a sale barn. Had four people drove trucks fer him. But you can lose it easy as you git it. You ought to see him now. We cain't even afford to put him in a rest home."

I got up and went over to the jukebox and put two quarters in. I played some John Anderson and some Lynn Anderson and then I punched Narvel Felts. I didn't want to have to listen to what she had to say.

She was lighting a cigarette off the butt of another one when I sat down beside her again. She grabbed my hand as soon as it touched the bar.

"Listen," she said. "That's my mama out yonder in that car. She's seventy-eight year old and she ain't never knowed nothin but hard work. She ain't got a penny in this world. What good's it done her to work all her life?"

"Well," I said, "she's got some grandchildren. She's got them."

"Huh! I got a girl eighteen, was never in a bit a trouble her whole life. Just up and run off last year with a goddamn sand nigger. Now what about that?"

"I don't know," I said.

"I need another beer!" she said, and she popped her can down on the bar pretty hard. Everybody turned and looked at us. I nodded to Harry and he brought a cold one over. But he looked a little pissed.

"Let me tell you somethin," she said. "People don't give a shit if you ain't got a place to sleep ner nothin to eat. They don't care. That son of a bitch," she said. "He won't be there when we git there. If we ever git there." And she slammed her face down on the bar, and started crying, loud, holding onto both beers.

Everybody stopped what they were doing. The people shooting pool stopped. The guys on the shuffleboard machine just stopped and turned around.

"Get her out of here," Harry said. "Frank, you brought her in here, you get her out."

I got down off my stool and went around to the other side of her, and I took her arm.

"Come on," I said. "Let's go back outside."

I tugged on her arm. She raised her head and looked straight at Harry.

"*Fuck* you," she said. "You don't know nothin about me. You ain't fit to judge."

"Out," he said, and he pointed toward the door. "Frank," he said.

"Come on," I told her. "Let's go."

It hadn't cooled off any, but the sun was a little lower in the sky. Three of the kids were asleep in the backseat, their hair plastered to their heads with sweat. The old woman was sitting in the car with her feet in the parking lot, spitting brown juice out the open door. She didn't even turn her head when we walked back to the car. The woman had the rest of the beer in one hand, the pack of Marlboro Lights in the other. She leaned against the fender when we stopped.

"You think your car will make it?" I said. I was looking at the tires and thinking of the miles they had to go. She shook her head slowly and stared at me.

"I done changed my mind," she said. "I'm gonna stay here with you. I love you."

Her eyes were all teary and bitter, drunk-looking already, and I knew that she had been stomped on all her life, and had probably been forced to do no telling what. And I just shook my head.

"You can't do that," I said.

She looked at the motel across the street.

"Let's go over there and git us a room," she said. "I want to."

The kid who had come into the bar walked up out of the hot weeds and stood there looking at us for a minute. Then he got in the car. His grandmother had to pull up the front seat to let him in. She turned around and shut the door.

"I may just go to Texas," the woman said. "I got a sister lives out there. I may just drop these kids off with her for a while and go on out to California. To Los Vegas."

I started to tell her that Las Vegas was not in California, but it didn't matter. She turned the beer up and took a long drink of it, and I could see the muscles and cords in her throat pumping and working. She killed it. She dropped the can at her feet, and it hit with a tiny tinny sound and rolled under the car. She wiped her mouth with the back of her hand, tugging hard at her lips, and then she wiped her eyes.

"Don't nobody know what I been through," she said. She was looking at the ground. "Havin to live on food stamps and feed four younguns." She shook her head. "You cain't do it," she said. "You cain't hardly blame nobody for wantin to run off from it. If they was any way I could run off myself I would."

"That's bad," I said.

"That's terrible," I said.

She looked up and her eyes were hot.

"What do you care? All you goin to do is go right back in there and git drunk. You just like everybody else. You ain't never had to go in a grocery store and buy stuff with food stamps and have everbody look at you. You ain't never had to go hungry. Have you?"

I didn't answer.

"Have you?"

"No."

"All right, then," she said. She jerked her head toward the building. "Go on back in there and drank ye goddamn beer. We made it this far without you."

She turned her face to one side. I reached back for my wallet because I couldn't think of anything else to do. I couldn't stand to look at them anymore.

I pulled out thirty dollars and gave it to her. I knew that their troubles were more than she'd outlined, that they had awful things wrong with their lives that thirty dollars would never cure. But I don't know. You know how I felt? I felt like I feel when I see those commercials on TV, of all those people, women and kids, starving to death in Ethiopia and places, and I don't send money. I know that Jesus wants you to help feed the poor.

She looked at what was in her hand, and counted it, jerking the bills from one hand to the other, two tens and two fives. She folded it up and put it in her pocket, and leaned down and spoke to the old woman.

"Come on, Mama," she said. The old woman got out of the car in her housecoat and I saw then that they were both wearing exactly the same kind of house shoes. She shuffled around to the front of the car, and her daughter took her arm.

They went slowly across the parking lot, the old woman limping a little in the heat, and I watched them until they went up the steps that led to the lounge and disappeared inside. The kid leaned out the window and shook his head sadly. I pulled out a cigarette and he looked up at me.

"Boy you a dumb sumbitch," he said.

And in a way I had to agree with him.

NIGHT LIFE

I decided a long time ago that it isn't easy meeting them, not for me. Some guys can just walk up to a woman and start talking to her, start saying anything. I can't. I have to wait and work up my nerve, have a few beers. I have to sit at a table for a while, or the bar, and look them over and find the one who looks like she won't turn a man down. This sometimes means picking one who is sitting by herself, who is maybe a little older than most, maybe even one who doesn't look very good. Sometimes I wait until she dances with another man, then go over and make my move after she sits back down. Sometimes, if I see one whose looks I like, I send a drink over to her table. But it isn't easy meeting them.

I'm in a bar just outside the city limits Friday night when three women come in and take a table next to the dance floor, the last table not taken. I order another beer and look out over the crowd, the band playing, the couples who have found each other drifting over the floor like smoke. Some of the tables have three and four women, some have couples, some have men, and one table has a girl by herself. I check her out.

She has on a black dress and white stockings, is dressed, I think, a little like a witch. She has a bottle in a brown paper sack sitting on the table and she holds onto her solitary drink with both hands. She seems to have eyes for only this. I sip on my beer for a while and eye the creeping clock above the taps and finally I go over. She looks up and sees me coming her way and looks away.

"Hi," I say, when I stop beside her chair. I wish the band wouldn't play rock and roll; you can't even talk over the noise.

She smiles but she doesn't say anything. I'm going to be shot down.

I lean over and shout above the music: "How you doing?" She says something that I think is "okay" and I feel completely stupid, leaning over her like this. She looks like she just wants me to go away quickly and leave her alone. I won't score. She won't dance. Friday night is flying away.

"Want to dance?" I shout in her ear. The black horn player is crouched on the stage in front of the mike, the spotlight on him, his cheeks ballooned out as he blows and sweats, his jeweled fingers flying over the valves. She shakes her head and gives me a sad look. Smoke two feet thick hangs from the ceiling.

"Hell, come on," I say, putting on my friendliest smile, feeling my confidence—what little I had to start with—ebbing away. They're all like this. They won't talk to you, they won't dance. Why do they come out to a place like this if they don't want to meet men? "I'm not going to bite you," I say.

She takes one hand off her drink and leans slightly toward me. "Thanks anyway," she says. The flesh around her eyes looks dark, it's bruised, she's hurt. Maybe somebody slapped her. Maybe she said the wrong thing to the wrong man and he popped her. I know it can happen between a man and a woman. It can happen in a second.

"You live around here?" I say. I don't know what to say; I'm just saying anything to try and keep her talking.

She shakes her head, closes her eyes briefly. Patience. She's weary of this, maybe, these strange men asking, always asking, never stopping. "No. I live at Hattiesburg. I'm just up here for the weekend."

"You waiting on somebody?"

She draws back and blinks. Now she'll tell me it's none of my business. "Not really," she says. "I'm just waiting."

"Well come on and dance, then," I say.

She opens a small brown purse that looks like a dead mole and pulls out a white cigarette. I fish up my lighter and give her some fire. She inhales and coughs, her tiny fist balled at her mouth. Maybe she's had a bigger fist at her mouth. Maybe she likes it.

"Thanks," she says.

"You going to school at Hattiesburg?" I say.

She nods, looks around. "Yeah."

"Just up here living it up on the weekend."

"Not really. I just came up to Jackson to sort of be by myself for a while."

Something's bothering her, I can tell. She only wants to be left alone. She doesn't want to dance. She has her own bottle and her own table, her own troubles of which I know nothing. So I draw back a chair and put one foot up in it, rest my elbow on my knee. "How come?" I say.

She cups her face in her other hand and dabs at the ashtray with the cigarette.

"Oh. You know. Just getting away from everything."

"Yeah," I say. I know the feeling. I begin wishing I'd never walked over here. "What's your name?"

"Lorraine," this Lorraine says. She doesn't ask me my name.

"You look sad, Lorraine. What's wrong?"

"Nothing," she says, apparently only mildly pissed. "Nothing's wrong. I just want to be by myself for a while. I've just got some things I have to deal with."

I know. I know all people have things they must deal with. I have things I must deal with. I must deal with lonesome Friday nights, and these little semihostile confrontations sometimes occur as a result. But I don't know when to stop.

"Don't you like to dance?" I say. I feel like a fool. Am a fool.

"Sure. Sure I like to dance. I just don't feel like it tonight."

"Well," I say. I hate to get shot down, blown out of the saddle. But most of the time, I get shot down. I hate to have to turn away and go back to the bar without even a dance. I hate for them to beat me like this. But she probably does have some problem. There's probably a man involved somewhere, somehow. Possibly even a woman.

"Don't take it personally," she says. "Maybe some other night."

"Sure," I say, and I turn away. I walk a few steps and stop. I look back at her. She's taking the top off the bottle. I don't know what's the matter with me. I go back to her table.

"You sure you don't want to dance?" I say.

"No," she says, not even looking up. "Not now. Please leave me alone."

She's just lucky is all. She doesn't know just how damn lucky she is. The last of the Budweiser is almost warm, so I raise it aloft and signal to the sullen barmaid. I know her. She knows me. Her wet swollen hands reach into a dark cooler. I give her money but she doesn't speak. She doesn't want to look at me. Her heavy breasts sway as she rubs the bar hard, her eyes down. I watch them move. I watch her move away. She finds something to do at the other end of the bar. I take a drink.

A large number of people are wanting in the bathroom. I wait for three or four minutes before I can get inside the door, and then it's old piss, wet linoleum, knifecarvings above stained urinals that shredded butts have clogged. Water is weeping out from the partitioned commode stall where there is never any toilet paper. Others in line behind me are now waiting their turn. Their faces are scarred and murderous; it won't do to bump into them. To these no apology is acceptable. They'll cut their knuckles again and again on my broken teeth after I'm on the floor.

I go back out, into the noise and the smoke and the dark.

A woman touches my wrist when I go by her table, one of the three I saw earlier.

"Hey," she says. "How come you ain't asked me to dance yet?"

And there she is. Dark hair. Pale face. Sweater.

"I was fixing to," I say. "You want to wait till the band starts back up?"

"Set down," she says. She pulls out a chair and I sit.

"Where's your friends?" I say. I hope they won't come back. I don't know why she's picked me, but I'm glad somebody has. Even if the night turns out wasted there is hope at this moment.

"They over yonder," she points. "I've seen you before."

"In here?" I need my beer. "Let me go over here and get my beer and I'll be right back." She nods and smiles and I can't tell much about her except she's got knockers. I get my beer and come back.

"I saw you in here other night," she says. "Last weekend."

That's not right; I worked all weekend last weekend, trying to make more money. But I say, "Yeah. I come in here about every weekend."

Dark hair. Pale face. Sweater. Knockers. Jeans. I look down. Tennis shoes. With black socks.

"I used to come in here with my husband all the time," she says. "You want a drink?"

I lift my beer. We sit for a while without saying anything. The band is coming back, moving around on the stage and talking behind the dead mikes.

"That's a pretty good band," I say.

"Yeah. If you like nigger music. I wish they'd get a good country band. You like country music?"

"Yeah," I say. "Sure." But I wish I knew George Thorogood personally.

"Who you like?"

I have to think. "Aw. I like old Ricky Skaggs pretty good. Vern Gosden, I like him a lot. John Anderson."

"I used to be a singer," she says.

"Oh really?" I'm surprised. "Where?"

She looks around. She shrugs. I watch her breasts rise and fall. "Just around."

"I mean, professionally?" I sip my beer.

"Well. I sung at the Tupelo Mid-South Fair and Dairy Show in nineteen seventy-six. Had a three-piece band. That's where I met my husband."

"You're divorced," I say.

"Huh. Wish I was."

Here's the one thing I don't need: to get hooked up with somebody who has more problems than I do. I'm already on probation. I don't need to get hooked up with somebody who will sit here all night telling me how her husband fucked her over. But she has some really nice, truly wonderful breasts. It won't hurt to sit here and talk to her for a while. Maybe she's as lonely as I am.

"What? Are you separated?" I say.

"Yeah."

"How long?"

"About two weeks. Listen. I don't give a shit what he does. He's a sorry son of a bitch. I don't care if I don't never see him again."

"You're just out to have a good time."

"Damn right."

I tell her I think we can have one.

By ten we're out on the parking lot in her new Lincoln (surprise) and she's braced up against the driver's door. I have her sweater and bra all pushed up above her breasts and I'm moaning and kissing and trying to get her pants down. We're half hidden in the shadow of the building, but the neon lights are shining on the hood and part of the front seat. People in certain areas of the parking lot can see what we're doing. I don't care; I'm hot. Her nipples have been in and out of my mouth and she's halfway or halfheartedly trying to fight me off. She smells of talcum powder and light sweat. We've been kissing for ten minutes, but she doesn't seem to be excited. I know already, deep down, that something is wrong. She keeps looking out over the parking lot.

"Oh baby," I moan. I kiss the side of her neck and taste makeup on my tongue, slightly bitter. Patooey. "Let's do it," I say.

"Not here," she says. She pushes out from under me and takes both hands and tugs her bra and sweater back into place. I look at her for a moment and turn away. Not here. That might mean maybe somewhere else.

"Oh we'll *do* it," she says. Sure. "We just can't right now."

She rubs the side of my face. "My husband might be around here."

"Your husband?" I say. What's this? "I thought you said you weren't worried about him." It's always like this. They all have some problem they have to lay on you before they'll give it to you, and even then sometimes they won't give it to you. "What? You think he might come around here?"

She brushes the hair up away from her eyes and pulls at her pants. She pulls down one of the visor mirrors and checks her face.

"He might. I told you we used to come over here."

"You said you didn't give a shit what he did."

"I don't."

"Then what are you worried about?"

"I'm not worried. I just don't want him to catch me doing anything."

"Aw," I say. "Okay." I understand now. She's another one of the crazy ones. I don't know why I'm the one who always finds them, goes straight to them like a pointer after birds. They're not worth the trouble. They drive me nuts with their kids and their divorces and their diet pills and their friends in trouble and their ex-husbands for whom they still carry the torch. They promise and promise and promise. I know she's crazy now, I know the thing to do now is just forget about it, go back inside, leave her out here. "Well, I'm going back in here and get me a beer," I say. "I don't want to get mixed up with you and your husband. I'll see you later."

I slide over to the door—I don't have to slide far—and open

it. I step out onto the parking lot and look back in at her. She doesn't look up. She has some secret hurt in her heart that matters to her and doesn't matter to me. I think about this for a moment. I weigh various possibilities and things in my head. For a moment I'm tempted to get back in and talk to her. But then I shut the door and walk away.

They call me in from the car bay the next day and tell me I've got a phone call. I figure it's probably my mother wanting me to bring home something from the store, eggs or milk. I have grease all over my hands, under my fingernails, too, where it's always hard to get out, so I tear off a paper towel and pick up the extension with that.

"Hello," I say.

"Hey!"

I answer slowly. "Oh. Yeah." I recognize the voice.

"This is Connie. What you doing?"

"Well," I say, "right now I'm trying to fix a Buick. What can I do for you?" I look around and eye the shop foreman watching me. They don't pay me to talk on the phone unless I'm ordering parts.

"I just wanted to see what you's doing tonight. I wanted to talk to you about last night. Can you talk?"

I slip the receiver down between my head and my shoulder and wipe my hands with the paper towel. "Yeah," I say. "I guess I can for a minute. What's on your mind?"

"Well, I just wanted to tell you I was sorry about last night. About the way I acted. I'd been drinking before I ever got over there and we—Sheila and Bonita and me—we'd been talking about Roland and me before we ever come over there."

"Roland," I say. "Your husband."

"Right," she says, seems happy to say it. "We been married eight years. We got two kids. You know the kids is the ones always suffers in something like this."

"Yeah," I say. Well, sure. Sure they do. "I guess so," I say.

"I'm at home and I was thinking about last night. I mean, when we was out in the car and all. I was just upset. I didn't mean to act like that."

She's talking like she did something wrong. But all she did was refuse to take her pants off. In a public parking lot. Where anybody could have walked up to the car and looked in, seen her in all her naked glory for free. I'm uneasy remembering this, my half-drunk horny stupidity. I could have gone too far. I'm not supposed to be in bars anyway.

"Well," I say. "Hell. You don't owe me any apology or anything. I mean. We just met. You know. Out in the car and all. . . . you don't have to explain anything to me."

"I feel like I ought to, though," she says. "I was just wondering what you were gonna do tonight. I thought I'd see if you wanted to get a drink somewhere. If you're not busy." She lowers her voice. "I mean I liked it. In the car."

I know now that I shouldn't have tried that anyway. She just had me so turned on. . . .

I say, "You did, huh?" I'm seeing it again now, how the light played over her breasts, how they looked when I pushed her bra up.

"Well," I say, "I don't have anything planned."

"Okay," she says. She sounds glad she called. "You want to meet me somewhere?"

"Sure," I say. "I guess so. Hell, we can drink a beer or something."

"I'd really like to tell you why I acted the way I did last night, Jerry."

"It's Gary."

"Right. Gary. I knew it was Gary. You want to go back out there? Where we were last night?"

I start to say no, let's go someplace else, but she says, quickly, "It's close to my house and all. I'll have to get somebody to keep my kids and they know the number there if anything happens."

"Okay," I say. "Listen. I've got a lot of work to do, so it may be late when I get off. Maybe around six or seven. I get all the overtime I can. Why don't we try to get out there about nine? That'll give me time to get home and get cleaned up and all. I've got to catch a ride."

"That's fine," she says. "I'll get us a table."

"Okay," I say. I think for a moment. I might as well go ahead and ask her. "Listen. You want me to get us a room?"

She waits three seconds before she answers. "Well. You can get one if you want to, Gary. I'm not promising anything. But you can get us a room if you want to."

She's already happy and high when I slide into a chair beside her. It looks like the only seat left in the place is the one she's been saving for me.

"Hey," I say, and I set a fifth on the table. She leans over and kisses me. Her eyes are bright even in the darkness; they seem to belong to a woman different somehow from the one I wrestled with in the car the night before. The table is no bigger than a car tire. "How long you been here?" I say.

On the floor to the music she moves with drunken feet, pressing herself against me, her washed hair in my face sweet and soft. We dance a few times and then she tells me she wants to talk.

"What it is, see, he's wanting to catch me. Messing around."

"I don't get it," I say. "How come?"

"He wants me to give him a divorce. But I ain't gonna do it. I ain't gonna do one thing that'll make him happy."

I don't care about any of this. I don't want to know her problems. She acts like she's the only one who has any.

"Let's talk about something besides you and your husband," I say. "Why don't you quit thinking about him? You'd probably have a better time. You know it?"

She seems to realize with sadness that what I'm saying is true. "I know it," she says. "I'll hush about him."

But she doesn't. She keeps bringing his name up and looking all around in the bar, trying to spot him at large. I know there is nothing to do but be patient. I have a motel key in my pocket.

We pull into a parking space next to the wall of a Day's Inn and she turns off the lights and ignition. The aluminum numerals on the red metal door read 214.

"Let's go in," I say. I open my door.

She turns her face away from me and stares at something across the parking lot. She's very quiet. Unhappy. Almost angry.

"What are you looking at?" I say. I see the back of her dark head move.

"Nothing." She pulls the keys out and opens the door. "Let's go on in. Now that you've got me out here we might as well."

I haven't twisted her arm to get her out here. She's driven us over here willingly. Now I don't know what's wrong with her. She gets out and comes around to the front of the car looking down, not looking at me. I slip the key in and unlock the door. I turn on the light. A motel room like any other. I set what's left of the fifth on the plastic woodgrain table and go back and lean against the door. She is standing below the sidewalk, hugging herself with her arms, facing away. She seems to be looking at a blue Chevy pickup parked across the lot.

"You coming in?" I say.

Without answering she turns and comes by me and goes to sit on the bed. I shut the door and bolt it. I'm a little drunk. She'd better be careful. I take the bottle out of the sack and open it, tilt a burning drink down my throat. I hold it out to her.

"You want a drink?"

She shakes her head violently and stares at the floor.

"Well," I say. I look around and see the TV. "You want to watch some TV?"

"It doesn't matter," she says. "Nothing matters."

"Boy ain't we having just loads of fun," I say.

I turn on the TV and kick off my shoes and stretch out on the bed beside her, turning one of the pillows around so I can prop my head against it. I find an ashtray and move it over beside me. I sip from the bottle and wish I had some Coke. CNN news is on. After a while she turns around and lies down beside me. She doesn't say anything.

"You didn't have to come over here, you know," I say.

"I know," she says.

I don't know why I always have to pick some crazy woman. I used to be under the impression that after a man has put up with one of them, that that will do it for the rest of his life, that the others will all be halfway normal.

"You want to go back?" I ask her.

I turn just my head and watch her. She's lying on her side with her legs drawn up. She's wearing light blue slacks and a black top with red flowers.

"No," she says. "I want to stay here with you."

"Oh yeah?" I say. "Damn if you act like it."

For answer she reaches out and takes my hand and puts it on her breast. She rubs the hand over it for a moment and then slips it inside her blouse. I lean over and kiss her and push my fingers down into the cup of her bra. She slides a hand up my leg and I break away long enough to set the whiskey on the table, then roll on top of her.

"Cut the light out," she says.

"What?"

"Cut the light out."

I get up and pull off my shirt and flick off the light and we are left in the blue glow from the TV. Some massacre in a foreign country is being documented on the television screen: swollen bodies, murdered livestock in the streets. Black bloodstains on shattered brick walls. I push her shirt up and reach behind her and unsnap her bra, the heavy round meat easing into my hands. I kiss at her with an urgency she doesn't seem to share. I rub at the waistband of her pants and run my hands all over her. But there is no feeling in her kisses. She's tense. I twist her thick nipples between my fingers and after five minutes I quit. She has worked her way upright in the bed and she sits now with her nice knockers poking out from underneath the twisted entanglements of her shirt and bra, looking not at me or the TV or her clothes but the wall.

I sit up and swing my legs to the floor and find my cigarettes. I light one and get my shirt off the floor.

"You ready to run me back to the club?" I say. "There's no need in us staying over here." Something is wrong with her. She doesn't even get excited. It's no wonder her husband has left her. She's cold as a fish.

"That's his pickup," she says.

"What?"

"That's Roland's pickup outside. He's got some woman over here. In one of these rooms." She looks at me. "Maybe right next to us."

I hate myself for being this way. For being so desperate. I already knew how it was going to turn out. I knew it would be exactly like this.

"Well, so what?" I say. "If he's screwing around on you, what are you so worried about?"

"I'm not worried," she says.

"The hell you ain't." I stand up and pull on my shirt. I know I need to get myself out of this room and away from her. It's not too late to go back to the bar and try to meet somebody else. Anybody will be better than her. Even the fat ones will be better than her. At least I can have a good time with them. They don't have problems. They don't waste the nights. "You're afraid he'll see you with me," I say.

"Would you just listen for one minute?" she says. "I been married to him since I was sixteen. We got some rental property we own together. He's a contractor. He didn't leave me. I left him! You don't understand."

"Yeah," I say. "I understand. I understand all of it. You're wanting somebody to listen to all your problems and I ain't no fucking head doctor. Just take me back to the club or let me out somewhere and I'll catch a ride home. Hell, it's Saturday night. I got to go back to work Monday. You know what I'm saying?"

She fastens her bra back together and pulls her shirt down. By the time I get out the door to the running car, I'm surprised she hasn't left me. The truck we saw earlier is gone, but she doesn't mention it. I get in with her and sit close to the door all the way back. I look at her breasts. They are magnificent. I want to suggest another scenario, but I don't.

I'm living with my mother again and Sunday is a chicken dinner, just the two of us. Mashed potatoes and English peas, gravy. I sleep late on Sunday, then go down to the road and pick up the papers, the *Commercial Appeal* from Memphis and the *Clarion-Ledger* from Jackson. The rest of my morning is taken up with reading these papers, especially the movie and book pages, and drinking coffee and smoking cigarettes until my mother comes in from church and calls me to dinner. I don't have a car now; a lawyer has the money it brought, so now I read the pages with the car ads, too. I want to buy a new one, have been toying with the idea, and try to save my money for that.

Sunday afternoon, I'm asleep in the bed that held me as a child when the phone rings. I wake and turn and hear my mother moving toward me in the empty house, her feet and weight ponderous on the old boards, hesitant. She's coming to see if I'm asleep and she probably hopes I am. She opens the door and sees me. She says there is some woman who wants to talk to me. I know somehow, freshly awake from dreams of erotica and hanging breasts, deliciously rested, ready for the last night of the weekend. I get up and go to the kitchen and shut the door. It's her.

"Gary?" she says.

"Yeah."

"It's Connie."

"Yeah. I know." What does she want and why has she picked me? Why can't she see that I'm bad for her? That I can't take much more?

"Did I wake you up?"

"Yeah, matter of fact you did."

"Aw, I'm sorry. I didn't mean to wake you up. I guess I shoulda called later. I didn't mean to wake you up."

"Listen," I say. "What do you want?" There's no need to be nice to her anymore. I'm through with her, I don't want her to start calling over here and bothering my mother when I'm not home. I don't even want her calling over here. My mother asks too many questions as it is. Any man twenty-eight years old ought to be able to come and go without his mother asking him where he's going every time.

"I just wanted to talk," she says, and she says that in a pleading voice. "Can you talk?" Suddenly she sounds cheerful and sober.

"I don't know," I say. "I mean, I don't see much point in it. I don't even know what you want. I don't think you know what you want." I can't see my cigarettes. "Hold on," I say. "I've got to find a cigarette."

I don't wait for her to answer. I go into the living room and get my pack and my lighter. I light one and look out the window at the passing cars, the uncut grass. My mother watches from behind her eyeglasses where she sits with the Bible of God cupped in her lap. She says nothing, but I see the fear she has. After a while I go back and pick up the telephone again. "All right," I say, making the weariness in my voice plain.

It's kind of hard, not having a car. I have to be careful to get with somebody who has wheels. I have to make sure of that early on. I don't mind paying for a room if the woman doesn't mind us going in her car. It complicates things, makes them more difficult. But I can't take them home, not while I'm living with my mother. She wouldn't allow it. I know what would happen if I tried it. I've imagined it before, and it isn't nice. It's awful. Doors jerked open and covers grabbed.

"Listen," she says. "I know I acted terrible last night. It was just his truck over there that did it. You got to understand, Gary, we been married ten years. You just don't throw ten years away without thinking about it."

"Right," I say. First eight years, now ten years. I must deal with her, get rid of her. "But it ain't none of my business. Let me explain something to you. When I go out on the weekend, all I'm looking for is to have a good time. All right? I mean I don't think I have to go to bed with every girl I meet. I've been married. Not as long as you, but I've been married. I know what it's like." I'm not saying what I mean to say. "You just act too damn strange for me, okay? You get depressed, and I don't need to be around somebody that's depressed all the time. It gets me depressed, too. Now that's all it is. If you still love your husband, fine. You need to try to work everything out with him. That's between you and him. I don't have anything to do with it. I just don't want you to call me anymore."

That should do it. That should make her mad enough to where she'll say something, then hang up on me. She doesn't.

"Oh, Gary. Don't be mad. I've been thinking over everything today. Listen. I called my husband and you know what I told him?"

"What?" I don't want to hear this shit.

"I told him I wanted a divorce. I told him I was going to try to get eight hundred dollars a month out of him. He started talking sweet then. He wants us to get back together now. What you think about that?"

"I don't know," I say. "I don't care," I say. I open the icebox and find a beer. Then I look a little longer and find the schnapps.

"I told him I saw him last night. At that motel. But anyway, that ain't what I called you about. I called you about something else."

"What?"

"I got us a room tonight. Just you and me. At the Holiday Inn. I already got it. I got the key right here."

I don't really believe that. "I don't really believe that," I say.

"Listen, Gary. I know I ain't acted right. I don't blame you for being disgusted with me. But it was just all that stuff with my ex. He's been going out on me for the longest. Friday night was the first time I'd ever been out without him. In ten years. Honest."

"Is that right?" I say. She's probably lying. She's probably just telling me all this so she can get me off again and drive me some more nuts telling me some more about it.

"I swear. Gary, I swear to God. May God strike me dead if I ain't telling the truth."

"Well," I say. I take a drink of my beer. Maybe she is telling the truth. Maybe they've had what she thought was a good marriage. It's happened before. You can go along fine for years and it can fall apart in a second. You can do things to each other that can never be forgiven. One word can lead to another word. You can lose control and a whole lot more. They can make you pay for one second of anger. They can make you pay with your house, and your car, and your money and self-respect. She doesn't have to tell me about marriage. I know already. Marriage is having to live with a woman. That's what marriage is.

But I won't have to see her after tonight. I won't put up with any more shit from her. I don't have to. I'm not married anymore. I won't be again.

"How's that sound?" she says.

"I guess it sounds all right," I say.

"Listen, baby, I'm gonna make up for everything tonight. I mean, everything."

"Well, okay," I say. She's convinced me. There's only one thing. I don't want her to pick me up here, at my mother's. "Where do you live?"

"I can come get you," she says.

"No. I'd rather you wouldn't," I say. "Listen. I've got a friend who'll give me a ride out to your house. You staying in the house?"

"Hell yes," she says. "I'm not gonna give it to my ex."

"I'll just get somebody to carry me out there, then. Where do you live?"

She tells me. I say I'll be there by seven. I feel a lot better about everything when I hang up the phone.

"You sure this is it?" I say to my friend.

The boy I'm riding with looks at the mailbox.

"That's the number. One hundred Willow Lane. Hell, Gary, there ain't nothing but rich people live up in here."

"Well damn," I say. "This is the address she gave me."

"Well, this is it then," my friend says. "You want me to wait on you?"

"I don't know. You might ought to."

"We'll just pull up in here and see if this is it."

We drive up a blacktopped lane to a house designed like a Swiss chalet. I guess that it's over four thousand square feet under this roof. It has big dormers and split shingles and massive columns of rough wood on the porch. There is a pool full of blue water in the backyard. The Lincoln I've been riding in and nuzzling her knockers in is parked in the drive.

"Hell. That's her car," I say. "I guess this is it."

She comes to the kitchen window and pushes the curtains aside.

"This is it," I say, when I see her. "I just didn't know it was this fancy."

"You better hang onto her," my friend says.

"Yeah. Maybe so. Well, thanks for the ride, Bobby. Let me give you some on the gas."

"Get outa here," he says.

I start pulling five dollars out of my billfold, but my friend leans across me and opens the door. "Get your butt outa here," he says. "Put that money back up."

"Hell, Bobby," I say. "It's a long way out here."

"I may need a ride from you sometime."

"You better take it."

"Go on. I'll see you later."

I get out, sticking the money back in my billfold, waving to my friend backing out of the driveway. The headlights retreat, swords of light through the motes of dust that hang and fall until he swings out and grabs low and peels away with a faint stench and high squeal of rubber. I listen to him hit the gears, to the little barks of rubber until he is gone. For a moment I wonder what I'm doing here. On another man's concrete. Another man's ride. Everything about this house is elegant. It's hard to believe this woman comes out of this place. But there she is, opening the door. I go up to her. She kisses me.

"Come on in," she says.

It's a dream room. High, vaulted ceilings, enclosed beams. Rams, bucks, bear heads mounted over the fireplace, and it of massive river stones. Carpet that covers my toes. I don't know what to say. I know now she wasn't lying about the contractor and the real estate. Or the kids. Two beautiful little girls are seated on the thick carpet in their nightgowns, one about two, the other about four. Dark hair like her, shy smiles.

"Hi," I say. They look up at me, smile, look down. They have toys, trucks, Sylvester the Cat on the floor. The remnants of their suppers are on paper plates beside them. Potato chips. Gnawed hamburger buns. They whisper things to each other and cast quick glances at me while they pretend not to watch.

"I'll be ready in just a minute, Gary," she says.

I look around. "Yeah. Okay," I say. I'm watching the little girls. They've taken my interest. They're so precious. I know they cannot comprehend what has happened to their daddy. I feel myself to be an intruder in this house, a homewrecker. The husband, the father, could come home and kill me this minute with a shotgun. Nothing would be said. No jury would convict the man. I don't belong here.

She has gone somewhere. I sit on the couch. The girls play with their trucks and croon softly to each other little songs without words, melodies made up in their own fantastic little minds. They move smooth as eels, boneless, their little arms and legs dimpled with fat.

"I'm ready," she says. I look around. She has her purse. She seems brisk, efficient. She has her keys. It's like she's suddenly decided to stop slumming. She has on trim black slacks, gold toeless shoes with low heels, a short mink jacket. Diamonds glitter in the lobes of her ears. Her breasts hang heavy and full in the lowcut shirt, and I know that tonight she will deny me nothing. She's smiling. She takes my arm as I stand up and she kisses me again. The children watch this puzzle in soundless wonder, this strange man kissing Mommy.

"Okay, girls, we'll be back after while," she says. They don't look up, don't appear to hear. "Sherry?" she says. "We're gone." She must be talking to somebody else in the house, somebody I can't see, the babysitter, I guess. "Sherry?" she says. "Did you hear me?"

"Let's go," she says to me, and she starts toward the door. She's searching for a key on her key ring.

"Bye, girls," I say. The oldest one gives me a solemn look, a dignified nod.

"Stay in here, now," she says. "Don't mess with the stove." We're halfway out the door when it hits me.

"Wait a minute," I say. She's locking the door, locking the

children into the house. I hear the lock click. "Where's your babysitter?"

"They're all right," she says. "We won't be gone long anyway. Not over a few hours."

"*Wait* a minute," I say. "You gonna leave them alone? Here?"

I've got my hand on her arm, I'm turning her to look at me in the lighted carport. She looks down at my hand and then up at me, surprised. She steps away.

"Well, it's not gonna hurt anything. They'll be all right."

"All right?" I say. "They're just little kids. I thought you said you had a babysitter."

"I couldn't get one," she says. "Now come on. Let's go. They've stayed by themselves before." She's going toward the car. I stand watching her dumbly, like a dumbass, like the dumbass I am.

"What if something happens, though?" I say. "What if the fucking house was to catch on fire?"

She stops and looks back. She holds her face up slightly, puts one hand on her hip. "Do you want to go or not?" she says.

"You told me last night the babysitter had your number so she could get ahold of you," I say. Then I realize. She's never had a babysitter. They've been locked up in this house the whole weekend, these children.

"Do you want to go or not?" she says.

I look through the curtains on the door. The girls have been watching it, but now they look back down at their toys. The youngest one gets up and walks away, out of sight. The oldest rolls her truck. I look at the woman standing by the door of a new Lincoln, waiting to carry me to a Holiday Inn. She's ready now, finally. And so am I.

"Come here," I say.

"What?"

"I said come here."

"Why? Get in, let's go."

I go around the hood after her, slowly. Her face changes.

"What is it?" she says. "What's wrong with you?"

"Come here," I say, and I know my face has changed, too.

"Hey," she says. "I don't know what you think you're doing."

I know what I'm doing. I have my hands on her now, and she can't pull away. She probably thinks I'm going to kill her, but I'm not. I'm going to keep my hands open this time, and not use my fists. I don't want to scare the little girls with blood. They would be frightened, and might remember it for the rest of their lives.

LEAVING TOWN

Her name was Myra and I could smell whiskey on her breath. She was nervous, but these days, you don't know who to let in your house. She'd seen my ad in the paper, she said, and wanted some new doors hung. We talked on the porch for a while and then she let me in.

It looked like she didn't have anything to do but keep her house clean. She gnawed her fingernails the whole time I was figuring the estimate. She kept opening and closing the top of her robe, like a nervous habit. Both the doors had been kicked out of their locks. The wood was splintered. She needed two new doors, some trim. Maybe two new locks. She wanted new linoleum in her dining room. I gave her a price for the labor and went on home, but I didn't think I'd get the job.

He was a polite young man. His name was Richard. He seemed to be very understanding when I explained that Harold had kicked the doors in. Of course I didn't tell him everything. All I wanted was to forget about Harold, and every time I looked at the doors I thought about him.

I tried to talk to him a little. I told him that I was divorced now and that it was a lot different when you're used to two salaries and then have to live on just one. I told him I didn't want to pay a whole lot for the work. He said the doors would run about forty dollars apiece. I had no idea they would be that high.

He had very nice-looking hands. They looked like strong hands, but gentle. I doubted if they'd ever been used to slap somebody, or to break down a door.

He didn't talk much. He was one of those quiet people who intrigue you because they keep so much inside. Maybe he was just shy. I thought the price he gave me was twenty or thirty dollars too high. I told him I'd think about it. But I needed the work done.

After he left, I fixed myself another drink and looked at the doors. They were those hollow-core things, they wouldn't keep out anybody who wanted in bad enough. I kept thinking about Richard. I wondered what it would be like to kiss him. I could imagine how it would be. How warm his hands would be. My life is halfway or more than halfway over. There's not much time left for things like that. I don't know why I even thought about it. He had the bluest eyes and they looked so sad. Maybe that was the reason. Whatever it was, I decided to call him back and let him do the work. I couldn't stand to look at those doors any longer.

I was feeding Tracey when she called. Betty was reading one of her police detective magazines. The phone rang three or four times. Betty acted like she didn't hear it. I got up with Tracey and went and answered it.

I was surprised that she called back. She'd already talked like I was too high. But people don't know what carpentry work is worth. You have to have a thousand dollars' worth of tools to even start.

She sounded like she was a little drunk. I guess she was lonely. When I was over there, she'd look at the doors and just shake her head. But I'd given her a reasonable price. It was cheaper than anybody else would have done it for. I didn't tell her that. She wouldn't have believed it.

I told her I could start the next night. She hadn't understood that I was going to do it at night. I had told her, though. She just hadn't been listening. She said she thought I was in business for myself. I told her I was, at night. I told her I had to work my other job in the daytime. Then she wanted to know all about that. She just wanted somebody to talk to. Tracey was going to sleep in my lap. I asked Betty if she'd take her but she wouldn't even look up. She was still reading her magazine.

She wanted to know didn't I get tired of working all the time, at night and on weekends. Hell, who wouldn't? I told her, sure, I got tired of it, but I needed the money. That was all I told her then. I didn't want to tell her about Tracey. I didn't want to tell her all my personal business.

She sat there for a while and didn't say anything. Then she wanted to know if there was any way I could come down on the price. That pissed me off. She wanted to know if that was the very least I could do it for. At first I told her I didn't see any way I could, but I needed the money. Hell, I have to put gas in my truck and all. . . .

I told her I'd cut it twenty more dollars but that was it. I told her if she couldn't live with that, she'd just have to find somebody else to do it. And I told her that if she found somebody cheaper, she wouldn't be satisfied with it.

I had to tell her a couple of times that I'd be there the next night. I told her I had to go by the building supply and get the doors. She wanted to talk some more, but I told her I had to put my baby to bed. Finally I got away from her. I wasn't really looking forward to going back.

I got up with Tracey and Betty wanted to know who that was on the phone. I told her a lady I was going to do some work for. Then she wanted to know what kind of work and how old a lady and was she married or divorced and what did she look like. I told her, Hell, normal, I guess, to let me put Tracey to bed.

She started crying when I laid her down and I had to stay in there with her and pet her a while. I guess her legs hurt. She finally went to sleep. Betty won't even get up with her at night. I have to. It doesn't matter if I've worked twelve hours or fourteen hours. She can't even hear an alarm clock. You can let one go off and hold it right in her ear. She won't even move.

She was smoking the last cigarette I had when I went back

in the living room. She said that kid hated her and I told her she just didn't have any patience with her. I picked up the empty pack and asked her if she had any more. She said she was out. I just looked at her. She'll sit in the house all day long and won't walk a half block to the store and get some, then smoke mine until she makes me run out. Then I have to go.

I got my jacket and told her I guessed I'd have to go get some. She told me to bring her some beer back. I told her I didn't have enough money to buy any beer. I wanted some too but I was almost broke. She told me to just write a check. She says that shit all the time. I told her we had enough to pay that doctor bill and that was it. Then she said something about the saw I bought. It was eighty-nine dollars. But good saws cost good money. And if I don't have a saw, I don't have a job.

She wanted to know when I was going to marry her. I told her I didn't know.

I went by the building supply the next day, after I got off from work. I priced the locks, but they were almost twenty dollars apiece. I decided to see if I could use the old locks on her doors and save her that much anyway. I signed for the doors and the trim, the linoleum.

I didn't want to go straight over there. I wanted to go home for a few minutes and see Tracey and get Betty to fix me something to eat. I'd asked Leon to let me borrow ten dollars until Friday, so I stopped at the store and got a six-pack of beer. You can't just go through life doing without everything.

I loaded up my sawhorses and left the linoleum in the carport. Tracey was sitting on the floor, wanting me to pick her up. I set the sack on the table and told Betty I'd brought her some beer. She was reading another magazine so I played with Tracey for a while. Then I got her building blocks and set her down with them and got one of the beers out of the sack. Dirty clothes were piled up everywhere. She won't wash until we don't have anything to wear. I lit a cigarette and just watched her. She didn't know I was in the room. I drank about half my beer. I had a lot of shit going through my head.

Finally I asked her if she could fix me something to eat before I went over there. I told her it would probably be late when I got back. I told her I was hungry.

She asked me what I wanted. I told her I didn't care, a sandwich, anything. She said she didn't know of anything we had to eat. She said I could go in there and look.

I told her I wanted some supper. She didn't look back up, and I thought, Work your ass off all day and come home and have to put up with some shit like this.

I sat there a while and then I got up and made out like I was going to the kitchen. She wasn't watching me anyway. She had her magazine up in front of her face, picking at the buttons on her blouse. I bent down behind the couch. I peeked over her shoulder to see what she was reading. THE LAUNDROMAT AXE MURDERER WOULDN'T COME CLEAN. I don't know how she can stand to read that shit. She gets so deep into it, she'll get her nails in her mouth. I got up on my knees right behind her. She was nibbling her bottom lip. I was just trying to have a little fun.

She jumped about two feet high when I went boo in her

ear. Turned around and slammed her magazine down. She was pissed. Bad pissed.

I told her I was just playing with her. She told me to just go on and leave. Said I was always hollering about saving money. Why didn't I go out and make some? Instead of worrying the hell out of her?

I got up in her face, said let me tell you one goddamn thing. You lay around here on your ass all day long and don't do nothing. Won't clean the house up. Won't even wash Tracey's face. I told her if I could go out and work at night, she could fix me something to eat.

She said there wasn't anything to eat.

I said by God she could buy something.

She said give her some money and she might.

I told her I gave her money, and she spent it on those stupid fucking magazines.

She whispered to me. Hateful. If I was so damn unhappy then why didn't I just leave? Just pack up and go right now?

I didn't answer. I picked up Tracey and she put her arms around my neck. We went into the kitchen. I looked in the refrigerator. There was some old bacon, and a half cup of chili in a Tupperware bowl, and a quart of milk, and a little brown hamburger meat, and one hot dog. I found some Rice Krispies under the counter. I fixed two bowls and ate with Tracey. I washed her hands and her face.

I didn't want to leave. I'd said some of the words I'd been wanting to say but I hadn't said all of them. My words wouldn't hurt her as bad as hers hurt me. I held onto Tracey and looked at my watch. There wasn't much time. Your life goes by and if you spend it unhappy, what's the point? If staying won't make you happy, and leaving ruins somebody else's life, what's the answer?

I didn't know. I still don't. But I'd told her I'd be there by six. And finally I couldn't wait in the kitchen any longer.

I was so nervous I changed clothes three times before he got there. I ended up wearing a dress that was too short. I cleaned the house twice, even though I knew there would be sawdust and tools on the floor. I'd been thinking about him all day, I couldn't help it. He was so quiet and mysterious and he had such lovely hands. I'd had a few drinks, and I was going to offer him a drink when he got there. Just thinking about him being all alone in the house with me excited me. Maybe if he had a few drinks, he'd loosen up and talk to me. I wanted to talk to somebody so badly. It's not easy being alone after being married for thirty years. It's not easy to come home to a house so quiet you can hear a clock ticking.

I kept waiting and looking at my watch, and I kept drinking. I thought it would calm me down. I was so nervous my hands were just trembling.

Finally he pulled up and I looked out through the curtain in the living room. He had two doors and two sawhorses in the back of his pickup. I watched him get out and put on a tool belt and lift the doors from the truck.

I opened the door for him and smiled and told him he was right on time. He said hi or something, and then started bringing everything in. He didn't have much to say. I just watched him and smiled. He brought in some kind of a crowbar and a power saw and a long orange extension cord. I couldn't get that idiotic grin off my face. I had a drink in one hand and a cigarette in the other. Harold used to tell me that if I didn't drink myself to death, I'd smoke myself to death. But he was always so cruel. Always so cruel.

I asked him if he would like a drink. He said he didn't like whiskey, and took the crowbar and tore the facing off the wall like he was mad at it. It made this awful screeching sound when the nails pulled loose. He just . . . attacked it. Within five minutes he had the frame and the door lying in the carport and was pulling finishing nails from the studs. The nails screamed when he pulled them. I said something about how he didn't waste any time. I was smiling. He said he wasn't making much money on this and had to get through as quick as he could.

I thought he was probably mad at me for talking him into coming down twenty dollars. But I'm single, I don't have Harold's money, I have to get by, too.

I told him I had some beer if he wanted one. He said let him get this door up and he might take one. He pulled a screwdriver out of his tool belt and stepped outside to the carport and closed the door behind him. Almost like he didn't have time to talk to me. Or was angry with me. I hadn't done anything to him. The paneling was rough and splintered where he'd taken the door off. You could see the wires inside the studs. You could see the nails. It all looked so raw.

I made myself another drink, and checked my makeup in

the hall mirror. You would have thought I was having a cocktail party the way I was acting. He was out in the carport and I watched him through the window. He was kneeling beside the door, doing something, I couldn't tell what. His shirt had come up and I could see the bumps of bone in his back. His back looked so smooth. I wanted to feel it with my hands, run my hands over it, up his ribs, down over his hips, I wanted him to put his mouth on my throat and slide it down to my breasts and take one of my nipples in his lips and say Myra, Myra. . . .

My goddamn back was killing me. If I bend over for more than five minutes at a time I can't straighten up. Sometimes in the mornings it hurts so bad I can just barely get out of bed. I have to get up and walk around and bend and stretch to get to where I can go to work. It usually stops hurting midway through the morning and starts hurting twice as bad around three. I'd been laboring for a bricklayer all that day, mixing his mortar and handing him his blocks. They just scab us out to whoever needs help on a big job. If you're not in the union you don't have any say. I can't stand the dues so I pay my own. But I'm afraid I'll get disabled. I'm afraid I won't be able to work anymore. I worry about that every day.

I fell three months ago. We were bricking a bank. A scaffold leg collapsed, one of those cheap ones they rent from the building supply. I was fourteen feet up, not that high, but I landed on a sheet of plywood that was propped up against a water cooler. I thought I'd broken my back. Everybody who saw me fall thought I'd broken my back. When the ambulance came for me, they treated me like a patient with a broken back. They pulled traction on me and immobilized me. I was screaming. I bit my tongue.

My foreman came to see me in the hospital. He told me the company took care of its employees. He only stayed a few minutes. I could tell he couldn't wait to get out of there.

I had to go on workmen's comp after I got out of the hospital. What I drew was about half my pay. You can't live on half money. You've got to have whole money. I went over to the job a few times, to talk to the guys I worked with, but I was just in the way. They couldn't work and talk to me, too. I stopped going after a while. I stayed home and drank beer with Betty and read those Little Golden Books to Tracey.

I'd never felt so useless in my whole life. There wasn't anything to occupy me. Betty didn't want to do it. I had to do the grocery shopping to make our money stretch. We fought over the money, over the TV, over anything and everything. I had to put up with these assholes every week in the office where I got my check. Some days I wanted to just go away somewhere and never come back again. I was supposed to stay off for four months, but I went back after two by forging my doctor's signature on an insurance release. They set me to mixing mortar and carrying twenty-pound blocks.

I got the knobs and the lock out of the old door and took them back into the house. She was sitting on an ottoman. She had on dark stockings. I told her I'd probably bring another boy with me the next night, to lay the linoleum. She just nodded. It was like she was listening to something in her head. I didn't know what I'd do if my back got to hurting so bad I couldn't work. I didn't know how bad it would have to hurt before it stopped me. I didn't know how I'd pay Tracey's doctor bills if that happened.

I told her I'd take that beer now if she didn't care. She nodded and smiled and went to get it. I watched her, and I thought about the twenty dollars she had talked me out of. I should have just told her to forget it. I should have just told her to get somebody else and keep her lousy twenty dollars.

He was certainly a fast worker. I didn't know if he wanted a glass or not. I figured carpenters usually drank theirs straight out of the can. He wasn't making it easy for me to talk to him. He acted like he had things on his mind. We couldn't talk at all with all that ripping and hammering going on.

I carried the beer out to him and he drank about half of it in one swallow. I sat down again to watch him work and asked him if he wanted a cigarette. He had some of his own. He picked up the lock and the knobs and started putting them into the door.

I asked her if she was going to be at home the next night. I had to ask her twice. She looked up and I told her that I'd probably get through with the doors that night. I told her that if she didn't care, I'd go ahead and tear out the old linoleum and lay the new the next night. If she didn't care.

She'd pulled her dress up over her legs. Her legs were kind of skinny but they weren't that bad. I didn't know if she meant to do it on purpose or not. Maybe she was so drunk she didn't notice it.

She didn't know if she was going to be home the next night or not. She asked me if I wanted to come back the next night. I told her I'd just like to get through. The quicker I got through, the quicker I got paid. She said she'd have to decide.

I knew he wasn't going to be interested in me. The only thing he was interested in was the money. He couldn't wait to get out of my house. And I'd been sitting there thinking such foolish things. I was ashamed of myself. I don't know anything about dating, I've been married so long. Going out to bars alone, hoping for some man to pick me up: I don't want that kind of life. My drink was almost empty.

I told him I needed a fresh one and got up to make it. I didn't know I was in such bad shape. My head started swimming when I got in the kitchen. I dropped my glass.

I heard a glass break and I stopped what I was doing. I got up and looked around. I didn't see her anywhere. Then I heard her. I thought maybe she'd fallen and hurt herself. She sounded like she was crying. I went down the hall and found her in the kitchen. She was down on her knees, on a towel she had folded underneath her. She was crying and picking up the broken pieces of glass. I didn't know what the hell to do.

I know you're not supposed to feel sorry for yourself. But I had always had somebody to take care of me and tell me what to do. It's so frightening to be alone. I was only trying to reach out to somebody. All I wanted was a little conversation. I was just trying to be nice to him.

I was so ashamed for him to see me crying. I'd just had too much to drink and I'd gotten depressed. He was standing behind me. He asked me if I was okay and I said I was. It was so quiet. The glass had gone everywhere. I wanted to make sure I got it all up so I wouldn't step on a tiny piece while I was barefoot one morning. I told him that it was okay, that he could go back to work, that I'd get him another beer in a minute. Then he knelt down beside me and started helping me pick up the glass.

She seemed so helpless and so weak. She wasn't anything like Betty. She wasn't hard like Betty. I know it embarrassed her for me to see her like that. And I was afraid she might cut herself, so I got down on the floor to help her. She was trying to stop crying. I didn't know what was wrong or what to say. I felt bad for her, and I wanted to help her if I could. All her mascara had run down from her eyes in black streaks. She'd smeared some of it wiping at her eyes. She said it was nice of me to help her. Then she said Richard. That was the first time she'd said my name.

I looked at him. He was just as embarrassed as I was. I thought about how I must have looked to him, half drunk, with my eyes red from crying. I had cried so much because of Harold. Nobody knows what I went through. He wasted so much of my life. All those years that were just thrown away. I wanted to tell him so bad about what had happened to me. I had so much on me that I wanted to unload. I turned to him and I put my hand on his shoulder. I wanted him to kiss me, or to put his hand on my breast. Or to at least hold me. I wanted to tell him what was wrong with me.

I didn't know what to say when she touched me. I stopped what I was doing and I looked at her. She was trying to smile. Her eyes were wet. I didn't know what she wanted. Maybe just somebody to listen to her. Maybe something else. But she was old enough to be my mother.

She said what if somebody asked you to do something. And it wouldn't hurt you, if it was just a favor that somebody wanted you to do, would you do it? If it didn't cost you anything and it would help the other person. She said if I just knew. She said he had other women. That he'd beaten her. That nobody knew what she'd been through.

She started crying again. She put her head on my shoulder and she took my hand and slipped it around her waist. I didn't know what else to do but hold her. She started sort of moaning.

I didn't have time to do anything. She said I want you. She put her mouth on mine. She was holding my ears in both her hands. I tried to pull back. I tried to tell her that she was drunk and she didn't know what she was doing. But she unbuckled my pants. It happened in a second. She pulled it out and started rubbing it with her hands, moaning. She leaned back and pulled up her dress and I ran my hands up underneath her. I couldn't help it. I didn't know what to do. I knew she was drunk and I was afraid she'd holler rape when she sobered up. We got up somehow and went back against the counter. She opened her dress and pulled my head down to her. I couldn't get away and didn't want to.

I just went crazy for a minute. Once I touched him I couldn't stop myself. He started running his hands all over me. I knew I should stop but I couldn't. I didn't even know him. I knew he was going to think I was a whore.

I just lost control of myself. I didn't even care what he thought. I just wanted someone to put his arms around me and hold me tight. I didn't want to stop. I knew if we kept on it was going to happen. I wasn't even thinking about how I'd feel the next morning, or how I'd feel after it was over. I was just thinking about how I didn't ever want him to stop. But finally he did. He stopped and backed away from me. He looked like he was scared to death. I don't know what I looked like. Half my clothes were off. I think I asked him what was wrong.

I finally got ahold of myself. I think I said shit or something. We were both breathing hard. I fastened my pants back up. She was staring at me like a wild woman. There was a chair pulled out beside the table and I went over to it and sat down. She didn't say anything for a minute. I think she was buttoning her dress. I waited until I thought she was done and then I turned around and looked at her. She was wiping her eyes with her fingers. She fixed herself another drink. Then she went to the refrigerator and got me another beer. I started to just get up and leave. But she brought the beer and her drink over and set them down and dropped into the chair beside me. She looked dazed. We almost did it, she said. Yeah, I said. We almost did.

He started talking about the little girl. At first I wasn't listening. I was almost in shock. It took a long time for me to calm down. My heart was beating too fast, and I was wet. I wanted to kiss him again but I was scared to try. He said she wasn't his. It was something about her telling him she was divorced and then later after he'd been living with her for a while, admitting that she had never been married. I think I was just staring at my drink when he started talking. But then what he was saying started sinking in and I started listening to him. I couldn't believe what we were doing, just sitting there in my kitchen talking and drinking after what we'd done. He said it didn't matter to him for a while about the lie she had told him because he loved the little girl and felt like she was his. He was the only daddy she'd known. But he didn't love the woman. I could tell that just from hearing him talk. He said he carried the little girl everywhere he went, even if he was just going to the store for something.

There was something wrong with her legs. She couldn't walk right. They had all these tests done on her and had her fitted with braces and then his insurance company wouldn't pay the bills because he wasn't married to her mother. I wondered what she looked like. I had this picture of black hair and a frowning face for some reason. He said he was afraid to leave her. He said he didn't love her, but he couldn't leave the little girl. He said he didn't know what would happen to her. I felt better about everything, about losing my head, after we talked for a while. But he was working all these jobs at night to try and pay the doctor bills. I felt like . . . I just don't know what I felt like. Cheap. Stingy. For getting him to lower his price. And I felt awful for drinking too much and having those daydreams about him, and then kissing him and all. He kept talking. The more he talked, the worse I felt over feeling so sorry for myself about Harold.

I asked him what he was going to do. He said he didn't know. He said if he left her there was no telling what would happen to them. He said the woman had never worked a day in her life and didn't finish high school and had been brought up on welfare. He said she didn't know what it was like to have to work for a living.

I shouldn't have talked so much. I didn't mean to tell her all my problems. I know everybody's got problems, and everybody thinks theirs are worse than everybody else's. I know she had it bad. Married to a son of a bitch that slapped her around. She felt like her whole life had been wasted. She talked some, too. She said she knew what it felt like to have to stay with somebody without love. She knew what I felt like. She was as miserable as I was.

I probably could have taken right back up where we left off. I was tempted to. I don't think I've touched a woman who was that hot ever. I thought when women got older they didn't care anything about sex. Or maybe she was just trying to reach out to somebody. She didn't come right out and say it, but just from the things she said, I could tell she hadn't slept with her ex-husband for years. I felt so goddamn sorry for her. But I didn't want her to feel sorry for me. I didn't want to work anymore, though. I just wanted to load my shit up and go somewhere. I thought about asking her if she wanted to go drink a few beers with me, but really I wanted to be by myself. I had to decide what I was going to do. I knew I couldn't keep going the way I was going.

I asked him what he was going to do and he said he didn't know. He said he'd keep on working. He was hoping she'd grow out of it. He said he didn't mean to dump all his problems on me. But he said the little girl would sit on the floor and hold her arms up to him when he came in from work and beg him to take her. He said he thought she sat on the floor all day because her mother wouldn't help her try to walk or even pick her up. He said all she did was read magazines and watch TV. I don't know how he could have gotten mixed up with somebody like that. I don't know why he couldn't have gotten somebody who deserved him.

I told her that if she didn't care I'd just leave the doors and finish up the next night, or the next. I had to get away. I hated to just leave her wall like that, but there wasn't any way I could finish hanging the door that night. She said it would be okay, that I could come back and finish it whenever I wanted to. She said she never had any company and nobody would see it anyway.

I watched him roll up his cord and put away his tools and get ready to leave. I wanted him to stay, but I didn't ask him to. I could tell he had a lot on his mind. His hands had felt so good to me. I knew I was going to cry after he left. I knew I was going to cry and I knew I was going to drink some more. I wanted him right then more than I've ever wanted anything in my life. I would have given him anything. But all he wanted was to leave. I wasn't going to try to hold him. I wasn't going to make a fool of myself again. But right up until the time he left, I would have made a fool of myself. Gladly. When he went out the door I knew I'd never see him again.

I rode around for a while. I didn't want to go back home just yet. I wanted to run but I didn't have any place to run to. Some people can just walk away, turn their backs and go on and forget about it. I couldn't. But it didn't stop me from thinking about it.

I went to a bar on Jackson Avenue and counted my money before I went inside. There was just enough left from what I'd borrowed from Leon to get a couple of pitchers of draft. There wasn't anybody in there I knew. I sat at a table by myself, in a booth in a dark corner. I thought that if I sat quietly by myself in the dark and drank, I'd be able to figure out what to do with the rest of my life.

Florida was the best place to go. There was no cold weather to stop you from laying brick. There was plenty of building going on. Jobs were supposed to be easy to get.

But I couldn't stop thinking about Myra down on the floor, crying. Or about how she felt when I was kissing her. I'd never had anybody want me that bad. I'd never had anybody so desperate reach out to me like that. And I'd turned her down. I regretted it.

I kept drinking. Betty didn't know what it was like to have to work, to be strapped into a job like a mule in a harness. The company I worked for didn't give a fuck if I broke my back. They'd just hire somebody else. There were people standing in lines all over the country wanting jobs. She didn't understand that. She didn't know what it was like to have to work when you were hurt. You either kept up or you didn't. If you didn't keep up they'd let you go.

She looked so awful down on the floor. I was still thinking about her by the time I finished the first pitcher. I had to scrape all my change together to make the price of the last one. I knew I'd be drunk by the time I finished it, but I didn't care. I wanted to get drunk. I felt like getting drunk would help me more than just about anything right then. So I got the other pitcher and sat back down in the corner with it. I knew by then that it had been wrong for me to turn her down. And I needed to talk to her some more anyway. She had listened to me and she had seemed to understand. She was so much kinder than Betty, so much gentler. Her body had been so soft. I wanted to take all her clothes off gently and touch her whole body and make her happy. I wanted to heal her. I kept drinking. The more I thought about it, the more it seemed like a good idea.

I know I was too drunk to remember what happened exactly. I came to in the parking lot. Somebody had hit me because there was blood in my mouth. I tried to stand. I made it up to my knees and then I passed out.

I woke up again. I was lying beside my truck. I got ahold of the door handle and pulled myself up with that. I leaned my arms on the bed and tried to remember what had happened. Somebody had been yelling at me. I remembered swinging one time. Then nothing until I came to in the parking lot.

I knew what I had to do. I knew where I had to go. I got in my truck and cranked it up. I had to close one eye to see how to drive. Some of my lower teeth were loose. There was a cut inside my mouth. But I knew somebody who would take care of me. I knew somebody who would be glad to see me.

All my crying was over with. You can only cry so much. You can't just keep on feeling sorry for yourself. I was lying in bed watching "The Love Boat" and hoping somehow that he'd come back. But I knew he wouldn't. I didn't know if he'd even come back and finish the work. I thought he would probably be too embarrassed to.

I was watching the show but I didn't believe in it. It wasn't like real life. There were too many happy endings on it. Everybody always found just exactly what they were looking for. And nobody on there was mean. Nobody on there was going to break down a door and slap somebody off the commode.

I wanted to talk to him again. He seemed to be such an understanding person, a person who would take the time to listen to another person's troubles. I was wishing I could see what his woman and his baby looked like. I was still having some drinks.

I knew there were nice men in the world, men who would love me for myself and not mistreat me. But how did you find them? How did you know they wouldn't change years later? There weren't any promises that would keep forever. Things altered in your lives and people changed. Sometimes they even started hating each other. I hated Harold so bad when I divorced him that I couldn't stand to look at him. But I can still remember how tender his hands used to be. I can still remember the first time he undressed me and how he looked at me when I was naked.

But who would want me now? I shouldn't have been surprised when Richard pulled away. I have varicose veins and my breasts are sagging. I've got those ugly rolls of fat around my middle. I've gone through the change. No, a young man doesn't want an old woman. It's the old woman who wants the young man.

I hoped he wouldn't tell anybody. I hoped he wouldn't tell his woman about it. I knew he wouldn't. Not a nice boy like him. I wanted to blame something, so I blamed the drinking. But I couldn't blame all of it on the drinking. I had to blame part of it on me.

I even thought about calling him. But I couldn't call him. What if his woman answered? What would I say then? He might have already told her and she might want to know if this was the old drunk bag who tried to get Richard in the bed with her. She might say, Listen, you old dried up bag of shit. . . .

But what if he answered? It wasn't late. It wasn't even ten o'clock. But what if the baby was asleep and it woke her up? It was stupid to even think about it. But I wanted him to come back so bad. Nobody thinks the things I think. The crazy things, the awful things, the insane things. That's what I was thinking when I heard him pull up.

I don't even know what I said to her. I was almost too drunk to walk. She turned the porch light on and came to the door. I talked to her. I guess I scared her with all the blood I had on me. I know I looked awful. I can't even remember what I said to her. There's no telling what I said to her. It's a wonder she didn't call the police.

I couldn't believe he came back. All that time of lying there thinking about him and wishing he'd come back and then he did. I just had on my housecoat and my underwear. I still had my makeup on. I couldn't wait to let him in.

I turned on the porch light and watched him try to get out of his truck. I didn't know what was wrong with him at first. He was staggering. And his face was all bloody. He'd been in a fight.

I got scared then. It took him about three tries to get up on the porch, and then he had to hold onto a post. He was the drunkest human I'd ever seen. I almost didn't recognize him.

He knocked on the door. I didn't know whether to open it or not. I hadn't been expecting him to be the way he was. I didn't know what to do. He kept knocking and finally I slipped the chain on and opened the door just a crack. I was scared to let him in.

He was weaving. He had blood all over his chin. He could just barely talk. It was hard to understand what he was saying, but he said something about it being so late. I said Yes, it was, and I asked him what he wanted. He said he just wanted to talk to me. I don't know what I could have been thinking of. He looked dangerous.

I told him he was drunk and I asked him again what he wanted. He kept saying that he'd sober up in a little bit. Then he asked me if he could come in. I told him it was awfully late. I didn't even really know him. I didn't know what he might do while he was drunk. He'd already been fighting, what else would he do? I knew that if I let him in he'd never leave, or he'd pass out and I wouldn't know what to do with him. Or what if he tried to rape me? I couldn't let him in.

I tried to be as gentle with him as I could. I told him it would be better if he went on home. I told him it was after ten.

He asked me if I had any coffee. He said if he had some coffee he'd sober up. But he could barely stand. And he was driving. I thought, What if he left in his truck and killed somebody, or himself, before he got home? Maybe I should have let him stay. But I was scared to let him stay. He looked so wild. His eyes were as red as blood.

He said something about a favor. He said something about if it wouldn't hurt you and would help the other person. I didn't know what he was talking about. I told him to please go home.

He said he needed to talk to me, that nobody understood. I told him I didn't want to do anything that would hurt him, but that he needed to go home right away.

I knew I had to be firm. I told him I was going to close the door. He hung his head. Then he looked up and looked into my eyes. Looked right into me. Everything changed in that moment. I saw how the rest of my life was going to be. I knew that I would always be lonely, and that I would always be scared. I told him to go home again and then I shut the door.

I don't remember driving home. I just woke up the next morning in bed with Betty. Tracey was crying. It was dark. I put my hand on Betty and I moved against her and I put my chin in her neck. She squeezed my hand in her sleep. She moved it down between her legs and moaned. Maybe she was having a bad dream. It all came back to me suddenly, what I'd done the night before. I just closed my eyes. I didn't want to think about it. I had to get up in thirty more minutes. I had to get up and fix myself some breakfast.

Some men showed up a few days later. One of them was short, with a red beard. His shirt was spattered with paint. He did all the talking. The other one just stood on the porch and looked around.

I let them in after they explained why they were there. They brought their tools in, and the linoleum in. I stayed in the bedroom while they hammered and sawed and nailed. I thought they never would get through.

Finally he knocked on the door and asked me if I wanted to come out and look at it. I went out and looked. The doors were hung and the new linoleum was down. They'd done a neat job, a good job. But I wanted them out of my house. I wrote him a check quickly, for the same price that Richard had named. They took his sawhorses. They said they could do other things: remodeling, build decks, paint my house. I thanked them and told them I didn't need anything else right now. I didn't ask them anything about Richard.

It was almost a month later when I saw them in the supermarket. I like to do my shopping at night, when the stores aren't full of people, when the aisles are clear and you can take your time. A young woman turned into the aisle ahead of me, a girl with a sweatshirt and blue jeans and fuzzy blue house shoes. I wouldn't be caught dead out like that. There was a little girl with yellow hair sitting in the cart, and she was reaching out for everything they passed. The woman slapped at the child's hands like an automatic reaction, without even looking.

I watched them for a while. And then I went on past them. I
wanted to finish and get out of the store quickly, as soon as possible, before it was too late. Their lives were things that didn't
concern me and the world is full of suffering anyway. How can
one person be expected to do anything about it?

I turned the corner and he was standing at the meat counter
with a pack of bacon in his hand. His back was turned and I
thought I might slip by. But he turned his head, just a little, and
he saw me. He didn't seem surprised, or even embarrassed. His
head bent just a little, and he said something. Hey, something.
I thought for a moment he was going to start talking to me.
But he didn't. He turned away. I thought that was nice of him,
to make it so easy for me to go on by. I didn't let myself
hurry. I stopped a little ways past him and looked at some dill
pickles in a display set up in the middle of the floor. There
were hundreds of bottles. I didn't want to buy any, but I picked
up one and read the price. It was fifty-nine cents. I looked
over my shoulder and he was looking at me. Richard. My hand
must have been trembling. I wanted him even then. I set the
jar back without looking and the whole display crashed down.
I jumped back. It was unbelievable the way it looked. Broken
glass everywhere, and thousands of tiny green chips. Green
juice that started puddling around my cart. It ran across the floor
and people stepped out of the aisles to look at me. I was trying
to think of something to say. I didn't look over my shoulder to
see if Richard was watching. I was scared of what I might see.

I put the groceries away and took a shower and put on clean clothes. Tracey was asleep in her bed and Betty was asleep in hers. I waited until she started snoring and then I started gathering things up. I had a week's pay in my pocket and the truck was paid for. I had the title in the glove box. I could trade it off, buy another one, whatever.

Tracey doesn't sleep well most nights, but that night she did. She slept through Grenada, through Jackson, on through Hattiesburg. The miles piled up behind us. I knew Betty wouldn't send anybody after us. I knew Betty would probably be relieved.

I had Myra's number in my pocket and I thought I might call her when we got to where we were going. I thought I might wish her some luck.

THE END OF ROMANCE

Miss Sheila and I were riding around, as we often did in those days. But I was pretty sure it was going to be the last afternoon of our relationship. Things hadn't been good lately.

It was hot. We'd been drinking all day, and we'd drunk almost enough. We lacked just a little getting to a certain point. I'd already come to a point. I'd come down to the point where I could still get an erection over her, but my heart wouldn't be going crazy and jumping up in my throat like a snake-bit frog. I wouldn't be fearing for my life when I mounted her. I knew it was time for me to book for a fat man's ass. She bitched about how much time I spent locked in my room, how my mother was bossy, when would I ever learn some couth? And you get them started nagging at you, you might as well be married. Well. I'd been out of women when I found her and I'd be out of women again until I found another one. But there were hundreds of other women, thousands, millions. They'd been making new ones every day for years.

"I ain't drunk," she said.

"Well, I'm not drunk, either."

"You look like you are."

"So do you."

"You got enough money to get some more? You can take all that Nobel Prize money and get us a coupla sixers, can't you?"

She was bad about chagrinning me like that.

"I magine I can manage it," I said.

So she whipped it into one of those little quick-joints that are so popular around here, one of those chicken-scarfing places, whipped it up in front of the door and stopped. She stared straight ahead through the windshield. Nothing worse than a drunken woman. Empty beer cans were all piled up around our feet. The end of romance is never easy.

"What matter?" I said.

"Nuttin matter. Everything just hunkin funkin dunky."

"You mean hunky dory?"

She had some bloodshot eyes and a ninety-yard stare. I'd known it would come down to this. The beginning of romance is wonderful. I don't know why I do it over and over. Starting with a new one, I can just about eat her damn legs off. Then, later, some shit like this. Women. Spend your whole life after the right one and what do they do? Shit on you. I always heard the theory of slapping them around to make them respect you, that that's what they want. But I couldn't. I couldn't stand to hit that opposite flesh. That slap would ring in my head for the rest of my life. This is what I do: take what they give and give what I can and when it's over find another one. Another one. That's what's so wonderful about the beginning of romance. She's different. She's new. Unique. Everything's fresh. Crappola. You go in there to shave after the first night and what does she do while you've got lather all over your face? Comes in and hikes her nightgown and then the honeymoon's over.

I'm not trying to get away from the story. I mean, just a few minutes later, some stuff actually happened. But sitting in that car at that moment, I was a little bitter. I had all sorts of thoughts going through my head, like: *Slapper. Slapper ass off*. I held that down.

She looked at me with those bloodshot eyes. "You really somethin, you know that? You really really really."

I knew it was coming. We'd had a bad afternoon out at the lake. Her old boyfriend had been out there, and he'd tried to put the make on her. I and seven of my friends had ripped his swim trunks off of him, lashed him to the front of her car, and driven him around blindfolded but with his name written on a large piece of beer carton taped to his chest for thirty-seven minutes, in front of domestic couples, moms and dads, family reunions, and church groups. She hadn't thought it was funny. We, we laughed our asses off.

I got out of the car. She didn't want to have any fun, that was fine with me. I bent over and gathered up an armload of beer cans and carried them to the trash can. They clattered all over the place when I dropped them in. I was a little woozy but I didn't think anybody could see it. Through the window of the store this old dyed woman with great big breasts and pink sunglasses looked out at me with a disapproving frown. I waved. Then I went back for more cans.

"Don't worry about the damn cans, all right?"

"I can't move my feet for them," I said.

"I'll worry about the damn cans," she said.

It sort of crumpled me. We were in her convertible, and once it was fun to just throw them straight up while we were going down the road. The wind, or I guess just running out from under them was fun. It was a game. Now it didn't seem to matter. I think we both had the creep of something bad coming up on us. She could have beat the shit out of me, I could have beat the shit out of her. It's no way to live. You don't want to go to sleep nervous, fearing the butcher knife, the revolver, the garrote.

"Just go in and get some beer," she said. "We got to talk."

Then she started crying. She wasn't pretty when she was crying. Her whole face turned red and wrinkled up. I knew it was me. It's always me.

"You're just so damn great, ain't you?" she said. "Don't even want nobody overt the house, cept a bunch of old drunks and freaks and whores."

My friends. Poets, artists, actors, English professors out at Ole Miss. She called them drunks and freaks. *Slapper. Slap shit out of her.*

"Just go on git the damn beer," she said. "I got something to tell you."

It's awful to find pussy so good that treats you so bad. It's like you've got to *pay* for it being good. But you've got to be either a man or a pussy. You can't just lay around and pine. I thought at that point that maybe I'd gotten out of that particular car for the last time.

I went on in. I was even starting to feel better. If she left, I could go home, open all the doors, crank up the stereo, get free. I could start sleeping in the daytime and writing at night again, nonstop if I wanted to, for eight or ten hours. I could have a party without somebody sullen in one corner. Everything would be different and the same again.

Well, hell, I wasn't perfect though, was I? I'd probably been a shitass a few times. Who's not? Even your best friend will turn asshole on you from time to time. He's only human.

I knew somebody else would come along. I just didn't know how long it would be. So I did a little quick rationalizing inside the store.

Whatever I was going back outside to wasn't going to be good. She was bracing herself up to be nasty to me, I could see that. And there wasn't any need in a bit of it. I could do without all the nastiness. I could take an amicable breakup. All I had to do was hang around inside the store for a while, and she'd probably get tired of waiting for me, and run off and leave me. So I went back toward the rear. The old bag was watching me. She probably thought I was a criminal. All I was doing was sitting back there gnawing my fingernails. But it was no good. I couldn't stand to know she was out there waiting on me.

So I got back up and went up the beer aisle. I figured I might as well go on and face it. Maybe we'd have a goodbye roll. I got her a sixpack of Schlitz malt liquor and got myself a sixer of Stroh's in bottles. The old bag was eyeing me with distaste. I still had my trunks on, and flip-flops, and my FireBusters T-shirt. I was red from passing out under the sun.

I could see Miss Sheila out there. I set the beer on the counter just as a black guy pulled up beside her car and got out. I started pulling my money out and another car pulled up beside the first one. It had a black guy in it, too, only this one had a shotgun. The first black guy was up against the door, just coming in, and the second black guy suddenly blew the top of the first black guy's head off. The first black guy flopped inside.

"*AAAAAAAAAAAHHHHHHHHHHH!*" he said. "*HHHH-HHWWWWWWWAAAAAAAAAAAAAAAHHH!*" Blood and meat and black hair had flown inside everywhere with him, glass. It stuck to the walls, to the cigarettes in the rack over the counter, to the warming oven where they had the fried chicken. I'd eaten a lot of that fried chicken. The guy flopped down the detergent aisle. "*WAAAAAAAAAAAAAAH!*" he said.

I just stood there holding my money. I'd been wrong. The top of his head hadn't been blown off after all. He just didn't have any hair up there.

"*HAAAAAAAAAAAAAAAAAAH!*" he said. He was flopping around like a fish. He flopped down to the end of the aisle, then flopped over a couple of tables where people ate their barbecue at lunchtime, (where I'd been sitting just a few minutes before) and then he flopped over in the floor. I looked outside. The second black guy had gotten back into his car with his shotgun and was backing out of the parking lot. I couldn't see Miss Sheila.

"Let me pay for my beer and get out of here," I said, to the woman who had ducked down behind the counter. "The cops'll be here in a minute."

The black guy got off the floor back there and flopped over the meat market. "*AAAAAAAAAAAAAAH!*" he said. He flopped up against the coolers, leaving big bloody handprints all over the glass. He started flopping up the beer aisle, coming back toward us.

"Come on, lady," I said. "Shitfire."

He flopped over a bunch of Vienna sausage and Moon Pies, and then he flopped over the crackers and cookies. Blood was pouring out of his head. I looked down at one of the coolers and saw a big piece of black wool sliding down the glass in some blood. He was tracking it all over the store, getting it everywhere.

I knew what the beer cost. It was about six dollars. I didn't wait for a sack. But I watched him for a moment longer. I couldn't take my eyes off him. He flopped over the candy and the little bags of potato chips, and across the front, and flopped across the chicken warmer and the ice cream box and the magazine racks. "*HAAAAAAAAAAAH!*" he said. I put some money up on the counter. Then I went outside.

The guy had shot the whole place up. All the glass in the windows was shattered, and he'd even shot the bricks. He'd even shot the newspaper machines. He'd murdered the hell out of *The Oxford Eagle*.

When I looked back inside, the guy had flopped up against the counter where the woman was hiding, flopping all over the cash register. Sheila wasn't dead or murdered either one.

I asked her, "You all right?" She was down in the floorboard. She looked up at me. She didn't look good.

"I thought you's dead," she screamed. "*OH, GOD, HOW COULD I HAVE BEEN SO FOOLISH?*"

I set the beer on the back seat and got in. "You better git this sumbitch outa here," I said. I reached over and got me a beer. I could hear the sirens coming. They were wailing way off in the distance. She latched onto me.

"*I WOULDN'T LEAVE YOU NOW FOR NOTHIN,*" she screamed. "*COULDN'T RUN ME OFF,*" she hollered.

"I'm telling you we better get our ass out of here," I said.

"Look out," she screamed. I looked. The wounded black guy was flopping through the door where there wasn't any door anymore. He flopped up beside the car. "*WAAAAAAAAAAH!*" he said. He was slinging blood all over us. But other than that he seemed harmless.

"What I wanted to say was maybe we should watch more TV together," she said. "If you just didn't write so much. . . ."

The cops screamed into the parking lot. They had their shotguns poking out the windows before they even stopped. Five or six cruisers. Blue uniforms and neat ties and shiny brass. They'd taken their hats off. They had shiny sunglasses. You could tell that they were itching to shoot somebody, now that they'd locked and loaded. The black guy was leaning against the car, heaving. I knew I wouldn't get to finish my beer. I heard them shuck their pumps. I raised my hands and my beer. I pointed to Miss Sheila.

"She did it," I said.

THE BRIGHT LEAF SHORT FICTION SERIES

"I think you're the one who'll charm her."

Emma said the words softly as she thought about the evening they'd met. Nathan's smile had made her toes curl. "Just like you charmed me."

His eyes darkened as he stared at her. "When was that, Emma? I haven't exactly been Mr. Suave lately."

In the quiet of the stairwell, his low voice echoed off the walls and felt like a caress. "The night we met," she said. "Before Harley came to live with me."

"What would have happened?" She didn't see him move, but he was closer to her. "If Sonya hadn't died? If Harley hadn't come to live with you?"

The weak winter sun streaming in through the windows turned his eyes into silvery-blue pools, deep and mysterious.

"I think..." She took a deep breath, trying to draw air into her suddenly tight chest. "I would have called you," she whispered. She wanted to lean closer. To test the fragile connection they'd woven between them.

Dear Reader,

One of the things I love about making up stories is that I can put my characters into impossible situations, then sit back and watch them squirm. And that's just what I did in *Bending the Rules*—start with a woman who desperately wants to adopt the child she's caring for, mix in the child's biological father, who wants to do the right thing, but isn't sure what that is, and season with an attraction that complicates everything.

Emma Sloan loves Harley Michaels fiercely and completely. She wants nothing more than to adopt the girl and make a family with her. But Nathan Devereux has just learned that he's the girl's father. She may be his daughter, but he's not sure how to handle this new family member. He's in a dangerous situation right now—he's in no position to welcome a child into his life. And Harley wants to stay with Emma. But Nathan is not going to simply sign away his parental rights. In the Devereux clan, family is everything.

I hope you enjoy reading Emma and Nathan's story as much as I enjoyed writing it. Happy reading!

I love to hear from my readers! Please visit my website, www.margaretwatson.com or contact me at margaret@margaretwatson.com.

Yours,

Margaret Watson

Bending the Rules

MARGARET WATSON

HARLEQUIN®SUPER ROMANCE®

Recycling programs
for this product may
not exist in your area.

ISBN-13: 978-0-373-71832-0

BENDING THE RULES

Printed in U.S.A.

HARLEQUIN®
www.Harlequin.com

ABOUT THE AUTHOR

Margaret Watson has always made up stories in her head. When she started actually writing them down, she realized she'd found exactly what she wanted to do with the rest of her life. More than twenty years after staring at that first blank page, she's an award-winning, two-time RITA® Award finalist who has written more than thirty books for Harlequin. When she's not writing or spending time with her family, she practices veterinary medicine. Although she enjoys that job, writing is her passion. Margaret lives in a Chicago suburb with her husband and three daughters and a menagerie of pets.

Books by Margaret Watson

HARLEQUIN SUPERROMANCE

*The McInnes Triplets

Other titles by this author available in ebook format.

Don't miss any of our special offers. Write to us at the following address for information on our newest releases.

Harlequin Reader Service
U.S.: 3010 Walden Ave., P.O. Box 1325, Buffalo, NY 14269
Canadian: P.O. Box 609, Fort Erie, Ont. L2A 5X3

For Meg, my charismatic, dazzling and extraordinary daughter.

You've grown into an amazing woman, and I am so proud of you.

CHAPTER ONE

NATHAN DEVEREUX SCOWLED as he hung the handicapped plac-
ard from his rearview mirror. He hated handicapped parking.
But if he didn't take this spot, he'd have to park a couple of
blocks away. That much walking and his leg would hurt like
a son of a bitch by the time he got home.

Which meant that physical therapy tomorrow would be difficult. Less effective.

Slamming the car door, he limped to the front of FreeZone.
Bright lights illuminated the interior of his sister's teen cen-
ter, and the groups of people mingling. Frankie and her fiancé,
Cal, were laughing and talking in the middle of one of them.

Nathan's dark mood slipped away. Frankie deserved this
happiness. She deserved to have all her dreams come true.

"It's not that scary, is it?" a low voice asked behind him.

He turned to see a tall woman standing behind him, smiling. Her blond hair was a mass of curls around her face, and
dangly silver earrings peeked out of the curls. A tan scarf was
intricately wrapped around her neck, and her brown eyes twinkled. "No teens in there right now. It's safe."

"Right. Because I can actually hear what you're saying."
He held the door and watched her walk in ahead of him. Her
black leather jacket clung to her curves, and her jeans-clad hips
swayed. Her scent was citrusy and sweet. "I was just admiring
the, um, the way Frankie and Cal pulled this place together."
As the woman turned to face him, he cleared his throat and
forced his gaze back to her face.

"You must be a friend of theirs, then. Most of the donors never saw the old place."

The blonde's low voice and direct gaze washed over him. The noise in the room faded. "Frankie's brother," he said, holding out his hand. "Nathan Devereux."

"Emma Sloan." Her hand was slender and cool, and her grip firm. "I work with Frankie occasionally."

Her eyes were the color of honey. They met his for a moment that stretched a little too long. When she gently tugged her hand away, he released her. "Good to meet you, Emma."

"You, too. Frankie has a bunch of brothers, doesn't she?"

"Three of us," Nathan said, his gaze lingering on those expressive eyes. "Which Frankie says is way too many. She claims we're overprotective."

"Nice to have someone on your side," Emma said lightly, but a momentary shadow swam behind her clear gaze.

"Feel free to remind Frankie of that," he said, wondering about the shadow.

Nathan registered the murmur of voices, the clink of champagne glasses passed by waiters and the slam of an air-hockey puck hitting the sides of the table. But he could focus on nothing but the woman in front of him.

The moment stretched out. Emma broke the eye contact and unzipped her coat. A swirly patterned aqua and green V-necked shirt covered soft curves. A silver pendant with a cutout pattern nestled above a hint of cleavage.

Nathan wanted to lean closer and examine the pendant.

"It's nice that you could come to Frankie's open house," Emma said in a husky voice.

"I wouldn't have missed it." He tore his attention away from Emma and glanced at Frankie, dressed in a blue suit and wearing heels. Even her spiky hair was under control. "Although I want to know who stole my sister and put that businesswoman in her place."

Emma followed his gaze and smiled. "Yeah. She cleans up nicely."

She glanced at him, and neither of them spoke for a beat. "Well," he began.

"Nice to have met you," she said at the same time.

They both smiled, and Emma gestured toward Frankie and Cal. "I guess I should say hello."

"Yeah. Right. I'll, ah, talk to you later?"

"I'd like that." She held his gaze for a moment, then turned and walked toward his sister. Maybe it was the heels she wore that made her hips sway like that. Whatever the reason, he admired the result all the way across the room.

"I know that woman." Darcy, his brother Patrick's fiancée, looped her arm through his and stared at Emma. "Can't remember how, though."

"She said she works with Frankie. Her name is Emma Sloan." She was laughing at something Frankie said, gesturing with her hands.

"You look smitten, Nathan," Darcy said, grinning.

"I don't even know her." He yanked on his tie. "We walked in the door together. Of course we introduced ourselves."

Darcy nudged him with her elbow. "Really? I guess you're all googly-eyed because you're awed at what your sister did with this place, then." She tugged at his arm. "Come sit down. You can admire…Frankie's place from the couch."

Nathan allowed her to lead him to one of the new, denim-colored couches, where Patrick was sitting. "Your fiancée has gotten real bossy, Patrick."

"You have no idea," Patrick said with a secret smile at Darcy.

"TMI, Paddy," Nathan said hastily. Patrick and Darcy leaned into each other as Nathan lowered himself carefully to the couch. He was thrilled that Patrick and Darcy had found each other, just as he was happy for Frankie and Cal, who were getting married in the spring. So what if it underlined his own loneliness? His problem. Not theirs.

Time to focus on something else. "How's the investigation going?"

Patrick's smile faded. "We came here to help Frankie celebrate. Let's not spoil the mood by talking about the case."

"Trust me—you're not going to spoil anything." The whole mess was never far from Nathan's thoughts—especially his responsibility for what had happened. "Just fill me in."

Patrick sighed. "Can't you let it go for one night?"

"Humor me, Paddy." He held up his left arm, still weak from the accident. "Or do I need to arm wrestle you for information?"

Patrick rolled his eyes. "We're stalled, okay?" He rested his elbows on his knees. "Alderman O'Fallon may be in jail, but he still won't talk, and neither will anyone else. It's as if the guy who gave O'Fallon the money is a ghost. Anyone who can hide like that has a lot of juice. It's not going to be easy."

"You're a forensic accountant for the FBI. There must be some way to follow the money."

"We're working on it. But they're not stupid. They know how to cover their tracks. It's not going to be easy unless we can get someone to crack. So far, that hasn't happened."

"I'm doing a little digging on my own. I gotta find this guy."

Patrick leaned toward him. "You ever hear 'don't do this at home, boys and girls'? This isn't your job, Nate. Leave it to the professionals."

"Yeah, it *is* my job," Nathan said quietly. "I'm the one who screwed up. I'm the one who took the money. Now I have to make it right."

"You're being way too hard on yourself. Yeah, you made a mistake. We all did. We're fixing it, and now we're moving on. We're *all* moving on."

"You do your thing and I'll do mine," Nathan said.

He eased back on the couch and accepted the glass of champagne a waiter offered him. He wouldn't be able to live with himself if he didn't make this right. He'd almost destroyed the family restaurant because he'd thought he was smart enough to make a sketchy deal and not pay the price.

Last winter, when he'd needed to remodel the restaurant kitchen, he hadn't been able to get a loan from a bank. Knowing that the building inspectors would close Mama's Place if he didn't remodel, he'd gone to his alderman—in Chicago, the alderman was the guy who made things happen. The go-to guy for bureaucratic problems.

The guy who could find a bank willing to lend money when others had refused.

Alderman O'Fallon had offered Nathan a special deal—he could get financing from a private individual. The interest rate would be higher than a bank's, but he'd get his money. Nathan had been so desperate that he'd agreed. And he'd been careful not to ask where the money came from.

His whole family had gotten sucked into the mess. Worst of all, because his brother Patrick had been distracted by the problem Nathan created, Darcy had almost been killed.

He'd known the deal with the alderman was suspect, but he'd taken it anyway. So there was no way he was going to sit back and let his brother handle it for him. He'd taken the money. He was going to find out who had given it to him.

"Here's a news flash, Nate." Patrick leaned over Darcy to get in his face. "Until we find out who gave O'Fallon the money, we don't even know if a crime has been committed. Maybe the ghost paid taxes on the interest he got from you. Maybe it was just a benefactor who wanted to help you out."

"Yeah, and maybe I'm really George Clooney in disguise," Nathan retorted.

Darcy pushed the two men apart. "Hey, Nate, Emma looks like she'd pick you over Clooney any day."

Distracted, Nathan glanced toward Frankie. Emma, standing on the edge of the group surrounding his sister, was sipping a glass of champagne and watching him. When their eyes met, she turned away. But not before he saw her flush.

"Fine," Nathan muttered, not looking at Patrick. "Let it drop." For tonight, anyway. He'd harmed the family and almost lost the restaurant. The FBI could investigate out the wazoo. He'd work his own contacts in the neighborhood.

No way had that loan been legal.

He'd known that when he took the money.

So what did that make him?

"I'm going to say hello to Frankie," he said, pushing himself off the couch.

"You sure it's Frankie you want to say hello to?" Darcy asked.

When Nathan glanced at her, she was grinning. "Funny, Darce."

As he walked away, she called after him, "I just want you to be happy, Nate."

Finding the guy who'd given him the money would make him happy. Being sure his family was safe would make him happy, too. So would getting away from the restaurant after everything was settled. He was going to Italy, and he was staying for a while.

Emma Sloan?

It had been a while since he'd felt the kind of spark that had arced between him and Emma. Any other time, he'd want to pursue it.

Right now, he had too many other things going on.

As he got closer, she laughed at something Frankie said.

Maybe he could find the time.

EMMA WATCHED NATHAN limp slowly toward her. His gait was uncertain, as if he were getting used to walking again. She'd noticed how carefully he'd moved earlier, and she wondered how he'd been injured.

"That's my brother Nate," Frankie said in her ear, and Emma started. Had she been that obvious?

"He was hit by a car a few months ago," Frankie continued.

"Nasty breaks in his arm and leg. The casts came off a couple of weeks ago. I told him to stay home tonight and put the leg up, but he never listens to me."

"I, ah, met him earlier." She glanced at Frankie. "He sounds pretty proud of you. Of course he wanted to come."

"He's my brother," Frankie said. "He has to say stuff like that."

A tiny burst of jealousy hit Emma squarely in the chest. "You're lucky to have brothers."

"Most of the time." She nudged Emma. "Go keep Nate company."

"I think he probably wants to talk to you," Emma replied.

"I don't think so," Frankie said with a grin. "I saw the two of you talking earlier. The little birds circling around your heads were very cute."

"Knock it off, Frankie." But Emma's heart beat a little faster as Nathan got closer.

She'd noticed his bright blue eyes the moment he turned to open the door for her. She'd seen the faint smile lines, too. The thick, wavy black hair. He was tall enough to tower over her—not many men could do that.

And his shoulders filled out his suit very nicely.

Then he'd smiled, and her heart had missed a beat.

She was thirty-one—too old to feel this giddy. Too old for little birds to fly around her head. But she hadn't been able to take her eyes off Nathan Devereux.

As he got closer, he glanced at her and smiled. She smiled back, her palms suddenly sweaty. While he was still several feet away, her phone rang.

She was tempted to ignore it. But she pulled her phone out of her bag to check.

It was her friend Sonya Michaels. "Can I call you back later, Sonya? I'm at the FreeZone reception."

"Is this Emma Sloan?" a male voice said.

"Yes." Her relaxed tone disappeared and she gripped the phone. "Who is this?"

"This is Officer Trenton of the Chicago Police Department. Are you Harley Michaels's aunt?"

She wasn't. Why did the officer think she was? "Is Harley okay?"

"There's been an accident. Harley gave us your number."

"What happened? Is Harley okay?" Emma's heart began to pound as she hurried toward the door, shrugging on her coat as she juggled her phone and purse.

"She's fine. Her mother had an accident. We need to talk to Harley's closest relative."

"That would be me." The lie slipped easily off her tongue. Sonya and Harley had no family. "Where are you?"

"We're at Ms. Michaels's apartment."

"Give me fifteen minutes."

As she opened the door and stepped into the cold wind, she glanced over her shoulder. Nathan stood alone in the middle of the floor, watching her. He wasn't smiling anymore.

She raised her hand briefly, and he nodded.

As she hurried toward her car, she glanced at FreeZone one last time. Nathan was standing where she'd left him. Still watching her.

Twelve minutes later, she was pounding on the apartment door. A police officer opened it. "I'm Emma Sloan. Where's Harley?"

"Emma?" Harley's voice wobbled from the living room, and Emma pushed past the officer.

Harley barreled toward her and threw herself in Emma's arms. Emma held her tight, the girl's wet cheek against her own. "I'm here, Harley," she whispered. "It'll be okay."

"No, it won't." Harley's fingers dug into her spine and her body shook with sobs. "M…Mom's dead."

"What?" Emma reared back and stared at Harley. "What happened?"

Instead of answering, Harley clung to Emma and sobbed into her chest. Emma held Harley protectively, stroking her back and her bright hair.

Over Harley's shoulder, a female police officer sat on the couch with Mrs. Vilnius. The older woman who stayed with Harley until her mother got home was weeping into a handkerchief.

The officer stood up and walked over to Emma and Harley. "Ms. Michaels lost consciousness on the bus," she said quietly. "By the time the paramedics arrived, she was already gone."

"My God." Emma felt as though she'd been punched in the chest. Sonya and Harley Michaels had started off as clients. But she'd become close to both of them, and now Sonya was one of her closest friends. Her throat tightened. *Had been.* "What… How…?"

"We're not sure," the woman said, glancing at Harley. "We'll…ah…have to wait for the results."

For an autopsy. Emma brushed her hand over Harley's hair, appreciating the officer's discretion. "What about Harley?"

The officer gave her an odd look. "That's why we called you. Harley said you were her only relative. We assumed you'd take custody of her. But if you're not able to do that, we'll call DCFS."

Harley tightened her grip on Emma.

"You don't have to call them—I work for DCFS," Emma said to the police officer. "And of course Harley will stay with me." She laid her cheek against the top of Harley's head and closed her eyes as grief washed over her. Sonya was gone. Dead, on a bus on her way home.

Harley was alone.

No. She had Emma.

"Good," the police officer said briskly. "You'll notify DCFS, then?"

"Yes." Emma was certified as an emergency foster parent.

Since Harley didn't have any other relatives, there should be no problem being named the girl's legal guardian.

The police officer nodded, Harley continued to sob and the enormity of it all began to sink in.

Emma dealt with children and families in crisis every day. She was always the outsider, though, schooled to stay detached and cool, giving advice and taking action according to a set of guidelines.

There were no guidelines for helping a child you loved deal with such a devastating loss. Emma didn't even have a parental role model to reference—she had pretty much raised herself.

So how was she supposed to help Harley? What did she say? Do?

She knew all the pat answers—get her into grief therapy. Be steady and patient with her. Encourage her to talk.

Love her.

She got the love part—she adored the teenager. It was everything else that was terrifying.

She held the girl closer. "I've got you, Harley. I've got you. You're not alone."

A muffled sob was her only answer.

The police officer turned to Mrs. Vilnius, still on the couch. "Thank you for staying with Harley until her aunt could get here, ma'am. We appreciate it."

The older woman nodded, her dark eyes liquid above the handkerchief. "If Harley needs anything…" She began weeping again, and Harley's arms tightened around Emma.

"I'll let you know," Emma said. She closed her eyes and held the crying girl as Mrs. Vilnius left the apartment.

The male police officer cleared his throat. "Ms. Sloan, if you'll give me your phone number, we'll be in touch."

Reaching one hand into her bag, Emma groped until she found her card case in one of the side pockets. She handed it to the officer, who took one out and handed back the case.

The police officers left, their footsteps retreating down the hall. The only sounds in the apartment were Harley's sobs.

What now?

Emma stood in the middle of the living room, rocking Harley as she cried. What did you say to a child who had just lost her mother? How did you ease her pain?

Tears trailed down Emma's cheeks and darkened Harley's red hair. She had no idea.

She and Harley stood there grieving, as the old apartment building creaked and groaned around them. The wind moaned through the ill-fitting windows and Harley shivered.

Emma held her more tightly.

Finally, with one last sniffle, Harley lifted her head. Her face was red and blotchy and her eyes swollen. She swiped the back of her hand across her face once, then again. Emma reached for a box of tissues that someone had set on the couch and handed Harley a wad of them.

The girl blew her nose and hiccuped. Her eyes were pools of devastation. "They…they just came to the door," she said. "Maybe they were wrong. Maybe Mom's not really dead. Maybe she's just sick, and they made a mistake. Or maybe they came to the wrong house."

"I'm pretty sure the police don't make those kinds of mistakes, Harley." Emma brushed damp strands of red hair away from her face. "But I'll make some calls and check, okay?"

Harley nodded and clung to Emma. "I lied to the police," she said, her voice faint. "But I did what Mom told me to do."

"What was that, sweetheart?" Emma continued to stroke Harley's hair.

"I told them you were my aunt. Mom said if she ever got… got sick, or hurt, that's what I should do. That you'd take care of me."

"She was absolutely right," Emma said, pushing Harley's tear-damp hair away from her face and holding her gaze. "I'm here, and I'm not going anywhere." Although she wondered why Sonya hadn't talked to her about the plan.

She'd probably thought it was one of those things that if you set it up, you'd never need it.

But she had.

Harley stepped away from Emma. She stared around the apartment, her arms wrapped around her waist. The couch and chairs were old and worn, the small television had been a neighbor's discard, and the rug had faded to a nondescript gray. But Emma had never noticed the Michaels' lack of possessions. The love that had filled this house had made everything else fade into the background.

"We had a fight last night," Harley said, her eyes filled with pain. "I told Mom I hated her."

"Oh, sweetheart, your mom knew you didn't mean it," Emma said softly, her heart aching. She held back tears as she tugged Harley onto the couch and wrapped an arm around her shoulders. "Kids say stuff like that to their parents all the time. Moms know better. Did you kiss her goodbye this morning before you left for school?" It was a safe question, because Sonya never let her daughter out of the apartment without a kiss and an "I love you."

Harley nodded.

"There you go. Trust me, honey. Your mom had forgotten all about the fight."

Harley looked away. "I don't think so. I was pretty mean to her."

The thirteen-year-old was moody sometimes, and Sonya could be impatient. Her friend would have been upset about the fight. Hurt by the ugly words. But Emma also knew the bond between mother and daughter was strong. They fought as much as any parent and child, but they'd been a unit, facing their problems together. "Your mom knew how much you loved her."

"What…what happens now?" Harley whispered, her voice hoarse with tears.

Emma had no idea. "Let's get some of your things and we'll go to my apartment." She kept her arm around Harley's shoulder and steered her toward the bedroom. "We'll figure it out together, okay? One step at a time."

CHAPTER TWO

Three weeks later

A FULL MOON glowed through the window as Harley sprawled at one end of the couch, texting her friends. Emma sat at the other end, pretending to read a book.

Every few minutes, Harley glanced at Emma, as if reassuring herself that she was still there. It was barely noticeable to anyone who wasn't watching for it.

Harley had been subdued and sad since her mother died. Emma had expected that.

It was the fear that broke her heart.

Emma picked her up every evening at six, and if she was even a few minutes late, Harley was looking for her with anxious eyes. Here at the apartment, if Emma disappeared into another room, Harley would make some excuse to come find her, as if afraid Emma would vanish once she was out of Harley's sight.

As she studied Harley's wavy red hair, Emma's heart thudded with a hard, painful beat. She hated to make Harley do this. The girl would have to bare her soul to a panel of people who'd decide on Emma's request to be Harley's legal guardian. Harley had to be ready.

The meeting was in two days. They had to talk tonight.

Taking a deep breath, Emma closed the book. "Harley, there are some things we need to talk about."

Harley's thumbs stilled on her phone. Without looking up, she said, "I already finished my homework."

"Yeah, I know." Harley didn't want to talk about it, either. But Emma was the adult. They needed to have this discussion. "It's about what's going to happen."

Harley's thumbs began moving furiously. "I don't know what you mean."

"Sweetie, put your phone down, okay?"

Harley kept typing and Emma waited. Finally, her expression carefully blank, Harley set the phone next to her. "I have to leave, don't I?"

Emma scooted closer, but Harley drew herself into a ball and resisted her touch. "No, you don't. I love having you here." She swallowed. "I *love* you."

Harley glanced at her out of the corner of her eye. "You're pretty cool, too."

Emma still wasn't used to the way Harley's words made her heart flutter. She reached for Harley's hand and squeezed it. "I need to tell you what's been going on. What I've been doing. Because you're old enough to make some decisions yourself." She took a deep breath. "Do you want to stay with me, Harley?"

"Yeah, sure."

Yeah, sure? That was all the enthusiasm she could muster? "You need to think about this, okay?"

Harley began texting again. "I've thought about it. I want to stay with you."

"Good. Because I want you to stay."

"Then we're all good, right?" she answered without looking up from the keyboard.

"I hope so. I'm pretty sure I'll be approved as your legal guardian, especially since it's what you want, too. Since you're thirteen, your wishes will be considered, as well. But the people making the final decision need to talk to you."

Harley glanced at her out of the corner of her eye. "So?"

"It won't be a big deal, but they'll ask you some questions. You have to be sure this is what you want. That's why I said you have to think about whether you want to stay with me."

Emma was pretty confident Harley would be convincing. But the thought of not being approved as Harley's guardian, of Harley living with strangers, had been keeping her awake every night.

It was hard to believe that after only three short weeks, Emma couldn't imagine life without Harley. Yes, they were still adjusting to one another. There were speed bumps and frustrations for both of them. But Emma wanted Harley with a soul-deep longing that was frightening.

She could do this. She could take care of Harley. She may not have had any experience raising children, but between the families she saw every day and her own experience growing up with an irresponsible, careless mother, she knew what *not* to do.

Harley had picked up her phone again. As her fingers flew over the keyboard, she glanced at Emma out of the corner of her eye. "I said I wanted to stay with you," the girl said. "I'll tell them, too. It's what Mom would want. Or why would she have told me to say you're my aunt?" She rubbed the back of her head. "Unless I have an aneurysm, too. Then you're not stuck with me."

"Harley, I am *not* stuck with you," Emma said, her heart aching for the girl. "I'll fight for you forever. And just because your mom had an aneurysm doesn't mean you're going to have one."

As soon as they'd found out what killed her mother, Harley had looked up aneurysm on Google and learned they could run in families. Emma had caught her rubbing the back of her head more than once, as if trying to massage a weak blood vessel.

Harley put her hand back on her phone. "Whatever. But my mom wanted me to stay with you."

"I'd like to think so." Emma had no idea what Sonya would have wanted. They'd never talked about it. "Maybe she had a will. That's why we need to go back to your apartment and sort through your stuff."

Harley wrapped her arms around her waist and shook her head. "Not yet."

They'd talked about this more than once. Harley needed the rest of her things, Emma needed to know if there was a will, and the apartment had to be cleaned out. It wasn't fair to the landlord to keep stalling.

Harley flatly refused to return to her apartment. It was the only time she hadn't gone along with what Emma suggested.

Harley didn't want to rock the boat. She was worried that Emma wouldn't keep her. Emma got it, and that was why she hadn't pushed about the apartment. But it had to be done.

"All right, you don't have to go. I'll do it by myself." She'd put all of Sonya's belongings in storage until Harley was ready to deal with them.

"When?"

"This weekend."

"You want me to stay here by myself?"

"If that's what you want. You can watch movies, or read a book."

"That's boring." Harley jiggled her toe on the carpet.

"What would you rather do, then?"

"I'll go see Mrs. Vilnius. She's probably sad about Mom."

"That's very thoughtful. I'm sure she'd like to see you."

Harley jumped off the couch and shoved the blind to one side to stare down at the street. Without looking at Emma, she said, "I've been thinking. Maybe you could, like, adopt me. Then you wouldn't have to worry that I'd leave."

"Would you like me to adopt you?" Emma asked carefully. She'd already considered the possibility, but thought it was too soon to ask Harley. She'd assumed it would be a too-painful reminder of what the girl had lost.

Clearly, she'd been wrong. In the chaos of her mother's death, Harley craved stability.

Harley lifted one shoulder. "It would be okay."

"Then we'll look into it."

Adoption wouldn't be as easy as Harley seemed to think. There was a ream of paperwork to do. References to line up. Home visits. Background checks. It took a long time to finalize an adoption. In the meantime, if she was Harley's legal guardian, that would reassure the girl. Make her feel more stable. "One thing at a time, okay? Let's get the guardianship settled before we start working on an adoption. But remember, I work long hours. Sometimes I have to go out at night. Maybe you'd rather be in a home with two parents." It would rip out her heart to send Harley to someone else. But if that's what would be the best for the girl, Emma would do it.

Harley narrowed her eyes. "I never had a father, and my mom worked a lot. She wasn't always home. Did that make her a bad parent?"

"Of course not. Your mom was a wonderful parent. She adored you and she took good care of you. But she had your whole life to figure everything out. I've had three weeks."

"You're better than some stupid stranger would be," Harley said fiercely. "I want to stay with you."

Maybe on-the-job training for parenting a grieving thirteen-year-old wasn't the ideal. But no one would love Harley more than Emma. "Okay, Harley. Once I'm your legal guardian, we'll talk to a lawyer and get the paperwork started."

NATHAN WALKED SLOWLY toward the back door, stopping to pick up the damn cane. It had been five weeks since the casts had come off, and it pissed him off that he still had to use it. But if he showed up at physical therapy without the cane, his therapist would lecture him about it.

The fact that she was right didn't make it any more bearable. After therapy, his leg ached enough to make the cane a necessity.

It didn't mean he had to like it, though.

The front doorbell rang just as he was about to step outside. He hesitated, tempted to keep going and ignore it. Then he sighed, slammed the back door and headed for the front of the house.

Before he got there, the door opened. "Nate?" Patrick called. "You here?"

"Yeah, I am," he said as he rounded the corner into the living room. "What are you doing here?"

"I'm taking you to therapy. I needed to talk to you, anyway, so I called Frankie and told her to stay home." Patrick frowned as he saw the cane in Nathan's hand. "You trying to ditch me?"

"Damn it, Paddy! I can do this myself. You guys don't need to baby me. You don't need to drive me every time."

"Yeah, we do." He stopped and put a hand on Nathan's shoulder. "Look, Nate, I get that you need to be in control. Those six weeks in the wheelchair were hell for you. You've had to be in control ever since Mom and Dad died, and it's scary when you're not. But there are times when you have to let go. Driving to physical therapy is one of them. And today we need to talk."

"I do not always have to be in control." Nathan glared at Patrick.

"Shut up and get in the truck."

Nathan shoved the front door open and stepped into the cold air. A tiny dusting of snow lay on the sidewalk, and he tightened his grip on the cane. Patrick stayed close, but he didn't make the mistake of trying to help him.

A few minutes later, as they drove toward the physical therapy facility, Patrick glanced at him. "Frankie said Emma asked how you were doing. Have you talked to her?"

Hearing Emma's name brought back memories of her sharp, citrusy scent and the dimple that flashed when she smiled. But he narrowed his gaze at his brother. "Is that why you're here? To grill me about my social life?"

"No. Just passing on a message from our sister." Patrick grinned. "Kind of fun messing with you, though."

Nathan scowled. "You're a laugh a minute, FBI boy."

Patrick's smile faded. "Speaking of which, tell me about the building permits you got for the kitchen remodel."

Nathan stared at his brother, puzzled. "Tell you what about them? I probably have them somewhere if you want to see them, but they were standard building permits. I went to city hall, filled out the applications, got the forms, stuck them on the door. That was about the easiest part of the whole job."

"You said you saved them. Are they at the house?"

"They should be, along with all the other paperwork."

"After your therapy, maybe you could find them for me."

As EMMA SAT in her office a week after her conversation with Harley, she glanced at the business card stuck into a corner of her desk calendar. David Sanders, Attorney at Law. She'd already memorized his phone number.

She'd found the card the night she'd cleared out Sonya's apartment, mixed in with the contents of Sonya's desk. That had been a tough night. Feeling tears prickle her eyes, she clasped her hands behind her head to force the memories away.

Eleven boxes. That's what it had taken to pack everything away. Considering the obstacles Sonya had overcome, the success she'd made of her life, it was depressing that eleven boxes were all that were left.

Eleven boxes and Harley.

Swallowing hard, she reached for her phone. She'd done it several times a day for the past week, and again let her hand drop.

She needed to call him. Sonya must have had a will, and it was Emma's responsibility to find out. But every time she'd picked up the phone, dread squeezed her chest.

As a single parent, Sonya would have chosen a guardian for Harley. The lawyer would have made sure of it. Once Emma called him, the wheels would be set into motion. It wouldn't matter what Harley wanted. What Emma wanted.

Maybe Sonya had chosen Emma. But what if she hadn't?

Harley wasn't ready to be handed over to a stranger. She needed more time.

So did Emma.

Emma had been named Harley's legal guardian earlier in the week, but if Sonya's will specified someone different, they'd have to figure out what to do. According to the people at DCFS, Harley had left no doubt about her desire to stay with Emma.

Swallowing hard, Emma stared at the card and picked up the phone. Clenching it tightly, she punched in the numbers before she could chicken out yet again.

The phone rang three times, and the weight on Emma's chest lightened. Maybe the voice mail would pick up. She could postpone the conversation with a clear conscience.

"David Sanders," a male voice said. Damn.

Emma closed her eyes and drew in a ragged breath. "Mr. Sanders, my name is Emma Sloan. I'm Harley Michaels's legal guardian. She's the daughter of one of your clients. Sonya Michaels. Sonya passed away and I just found your card. I thought you might have a will or…or something."

"God, I'm sorry to hear that. I liked Sonya so much. Hold on. Let me see what I have."

Emma heard the sound of a metal drawer opening, then paper rustling. A minute later the attorney picked up the phone. "Ms. Sloan, I have a will and some financial documents. Give me a day or so to look everything over, then I'll call you back."

"All right." She gave the attorney her phone number. "Maybe you could call during the day so Harley isn't around."

"I'll do that. Talk to you soon."

Emma was leaving a client's home later that morning when her phone vibrated. She saw David Sanders's name on the screen, making her hand shake as she connected. "Emma Sloan."

"David Sanders. I've looked over Sonya Michaels's paperwork. Can you come in to discuss it?"

Her mouth went dry and her heart battered against her chest.

"Can't you just tell me over the phone? Did Sonya name a guardian in the will?"

"It's complicated. We need to discuss this in person."

"When are you available?"

"I can see you late this afternoon. Would five o'clock work for you?"

"Yes, I can make that."

"Good. I'll see you then. And, Ms. Sloan? Come by yourself. Don't bring Harley."

"Why not?" She gripped the phone so hard her fingers ached.

"I'll see you at five, Ms. Sloan."

SEVERAL HOURS LATER, Emma shifted on the uncomfortable plastic chair in the tiny waiting area of David Sanders's office. The inner door was closed, and the low murmur of voices drifted out to her.

She glanced at her watch. Five-fifteen. In forty-five minutes, she had to pick up Harley. Grabbing her phone, she dialed Frankie's number. It went right to voice mail, and after the beep, she spoke quickly.

"Hey, Frankie, this is Emma. I might be a little late picking Harley up tonight. Could you tell her I had a meeting and got held up? I know she worries if I'm not there on time."

As Emma put away her phone, the door opened and an older couple walked out, followed by a young man wearing oval glasses. His brown hair was pulled into a short ponytail and he wore a dress shirt with faded jeans.

"I'll call you when I have more information," he said.

"Thank you, David," the older man said.

As the door closed behind the couple, the attorney looked at her. "You must be Emma Sloan." His words were formal and appropriate. But there was a spark of interest in his eyes, quickly hidden.

"Yes." She swiped her damp palm on her pants, stood and shook his hand. "Nice to meet you, Mr. Sanders."

"Please, call me David." He stepped to the side. "Come on in."

The small office was lined with bookshelves, leaving barely enough room for a shabby desk and two wooden chairs in front of it. Two battered filing cabinets sat against the wall, with framed diplomas displayed above them.

Emma sat in one of the hard chairs. As David swung into his chair and plucked a folder from a bookshelf behind him, her foot tapped on the floor in a staccato beat. Her hands were still sweating, and she twined them together in her lap. She cleared her throat and said, "What's going on, David? And why did you tell me not to bring Harley?"

He looked up from the open file folder. "Because what I'm going to tell you will be a shock. And I didn't want to spring it on a grieving child."

Oh, my God. What was in that folder? She swallowed again. "I'm not Harley's guardian, am I?"

He hesitated. "You are for now. But in her will, Sonya named Harley's father. And she wants you to introduce the two of them. Help them get to know one another."

"Harley's father?" She frowned. "Is he in Chicago?"

His eyes wary, he nodded slowly. "His name is Nathan Devereux."

CHAPTER THREE

"WHAT?" EMMA STARED at the attorney, so shocked she could barely speak. *"Nathan Devereux?"*

"He lives on the north side of Chicago and owns a restaurant."

No way was this a coincidence. "I…I met him a few weeks ago. The night Sonya died, actually. I know his sister, Frankie. Harley goes to her after-school program."

"Yes. Sonya explained that she'd enrolled Harley at—" he looked down at the papers "—FreeZone because she knew the woman who ran the program was her daughter's aunt."

"But…but how? Why? Does Nathan know?"

"According to Sonya, Mr. Devereux has no idea." He set two envelopes and a DVD on the desk. "She did leave two letters, though—one for you and one for Mr. Devereux. As well as a DVD for her daughter."

Emma stared at the three bombs lined up on the desk in front of her. Sonya's neat handwriting scrawled across the two envelopes and the DVD case. Questions tumbled through her brain. "Why didn't she tell Nathan about Harley? What's going on?"

"Sonya didn't share her thoughts with me. She wanted me to draw up legal documents, and that's what I did. She left a will, her financial records, the two letters and the DVD. That was it."

"You didn't ask her about it?"

"That wasn't my job," he said calmly. "She wasn't here because she wanted a therapist. She was here to make legal arrangements." He cleared his throat. "She came in shortly after she moved to Chicago. She said she'd had a medical incident and needed to get her affairs in order."

Emma stared at the letters but didn't touch them. "So what happens next? Harley has no idea who her father is. As far as I know, her mother never told her anything."

"Mr. Devereux has to be informed, obviously. As Sonya's attorney, I'll contact him and give him the letter."

No. "I think…it sounds as if Sonya wanted me to do that." *You couldn't have told Harley yourself? And why didn't you ever tell Nathan? What were you thinking, Sonya?*

David leaned forward and touched her hand. Let his fingers linger. "I'm trained to handle this."

She eased her hand away from his. "I am, too. I'm a social worker for the Department of Children and Family Services." Her head whirling, she added, "And I know Nathan." *How was she supposed to tell him he had a child?*

"Sonya does say she wants you to facilitate the meetings between Harley and her father." He drummed his fingers on his desk. "I strongly discouraged Sonya from doing this. I told her it wasn't fair to put this burden on you. She seemed to think you'd be able to handle it, though."

"Of course I can handle it," Emma said. She steadied her voice. "It's just a surprise." What would this do to her plan to adopt Harley? Now that her father was known, most judges would grant him custody if he wanted it.

"Emma, this has been a huge shock to you. Before you do anything, let's give it a little thought." He consulted an appointment book in front of him. "Would you be able to come in again two days from now?"

"I'm not sure what that would accomplish. It doesn't change anything."

"We could brainstorm strategies."

"Forgive me, David, but how often have you handled this kind of situation?"

He hesitated. "I've been involved in custody disputes before. Adoptions. But this particular situation is a first."

Emma nodded. "In my work for DCFS, I've had to tell men the result of paternity tests and deal with the fallout. I appreciate your offer, but this is my job. And it's clearly what Sonya wanted." She forced a smile. "I'll give you a call in a few days. Would that be all right?"

"Of course. You can call me anytime." The earnest young attorney leaned across the desk, but she focused on the frayed cuffs of his shirt. "You obviously care about the child, and your determination to do what Sonya wanted is admirable. But it will be less…messy if I handle this."

"I don't care about messy," she said fiercely. "I care about Harley. I want to make sure that *she's* protected in all this. And although I know Mr. Devereux, Harley is my concern."

"That's why I should break the news to Mr. Devereux. I can stick to the legal issues."

Implying that she would be ruled by her emotions. She swallowed the ball of dread and fear growing in her throat. "I can, too, Mr. Sanders."

David watched her for a few moments. "I know this is a shock," he said quietly.

"You're damn right it's a shock. I wanted to adopt her," Emma said, clenching her teeth to keep her tears at bay. "That's what Harley wants, too." *Sonya, what were you thinking?*

"That's going to be very complicated now." His voice was gentle. "I'm sorry."

"I know it's complicated." *What would she say to Harley?* "But Harley and I and…and Nathan…will figure it out." She shoved away from the table, grabbed the envelopes and the DVD and stuffed them in her bag. "I have to go, or I'll be late picking up Harley. She worries if I'm not there on time. Thank you for your help."

She fled the office. *Yes, thank you for dropping this bombshell on me. On Harley. Thank you for shattering her world.*

Twenty minutes later, Harley stared out the windshield of the car, clutching the armrest. She'd barely spoken since they'd left FreeZone.

"What's wrong, sweetheart?" Emma said. She had no idea how she'd managed to sound calm.

What would Harley's reaction be when she found out about her father? Would she be excited? Happy? Eager to get to know her new family? Especially since she already knew Frankie. Her aunt.

What would Emma have done if she found out who her father was when she was thirteen?

She would have been thrilled, she admitted. Maybe Harley would be, too.

Emma's grip tightened on the steering wheel. This probably meant the end of any ideas about adopting Harley.

Harley toed the worn mat on the car floor. "I was worried when you were late."

Emma reached over and squeezed the girl's hand. She knew that feeling all too well from her own childhood. Her mother would promise to pick Emma up from school, from a friend's house, then fail to show up. "I'm sorry, honey. I was in a…in a meeting. That's why I called Frankie."

"What was the meeting about?"

Oh, God. Emma took a deep breath. "It was a custody discussion. About two people who both wanted their child."

"Can't they share her?"

"Sometimes that's not easy."

Harley's shoulders relaxed. "I'm glad you're going to adopt me." She glanced at Emma. "I won't have to call you 'Mom,' though, will I?"

"Of course not. You already have a mom. You can just keep calling me Emma."

A corner of Harley's mouth turned up just a little. "Mom didn't like that, you know."

"What didn't she like?"

"That you said it was okay to call you Emma. She thought adults should be called by their last names."

"That's what you should always do unless the adult asks you to call them something else." This was the first time Harley had talked about Sonya this way—remembering her. Almost reminiscing. "I wanted you to call me Emma because friends call each other by their first names."

"But are you sure it's okay for me to call you Emma after you adopt me? Won't people think it's weird?"

Emma's throat swelled and she bit her lip. "I don't really care what people think. Do you?"

Stupid question, she realized immediately. Harley was thirteen. Girls that age worried constantly about what everyone thought of them.

"I guess not." She didn't sound convinced.

"Give it some thought," Emma said. "Figure out what you're comfortable with. The adoption will take a while." Her voice caught on the last word. The bus in front of her blurred, and the red of the traffic light looked as if it was underwater.

She felt Harley swivel in her seat to face her but kept her eyes on the road. Finally Harley said, "Are you okay? Your voice sounds funny."

Emma cleared her throat. "I was talking a lot today. Maybe I'm a little hoarse." She needed to change the subject before she broke down and began sobbing. "How's the homework situation?"

"I finished most of it at FreeZone. I still have to write a book report, though."

"Did you finish the book?"

"Duh, Emma. Of course I did." Harley froze. "I'm…I mean, yes, I finished it at FreeZone."

The traffic light turned green and the car lurched forward as Emma let the clutch out too fast. "Harley, you don't have to watch what you say to me." Her face felt stiff and her smile was forced. "That sounded like the old, mouthy Harley. I've missed her."

"Mom always said…" Her voice caught, and Harley stared out the window. "She said my mouth would get me in trouble."

She reached over and smoothed Harley's hair. "Not with me." Her throat closed. After only four weeks, she couldn't imagine life without the girl.

Would Nathan even know how to handle a conversation like this? Would he understand what was happening? "You can…you can say whatever you want. But then, I get to say anything I want to you."

Harley frowned. "Like, if I was mean to you, or called you a name, you'd call me one back?"

"I would never do that. Name-calling hurts people's feelings and makes them feel bad." She tightened her grip on the steering wheel, wondering how Nathan would answer that question. "I hope you won't ever do something so mean to anyone. But if you were mean to me, I'd let you know I was disappointed in you. That you'd hurt my feelings."

"Mom did the same thing," Harley muttered. "I always wished she'd just yell at me and get it over with. I hated it when she made me feel like a jerk."

Emma reached for Harley's hand. "So I guess her method worked, then."

There was a beat of silence. "Yeah, I guess it did," Harley said grudgingly. "But she cried sometimes when she thought I wasn't looking."

Emma's eyes swam with tears, and she pulled over to the curb.

"Why are we stopping here?"

"I thought…" She cleared her throat. "I know you were going to cook something tonight, and I love your food. But since we're running late, I thought maybe we could order some Chinese and pick it up on the way home."

"Chinese?" Harley glanced at Emma. "Mom didn't like Chinese. We hardly ever got it."

"Yeah, I know." Her voice too wobbly to say more, she handed Harley her phone. "Kung Pao vegetables for me. Whatever you want."

"Your voice sounds funny again, Emma."

"Must be getting a cold."

She struggled to suppress her tears as Harley scrolled through her phone. "You listed the phone number under Chinese? That's lame."

"That's me. The queen of lame."

As Harley ordered their dinner, she seemed better. More solid. Which was ironic, because Emma's world had exploded into pieces so tiny, there would be no putting them back together.

THE NEXT NIGHT, Emma sat at a table in Mama's Place, her heart thumping erratically, and watched Nathan at a table with a group of people. They were clearly employees, and a younger version of Nathan was serving them all small plates of food. There was a lot of discussion and laughing. From the expressions on the faces of the people she could see, they were enjoying the food.

Emma had called earlier and asked when would be a good time to speak to Nathan privately. The woman who'd answered had sounded surprised, but she'd suggested four-thirty. When Emma arrived, Nathan had been sitting at the round table already, his back to the room. Emma had slipped into a seat in the corner and watched.

As everyone was pushing away from the table, a woman said something to Nathan, nodding in Emma's direction. Nathan turned around and stilled when he saw her. Then he smiled and walked toward her.

Emma's heart jumped, just as it had when she'd met him at FreeZone. Her palms got sweaty, and her mouth got dry.

Nerves. That was all. But she noticed how his eyes were twinkling. How his dress shirt made his eyes look so vividly blue. How narrow his hips looked in the dark pants he wore.

How happy he was to see her.

She swallowed again and forced a smile to her face. Would he be just as happy when he heard what she had to say?

She doubted it.

EMMA SLOAN SAT at a table in the corner, watching him with a tense smile on her face. Her blond hair was tucked behind her ears, showing off her dangly silver earrings. Her hands were clasped together on the table, thumbs circling each other.

She was nervous. Was it because she'd taken the initiative to come and see him, and wasn't sure how he'd react? His smile widened as he slid into the chair across from her. "Emma. It's good to see you." He gestured toward the table behind him, where the staff was cleaning up. "Are you hungry? We all taste the day's specials before we open. I can get you a plate."

Turning pale, she said, "Thank you, but no. I'm fine." She cleared her throat. "It's good to see you, too, Nathan."

"I wanted to call. But Frankie told me about your friend, and I didn't want to intrude. I'm so sorry."

"Thank you. I would have… That is, I wanted to…" Her voice drifted away.

He started to reach for her hand, but drew away. "Frankie told me you're taking care of your friend's daughter. How is she doing?"

"Her name is Harley. She's thirteen. This has all been really hard for her."

He remembered the weeks after his parents had been killed. The shock. The uncontrollable grief. The fear of not knowing what would happen. "I know it has."

She looked down and nodded. "For me, too." Then she swallowed and seemed to brace herself. Looked at him directly. "Actually, Harley is the reason I'm here today."

"Is there something I can do to help?"

She gave a small, strained laugh. "I guess there is." She gripped the edge of the table and watched him carefully. "There's no easy way to tell you this, Nathan. The reason I'm here today is that Harley is... She's your daughter."

CHAPTER FOUR

"WHAT?" NATHAN MUST have misunderstood her. "What are you talking about?"

"Harley Michaels is Sonya Michaels's daughter. You're her father."

He reared back as if she'd punched him in the chest. "What the hell?"

"I spoke to the lawyer yesterday. David Sanders." She slid a business card across the table. "You can call him and confirm it, if you want."

She reached into her purse and pulled out an envelope. "Sonya left a letter for you."

Nathan heard the frustration in her voice as he stared at the envelope, starkly white against the red-and-white checkered tablecloth. He didn't touch it. Couldn't. It was as if he'd fallen asleep and was having a nightmare. If he didn't pick up the envelope, he'd eventually wake up.

Emma wouldn't be sitting across from him. She wouldn't be handing him an envelope with his name in neat handwriting on the front. Handwriting he didn't recognize. She wouldn't be saying something crazy about him having a thirteen-year-old daughter.

"I had the same reaction when the lawyer told me," she said, her voice low and trembling a little. "I couldn't wrap my brain around it."

He shoved the envelope across the table too hard, and it slid off the edge into Emma's lap. "This is insane. I don't have a daughter. And I've never heard of Sonya Michaels."

Emma put the envelope back in her purse. "Apparently, you knew Sonya well enough to conceive a child with her."

"Not possible." No way. He'd never heard the woman's name before now. He'd certainly never had sex with her.

And even if he had, he always used a condom. *Always*.

Hell, thirteen years ago, he wasn't even *having* sex. He was trying to keep the restaurant going and hold his family together while dealing with the grief of losing his parents. Most nights, he was lucky if he got a few hours of sleep.

"I'm sorry, Emma. But there's no way this could be true. I wasn't having...didn't have a girlfriend back then."

"Harley will be fourteen in March. So it would have been closer to fifteen years ago."

His nails digging into the tablecloth, he stilled. March. So she would have been conceived in early summer of the year before. Tension eased in his shoulders. "Exactly why it's not possible. I know exactly what I was doing then. I wasn't out having one-night stands or screwing strangers."

Instead of recoiling at his harsh words, she nodded. "Maybe not, but you had sex at least once. Because Harley is your daughter."

He'd expected to shock her with his blunt words. Throw her off, make her stop talking nonsense. Apparently, Emma was made of stronger stuff than that. "Is that what her mother told you?"

Her throat rippled as she swallowed again. "It's what Sonya told the attorney. She didn't say that *maybe* you were Harley's father. She didn't say it was a *possibility*. She said you were. Period."

"And you believe her."

"Yes. She was one of my closest friends. I've known her and Harley ever since they moved to Chicago." She leaned toward him, and her cloud of blond hair brushed her shoulder. "Sonya was one of the most honest and straightforward people I know."

"Not always."

She nodded slowly. "No. She never told me who Harley's father was. But that was her business, not mine."

"Aren't you forgetting something?"

She cocked her head to the side. "What?"

"She also never told me. If it was true, why wait until she died? Why not tell me right away? I had a right to know. Besides that, she could have claimed child support. Or was she independently wealthy?"

"No." Emma's skin was so pale that the tiny freckles dusted over her cheeks stood out like spatters of brown paint. "Sonya didn't have much money. She was going to school part-time to become a nurse, but she worked in an office as a manager's assistant to support herself and Harley."

Nathan frowned. Something about Emma's story rang a bell.

He rolled his shoulders. It didn't mean he'd actually known this Sonya Michaels. This story would apply to a lot of single mothers—working a low-paying job, trying to get an education. "So she could have used child support. But she never asked for it. Why?"

"I have no idea. Sonya was very closemouthed about her past."

"And you never asked one of your closest friends about the kid's father?"

"The 'kid' has a name," she said sharply. "Harley. Your daughter's name is Harley."

"If I thought she was my kid, I'd remember that," he said evenly.

"Will you take a paternity test?"

"I'll need to talk to my attorney about that."

For the first time, he saw contempt in Emma's expression. "If you're so certain you're not her father, you have nothing to worry about."

"I'll rely on my attorney's advice. Not yours."

She fumbled in her bag and pulled out a small silver rectangle. She flicked it open and laid a second business card on the table, next to the one from the lawyer she'd mentioned earlier. "If you decide to have a paternity test done, please let me know. I'll arrange for Harley's blood test." She studied him out of cool eyes that were no longer friendly. No longer interested. "If I don't hear from you in a week, I'll send you some papers to sign. You'll need to relinquish your parental rights so Harley can be adopted."

"Can't relinquish rights I don't have," he said.

"Then I guess you'd better have the paternity test." She shoved away from the table and slung her bag over her shoulder. "You're not the man I'd hoped you were, Nathan."

"Sorry to disappoint you." He wasn't the man he'd thought he was, either. Everything he'd done over the past year had shown him that. But it didn't mean he was going to accept responsibility for someone else's kid.

She nodded. "I'll be in touch. One way or the other."

As she headed for the door, he hurried to open it for her. A blast of cold air swept inside and swirled around his legs.

Emma didn't look back.

As the door whooshed shut behind her, Nathan studied the card she'd left on the table. Emma Sloan was a case manager for DCFS. That was where the contempt in her amber eyes had come from.

She must see men every day who refused to take responsibility for their children. Refused to support them.

He wasn't one of those men. If he thought there was even a remote possibility that he was Harley Michaels's father, he'd do the right thing. But there wasn't.

Once again, something nudged at the edge of his brain. He tried to pry it loose, but it slithered away.

No way was he the kid's father.

The door opened again, and for an instant he thought it might be Emma, coming back to tell him she'd been joking. Then a couple walked in, holding hands. Plastering a smile on his face, he led them to a table.

For the next several hours, a steady stream of customers trickled in, and he was busy enough that he didn't have time to think about Emma or what she'd said. Finally, around nine o'clock, the crowd thinned. His leg ached, and so did his arm, so he eased onto a stool at the bar and motioned Jesse, the bartender, over. "Let me see the inventory list, Jess."

As he worked through it, someone slid onto the stool next to him. He glanced over and saw Danny Kopecki. "Hey, Danny. How's it going?" he asked, setting the inventory aside.

"Good," the tall, dark-haired detective answered. He motioned to the man on the stool next to him. "You remember my dad, right?"

"Of course." Nathan reached around Danny to shake the older man's hand. "How are you, Mr. Kopecki?"

"I'm good, Nathan." His grip was firm. Friendly. "But stop with the Mr. Kopecki crap. Makes me feel like an old man. My name is Mitch."

"Okay, sir." Danny's father ran his hand over his fringe of white hair and rolled his eyes. "I mean Mitch."

Jesse walked up and asked, "Guinness?"

"Yeah, thanks," Danny said.

"Cola for me," Mitch said.

Nathan turned to face the detective. "Jesse knows what you drink?"

Danny shrugged. "I was here a few times while Patrick was running the place. Guess the kid has a good memory."

"Thanks again for what you did with Chuck."

Danny lifted one shoulder. "You're welcome. Glad I could get a dirtbag like Chuck Notarro off the street."

Nathan knew far too well what a dirtbag Chuck was. The guy had collected the loan repayment money from him every week. "He still in jail for bringing a gun into my restaurant?"

"Nah. Finally got bailed out. Disappeared. Probably stashed somewhere out of sight."

"No loss," said Mitch.

"None at all."

Jesse set the drinks in front of the two men, and Danny swallowed a gulp of his beer. "Based on my extensive research, Mama's has the best Guinness in the city," he said as he set it down. "You must sell a ton of it."

"We do, but there's a place out in Naperville called Quigley's that sells a lot more. Those suburbanites know how to put away their Vitamin G."

"Who'd have thought a bunch of suburban nancies could outdrink us?"

"Hard to believe," Nathan said, his voice light.

Mitch smiled and took a drink.

"So Dad wanted to get a drink, and I have some information for you. Thought we'd kill two birds with one stone," Danny said. He shoved a hand through his thick hair. "Nothing solid yet, but a few leads." He leaned closer to Nathan and lowered his voice. "Something happened a few years ago with Alderman O'Fallon's kid. He would have been fifteen or sixteen at the time. I checked with his school, and he was yanked out without any explanation. Disappeared from the neighborhood. Found out he was in drug rehab."

"That was way before I approached O'Fallon for the money I needed," Nathan said.

"Yeah, but maybe someone did him a favor. Got the kid out of drug charges, or something like that. Maybe O'Fallon owed that guy. Maybe that's why O'Fallon won't give up the guy who gave him the money. Maybe they're connected."

Mitch tugged his tie loose. Nathan nodded. A spark of excitement swept through him. It was the first real lead they'd had in the two months since the alderman was arrested. "Can you follow it up?"

"I'm running into walls. Maybe Patrick would have better luck."

"I'll let him know. Thanks, Danny."

The detective took a drink of his beer. "We're gonna nail this bastard, Nate. Just a matter of time."

"God, I hope so." It was time to get his life back on track.

Jesse handed him the order sheet to sign. When he reached for his pen, his fingers brushed the edge of Emma's card. "Hey, Danny, what would you do if someone came to you and said you had a kid and you didn't even know who the woman was?"

Mitch set his glass abruptly on the bar and stared at Nathan, and Danny narrowed his eyes. "Get a paternity test, then tell her to get lost." His eyes sharpened. "Why? Someone calling you a daddy?"

"Trying to."

"Paddy could run a background check on the woman. She's probably pulled scams like this before."

"You have such an elevated opinion of the general public," Nathan said.

Kopecki snorted. "I've been a cop for over ten years. Nothing surprises me anymore."

"You want me to look into it, Nate?" Mitch asked.

"Nah," he answered. Danny's father was an assistant state's attorney. "You've got better things to do than worry about my situation."

Danny nudged Nathan's shoulder. "Turn it over to your brother," he said.

"Really? Ask my younger brother to check out a woman who says I fathered her kid? Think I'll handle it myself."

Kopecki grinned. "Probably smart. Paddy wouldn't let you live that one down."

"He would not."

"Sometimes families are a pain in the ass, you know?" Danny laid a twenty on the bar and slid off the stool. "Good talking to you, Nate. Keep in touch."

"Thanks for the update." It was the first glimmer of hope since the mess with the restaurant had started.

The tall detective waved as he walked out of the bar, and

Mitch nodded goodbye. Nathan looked at Emma's card again. *Get a paternity test, then tell her to get lost.*

Problem was, he couldn't tell Sonya Michaels to get lost and he didn't want to tell Emma to, either. In spite of what she'd sprung on him tonight, she intrigued him. He wanted to see if her mouth tasted as good as it looked. Wanted to know what her lush body would feel like pressed against his.

He tapped the card into his shirt pocket. There was about as much chance of that happening now as seeing pigs soaring over Wildwood.

He'd get the paternity test. Then *she'd* tell *him* to get lost.

A FEW DAYS after her meeting with Nathan, Emma pulled out the certificate she'd found in one of Sonya's boxes. It was an employee of the month award from the dean's office at the College of Liberal Arts at the University of Illinois.

It was the only thing that had shed any light on Sonya's past.

The letter Sonya had left for Emma hadn't held any answers.

Sonya had thanked Emma for taking care of Harley. Asked if she would consider adopting the girl if Nathan Devereux was unable to take care of her. Told her how much their friendship had meant to her. Asked her to tell Harley every day that her mother loved her.

Nothing about Nathan and their connection.

Maybe Nathan's letter would have more information.

Sighing, Emma set the certificate aside and opened her email. There was a message from Nathan. Curt and to the point, he'd informed her that he'd had the blood test done several days earlier. Since she would arrange for Harley's test, he gave her the lab name and his account number and said that the lab would send her the results. He was confident she'd let him know as soon as she received them.

He sounded pissed off. But if he was convinced he couldn't be Harley's father, that was understandable.

She'd been thinking about him since the night she'd walked

out of his restaurant. At first she'd been angry. She'd lumped him in with all the other men who'd tried to duck their responsibilities. All the jerks who denied they were the father of their longtime girlfriend's baby.

As she'd calmed down, though, she'd been able to see his point of view. If he really had no memory of Sonya, of course he'd be suspicious. Of course he'd deny he was Harley's father.

It didn't say much for his morals if he'd slept with so many women that he couldn't remember them all. But her job wasn't to judge him. Her job was to establish if he was Harley's father. And if he was, to then make sure he was the best choice to be her guardian.

For a moment, she couldn't help wondering what would have happened if Sonya hadn't died. Would Nathan have called her? Would she have called him?

Yes. She'd been attracted to him that night. And from the way he'd looked at her, he'd felt the same. If he hadn't called first, she would have called him.

What would have happened in the past month? Would they have connected on a deeper level, or found their attraction to be fleeting?

She'd never know. Now they were adversaries. Harley stood between them—Emma wanted to adopt the girl, Nathan was her father. And attraction or not, she'd always choose Harley over Nathan.

Tomorrow, she'd take Harley to have a blood sample taken. She'd tell her it was for school, but the thought of lying to Harley made her ill.

Emma's mother had lied to her on a regular basis, and Emma had sworn she'd never lie to a child of her own. She'd tell the truth, no matter how difficult.

But there was no way she could tell the girl why she was having blood drawn. Not yet.

If Nathan was right, and he wasn't her father, it would be cruel to put Harley through that emotional wringer.

If it was true, there was no reason to tell her yet. Emma would need time to talk to Nathan. To find out how he wanted to proceed. Then she'd have to prepare Harley for the shock.

In this situation, there were no simple answers.

She still hated to lie.

She wondered if *her* mother had ever had a twinge of conscience about lying to Emma. She suspected not.

Just another reason why she'd be a very different parent than her own mother had been.

THE NEXT AFTERNOON, as she and Harley sat in the crowded reception area of a local lab, Emma's cell phone rang. Glancing at the screen, she saw an unfamiliar number. Probably work-related. She answered warily. "Emma Sloan."

"Emma, this is Peri. How are you?"

Her stomach twisted and she glanced at Harley out of the corner of her eye. "Mom. I'm good. How are you?"

Harley turned to stare at her, and Emma smiled reassuringly.

It figured that when she was sitting here, obsessing over the lie she'd told Harley, her mother would call. Her mother's new-age woo-woo mindset would claim she'd been able to tell Emma was thinking about her.

Emma knew it was nothing more than really bad luck.

"I'm wonderful," her mother said. "Missing my baby girl."

"Sorry I haven't called. I've been really busy." Before her mother could pursue it, she added, "What have you been up to?"

"I met a man who owns an organic farm, and I've taken over his tomato plantings. I feel as if I've found my calling."

Periwinkle Sloan had found her calling many, many times before. There had been the yoga classes. The unfortunate organic cheese experiment.

The alpaca farm had been particularly disastrous. She and Emma had had to sneak away in the middle of the night to avoid bill collectors and the angry farmer who'd leased them the land.

"That's good, Mom. I'm glad to hear it."

"I'd love for you to visit. Can you get away for a couple of weeks?"

"Sounds like fun, but, like I said, I'm really busy right now." She glanced over at Harley, who was listening avidly. "One of my best friends passed away, and I'm taking care of her daughter. So there's no way I can leave."

"Bring the girl with you. She'll enjoy the farm."

"Harley is in school, Mom. I can't take her out for two weeks. And I have a job, too."

"Always so responsible, Emma."

Her mother made it sound like a moral failing. "Yeah, well, there are bills to pay. And lawyer's fees."

"Lawyer's fees? Are you in trouble?"

"No." She wrapped one arm around Harley and pulled her close. "I want to adopt Haley." It was true. She just wasn't sure it would be possible now. But she smiled at the girl, and Harley's tense shoulders relaxed.

"I'll be a grandmother! How exciting."

Strategic mistake. "Not for a while. Adopting takes time."

"I can't wait to tell my friends! A granddaughter!"

"You're not a grandmother yet, Mom. I'll let you know what happens." Emma glanced at her watch. "Listen, it's been good talking to you. But I'm waiting for an appointment, and I think they're about to call my name." God! Was lying contagious, even over the phone?

"Take care, Emma. And give my granddaughter a big kiss from me."

"I'll do that." It was easier to go along than to try and alter her mother's perception of reality. "I'll talk to you again soon."

She added her mother's new number to her contact list, then dropped the phone in her bag.

"Was that your mom?" Harley asked.

"Yes, it was. She's very excited to meet you."

"I never had a grandmother. Is she old? Does she have white hair and, like, granny shoes?"

Emma wondered if Nathan's parents were still alive. She took Harley's hand. "The last time I saw her, her hair was bright red. The time before that, it was that burgundy color I've seen on some of the high school girls. She wears Birkenstock sandals, long floaty skirts and peasant blouses."

"She sounds like fun."

She probably was, if you weren't related to her. "Maybe you'll meet her someday," Emma said lightly. "Right now, she's busy on an organic farm. Growing tomatoes."

For Harley's sake, if nothing else, Emma was glad she was nothing like her mother.

NATHAN SLOUCHED ON the leather couch in his living room, not paying a lot of attention to the football game. Frankie and Cal were here, along with Patrick, Darcy and Marco. Watching the game together on Monday nights had evolved into a tradition since Nathan's injury.

Cal had begun coming over on Sunday afternoons to watch the Cougars games with Nathan, to distract him from the misery of being stuck in a wheelchair. Once he was back working, they'd begun to get together on Monday nights, when the restaurant was closed.

Tonight, most of Nathan's attention was focused on his laptop. He was checking airfares to Italy, just as he'd done every week for the past few months. He was in the process of hiring a manager for Mama's, and once this mess with the alderman and the loan was cleared up, once his leg was stronger, he was going away. He needed some time to himself. Some time to figure out what he wanted to do with the rest of his life. Connecting with potential suppliers in Italy was a great excuse.

As he clicked on a link to one of the international airlines, the doorbell rang. Nathan looked up at his siblings. "You guys invite someone else to watch the game?"

"Nope." "Uh-uh." Cal hit the mute button on the remote as Nathan set his computer aside and headed for the door.

A short, rail-thin man stood on the porch. The barest hint of gray stubble covered his head, as if he'd been shaving it and now it was growing out. He looked vaguely familiar, but Nathan couldn't place him. He swung the door open. "Yes?"

The man studied his face, as if assuring himself that he had the right person. "You're Nathan Devereux."

"Yes. And you are…?"

The guy shoved his hands into his pockets and shuffled his feet, but he didn't look away. "My name is Peter Shaughnessy. I'm the driver who hit your parents' car. The guy who killed them."

"What?" Nathan stared at him in disbelief. He hadn't seen the man who killed their parents since the trial, but that guy had been seriously overweight, with a huge beer gut. He'd also had flaming red hair.

Shaughnessy smoothed a hand over his head. "Yeah. I know I look different. Lost a lot of weight in prison, then I had liver problems."

"What do you want?" Nathan asked. By now, his siblings were standing behind him, staring at Shaughnessy. Frankie and Marco hadn't gone to the trial. Nathan had tried to stop Patrick from going, as well, but he'd been driving their parents' car when the accident happened and he'd insisted on watching.

"Look, I know you don't want nothing to do with me. I understand that. But I'm going through the program." At Nathan's puzzled look, he added, "A.A. And one of the things we have to do is apologize to the people we harmed with our drinking." He straightened. "That would be all of you. I'm sorry for what happened that night. Sorry your parents were killed."

"Fine." Nathan's face felt like stone. "You've apologized. Now don't come here again."

He began to close the door but Shaughessy stuck his foot in. "Wait. There's…there's more stuff I need to tell you."

Nathan waited, but instead of speaking, the man glanced over his shoulder.

"What? What stuff?" Nathan demanded.

"Not now." His voice trembled. "I gotta go. I think…I think they're watching."

"What the hell…?"

The man scurried down the steps and walked down the sidewalk, his head swiveling from side to side, until he was out of sight.

Nathan slowly closed the door and turned to face his siblings. "You hear all that?"

Marco was the first to speak. "The guy has the nerve to come here? To tell us he's goddamned sorry?"

Patrick's eyes were narrowed. "What other 'stuff' is he talking about? And who's watching?" He stared at Nathan. "You have any idea? You were the one who dealt with the legal side of it."

"No. I don't have a clue." He'd tried to bury those memories as far down as he could.

Patrick stepped outside onto the tiny porch, scanned the houses on the other side of the street. "I don't see a damn thing." He came inside and slammed the door. "Lucky I'm an FBI agent. We've got resources, and I'm going to use them."

"Good," Nathan said. "Start with where Shaughnessy lives. Where he works. I need to talk to him."

EMMA BEGAN WATCHING her mailbox at work. Five days later, as she returned late in the afternoon, she saw an envelope in her slot. Hands shaking, she pulled it out and glanced at it. The return address was Who's Your Daddy.

Dumping her purse and coat on the desk in her cubicle, she hurried to the only place she would have privacy. She locked the restroom door behind her.

Her fingers shook as she lifted the flap. Pulled out the single sheet of paper. Read it.

CHAPTER FIVE

HARLEY WATCHED EMMA HESITATE. "I hate to leave you alone," she said. "Are you sure you don't mind?"

Emma sounded all worried. If her mom had asked her that, Harley would have rolled her eyes. But she couldn't do that with Emma. So she said, "I'm fine. I stay by myself all the time."

Emma chewed on her lip. "I can get back here in twenty minutes if you need me for anything."

"Okay. But I'm good." Her mother had said the same stuff when she'd gone out. Like Harley was a little kid or something. She'd say something rude, her mom's eyes would narrow, then she'd slam the door as she left.

Harley couldn't be rude to Emma. Emma might change her mind about adopting her. And tonight, she really wanted Emma to leave. So she gave her the innocent look and Emma smiled.

"I love you, Harley."

"Yeah, me, too."

Emma stood watching her, and Harley pretended to be texting a friend. Finally the door clicked shut. Emma was gone.

Harley hurried to the window and watched Emma get into her car. She looked up and waved, and Harley waved back. Emma was such a dork sometimes.

She watched until Emma had driven out of sight, then hurried to the desk in the corner and rummaged in the bottom drawer. She'd found the DVD a few days ago, way in the back. All it said on the case was "For Harley." In her mom's handwriting.

She had no idea what it was about. But she was pretty sure it hadn't come from their apartment. She would have recognized it if it had. The last time Harley was alone, she'd looked through Emma's desk to see if there was anything of her mom's. She'd found this, but hadn't had time to do anything about it.

Tonight she was going to watch this DVD. She missed her mom so much. When Emma tucked her into bed at night, she pretended it was her mom, smoothing her hair and whispering, "I love you."

But Emma didn't sound anything like her mom. So, after Emma left the bedroom, Harley muffled her sobs in the pillow, until it was hot and damp and her chest hurt.

Why was Emma hiding this DVD? Was there some big secret? Did Emma think Harley should forget about her mom? Was it a social worker thing?

She slid into Emma's desk chair and loaded the disc into the DVD slot on the computer. Clicked the mouse to open it. And there was her mom.

"Hey, sweetie," her mom said softly. "I love you so much. I know you miss me. I miss you, too. I miss hugging you. Giving you kisses and watching you squirm. Helping you with your homework. Cooking with you."

Her mom swallowed twice and her eyes looked shiny. Harley put her hand on the screen, but instead of her mom, there was nothing beneath her fingers but the cold glass of the monitor.

"I miss tucking you into bed at night, even though you told me you're too old for that. I miss picking you up at FreeZone and hearing about your day. I miss everything."

Her mom wiped her eyes with a tissue. "This isn't fair to you. But bad stuff happens and I knew I could die. Remember when I got sick when we lived in Milwaukee? That's when the doctor found out about the aneurysm. He said it might be fine. But he warned me that I could die, too. That's when we moved to Chicago and I made this DVD."

Her mom leaned forward and it felt as if she was reaching out for Harley. Harley wanted to hug her mom, just once more.

She wanted to tell her mom she was sorry about the mean things she'd said the night before her mom died.

She wanted to tell her mom she loved her one last time.

"I want to tell you about your father, Harley. We moved to Chicago because he lives here."

Harley shot up straight in her seat. Holy shit! Her dad? In Chicago?

Her mom cleared her throat and tried to smile. "I'm pretty sure that Emma is your legal guardian now. But I want you to meet your father. And I want Emma to help you get to know him." She swallowed. "He's a good man. A kind man." She smiled, but her mouth trembled. "And you already know and like his sister. Your aunt. You have two uncles, as well."

"What?" Shocked, Harley stared at her mother's image on the screen. She had an aunt? Two uncles?

"Your father's name is Nathan Devereux. He owns a restaurant in Chicago. Give Nathan a chance. I never told him about you, so he's going to be surprised. But once you get to know him, I'm sure you'll love him. And I know he'll love you just as much as I do."

Still staring at the screen, Harley grabbed a small pillow from the couch. Clutched it to her chest to keep the pain from exploding.

"You're a strong girl, Harley. You're smart and you're funny and you're kind. I wish I could have watched you grow up. I wish I could have known the interesting, wonderful woman you'll become. I know this is so hard for you. I know nothing feels right. But I'll be watching out for you. If you get sad, or lonely, or when you miss me, think about the fun we had together. Think about the things we did together. Think about how much I love you. And I'll be right there with you again. I love you."

The video faded away, but not before Harley saw the tears on her mom's face.

She slumped in the chair, staring at the darkened screen as

hot drops of moisture landed on her hands. Her heart pounded. It was hard to breathe. *Her father.*

Ms. Devereux was her aunt.

She'd asked her mom about her father so many times, but all her mother told her was that they'd loved each other. Her mom had never said that Harley's father didn't know about her.

Had Emma watched this DVD? Did she know about Harley's father?

A cold fist tightened inside her. Had Emma lied about adopting her? Was she trying to make Harley feel better until she turned her over to this Nathan dude?

Her throat was thick and hot. Her chest got tighter. Her head pounded.

No. Emma wouldn't lie to her. Emma had promised to be straight with Harley.

She grabbed the mouse and opened Google. Typed in Nathan Devereux's name. Found his restaurant, called Mama's Place.

There was a picture of him with a bunch of waitresses, and she studied it for a long time. He didn't look anything like her.

She memorized the address, then ran to get her coat. Emma would be gone for a few hours.

Harley could take the bus to his restaurant and check out her father. See what he looked like. She'd be back long before Emma got home.

THE BACK DOOR SLAMMED behind Nathan as he hurried through the kitchen. He was late. He'd been looking for information on Peter Shaughnessy online, and he'd lost track of time.

Marco stood talking to Frankie, and they looked as if they wanted him to join them. He held up his hand. "Already late. I'll catch you in a few."

With any luck, Frankie would stay back here with Marco until he and Emma finished talking. It would be awkward to have her find them together. Even worse if she found out what the conversation was about.

Unless, of course, the test was negative. Then the meeting would be over quickly. And his life could go back to what passed for normal these days.

"You want me to bring a plate of the specials over when we do the tasting?" Marco called.

No way in hell could he eat right now. "I'll try them later," he said as he pushed through the door.

Emma was sitting at the same table as last time. She toyed with a glass of water on the table. Stared at it as she stirred slowly with the straw.

Ice filled his veins as he watched her. She didn't look happy. What would she consider bad news—that the test was negative? Or positive?

She must have felt him staring, because she lifted her head and their eyes met. Her expression didn't change.

He took a deep breath and headed toward her. His stomach churned as he braced himself for the news.

Emma straightened as he slipped into the chair across from hers. "Hello, Emma."

"Nathan." She moistened her lips, then reached into her purse and pulled out an envelope. "The results came today."

He stared at the envelope for a long moment. Such an innocuous-looking rectangle. But it could change his life forever.

He couldn't be the girl's father, he reminded himself. That had been his mantra all week. He'd racked his brain but hadn't been able to remember Sonya Michaels. Looked her up on Google and found nothing.

"I expected David Sanders to contact me."

"He's angry that the results were sent to me. I didn't care."

Using one finger, he tugged the envelope across the table. The flap was open, and he played with it for a moment. Finally he slid the plain white sheet of paper free.

Taking a deep breath, Nathan unfolded it. He ignored the paragraph about the testing method and focused on the numbers in the center of the page.

Ninety-nine point nine percent likelihood of a match.

He stared at the number, trying to process the news. Emma leaned toward him. "It means you're Harley's father."

"Yeah, I got that." He tossed the paper to the table. "What I want to know is, how did this happen? Sonya Michaels is a complete blank in my mind."

"Did you, ah, ever contribute to a sperm bank?" Her face got a little pink, but she held his gaze.

"If I had, don't you think I would have mentioned it before now?"

Emma stared at him for a moment, her expression closed. Impossible to read. She pulled out another envelope and removed a picture. "This is Sonya."

He stared down at an attractive woman with long dark hair and blue eyes. She was sitting at a table, and she'd looked over her shoulder to laugh into the camera.

"Does that ring any bells?"

"Honestly, not really." He continued to study the woman. "Yeah, she might look a little familiar. But I have no idea if it's because I've met her or if she just has one of those faces."

Emma took another photo out of the envelope and pushed it across the table. "This is Harley."

The girl had long, wavy red hair and bright blue eyes. Devereux eyes? He swallowed. Her face was angular and interesting in the unformed way of children. But she was going to be a knockout when she got older.

"No one in my family has red hair," he said. As if that would make a difference.

"Someone does now."

He set the picture down on the table. He was a father. That was his daughter. The realization was too much to take in.

He glanced up at Emma, who was watching him with somber eyes. "You should be happy. This is what you wanted, wasn't it?"

Her lips tightened and she studied the cars driving past on Devon. Finally she faced him. "Frankly, Nathan, no. I didn't want this. I desperately hoped you wouldn't be a match."

He had, too. "Hey, I'm not that bad," he tried to joke.

She held his gaze steadily. "I wouldn't know. But I wanted to adopt Harley." She blinked hard. "This changes everything. How do I explain why her mother never told her about you? Why her mother never told *you* about *her.*"

"You think I'm any happier about this?" He tried to close his left hand into a fist and stared at his fingers as if his will alone could force them to bend. "I have plans for…" He could say goodbye to his trip to Italy. His time away from the restaurant. "I didn't want children."

"So you can sleep with a lot of other women you won't remember?"

Her words struck him like a blow. Then they made him angry. "Are you always so judgmental, Ms. Sloan? Especially about people you know nothing about?" His left hand curled around the edge of the table. He'd managed to bend his fingers slightly—all it had taken was getting pissed off.

At least his physical therapist would be pleased with the results of this evening.

Emma dropped her gaze and fiddled with the sheet of paper. Lined it up precisely with the red-and-white squares of the tablecloth. "You're right. I apologize. I have no right to judge your choices. I'm…upset."

"That makes two of us."

"Look, Nathan, if you don't want the responsibility of being Harley's father, you can sign away your parental rights. Clearly, that would solve a lot of your problems." Contempt filled her eyes again, making their amber depths hard and brittle.

He leaned toward her, moving from a little pissed off to flat-out angry. "You actually think I'd just sign away my rights to my child and go on like nothing had changed?" He crumpled the tablecloth in his right hand as he tried to control his temper. Smoothed the wrinkles. "Even if I don't remember her mother, she's my daughter and therefore my responsibility. I'm not going to forget I have a kid." Even though he wanted to. What kind of man did that make him?

"No one should be a parent out of a sense of responsibility. Or because they feel trapped." She threw the words out like a weapon. "Harley deserves better than that."

"Yes, she does. But did you expect me to jump for joy? To be thrilled at the prospect of a thirteen-year-old daughter I've just learned about?"

Some of the hardness in her eyes softened. "I'm handling this badly. I'm concentrating on my own disappointment instead of thinking about you." She sounded like a damned therapist, and that made him even angrier. "I'm sorry."

"Don't worry about it. I'm not feeling so friendly toward you right now, either."

To his surprise, a tiny smile curved her mouth. "Now that we've both had our little tantrums, can we concentrate on Harley and what's best for her?"

Damn it, how could he still want Emma Sloan? She'd just derailed his life. Changed it forever, and not in a good way. Made ugly assumptions about him. "Yeah, let's do that."

"Right now I'm Harley's legal guardian. Sonya didn't say anything about giving you custody of her, just that she wanted me to…help the two of you get to know each other. But if you want custody, you could probably get it."

Right now Nathan was consumed with finding the guy who'd lent him the money to rehab the restaurant. His attempt to cut corners to get the loan he needed had gotten him involved with thugs and criminals. In trying to get to the bottom of the mess he'd created, he was stepping on toes. Poking a stick into the hornet's nest. He didn't want his daughter caught up in the middle of a dangerous situation. "God, no. I'm not prepared for that. And it wouldn't be fair to her."

"No, it wouldn't. Do you have any idea how hard it is to lose a parent at her age?"

As much as he wanted to throw the truth at her, he simply nodded. "I know what she's going through."

"I doubt it. Unless you've been through it yourself, it's impossible to really understand."

"I'll defer to your greater knowledge." *Don't get angry. She doesn't know anything about you.*

"If you want to pursue this, I think we should move slowly."

The anger spilled out in a wave. "If I want to pursue this? You mean like I'd pursue buying a car? Or figuring out what brand of cat food to buy?"

She flushed. "It was a figure of speech."

"A lousy one."

"Agreed." She sighed. "Look, Nathan, we've clearly gotten off on the wrong foot here."

"Fueled by your assumptions about me," he said steadily.

"Yes. And I apologize." She shoved a hand through her hair, and the blond waves clung to her fingers. "I do this every day in my job. But I've never been personally involved. I had no idea it would be so hard when it's a child I love."

The pain in her eyes almost made him regret his sharp words. She was right, after all. He'd done a lot in his life recently that wasn't admirable. But he'd never skipped out on his responsibility to his family. He might not want to be a father to a teenage girl, but he'd do what he had to do.

"What's the next step?" he asked.

She fiddled with the handle of her bag, then drew out the letter. "Maybe you should read what Sonya wrote to you. Maybe that would help us figure it out."

Us. She was assuming they were in this together. He wasn't sure why, now that he knew her opinion of him, but that made him feel marginally better.

Unlike when he'd stepped up to raise his siblings, he'd have someone in his corner. Someone to help him figure stuff out. Which he was going to need. Because the only thing he knew about raising a grieving thirteen-year-old girl was how to botch it completely.

He touched the envelope gingerly. "Why didn't David send this to me?"

"Since we have to work together to help Harley, I wanted to give it to you myself. He wasn't happy, but he agreed it made sense."

"Have you read it?"

"It's addressed to you. I got my own letter."

"What did yours say?"

"You should probably read yours first."

He tugged the letter closer, studied the neat handwriting. It still didn't look familiar. He slid his finger beneath the flap and pulled. The edge of the envelope sliced into his finger, leaving the sharp sting of a paper cut.

Ignoring the pain, he opened the letter and slid out the single sheet of paper. Unfolded it slowly.

There was one small paragraph, in the same handwriting as the envelope.

Dear Nathan,

If you're reading this letter, it's because I've passed away and you've found out about Harley. Forgive me for not telling you about her, but I knew about your situation and decided it would be better for all of us if you didn't know about Harley. You already had too much to deal with, and I knew you were overwhelmed.

I never intended to disrupt your life, but I had no choice. Please take good care of her. I hope you can find it in your heart to love her.

Sonya Michaels

A fresh wave of anger made his head pound. "What kind of bullshit is this?" He tossed the piece of paper across the table toward Emma. "This doesn't tell me anything."

She scanned the letter, then set it on the tablecloth. "This isn't like Sonya. But then, neither was the letter she left for me."

"What did she say to you?"

"Just asked me to adopt Harley if you—" she swallowed and glanced away "—weren't able to take her. Told me how much our friendship had meant. Asked me to tell Harley that she loved her. Nothing about why she didn't tell you." She hesitated. "What was 'your situation'? Why were you overwhelmed?"

"It was irrelevant. She should have told me she was pregnant, but she chose not to." He shoved his hand through his hair. "I know she was your friend, but she was wrong on so many levels."

"I know." She slid her hand along the strap of her purse. "How are you going to explain to Harley why she didn't tell you?"

He'd passed beyond anger to numbness. "What am I supposed to say? 'I had sex with your mom and don't remember her? She didn't respect me enough to tell me about you?' I have no idea. Any suggestions?"

"When the time comes, we'll figure something out." She reached into her purse and drew out a small framed certificate. "I found this in her stuff. Does it ring any bells?"

He took the cheap brown frame and studied the yellowing paper. "Employee of the month." The dean's office of the college of Liberal Arts and Sciences at the University of Illinois. He glanced at the date.

"I was at the University of Illinois then," he said slowly. "In LAS. I might have met her in the dean's office. I honestly can't say."

"I think it's a fair assumption that you did," Emma said dryly.

"I guess it is. Still doesn't explain why I can't remember anything about…"

"About sleeping with her? Maybe you were drunk. High. Who knows? All we know is that you had sex with her."

"Fine." She made it sound so sordid. So dishonorable. "I'll do some digging and try to figure it out. But in the meantime, what about Harley?"

She reached across the table, took the certificate and placed it carefully back in her bag. "I suppose you should meet her."

"I suppose I should. But don't…don't tell her I'm her father. Maybe we should get to know each other first."

She studied him for a long moment. "I swore I'd never lie to her. Meant it, too. But less than a month later, this will be the second big lie I've told her. There've been a few small ones, too."

"Being a parent isn't black-and-white. There's a lot of gray in there."

"Like you'd know."

Yeah, he would. "Doesn't take a genius to see that," he said, his voice even. "Not telling her right away would be easier for Harley. Less pressure."

"Easier for you," Emma said.

"For you, too," he retorted. "Or are you that eager to explain to her why her mother lied?"

Faint pink tinged her skin again. "Fine. You're right. So what do you suggest we do?"

"Why don't you bring her here for dinner one night? I'll sit with you for a while. We can tell her the truth about how we met—that should ease your conscience."

"Are you suggesting we pretend to be dating?"

"You don't have to sound so horrified by the idea." When they'd met that night at FreeZone, he'd been all for dating her. He was pretty sure she had been, too. "And that's not what I'm suggesting, anyway. You know Frankie. Frankie's my sister.

Frankie told you about the restaurant. You wanted to try it out. Okay? That's all true."

Emma stood. "Fine. I'll figure out a day that will work and give you a call. We'll have dinner."

He stood, as well. "Good." He hesitated for a moment, then reached across the table to shake her hand. "No matter what we think of each other, we need to work together. You want what's best for Harley, and I do, too." Her hand was warm and soft. Small. Almost fragile.

It was the only fragile thing about Emma Sloan.

"But who gets to decide what's best for her?"

"Maybe she does."

She held his gaze as she let go of his hand. "I'll be in touch, Nathan."

The front door opened, but he knew Phyllis would seat the customers. "Thanks for coming by."

He heard the sound of feet approaching behind him. Emma paled, and he turned to see a redheaded girl standing behind them, a devastated expression on her face and tears streaming down her cheeks. She stared at Emma, her blue eyes miserable with betrayal. "You lied to me."

CHAPTER SIX

OH, MY GOD. Emma reached for Harley, but the girl jerked away. "Harley. What are you doing here?"

"I came to check out my so-called father. Is that him?" Harley's gaze swept over Nathan. "Or is that another lie? He doesn't look anything like me."

She pivoted back to face Emma. "And you *lied* to me." Her voice caught on a sob, and Emma reached for her. Harley backed up, bumping into a table. "The whole adoption thing was crap, wasn't it? You knew about him all along. You were planning to dump me on him."

Emma pushed past Nathan and put her arm around Harley's shoulders. "Harley, I…"

The girl shoved her arm away. "Don't touch me. You never wanted me. You were just looking for someone to take me off your hands."

"Harley, stop it! That's not true. I just found out myself." She grabbed the teen's shoulders and held on tightly as Harley tried to squirm away. "I came here tonight to tell Nathan he was your father. I got the results of the paternity test…." Her voice faded away. The paternity test she'd lied to Harley about.

"*What* paternity test?"

Emma swallowed. Held on more tightly. "That blood test you had a few days ago."

"You said that was for school. You lied about everything!"

"Of course I did," Emma shouted back. Every last one of her social worker skills vanished in the face of Harley's pain and anger. "What if it had been negative? Why would I want you to get your hopes up?"

Harley wrenched herself away. "Hopes? Hopes for what? That I'd go live with a stranger? You said you'd adopt me. You promised."

"Yeah, I did. That was before I knew about Nathan."

Nathan stepped between them, his face pale. "Harley, I'm Nathan." He swallowed. "Your father. This isn't the way Emma and I wanted you to find out about this. About me. She lied to protect you. You've had enough disruptions in your life already." He extended his hand to Harley and she flinched. Nathan curled his fingers into his palm. "I'm sorry about your mother."

"Don't you talk about my mother." Harley began to sob. "She always said you loved each other, but you didn't care about her at all. If you had, you wouldn't have left us."

Emma elbowed him aside and wrapped her arms around Harley. She knew how to deal with wounded children, but that was…clinical. Harley was a child she loved. She spoke without analyzing it first. "I love you, Harley. I wasn't trying to hide this from you. We just wanted to figure out the best way to tell you."

Harley twisted her fingers in Emma's sweater at the same time as she tried to shove her away. Her tears were hot on Emma's shoulder, and she wept as though her heart was breaking all over again.

Beyond those first couple of days after her mother died, Harley hadn't cried at all.

"Why don't we take this into the office?" Nathan said in a low voice. "I don't want to…disturb our customers."

He met Emma's gaze over Harley's head. He looked as lost as she felt. As desperate to regain some control of the situation. Emma nodded. There was no reason to broadcast their drama to the whole restaurant.

Harley didn't lift her head. Didn't acknowledge Nathan.

Her fisted hands still clutched Emma's sweater. Emma held her more tightly, rubbed her hands down her back.

"Harley, would you, ah, like something to drink?" Nathan asked.

For a moment, Emma thought she'd continue to ignore him. But she lifted her head and stared at him for a moment. "A Coke."

Then she turned defiant eyes on Emma, as if daring her to say, "no caffeine."

"A Coke would be good," Emma said, trying to sound calm. "Thank you, Nathan."

"This way," he said, hurrying ahead of them. He stepped into a waitress's station. Ice clinked into the glass, followed by the soda. He handed it to Harley, then asked, "How about you, Emma?"

"I'm fine."

"What's wrong with your leg?" the girl asked.

"That was rude, Harley," Emma said.

"No, it's all right," Nathan said. He turned to Harley. "I was hit by a car. I broke my left leg and left arm." He wiggled his arm back and forth.

"Oh," Harley muttered.

Emma kept her arm around Harley as they walked into the kitchen. It was hot, and several men worked at the stoves on the left side. On the right side, a guy slid a pizza into one of two wood-burning ovens.

And just to make the evening complete, Frankie was here, too. She stood in front of them, talking to a man who looked like a younger, leaner version of Nathan.

Harley stopped moving and stared at Frankie. Emma wanted to turn and run. To drag Harley away from Mama's Place, away from the Devereux family, away from the stew of emotions that swirled around them.

She wanted a chance to talk to Harley, alone, to make the girl understand why Emma had lied.

Too late. They'd tried to do the right thing. To be so careful. But all she and Nathan had done was hurt Harley.

Frankie glanced over her shoulder. Smiled. "Harley. Emma. What are you doing here?"

"Later, Frankie," Nathan said, trying to hurry past them.

Harley dug in her heels. "Did you know, too, Ms. Devereux?"

Frankie's smile faded. "Did I know what?" She glanced at Emma with a puzzled expression.

"That *he's*—" Harley gestured toward Nathan "—my father." The girl's gaze whipped from Frankie to Nathan and back again, and her voice took on an edge of hysteria. "My mom said I already knew my aunt." Harley's nose was red and she didn't seem to notice the tears streaming down her cheeks.

"What?" Frankie stared at Nathan, her eyes narrowed. "What the hell is going on?"

"Really, Nate?" The other man, the one who must be another brother, scowled. "Are you frickin' kidding me?"

"Shut it, Marco," Nathan yelled. "There's a kid here." He shoved his hands through his hair, leaving it sticking up. "God! Could this get any worse?"

HARLEY'S HEART SHRIVELED. *He* didn't want her, either. Then the jerk guy yelled at Emma. "You had a fling with Nate, and now you're trying to pass this kid off as his? What kind of scam are you pulling?"

"What the hell's the matter with you?" Nathan shoved jerk guy backward. He fell into a wire shelf, and pots and pans clattered to the floor.

Harley began to shiver. She'd done this. They were yelling and hitting each other because of her. Emma glanced at Harley and frowned. She knew this was Harley's fault, and now didn't want her, either.

Harley tore away from Emma and ran toward the door. Something on the floor made her slip and almost fall. She slid into the counter and grabbed the edge, steadying herself. Then she shoved at the door and it swung open.

As she ran through the restaurant, everyone watched her as if she was some kind of freak. She ran faster and banged through the front door, hurtling onto the sidewalk.

"Harley! Wait!"

Emma. Behind her. Running. Needing to escape, Harley bolted into the street. A car flashed past her, just a few inches away. Its horn blared, and Emma screamed.

More cars were coming from both directions, but she ran anyway. Emma would be sorry if she died. Harley didn't care. She wanted to die. Then she could be with her mom.

A car swerved, skidding, and Harley darted across the remaining two lanes of Devon Avenue. Horns honked behind her and tires squealed. Emma was chasing her. Maybe Emma wanted to die, too.

Harley stopped on the sidewalk, panting, her lungs burning. She looked behind her, and Emma was almost across the street. Harley took off down the sidewalk. She didn't know where she was going. She didn't care. She just wanted to be away from Emma, who'd lied to her. Nathan, who was her father but didn't want her. The jerk who said awful things. Frankie. Her *aunt*.

Harley galloped down the sidewalk, crossing the side streets without even looking. The pavement was old and crumbling, and some of the pieces were uneven. She caught her shoe on one and stumbled. She almost fell, but she braced herself with her palm, which slid along the cement. It stung, but she didn't care. She didn't care about anything.

"Harley, stop." Emma's voice, breathless. Close behind her.

Harley rounded a corner and headed down a street with big houses. Her chest burned and her side ached, but she couldn't stop. Then arms closed around her from behind. "Stop, Harley," Emma begged. She sounded out of breath, too.

Harley tried to twist away, but Emma was too strong. She

pulled Harley close and buried her face in her hair. "God, Harley! You could have been killed."

"I wish I was dead." Snot mixed with the tears on her face, and she swiped the sleeve of her hoodie across her face. "Everyone lied to me. You lied. My mother. Frankie. I hate all of you."

"Yeah, I know," Emma said. She held Harley tight, and Harley felt drops hit her hair. Was Emma *crying?* "I don't blame you. I'd feel the same way."

EMMA TIGHTENED SPAGHETTI-LIMP arms around Harley, and the girl eventually stopped struggling. She drooped against Emma's chest, panting. Finally she lifted her head. "I hate you, Emma." Her quiet voice was brokenhearted.

"Yeah, I guess you would." She tucked Harley's head closer and dropped a kiss onto her hair. It smelled like the outdoors and shampoo. The same shampoo Emma used.

I hate you. Those words were new to Emma. They hurt, but she tried to ignore that. This wasn't about her. It was about Harley.

"Your fa…Nathan and I didn't mean to hurt you," Emma said, stroking Harley's damp red hair away from her face. "We couldn't tell you he was your father until we knew for sure. What if…" What? What if her mom had made a mistake? Is that what she wanted to tell Harley? That her mom slept around? Wasn't sure who Harley's father was?

"What if what?" Harley asked.

"What if it wasn't official?" Emma said, scrambling for the right words. "There's all kinds of paperwork. The paternity test was one of the steps. What if we hadn't done it? Then the paperwork would take even longer."

She was making this up as she went along, and it didn't make sense. But what was the alternative? A young girl shouldn't have to think about her mother having one-night stands with strangers.

If Harley was a client, it would be so much simpler. Explain what they were doing. Do it with compassion and gentleness, but tell the truth.

But Sonya's truth would hurt Harley deeply. And Emma loved Harley too much to do that.

"You lied to me about that blood test. You said it was for school."

Emma closed her eyes. "Yes, I lied to you. I didn't know what else to say."

"You lied about everything." Harley's voice trembled. Her expression was closed off. Despairing. As if her mother's death wasn't enough of a blow. Now the rest of her world was falling apart, too.

"Not about everything. I love you. I want to adopt you. Then I talked to your mom's lawyer and found out that Nathan was your father. Found out that Frankie was your aunt." She swallowed and took a trembling breath. "The things I lied about— it was only to give Nathan and me time to figure out how to tell you the truth. It was to protect you, Harley. That's all."

"He doesn't want me," Harley said, and she swallowed. "He even said so. He said it couldn't get any worse."

"He didn't mean you. He meant the situation." Everything was overwhelming to Harley. She was a child—she'd never had to deal with anything like this.

Sonya, how could you dump this in my lap? In Nathan's? How could you do this to your daughter?

"Yeah. I know what the situation is—he's stuck with a kid he doesn't want."

"That's not true." At least, she hoped it wasn't. She tightened her arms around Harley. "You're upset and shocked to find this out. So is he."

"He said it was as bad as it could get."

"The restaurant is his business," Emma said, leaning back and grasping Harley's shoulders. She had to make the girl understand. "You…we all made a scene. Disturbed his customers. That's what he was talking about. And then his brother…"

His brother had been an ass.

"He was a jerk," Harley said passionately.

"Yeah, he was. But sometimes, when people are shocked or surprised, they say things they don't really mean."

"I don't care," Harley said sullenly. "I don't want him to be my uncle."

"You can't pick your relatives," Emma said, trying to sound calm. "He *is* your uncle and you can't change that." She thought briefly of her own mother. "But you have to learn to deal with him. Be civil, at least."

"He thought you were my mom. He thought my mom was pulling a scam."

"We know that's not true."

The girl sniffled and wiped her nose on the sleeve of her jacket. Emma dug in her pocket for a tissue and tried to hand it to Harley.

The girl jerked her arm away. "Leave me alone. And go away. I don't want to live with you anymore."

"I understand why you wouldn't," Emma said, her heart breaking into tiny pieces. "But you don't have any other choice, sweetie."

"And don't call me 'sweetie,'" Harley yelled. "I'm not your sweetie. I'm not anyone's sweetie."

How had everything gone so terribly wrong? She'd been trying to protect Harley. Do the right thing. And now Harley was devastated. Nathan must be, too. And Emma?

Every inch of her body throbbed with remorse. She'd give everything she had to go back in time and handle this better. Do it in a way that wouldn't hurt Harley.

She had no idea of what that would be. She, the social worker who handled everything calmly. When it was a child she loved, she was a complete disaster.

Speaking of which… "Tell me something, Harley. How did you find out about Nathan?"

"I watched the DVD my mom left for me."

"That was at the back of a drawer. You searched my desk?"

"It had *my* name on it," Harley said defiantly. But she didn't look at Emma. "You had no right to hide it from me."

This wasn't the time for a discussion about snooping. "I had a lot of reasons to hide it," Emma said quietly. "The biggest one was protecting you. I wasn't going to tell you about Nathan until I told him."

"You should have told me first!"

"That wouldn't have been fair to him," she answered. "How would you have felt if I took you to meet him without telling you who he was? You'd have been upset and angry, and you'd have had every right to be."

But that's exactly what she and Nathan had been planning. Heat burned in her cheeks. Could she have handled this any worse?

Instead of answering, Harley was stone-faced. Taking a deep breath, Emma continued, "I wouldn't do that to Nathan, either. So, no, I didn't tell you first. I needed to talk to him alone.

"Think about how you feel right now. Wouldn't it have been easier if I'd told you myself when we were both calm?" Although Nathan hadn't exactly been calm, and neither had she. "Answered your questions? Helped you figure out what you wanted to do?"

"You don't care what I want. Mom didn't, either, or she would have told me about *him*. I asked her all the time, but she never said a thing." Harley clenched her fists as her voice grew louder. "Now I'll have to live with him and I'll never see my friends again. I'll have to go to a new school. They're probably all rich snobs and no one will want to be my friend. I hate you! I hate my mom, too."

Harley tensed, and Emma grabbed her before she could run again. "Harley, stop it. You're not moving anywhere yet. Maybe not for a long time. Maybe never. Do you really think I'd just drop you off at Nathan's house and drive away?"

She held Harley's shoulders, forcing her to meet her gaze. Harley sniffled and turned her head to rub her face on her shoulder. "How would I know?" she finally said, her voice sullen.

"I think you do," Emma answered. "I love you, Harley. I'm not going to do anything to hurt you."

Harley lifted her head to meet her gaze. "You already have."

Emma's heart wrenched. God! Kids knew exactly where to stick the knife in and twist it. "I'm sorry this happened." She didn't add that it wouldn't have if Harley hadn't snooped. Harley was smart enough to realize that herself. "Let's go back to the restaurant. It's cold out here."

Harley slowly retraced her steps along the sidewalk, shoving her hands into the pockets of her hoodie and hunching her shoulders. They passed a Baskin-Robbins that was open, but only a couple of people sat in the pink plastic chairs eating ice cream. A hairdresser, a Realtor's office and a hardware store were all closed.

The neighborhood looked like a small town in the middle of the city. A nice place for kids to grow up. Was Emma selfish for wanting Harley to grow up with her instead? She caught up with Harley as they crossed a side street, and she noticed a grocery store that was still open. Happy Foods. That sounded small town, too.

Two people stood on the sidewalk in front of Mama's Place. Nathan and Frankie. Frankie was wearing a T-shirt, and she had her arms wrapped around herself. Nathan looked frozen in place as he watched the two of them make their way back to the restaurant.

Harley noticed them, too. She stiffened, and her steps slowed. Emma put her arm around Harley's shoulders, but the girl shook her off.

Emma wanted to let Harley know she wasn't alone. But the hurt and angry child didn't want comfort. Emma understood that.

Harley had trusted her, and she'd let the girl down.

It would take time to regain her trust. In the meantime, all Emma could do was show up and love her.

"What are they doing out here?" Harley muttered.

"They want to make sure you're okay," Emma answered.

She hunched her shoulders higher. "I can take care of myself."

"Everyone needs help once in a while."

Harley scowled. "I don't need them. I don't need you, either. I'll be fine on my own."

Oh, God. What was Harley thinking about? "You're not going to be on your own, Harley," she forced herself to say calmly. "You'll still be living with me. You'll still go to school, still go to FreeZone afterward. Everything will be the same while we figure this out."

"Who says I want to figure anything out?"

"You can't ignore the fact that you have a father now. Uncles. An aunt."

"What?" Harley stopped and whirled around to face her. "You think I'm supposed to, like, *love* them or something? Just because you tell me they're my *family?*"

She made it sound like a dirty word. "Of course not. They'll have to earn that. But you have to at least make an effort to get to know them."

"I already know Frankie."

"And you like her," Emma replied.

Harley kicked a stone. "That was before."

"You think she's changed because now she knows you're related to her?"

"She'll probably try to tell me what to do. Think she can boss me around."

"Maybe you should give her a chance."

"I don't want to go to FreeZone anymore," she muttered. "Everything will be different."

Was Harley afraid her relationship with her friends would

change if they knew Frankie was her aunt? "You don't have to tell anyone that you're related," Emma said.

"You think I should lie to them? Just like you lied to me?"

"I think you should take some time to sort out your feelings before you do anything. You're tired. Things will look different in the morning."

"Leave me alone!" Harley cried. "You're talking to me like a social worker, just like you did when you first came to our place. Mom didn't like it. She said you talked down to her."

"No, I didn't. I talked that way because I *am* a social worker." Emma's head pounded, and she struggled to maintain her frazzled composure. She couldn't lose it now. She'd been calm so far. Tried to handle the whole ugly mess in a rational way. But she'd had no idea being a parent was this hard. This painful. "And I was seeing you and your mom for my job. It wasn't until later that we became friends."

"Whatever."

They were approaching the restaurant, and Nathan and Frankie hurried toward them. "You must be cold," Nathan said, leaning on his cane. "Come inside and get warm."

"I don't want to go back into your stupid restaurant. I want to go…" Harley stopped abruptly and kicked the side of the building.

"You want to go home, and I do, too," Emma said. She glanced at Nathan, and he nodded. His posture relaxed. "We'll deal with all this another time." She touched Harley's shoulder. "We need to go home."

CHAPTER SEVEN

HARLEY DIDN'T SAY a word on the drive home. Streetlights illuminated the tear tracks down her face. Every few minutes, in the silence of the car, Emma heard her breath hitch.

When they got home, Harley went straight to her room and locked the door. Emma stood on the other side, one hand pressed to the wood.

"Harley, let's talk about this." The only answer was muffled sobs. "Unlock the door, Harley. Please."

"Go away." Harley's voice was thick and indistinct.

Emma's throat swelled. How did parents do this? How did they handle heartbreak in their children? How did they even know where to begin?

She'd always looked at parenting clinically—how was the mother's temperament? The father's? What was the child's emotional health? Did they interact well?

Everything was different now. When your child was hurt, there was only helplessness. The pain of listening to her cry on the other side of a locked door.

She slid down the wall and rested her head on her knees. Sooner or later, Harley would come out.

Emma woke in the middle of the night with a crick in her neck and an aching back. She stood up and tried Harley's door. It was unlocked.

Easing it open, she peered into the dark room. Light from the hall spilled over Harley's still form. She'd changed into her pajamas, and her red hair clashed with the orange T-shirt.

She'd kicked off the blanket, and her knees were drawn up to her chest.

She looked so vulnerable. So defenseless. Emma wanted to gather her against her chest and soothe all her pain away.

Instead, she drew the sheet and blankets up to Harley's chin, pressed a kiss to her hair and tiptoed out. Tomorrow, they'd both be calmer. They would deal with this in the morning.

OR NOT.

Emma sat at her desk at work and rolled her shoulders. They still hurt from her night on the floor. A headache pounded behind her eyes, and she'd drunk so much coffee her hands shook.

Harley hadn't spoken a word that morning. Every overture from Emma, every question, had been ignored. Harley had eaten breakfast, gotten dressed and waited for Emma to drive her to school. When they arrived at the building, she'd slammed the car door and walked away without looking back.

If one of her clients was facing this problem, Emma would have all kinds of advice. But the stew of emotions roiling in her stomach made it impossible to think logically.

She stared at the report she'd been writing and realized it made no sense. Deleting everything, she closed her eyes and tried to focus on the Jeffry family.

The phone rang and she reached for it eagerly. "Hello?" School was just getting out. Maybe Harley was calling.

"Ms. Sloan, this is David Sanders. How are you doing?"

"David. I'm fine," she said, trying to mask her disappointment. "You?"

The lawyer let the moment of silence stretch too long. Emma gripped the phone more tightly. "What's wrong?"

"Maybe nothing." He sighed. "But I…liked you the moment I met you, Emma. And I'm concerned."

"How come?"

"You'll be spending a lot of time with Nathan Devereux. I came across some information you need to know."

She frowned. "What's going on, David?"

Another pause. "I worked for the Public Defender's office in Cook County for three years before I started my practice. I still know a lot of people in the court system. I called a few of them and asked about Nathan."

"Why would you do that?" Emma didn't know whether to be angry or nervous about what he might have found.

"You already knew Devereux and you seemed...ah, positive toward him. I thought maybe you were...well. I wanted to make sure he was...trustworthy."

Suddenly chilled, she said, "And?"

"I'm not sure he is. Two of my friends have heard rumors. Something about problematic business arrangements. Relationships with inappropriate individuals. That the FBI was involved."

One of Frankie's brothers was an FBI agent. "I don't believe that," she said. Nathan might not be excited about being a father, but that didn't mean he was a crook.

"I have no proof," David said carefully. "I just thought you should know."

"So you're trashing his reputation based on rumors and hearsay."

"No. Just telling you to be careful."

"I'm meeting with him because he's Harley's father. It's not like I'm dating him." After all that had happened, that ship had sailed. She still regretted that it had.

"Yes. Well. Just wanted to let you know what I'd heard."

David was trying to watch out for her. Give her a heads-up. She should be grateful. But instead she was irritated. "Thanks for calling, David," she said a little too sharply. "I appreciate the effort you've made."

He sighed. "I've pissed you off. I'm sorry. I was just concerned."

"I know." Her voice softened. "Thank you."

"Keep me posted," he said, and she heard the resignation in his voice.

"I will. Bye."

She ended the call and dropped her phone into her bag. She didn't believe Nathan would be involved in anything illegal.

But why were people in the court system talking about him?

She needed to give him a chance to respond to David's insinuations. She reached for the phone. Hesitated.

No. She needed to talk to him in person. She needed to see his eyes when she asked her questions.

A half hour later, she walked through the front door of Mama's Place. It was midafternoon and the dining room was dimly lit. But lights were on in the kitchen, and she heard the clank of large pots and voices behind the swinging door.

She pushed the door open and poked her head inside. Marco stood at a stove on the left side of the kitchen, stirring something that smelled of garlic and butter. There was no sign of Nathan.

"Excuse me," she said, stepping all the way in. "Is Nathan here?"

Marco glanced at her, and the flash of recognition was followed by what looked like shame. He jerked his head toward the back of the kitchen. "In his office."

"Thanks." She skirted the work area without looking at him again. But she felt his gaze follow her all the way to Nathan's office.

The shades over the window looking into the kitchen were closed, but the door was ajar. She knocked once.

"What?" he barked.

She poked her head in the door to see him seated behind his desk, scowling at the door. "Looks like I caught you at a bad time."

"Emma." He jumped to his feet. "Sorry. I thought it was… Anyway, come in." He held a chair for her, then pushed the door closed.

He sank back into his desk chair and studied her for a moment. She tucked her hair behind her ear and smoothed the tangled waves. It was windy outside, and she knew her hair was wild. Not the look she wanted for a serious conversation. "How are you doing?" she asked finally.

"Tired as hell," he said, and the weariness showed on his face. "After you and Harley left last night, I called my brother Patrick and asked him to come over. Everyone else knew what was going on. Only fair that he did, too."

"How did that go?"

"Mr. FBI agent wanted to do a background check on Sonya and rerun the paternity test."

"And you told him…?" Emma gripped the arm of her chair.

"I told him to back off. God! Families can be a pain in the ass."

"I guess they can," she said, her spine stiffening as she remembered Nathan's own reaction to the news.

He pressed his fingers to the bridge of his nose. "I wasn't talking about Harley or our…situation." He leaned forward. "I was talking about my siblings. At least Frankie is being rational."

Emma moved a colorful paperweight on his desk, lined it up with the edge of a desk calendar. Part of the responsibility for last night's scene was hers—she'd left that DVD where Harley could find it. "I'm sorry about what happened yesterday."

"How *did* it happen?" He leaned forward. "I thought you weren't going to say anything to Harley until we'd talked and figured out what to do."

He thought she'd *told* Harley? "I underestimated a thirteen-year-old's curiosity," she said coolly. "Her mother left a DVD for Harley with the attorney. I hid it in the back of a desk drawer, but she found it."

"What did…Sonya say?"

His hesitation before saying Sonya's name made her grit her teeth. "I get that you don't remember sleeping with Sonya.

But don't you think you should remember the name of your daughter's mother? In case it, you know, comes up in a conversation with Harley?"

Nathan kept his gaze on her. "Based on last night, I doubt that's going to happen anytime soon."

"It's going to have to happen sometime."

"What are you going to do? Drop her off here and run like hell?"

"I'd hoped we could have a civil conversation," she said, standing up. "Clearly, this isn't the right time."

"I'm sorry, Emma. That was uncalled-for." He closed his eyes for a moment. "Sit down. Please." One side of his mouth began to curve. "Haven't we had enough drama in the last twenty-four hours?"

She hesitated, but finally sank back into the uncomfortable plastic chair. "I guess we're both on edge. I didn't get much sleep last night."

"What happened after you left?"

"Nothing. She cried all the way home. Locked herself in her room and wouldn't speak to me. I got the silent treatment this morning, too."

He sighed. "Thirteen is a tough age. To have your mom die and all this stuff thrown at you? Hard enough for an adult to handle, let alone a hormonal kid."

Emma frowned. "What would you know about hormonal thirteen-year-olds?"

"I have a sister. Hard as it is to believe, Frankie was once completely out of control."

"After what happened to her when she was in juvie, she had a right to be."

"So does Harley. So. Did you come here to figure out our next move?"

"That was part of it." She hesitated, suddenly reluctant to ask Nathan about his "sketchy activities." But she had to, for Harley's sake. "David Sanders called me this morning. He

said he'd heard some rumors that you were involved in something…shady. 'Inappropriate business relationships' was how
he put it."

Nathan turned to stone in front of her. Stared at her as the
moment stretched longer and longer.

Emma tucked her coat around her legs, fiddled with her
purse as she held his gaze. Finally he asked, his voice tone-
less, "Where did he hear that?"

"He said he used to be a public defender. That he still has
contacts in that part of the judicial system." She gripped the
purse strap more tightly. "Nathan, are you being investigated
for something?"

"No. I am not."

"Then what was David talking about?"

"I can't say."

"You don't know, or you won't tell me?"

"I can't say." His eyes were as icy and cold as Lake Michi-
gan in the winter. A muscle twitched in his jaw. "You were
right earlier. This isn't a good time for a conversation. We'll
talk soon, Emma."

She stood, clutching her purse like a shield. "I wasn't accus-
ing you. I was asking. I'm responsible for Harley. If you're a…"

"Is the word you're searching for *criminal?*" He rose to his
feet. "The answer is no."

"I didn't mean that," she said, reaching for the door. "I
just…"

"I'll talk to you later, Emma." He watched her steadily. Beneath the anger, there was hurt. As if he couldn't believe she'd
accused him of something like that.

She was shocked at herself, as well. What had she been
thinking?

She hadn't been. She'd been upset by David's accusation and
wanted Nathan to deny it. Laugh it off. Act puzzled.

Anything besides this cold anger.

She stepped away from the door, then hesitated. She couldn't leave like this. Not only had she offended him, but she'd hurt him, as well. As she turned to go back into the office, she heard Nathan's voice.

"Patrick? I need to talk to you." Silence for a few moments. "Yeah. Can you come over? ASAP."

He was calling the FBI agent.

NATHAN PROWLED THE kitchen while he waited for Patrick. Marco raised his eyebrows, clearly wondering what was going on, but Nathan ignored him. He was still pissed at his youngest brother.

Finally, the back door banged open and Patrick rushed in. The buttons on his shirt weren't lined up correctly and his hair was mussed. He'd forgotten his belt, too.

Nathan raised one eyebrow. "Darcy not working today?" Patrick's fiancée, Darcy, had recently returned to work as an E.R. nurse.

Patrick scowled. "No, she's not. This better be good."

"It is." He glanced at Marco and the cooks, who were openly listening. "Come in the office."

Patrick slouched down in the chair Emma had been sitting in. She'd looked at him as if he was the scum of the earth. As if he kicked puppies for fun.

Throwing himself into his own chair, Nathan shoved both hands through his hair. "Emma Sloan was just here. She'd heard some rumors and wanted to ask me about them."

"What kind of rumors?" Patrick asked.

"Rumors from the courts. That I was involved in inappropriate business relationships." He made quotation marks in the air.

Patrick shot upright. "What the hell? Who did she hear that from?"

"The damn lawyer who handled the Michaels woman's will. Used to be a public defender. Said he still knows people."

Patrick slapped a hand on the desk. "Okay. I can work with

that. We know people, too. I'll do some nosing around. This is good, Nate. It's movement."

"In what direction?" Nathan kicked away from the desk and stood up. He opened the blinds to the kitchen and stared at Marco, who was stirring something on the stove and talking to Luis at the same time. "Now, not only am I a guy who can't remember his kid's mother, but she thinks I'm a crook, too. This is a huge cluster, Patrick."

"What the hell are you talking about? The kid? Why would she think you're a crook?"

"Not Harley," Nathan said impatiently. "Emma."

Patrick looked puzzled for a moment. Then he smiled. "The woman from Frankie's open house? The one you were interested in?"

"Yes." He turned to face his brother. "That woman. I told you she's taking care of Harley."

Patrick's smile faded. "What a mess."

"Tell me about it."

"I'll get on it right away. If we can find the person Sanders talked to, maybe we can follow the rumor to the source. That would tell us a lot."

Nathan hesitated. "Odd that the guy who killed Mom and Dad shows up in the middle of this. You find out anything about Shaughnessy?"

"He was paroled six months ago and lives in a halfway house now. He's got a job, but I don't know where yet. I'm working on it, though." Patrick scowled. "I don't believe in coincidences."

"Let me know when you get more information." Nathan waved toward the door. "Go back to Darcy. And keep me posted."

Nathan watched his brother leave. The information from Emma was a good break. But why did it have to be Emma who delivered it? Emma, who now thought he was a crook.

STILL SHAKEN FROM her encounter with Nathan, Emma pulled her car into a parking spot, several buildings down from Free-Zone. As she trudged down the sidewalk, she kept her head down to protect her face from the biting wind and the sharp sting of sleet.

As Emma reached the door of the teen center, Harley stepped outside with a girl with short, shaggy brown hair. Harley's shoulders were tense and her eyes weary.

Harley probably hadn't gotten a lot of sleep last night, either.

"Hi, Harley," Emma said when she got closer.

"Hey."

Harley continued talking to her friend. Emma heard something about "gym" and "dork" and "stinky socks." Discussing a boy? Oh, God. She *so* wasn't ready to deal with that, on top of everything else.

As they stepped outside, Harley said, "Bye, Lissy. See you tomorrow." She watched the girl walk in the other direction until she climbed into a car. Then she turned around, reluctance clear in every stiff line of her body.

"Down there," Emma said, pointing at her car.

Harley sprinted toward it, and Emma unlocked the door with her remote. The girl yanked the door open and threw herself onto the seat.

Emma knew better than to assume Harley was anxious to get home. She'd seen the girl shivering in her thin hoodie.

She turned up the heat as she pulled away from the curb. "How was your day?" she asked.

Harley lifted a shoulder. "Okay."

One word, but more than she'd gotten out of Harley last night and this morning. "School good?"

The same shoulder went up again. "Lot of homework." She was quiet for a while, then burst out, "Stupid Kevin Diller ran around in gym class, shoving his smelly socks in all the girls' faces. It was totally gross. He got a detention."

She *was* going to have to deal with the whole boys thing. But at least it got Harley talking to her again. Emma relaxed her grip on the steering wheel and her stomach uncoiled. "That's disgusting."

"You wouldn't believe how bad they smelled. It was like someone left their lunch in their locker for a—"

She stopped abruptly. Probably remembered she was angry at Emma. Emma glanced at her out of the corner of her eye. Not the best time for a conversation about boys.

"You want to get something and take it home for dinner? Since you have a lot of homework?"

"No. I want to make dinner."

"Okay. I think we have chicken in the fridge. There are potatoes and rice. And broccoli and green beans."

Harley frowned. "There's a recipe I want to try. I can use some of that stuff."

"Great."

An hour later, they were sitting at the kitchen table, eating chicken and rice with a sauce made from sherry and butter and some spices. "This is delicious, Harley," Emma said.

"It's okay." She took another bite. "It needs a little more basil, though. Maybe some lemon juice."

"Did you make up this recipe?" Emma asked casually. Anything to keep Harley talking.

The girl shrugged, the same indifferent gesture she'd used in the car. "I saw something like it on one of the cooking shows. Tried a few different things."

"It's amazing." She smiled at the girl. "You have great instincts for what tastes good together."

The tips of Harley's ears turned red and she took another bite. "It needs work."

Harley had apparently always had a sensitive palate. Emma remembered Sonya telling her how, when Harley was barely more than a baby, she could always tell if her mother bought the wrong brand of American cheese. "Can you manage to choke it down?" she teased. "Or do you want a PBJ?"

Harley scowled again. "It's edible."

After Harley had finished eating and was leaning back in her chair, drinking a glass of milk, Emma said, "Harley, I'm sorry about the way everything happened yesterday."

The girl set the glass on the table, picked up a piece of green bean on her plate and dragged it through a blob of sauce. "You should have told me," she said. Her voice was quiet. Sad.

"You want the truth? Can I tell you my side?"

Harley looked directly at her with a surprised expression. "Okay."

Emma set her fork carefully on her plate. "I didn't tell you because I knew hearing about your father would upset you. But mostly, I didn't want anything to change." She reached toward Harley and tried to take her hand, but the girl snatched it away. Emma sighed. "And, frankly, I was hoping the test would be negative. That there had been a mistake and some other Nathan Devereux was your father. Then we could go through with our adoption plans."

Harley concentrated on picking up one grain of rice with her fork. "You probably don't want to adopt me anymore, anyway."

"Of course I do. Why would I have changed my mind?"

"I was a brat last night. I saw the way you looked at me. You were mad that I made a scene. Mothers have to put up with crap from their kids. But you're not related to me. And now there's someone else to dump me on."

"Harley." The girl continued to poke at the rice. "Look at me, please."

Harley raised her head, her face blank.

"Yes, you acted badly last night. That doesn't change how I feel about you." Emma touched the back of the girl's hand. "And there will be no dumping. I want to keep you. Are we clear on that?"

She stared at Harley until the girl shrugged. She still didn't answer, but her jaw relaxed a little. So did her hand, which was clenched into a fist around the fork.

"But no matter what I want, Nathan is your father. His rights trump my desire to adopt you. So we have to figure out what to do. Okay? You don't like this. Neither do I. But we have to deal with it."

"I don't want to deal with anything," Harley said, so softly that Emma could barely hear. "I want things to be the way they were." She looked at her lap, and a tear fell on her jeans. "I want my mom."

Emma wanted to hold Harley tight and make everything better.

But she stayed in her seat. Harley would shove her away if she tried to hug her. "I know you do, sweetheart. I miss her, too." Her throat tightened. In the weeks since Sonya had died, Emma had focused on Harley. But seeing the sorrow in Harley's expression made her own heart ache. She missed her friend.

"It's not fair that she died," Harley said.

"No, it's not. Life can be terribly unfair." God, she hated that Harley had learned that lesson when she was only thirteen.

Harley lifted her head, tear streaks on her face shiny in the bright light of the kitchen. "I need to do my homework."

"Okay."

Harley went into her room, closed the door gently. The lock clicked into place.

CHAPTER EIGHT

NATHAN BOUNCED A pencil off the desk calendar as he fingered the telephone. He needed to call Emma and apologize for the way he'd acted yesterday. He'd been out of line.

She'd accused him of being some kind of criminal.

Damn David Sanders. He wanted to go to the lawyer's office and kick his ass. Nathan scowled at the phone. What the hell had the guy been thinking?

Maybe Sanders hadn't been thinking. Maybe he was just reacting to Emma's big golden eyes. Her undisciplined hair. The body hiding beneath her funky clothes.

Was Emma just as unconventional in other parts of her life?

Not that he would ever know. That initial attraction, the chemistry that had boiled between them, was gone, at least on Emma's side. In her eyes he was the guy who'd slept with so many women he couldn't remember them all.

The truth was so far from that, it was laughable. But he wasn't about to humiliate himself by explaining his pitiful dating life to Emma.

But, damn it, he still wanted to see her again. Alone, this time. So he could apologize. Find out if the attraction between them was completely dead. Maybe it was on life support, and they could resuscitate it.

He punched in her number before he could chicken out and counted the rings. Just as he was about to give up, she answered.

"Emma Sloan." Brisk. Businesslike.

"Hi, Emma, this is Nathan Devereux." He swallowed. "I'm calling about yesterday."

"Yes?"

How did she go from professional to ice-cold in one word? "I need to apologize. I was out of line." *Even though she'd pretty much called him a dirtbag.* "I shouldn't have reacted that way."

Silence. Then she said, "I shouldn't have repeated what David said. So we're even, I guess." Her voice was cool and impersonal. As if he was a stranger.

"I'd like to talk to you," he said in a rush. "Can you meet me for lunch?"

"Not today. I have several appointments this afternoon. I can't drive all the way to your restaurant."

"I wasn't asking you to meet me here. Pick a place that's convenient for you."

She hesitated a moment too long. "I'll be on the north side this afternoon," she finally said. "We could meet at Oscar's in Lakeview." She gave him the address. "Would that work for you?"

"That's fine." They arranged a time, and ended the conversation. Nathan hadn't planned on asking her to meet him—the words had spilled out before he could stop them. He couldn't tell Emma about the investigation or why he'd been so stunned at her question. So what the hell was he going to say to her?

He had an hour to figure it out.

As he was walking out the back door, he spotted Jerry Fullerton, the health inspector who came by a few times a year to make sure the restaurant was up to code.

"Hey, Jerry," Nathan said, holding the door open for him. "I wasn't expecting you today."

"I was working in this area and figured I'd save a little time." He winked at Nathan. "More efficient this way."

Nathan glanced at his watch. "I wish I could stick around, but I have an appointment. Wouldn't have made it today if I'd known you were coming."

"Not a problem," Jerry said breezily, flipping open his metal clipboard and pulling out a sheet. "Haven't gotten your envelope yet, but I know you're good for it." He raised his eyebrows. "Right?"

"Uh, yeah," Nathan said, his mind scrambling. "Same place as always?"

The inspector's forehead wrinkled, as if he was puzzled. "Mail slot in my door. What happened? You hit your head when that car smashed into you?"

"Too much on my mind," Nathan said, his skin prickling. He clapped Jerry on the shoulder. "You know how crazy it can get sometimes."

"You're telling me." Jerry relaxed into a smile and he held his fist out for a bump. "I know I can count on you."

"You can, Jerry." He needed more information. "There isn't a late fee, is there?"

"Nah," Jerry said with a grin. "You still get the old-timer's rate. Three hundred bucks."

"Hey, I'm not that old," Nathan said.

"Old-timers as in long-term contributor." Jerry's smile faded. "You telling me something here, Nate?"

"Course not," Nathan said. He managed a smile. "Like I said, lot of stuff on my mind lately."

"Know what you mean." Jerry winked again. "Go ahead to your meeting. If there's anything needs to be taken care of, I'll talk to Marco."

"Great. Thanks." Nathan watched the inspector run through his checklist for a moment, then let the door close behind him. As soon as he was in his car, he dialed Patrick.

"Devereux." Patrick sounded impatient.

"It's Nathan. You got a minute?"

"Yeah. Hold on." Nathan heard the sound of a door closing. "What's up?"

"The health inspector is here. Jerry Fullerton. Same guy

who's been doing it for years. Someone's paying him off, Paddy. Or has been, up until now."

"You sure?"

"He said he hadn't gotten his envelope yet, but he knew I was good for it. Three hundred bucks. Hard to misinterpret that."

"You sure Marco isn't paying him?"

"Marco doesn't pay any attention to the day-to-day stuff. I'm not sure if he even knows Jerry's name. All he thinks about is the food." Nathan started his car, and the vent streamed cold air on him. He slapped it off.

"Tell me the guy's name again. I'll try to get a warrant to check his bank account."

"Jerry Fullerton. Should I tell Danny Kopecki, too?"

"Can't hurt. The more information everyone has, the better."

"Thanks, Paddy."

"Yeah. Got to go."

By the time Nathan got to Oscar's, he'd called Danny Kopecki and told him about the inspector and the bribes. Now it was time to concentrate on the other issue in his life.

In the ten minutes before Emma walked through the door, he'd read all the Oscar Wilde quotes on the pub's dark-paneled walls and practically memorized the menu. But he still wasn't sure how to explain his reaction to her question about what had happened at the restaurant.

He stood as she reached the booth, bracing himself with a hand on the table. He'd had to park two blocks away, and his leg ached. Thank God he'd brought the damn cane. "Hi, Emma. Thanks for coming."

She tucked her long skirt beneath her as she slid into the opposite bench. Her hair was piled on top of her head today, and instead of her usual dramatic earrings, she wore simple gold hoops in her ears. But he noticed the flash of red on her feet as she sat down.

"We needed to talk," she said. She smiled at the waitress

approaching the booth and said, "Hey, Abby. I'll have iced tea, please."

"We have the blackberry sage you like. That okay?" the woman asked.

"Sounds great. Thanks."

Nathan raised his eyebrows as the waitress hurried away. "You're a regular here?"

"I was, until a few weeks ago." She lined up the fork and spoon with the edge of the table, then straightened her menu.

Until her friend died and Harley came to live with her.

His life wasn't the only one that had been disrupted by Sonya Michaels's death.

He knew nothing about Emma, he realized, other than she was a social worker and now Harley's guardian. What did she do for fun? Did she have any hobbies?

A boyfriend?

He pushed his silverware to the side and leaned forward. "Emma, I was an ass yesterday. I'm sorry. There's no excuse for the way I acted. It was a bad day, but I shouldn't have taken it out on you."

A stray curl had fallen from the mass on her head, and she tucked it behind her ear. "You've already apologized and I've accepted. Neither of us was at our best."

"Why would David Sanders even tell you something like that? And why was he asking his contacts about me?"

Color spread from her neck to her face. "I'm not sure, but from the way he talked, I think he was…he is…I think he's, ah, interested in me."

"Really." Nathan clenched his fists together in his lap. "And are you interested in him?"

Her color deepened, but she lifted her chin. "Why do you ask?"

Because he was an idiot who couldn't stop thinking about her. "You're a smart woman, Emma. Why do you think?"

She held his gaze for a moment, and the pulse at the base of her neck fluttered. Her lips parted and she swallowed. "I have no idea." Her voice was breathy. Soft.

"I bet you can figure it out."

She swallowed again. "You're a dangerous man, Nathan."

Her eyes had dilated. Her chest rose and fell a little faster. He wanted to taste her mouth. He suspected that, beneath the sweetness, she'd be a little tart.

Not the time. Or the place. "Dangerous? Me?" he managed to say. "What do you think I'm going to do? Trip you with my cane?"

Her gaze moved to the handle of the damn cane, propped against the side of the booth, before returning to his mouth. "I don't think your cane has anything to do with it."

Oh, God. Time to dial it down. If they didn't, he'd lose the last scraps of his self-control. He'd be across the table and kissing her before she drew her next breath. "I'm looking forward to discussing exactly how I'm dangerous to you. In detail." He curled his fingers around the edge of the vinyl bench seat. "But I asked you to meet me to talk about Harley. Not... other things."

"Right." She blinked. Drew a deep breath, then another. Tucked the stray curl behind her ear again with a trembling hand. Shrugged out of her jacket and dropped it on the seat next to her. "Harley. What do you want to know?"

Tearing his gaze away from Emma's sweater, he said, "I want to know who she is. What does she like to do? Where does she go to school? Is she a good student? Before her mother died, was she a happy kid?"

Emma nodded. "Happy. Yeah, she was. She and Sonya were close. Harley has a mouth on her—which you probably figured out the other night. Sometimes I want to laugh at the stuff she says, but I know I shouldn't.

"She loves to cook. And she's good at it. She plays indoor soccer once a week. She has a lot of friends—she's texting constantly. And she's a good student—A's and B's on papers and tests."

"How well did you know her mother?"

"Sonya and I were close." She slid her hands, palms down, onto the table. He wanted to cover them with his. Feel the softness of her skin, the beat of her pulse in her wrist.

But she wasn't looking at him now. Her gaze was miles away. "I met her because her downstairs neighbor called in a complaint to DCFS—the woman thought Harley spent too much time alone. Turned out there wasn't really a problem—Harley was alone after she got home from school and had been playing music too loud." She smiled. "Dancing, too, and the thumping drove the woman crazy. It was one of my easier cases."

Emma's smile faded. "I liked Sonya a lot. Harley, too. We got to be close, and I spent a lot of time with them. I...I'm surprised she never told you about Harley. But I guess I shouldn't be. She never told me about her aneurysm. That it could kill her. Apparently she was good at keeping secrets."

"Too good. She should have told me about Harley."

"Yes, she should have." Emma drummed her fingers on the table. "But you know now, and all three of us have to deal with it. We need to figure out what to do." The sexy, flirty woman of a few minutes ago had disappeared completely.

Businesslike Emma was back.

He could discuss this calmly, too. "This stuff going on at the restaurant—I'd rather not get into it right now. But it's one of the reasons I wasn't thrilled when you told me about Harley."

She narrowed her eyes. "You don't have time for your daughter?"

"That's part of it," he said bluntly. "There are criminals involved. I don't think it's dangerous, but do you want to take that chance? I don't. It's the time part that's the problem. This is something I need to focus on. To deal with. And it's taking all my spare energy."

"That sounds mysterious. Convenient, too."

"It's not convenient at all," he said evenly. She was irritated. That was okay. He was, too. "But I can't ignore it, or wish it away."

She leaned forward, and that stray curl slipped over her shoulder. "You have something else to deal with now," she said. "A daughter. And you can't ignore her, or wish her away, either."

"But I could have put off dealing with it, if you hadn't left that DVD where she could find it."

She sucked in a breath. "So it's my fault that you're inconvenienced?"

"Of course not." He sighed. "God, Emma. I'm not blaming you for anything. You're trying to do your best for Harley. I get that. I want the best for her, too. And right now, I'm not sure it's me."

"And you can't even sign away your parental rights, can you?" she murmured. "Not now that Harley knows about you."

"That was never an option. Which I told you the first time we talked."

"Maybe it would be better for Harley if you did."

"Really? That's what you think? That I should just forget that I have a daughter? Let her think I don't care about her? That I don't want her?"

"Isn't that the truth?"

"No, it's not. Just because the timing is bad doesn't mean I don't want her. And even if I didn't, do you think I'd hurt her like that?"

"I have no idea."

"Just so it's all on the table, I'm planning a trip. I might be gone for a while."

"And where does that leave Harley?"

"That's one of the things we have to figure out." That made him sound cold and heartless. As though a vacation was more important than his child. But he needed to get away, damn it. Needed to clear his head.

The waitress slid Emma's iced tea on the table and poured him more coffee. "Are you ready to order?" she asked brightly.

"Give us a few more minutes, Abby," Emma said. "Okay?"

"Sure."

Emma stared at the menu for a long moment. Nathan shoved his away. He'd lost all interest in eating.

Finally she lifted her head. "I know I'm not being fair to you. It's just…" She adjusted the silverware on the table, lining everything up again even though nothing had moved. "Harley is so sad. So scared about what's going to happen." She hesitated. "And so am I. I love her. I want to adopt her. And now I'm going to lose her."

"You're not going to lose her," he said. He started to reach across the table to her, then curled his fingers into his palm. "Whatever happens, you'll be part of her life." Which would keep Emma in his life, as well. It was selfish of him to consider that, but he couldn't help it.

"It won't be the same." She tucked her curl behind her ear again, and her hand shook. "Yeah, I'll visit her. We'll talk on the phone, have a sleepover now and then. But she'll settle into a routine with you and your family and we'll drift apart. It's inevitable."

"It doesn't have to be."

She shrugged. "I've spent a lot of time with children in the system. I know how quickly things change with the kids. How quickly they can adapt and move on."

"We'll have to make sure it doesn't happen with Harley," Nathan said. "Can we agree about that?"

"Sure." But the expression on her face said she didn't believe it.

"Good." He cleared his throat. "Which brings me to the other thing we need to talk about. First of all, how is Harley doing after that disaster the other night?"

"She feels betrayed by everyone—me, her mother. You. She doesn't want anything to do with us."

"So how do we fix this?" he asked.

"I think she has to get to know you." She kept her gaze steady on him. "Even though it's *inconvenient*. The two of you need to meet again under better circumstances."

He tried to ignore Emma's snarky reference to his earlier words. They had to work together on this. "I agree. Any ideas?"

"Maybe the three of us could go out to dinner. Low-key, to start out."

"Monday is the only night that would work for me. Mama's is open every other night."

She frowned. "You don't have anyone to cover for you?"

"You sound like my brother," he muttered. "And no, I don't. I was gone for too long while I was injured, and I need to spend time at the restaurant to get back up to speed. I'm hiring a manager, but she hasn't started yet."

"Mondays don't work for us. Harley has soccer. Any other ideas?"

"Why don't you bring her to Mama's for dinner? If you come early, on a Tuesday, maybe, it won't be too busy and I can spend some time with you."

"I'm not sure that's a good idea after what happened there."

"Mama's is part of her heritage. She's going to be seeing a lot of the place as she gets to know the family. Might as well get used to it."

"I'm not sure how Harley will feel about that," Emma said.

"You're her guardian right now. You're the one who makes those decisions. If it's her choice, she'll probably never want to see me again."

At thirty-two, Emma had been a social worker, concentrating on kids, for almost ten years. And Nathan was telling *her* how to be a parent?

Before she stopped to think, Emma said, "I've known her for two years and I've been living with her for over a month.

You met her once, under less than ideal conditions. And you're the expert on parenting?"

A muscle in Nathan's jaw twitched as they stared at each other. The connection that had rippled between them just a few moments ago was gone.

"Yes, as a matter of fact," he said. "I have a lot more parenting experience than you do."

"Really? A single guy knows all about teenagers?"

His hands clenched the edge of the table before he pressed them flat. "My parents died when I was twenty-two. It was in May, just before I came home from college for the summer. I was a semester short of graduating, but I dropped out of school. I took over running the restaurant and took responsibility for my siblings."

Emma sucked in a breath, appalled at herself. She'd dredged this up with her snarky remarks.

She opened her mouth to speak, but he continued, "Patrick was seventeen. He was driving the car when a drunk ran a red light and hit them. Frankie was almost thirteen. Marco was eleven."

His eyes clouded. "Marco was the easiest. He missed them, but the rest of us tried really hard with him. Patrick blamed himself for killing our parents. And Frankie..." He stared at the table. "She kept her grief hidden, and I assumed she was okay. Then she started acting out, getting in trouble, running wild. Until she ran away when she was fifteen. And you know what happened to her then."

He looked at Emma. "Worst month of my life. I spent every night at the restaurant, worried sick, resenting that I had to be there. Every day I scoured the streets, looking for Frankie. Talking to her friends, trying to figure out where she was. Afraid she was dead."

He swallowed. "So, yeah, I know what it's like to raise kids. Especially kids who are grieving. Which, by the way, I hope you have covered. I hope Harley's getting grief counseling."

"Of…of course she is." God, what could she say to him? Any apology would be completely inadequate.

He closed his eyes, and when he opened them, it was as though Emma was facing a stranger. "You know, Emma, you're right. You're Harley's legal guardian. She's your responsibility. So you figure out what you want to do and let me know." He pulled out his wallet and threw some money onto the table. "I have to get back to work, and I'm sure you do, too. I'll talk to you later."

He grabbed his cane and pushed himself to his feet. He limped out of the pub without looking back.

Emma watched him walk past the windows and disappear from view. God. She'd had no idea.

No wonder he'd been less than thrilled when he'd found out about Harley. He'd raised three kids already, and it must have seemed as if Harley was Frankie all over again. Grieving, hormonal, lost.

On top of whatever was going on at the restaurant.

Once again, she wondered what would have happened between them if Sonya hadn't died. When he'd stared at her this afternoon, the heat in his eyes had been as intimate as a caress.

She'd wished it had been. She'd wanted him to kiss her. Wanted to kiss him back.

And wasn't that foolish? She had to maintain her objectivity. As Harley's legal guardian and a DCFS social worker, she'd eventually be asked her opinion of Nathan's parenting skills. Of the bond between him and Harley. How could she do that if she was…involved with him?

Abby stopped next to the booth. "Your friend couldn't stick around?" she said, her expression sympathetic.

"He had to leave." Emma forced a smile. "Maybe you should just bring the check."

"Be right back."

A few minutes later, the waitress dropped off the bill for her iced tea and Nathan's coffee. Nathan had left far too much money. She slapped the twenty into the folder with the bill and slid out of the booth.

She thought she'd known so much about being a parent. Compared to Nathan, she knew nothing. A sharp, cold wind whipped at her hair as she hurried to her car. Harley needed to spend time with Nathan, getting to know him. And she had to make it happen, even though it brought her closer and closer to losing Harley.

Even if it broke her heart.

CHAPTER NINE

HARLEY SLOWED HER steps as they reached the front door of Mama's Place. "I don't think this is a good idea."

Right now, Emma didn't, either. "Why not?" she asked, wishing desperately that they were back in her cozy apartment. Her heart was racing and her damp hand slipped off the door handle.

"We can't, like, just surprise him."

"He suggested we have dinner here," Emma said. "We didn't have a chance to arrange a day." Because she'd made one too many snarky remarks and he'd walked out of Oscar's.

"This is stupid," Harley muttered.

Emma had been the stupid one. Irritated because Nathan wouldn't tell her what was going on at the restaurant. Hurt that he questioned her parenting skills, although he had every right to do so. And disgusted with herself because she'd still noticed the blue of his eyes, the width of his shoulders and the way his face softened when he smiled.

Appalled that she'd wanted to kiss him.

It had been several days since the fiasco at Oscar's. Emma realized she had to make this move, but she'd been dreading it. Which was why she was determined to get it over with. "Look, Harley, you have to talk to him. Get to know him. He's your father. And starting tonight, we're coming here for dinner once a week." Emma had to talk to him, too.

"I don't want to be here." Desperation filled Harley's voice. "Not after last time." She pressed a hand to her stomach. "We should go home. I don't feel good."

"I know you're nervous." Emma smoothed her hand down Harley's back. "Maybe you should just tell him you're sorry for making a scene in his restaurant."

Harley's face reddened. "I was angry."

"I know you were. And I don't blame you. But this is where he works. You embarrassed him in front of his customers."

Harley shoved her hands into the pockets of her fleece jacket. "Fine. Let's get this over with."

Great. A sullen kid and an embarrassed woman. The perfect way to begin Harley's relationship with her father. "Come on, Harley. Maybe you'll have a good time."

"Yeah. Right."

Emma took a deep breath, opened the door and walked in. The restaurant smelled like garlic, tomatoes and cheese. Comforting, homey scents. It was just after five—she'd picked Harley up early from FreeZone—and the restaurant was empty.

Harley was right. This was a bad idea. It would be just the three of them. She should have called Nathan to set up a specific time to get together. But every time she'd reached for the phone, she remembered how she'd behaved at Oscar's and couldn't bring herself to call.

"There's no one here. Maybe it's not open," Harley said hopefully.

Emma scanned the tables. Last time she was here, she'd been too nervous to notice the decor. Now she saw that all the tablecloths were covered with sheets of butcher's paper. Small lights twinkled on the ceiling. Photos of Italy, sports figures, children, hung on the walls. Laminated newspaper articles and restaurant reviews, yellowing with age, were displayed by the entrance. A photo of a smiling, middle-aged couple hung in an old frame close to the door. Reminders of family were everywhere.

Harley's family.

"It's open every day but Monday," Emma said, trying to sound as though she was glad to be here. She heard voices in the kitchen, then the door opened and a waitress walked through. She had bright red hair and carried a tray loaded with small cheese dishes.

She stared at them for a moment, then smiled. "Welcome to Mama's," she said. "Let me get Nathan." She bumped the door open with her hip and yelled, "Customers waiting."

The door swung closed behind the waitress and she began to set the dishes on the tables. Emma's stomach twisted and she wanted to run out the door, the way Harley had done last time they were here.

The door swung open again and Nathan came into the dining room. He wore a dark gray suit that emphasized his muscled chest and flat abdomen and a light blue shirt that made his eyes look even brighter. He started toward them, smiling. His smile faded when he recognized them.

"Harley. Emma. I wasn't expecting you."

Apparently Nathan didn't like surprises. At least this kind. "You, ah, said that Tuesdays were good."

"I did, didn't I." He shifted his gaze to Harley and his face softened. "How are you doing, Harley?"

The girl shrugged one shoulder. "Okay."

"I'm glad to see you." He fumbled a couple of menus off the top of the stack. "Let's find you a table."

Harley elbowed her in the side. Hard. "This was a bad idea," she whispered.

Emma privately agreed, but they'd have to muddle through it. "It'll be fine."

Harley rolled her eyes and lifted her hand to her forehead. Pretending to brush her hair to the side, Harley's fingers formed an *L* .

Loser. An hysterical laugh bubbled up in Emma's throat, and she clenched her jaw to suppress it. She glanced at Nathan, hoping he hadn't noticed. But his lips twitched. Great. Would he think she was allowing Harley to be disrespectful? Would it be proof that she was the bad parent he'd accused her of being?

Nathan pulled out Emma's chair, and she sat down. His fingertips brushed her back as he let go of the chair. She stilled. His hand lingered for a moment, then he let it drop with a final, tiny caress.

Harley had already sat down, so he placed the menus carefully in front of them. "What would you like to drink?" he asked politely. He glanced at Emma for a heartbeat, then looked away.

"Iced tea, please," Emma said, wishing for something stronger.

"Coke," Harley said, with a sidelong glance at Emma.

Emma shook her head. Harley hunched her shoulders. "I mean lemonade. Please," she added after Emma narrowed her eyes.

"I'll be right back."

As Nathan hurried away, Harley leaned toward Emma. "He doesn't want us here." Hurt lingered beneath the girl's I-don't-want-to-be-here-either expression.

"Yes, he does," she whispered back. "He's the one who suggested it."

"I don't believe you." Harley crossed her arms over her chest and watched as the redheaded waitress walked toward them, carrying their drinks.

"Here you go." The waitress set glasses on the table. "I'm guessing you're not ready to order yet." Her gaze settled on Harley for a moment, then switched to Emma. "Here's the list of Marco's specialties for the day." She set a laminated card on the table. "Your…our chef is really good. I think you'll enjoy his food."

"Thanks," Emma said with a strained smile. Clearly, the woman remembered them and knew who they were. "I'm Emma, by the way. This is Harley."

"And I'm Phyllis. Nice to meet you both."

After Phyllis walked away, Harley said, "Why did you introduce us? That was weird."

"Because she remembers us from last time," Emma said. "It was the polite thing to do."

Harley's pale cheeks turned bright red, highlighting the sprinkling of freckles. "Does everyone here know he's my father?"

"Probably everyone who works here. You were pretty, ah, loud."

Harley looked around wildly, but there was no one else in sight. "Let's get out of here."

"No. This time we're facing the situation. We're going to have dinner and talk to Nathan. You're going to show him you weren't raised by wolves." *And I'm going to choke down a large helping of crow.*

Nathan reappeared, carrying two plates. They each held three small servings of different foods. "I thought you might like to try Marco's specials. Everyone who works here samples them before we open. We've been doing it forever." He glanced at Harley as he set the plates on the table. "My parents used to do the same thing when they ran the restaurant. My dad was the chef then."

Harley was studying the plate and didn't respond. Emma wondered if she realized Nathan was trying to tell her something about her family. About their traditions.

"Smells okay." Harley glared up at Nathan. "Your brother's the chef? I guess even jerks can cook."

Instead of getting annoyed, Nathan smiled. "Marco is a little excitable. But he knows what he's doing in the kitchen."

Harley picked up a fork, and Nathan sat across from her. He leaned forward, as if genuinely interested in her opinion. Nathan couldn't know it, but giving Harley food to taste was a perfect way to get her talking.

Emma tried some of the first dish. It was a pasta with a rich red sauce. Tiny pieces of carrots and celery nestled in the curves of the pasta. It was delicious. "That's really good," she said.

Nathan smiled. "I'll tell Marco."

Harley tried it and nodded. "It's okay. Bolognese sauce is so last year, though."

Nathan's smile faded. "What?"

Harley shrugged. "That's what all the cooking shows were doing last season. They've moved on. Your brother probably should, too."

"Harley." Emma's fork clattered to the plate. "That was rude."

"It's the truth." Harley gave Emma an innocent look. "We're telling the truth now, aren't we?"

Emma shot a horrified look at Nathan and was shocked to see him struggle to hide a grin. "Yeah, Harley. You're right. We're all about the truth." He leaned back in his chair. "What about the gnocchi with the brown butter sage sauce?"

Emma took a bite and savored the flavor for a moment. "That's great. I really like it."

Harley took a bite, chewed. "It's good. But I think he browned the butter a little too much." She tasted the third sample, a red sauce with roasted vegetables. "This one needs more basil."

"You've got quite the palate," Nathan said. He wasn't smiling now.

Harley raised her eyebrows. "Just saying."

"I'll pass along your comments to Marco. I'm sure he'll appreciate them."

It was impossible to read Nathan's expression. But Emma would love to be a fly on the wall when the "excitable" Marco heard his new niece's snarky remarks. "I guess I'm missing the subtleties." Emma took another bite. "I love all three of them."

"Thanks," Nathan said, his expression softening as he glanced at her. "Marco is good at what he does." He turned back to Harley, watching as she finished the samples. "My mother used to do that," he murmured.

"Do what?" Emma asked.

"What Harley did." He kept his gaze on the girl as he spoke. "I remember her telling my father when a dish wasn't quite right. She could identify every ingredient, and she wasn't shy about pointing out his mistakes. Looks like you inherited the family palate, Harley."

Harley scowled. "That's stupid. Emma was just being polite. Anyone could tell there was a problem with those samples."

"No, they couldn't," he began. The front door opened and a family of five came in. The oldest child, a girl of about ten, said something to the youngest boy. He shoved her and she bumped into the podium.

"Excuse me," Nathan said, pushing away from the table. As he walked to the front of the restaurant, the mother grabbed the girl and said something in a low voice. The girl smirked.

Nathan took menus, paper place mats and a box of crayons and led the family to a table in the adjoining room. It was separated from the room where Emma and Harley sat by a low wall and arches that were supposed to resemble windows. Tiny white lights outlined each of the arches.

Emma watched as he seated the mother, then held a chair for the girl. By the time he was finished, he'd skillfully maneuvered her between her parents and put the younger boys across from her.

He crouched next to the girl and asked her something. She nodded vigorously and grinned. Then Nathan walked around the table and spoke to the boys. They nodded, too.

By the time Nathan left them, the tension at the table had eased. The mother was smiling, talking to the father. The three kids were coloring on their place mats.

All because of some deft handling by Nathan.

Hard-learned, Emma reminded herself. Unlike her professional experience with kids, Nathan had actually raised them.

Emma's face burned as it did every time she remembered her crack about a guy without kids knowing what to do with them. Instead of jumping down her throat, Nathan had been remarkably low-key while telling his story.

Emma took a sip of iced tea and watched Nathan seat another couple with a baby. He'd said Tuesdays were quiet. Maybe, at the rate people were coming in, he wouldn't have a chance to talk to them after all.

Irritating that she was disappointed rather than relieved.

NATHAN DELIVERED ANOTHER round of kiddy cocktails to the three kids who'd come in fighting. "Thank you," their mother murmured. She leaned closer to Nathan. "I'm pathetically grateful."

"You're more than welcome. A lot of arguments can be smoothed over by a glass of Seven Up and grenadine." He smiled as he watched the kids pull the orange slices and cherries off the little swords and slurp them down. The two boys began a swordfight with the plastic picks, and their father just barely rescued the youngest boy's bright red drink. "Let me see if your dinner is ready," Nathan added quickly.

As he hurried toward the kitchen, he glanced at Emma and Harley. Emma was leaning toward Harley, saying something. From the mulish look on Harley's face, they weren't exchanging pleasantries.

Then Emma held out her hand. Instead of giving her whatever she was asking for, Harley slipped a phone into the back pocket of her jeans, then held her hands up.

Emma stared at his daughter for a moment, then nodded once.

His daughter. It still sounded so foreign. So strange. The thought brought a familiar surge of anger. Why hadn't Sonya Michaels contacted him? She'd known where he was.

He'd probably never get any answers. It didn't matter now, anyway.

Emma wanted to adopt Harley. For a lot of people, that

would have been an easy solution. But Nathan would never forgive himself if he turned his back on his child.

But, God. Why couldn't this have happened a year from now? If he'd gotten this mess with the restaurant straightened out, if he'd taken his trip, he'd be able to focus on being a father.

Now all he could think about was getting away from Mama's. From all his responsibilities. And Emma had just given him another one—the biggest responsibility of all.

It wasn't Emma's fault, he reminded himself. This was painful for her, too. She looked completely engaged with Harley, touching her hand, smiling at her.

Lucky Harley.

The overhead lights made Emma's hair shine. She'd pinned the sides away from her face and the curls tumbled down her back. His fingers itched to feel them slipping through his hands.

He transfered his gaze to Harley. When she'd walked into Mama's last week, his first thought was that she looked nothing like a Devereux. Then he'd noticed her eyes. It had been spooky to see his sister in that unfamiliar face.

After he'd gone home that night, he'd dug out his parents' old photo albums. He'd been turning the pages, looking at pictures of long-forgotten great-aunts and uncles, when he'd found one of his father's mother.

Nathan barely remembered her—she'd died when he was young. But in a photo of his grandmother holding him shortly after he was born, her bright red hair had been as vivid as Harley's and just as curly.

He turned away from Emma and Harley as he pushed into the kitchen, but not before he spotted Harley talking to Emma, gesturing at her empty plate. Clearly discussing Marco's specials.

Phyllis was at the counter, collecting two pasta dishes. "Are those for the table in the corner with the three kids?" he asked.

"Yeah, thank God. The parents are looking a little frazzled."

A pizza sat on the high counter surrounding the wood-burning ovens. "This theirs, too?"

She nodded. "Be right back."

"I've got it."

As he carried the pizza to the table, he sneaked another glance at Harley and Emma. Harley was studying the walls, and her gaze had zeroed in on the autographed picture of Ron Santo, the Cubs' Hall of Fame third baseman.

He wondered if Harley was a Cubs fan. That would be something they had in common. Something to build on.

After delivering the pizza, he strolled over to Emma and Harley's table. They were the only ones seated in that small section, and he hoped he could keep it that way.

"Hey," he said as he reached them. "Did Phyllis get your order?"

"She did." Emma smiled, but she appeared nervous. "You're busier tonight than I thought you'd be."

"The early rush—mostly families with kids." He pulled out a chair and sat down, then nodded at the Santo picture. "Looks like you're a Cubs fan," he said to Harley.

Harley glanced at the photo again and scowled at him. "My mom liked the Sox. I do, too."

"I'm sorry," Nathan said, trying not to smile. "My condolences."

Harley rolled her eyes. "That's so lame."

Nathan settled back in the chair. "Have you been to many games?"

Harley kept her expression carefully neutral. "A few."

"Don't let her fool you," Emma said with a smile. "She can probably dissect every player on the roster and tell you more than you'd ever want to know."

"Emma, he's a *Cubs* fan," Harley said, disgusted. "They don't care about that stuff. They just want to look good for the TV camera."

"Whoa." Nathan bit his lip to hide a smile as he narrowed his eyes. "Are you talking smack about my baseball team?"

Harley sneered. "Baseball team? Bunch of losers is what they are."

"At least they lose with style."

Harley snorted. "Right. Like you get style points in baseball. What are they, ice dancers?"

Emma lifted the menu so it covered the lower half of her face. Above it, her eyes were laughing. "Harley, maybe that's enough baseball talk."

Nathan swallowed a grin. "Wait until next year, baby."

"Like we haven't heard *that* before." Harley rolled her eyes, looking eerily like Frankie at the same age.

Nathan's smile faded. Harley was more than some kid in his restaurant he had to tease into a good mood. She was his daughter.

Was he supposed to recognize her as his immediately? Feel some kind of parental bond? Fall in love with her at first sight? Because that sure as hell hadn't happened.

She'd charged into his restaurant and made a huge scene. After she and Emma had left, he'd passed out free desserts to every customer to apologize for the disruption, but the damage had been done. By now, everyone in the neighborhood probably knew about his surprise daughter.

The front door opened again, and his shoulders relaxed. He could escape. "Maybe we'll catch a game sometime this spring," he said.

"A Cubs game?" she sneered. "Big whoop."

"We can go to a Sox game if you'd rather. I'll just bring a book for the boring parts." He nodded toward the couple waiting at the podium. "Guess I have to get to work. I'll stop by again when I can."

Several minutes later, while still at the podium, he watched Phyllis deliver Harley's and Emma's meals. Emma had chosen the brown butter sage ravioli. Harley had a plate containing portions of all three of Marco's specials.

Either she'd enjoyed them after all, or she was looking for more talking points. From everything he'd seen already, Nathan guessed it was the latter.

The next time he swung through the kitchen, he called to Marco, "Hey, got a couple of comments on your specials."

"Yeah?" Marco turned away from the stove, his face red, sweat pouring down his cheeks. "Do they want to come back here and kiss me? And are they beautiful babes?"

"I think she's pretty. She doesn't seem to have any interest in kissing you, though. She said that you'd browned the butter too long on the gnocchi, and the pasta with roasted veggies needs more basil in the sauce. And by the way, Bolognese sauce is so last year. The cooking shows have moved on."

Marco's knuckles turned white on the spatula. "Who the hell said all that stuff?"

"Your niece. Harley."

CHAPTER TEN

"HARLEY? THAT SO-CALLED kid of yours said all that shit about my food?" He pointed the spatula at Nathan. "What kind of crap is that?"

Nathan stepped around the counter and yanked the spatula away from Marco. "First of all, she's not my *so-called* kid. There was a paternity test. She's mine."

"So all your talk about condoms when I was in high school was 'do as I say, not as I do'?"

Since he didn't remember the event, he had no idea whether he'd used a condom with Harley's mother. But that was none of Marco's business. "Bite me." He grabbed his brother's arm and pulled him away from the stove. "Javier," Nathan yelled. "Take over whatever Marco was doing."

"You're pissed off because I'm saying stuff about a kid you don't even know?" Marco shoved Nathan's hand away. "She *is* going to be a problem."

Nathan studied his angry brother. He could keep fighting with him or defuse the situation. He didn't have the energy for a fight, so he rolled his eyes and went for détente. "Right. Because no one in this family would know anything about being a smart-ass."

"Being a smart-ass is one thing. Some *kid* criticizing my food is something else."

Nathan hauled Marco toward his office. When they were in a quieter part of the kitchen, Nathan let him go. "Are you really throwing a tantrum because someone questioned your food? How do you know she's wrong?"

"She's what? Twelve? Thirteen? Kids that age eat nothing but pizza and macaroni and cheese."

"For God's sake, Marco! Grow up!" He scowled at his brother, wondering when he'd become so arrogant. "You were probably too young to remember, but Mom was just like Harley. She had extrasensitive taste buds. She'd taste all the dishes and would say the same kind of stuff to Dad. He'd get just as mad as you did. Then he'd calm down and fix what she said needed fixing."

Marco was looking less angry and more intrigued. "Yeah? I didn't know that."

Nathan's shoulders relaxed. "Patrick and I thought it was hilarious. But a little spooky, too. I mean, how could Mom tell that Dad had used a different brand of oregano in the pizza sauce?"

"They're called supertasters," Marco said.

"Who are?"

"People who can do that. They have a bunch more taste buds than everyone else. I've met a few of them. Chefs, mostly." He narrowed his gaze. "Still doesn't mean I'm going to listen to that kid talking smack about my food."

"Maybe you ought to. Maybe she's right."

"Everyone loves tonight's specials. I've had a few orders already, and no one's complained."

"I guess none of them are supertasters."

"Very funny. What do you want me to do? Hire the kid?"

Nathan stopped smiling. "Of course not. But it might be a good opening for the apology you owe her. And Emma."

EMMA PUSHED HER plate away and sighed with satisfaction. "I really liked that gnocchi."

Harley gave her a pitying look. "Yeah, I guess if you couldn't tell the butter was almost burned, it would taste pretty good."

"Those were some snarky things to say about Marco's food," Emma said mildly.

Harley ate the last bite of her Bolognese pasta and shrugged one shoulder in the way Emma was starting to find annoying. "They were true."

"You were trying to get a rise out of Nathan, weren't you?" It was rude and ill-mannered, but Emma understood. She'd seen plenty of other kids do it when faced with a new situation. They acted out, pushed the limits, all to test how far they could go before being rejected. Nathan wouldn't turn his back on his daughter—he'd made that more than clear at Oscar's. But Harley didn't know that.

"Maybe," Harley muttered. "I think he's still mad at me."

"I'm guessing he is, a little." Emma leaned closer and touched Harley's hand. "Wouldn't you be upset if someone made a scene at your school, in front of your friends?"

"That's different." Harley stared at her plate, avoiding Emma's eyes. "Kids aren't the same as adults."

"Sometimes they are. Adults get embarrassed, too." Emma was mortified about the way she'd acted at Oscar's. "They get their feelings hurt. They say stupid things and regret them later."

"Yeah? So?"

"This might be a good time for that apology we talked about." For her, too. She'd lashed out and said some things to Nathan she wished desperately she could take back.

"He's pretty busy," Harley said. Two more groups had arrived in the past fifteen minutes.

"Not that busy." She rubbed Harley's back. "Get it over with. You'll feel better. And so will…Nathan."

Should Emma refer to him as Harley's father? Use his first name? There were so many delicate issues to navigate.

Her face heated as she remembered those moments at Oscar's. The desire in Nathan's eyes. The way he'd stared at her mouth.

The way she'd stared back.

Spending time with Nathan was going to be challenging for her as well as Harley.

As if she'd conjured him with her thoughts, Nathan appeared next to the table. "Did you enjoy your meals?"

"Mine was great," Emma said. She glanced at Harley, who was dragging her fork through the sauces remaining on her plate.

"They were good. Your brother's an okay chef." She poked at a piece of gnocchi on her plate.

"I'll tell him. He'll be happy to hear it."

Harley looked up at him and took a deep breath. "I'm sorry for making a scene here last week. It was really rude of me." The words came out in a rush, as if she needed to get them said before she chickened out.

Nathan sat across from her. "Thank you," he said. "I was surprised when you showed up. Maybe I didn't handle it as well as I could have."

Harley hunched her shoulders. "I was the one yelling," she muttered.

"Yeah, you were. But if I were in your shoes, I might have done the same. So let's agree that it was a mistake and move on."

Finally she looked at him, surprise and relief in her gaze. "Yeah?"

"Of course." He reached toward her, hesitated, then drew back. "In the grand scheme of mistakes you can make, that was a pretty small one."

"Okay." Harley's shoulders relaxed and she sat up straighter.

Emma wanted to hug Nathan. He'd said exactly the right things to Harley. Another example of his experience with kids. She was mortified all over again.

Nathan cleared his throat. "Let me get those dishes out of your way."

"You're the owner and you have to clear tables?" Harley asked.

He stacked the dishes efficiently, then swept the crumbs from the table. "Owning a business means you have to do everything sometimes. Our busboy has a late class on Tuesdays and doesn't come in until seven. Would you like some dessert?"

"No, thank…" Emma started to say.

"Yes, please," Harley said. "Do you have cannoli?"

Nathan studied her for a moment. "You like those?"

"Love them."

"We have them, but after what you said about Marco's specials, I'm afraid to serve them to you. They're frozen."

Harley frowned. "Really? In a nice place like this?"

Nathan smiled. "Thank you. I think. We can't afford a pastry chef right now, so we buy from bakeries. The frozen cannoli are the best we've found."

"I'll take a frozen cannoli, I guess."

Emma swallowed a bubble of laughter. "Don't do Nathan any favors, Harley."

Nathan shot her an amused glance. "Nothing for you, Emma?"

"No, thanks. I'm stuffed."

"Be right back."

As he walked away, Emma touched Harley's hand. "Nice job. I think Nathan appreciated it."

"Whatever." But Emma noticed she wasn't hunched in her chair anymore.

Before she could say anything else, Marco appeared next to the table. He was as tall as Nathan, with blue eyes and dark hair like his siblings, but lean and wiry. His white apron was spattered with red sauce, with a few dots on his white shirt. The back of his hand sported a pink mark that looked like a healing burn.

"Hey," he said, glancing from Emma to Harley. "Okay if I sit down for a minute?"

"Of course," Emma said, moving her iced tea out of his way.

He propped his elbows on the table. "I was out of line the

other night, and I'm sorry," he said gruffly. "I spoke before I thought. I know you're not trying to pull anything. I was just surprised."

Before Emma could answer, Harley said, "You were a jerk."

Marco looked startled, as if he hadn't expected Harley to be so blunt. After a moment, though, he nodded. "Yeah, I guess I was."

Harley seemed taken aback. Had she expected Marco to deny it? To start another fight?

"It was a rough night for all of us," Emma said quietly.

He looked at her gratefully. "And then some." He turned to Harley. "Nathan said you had some comments about my sauces."

Harley watched him cautiously. "Yeah. I did."

"You want to come back to the kitchen and we can try them together? You can tell me what you think."

Harley's eyes narrowed. "Are you making fun of me?"

"God, no." Marco held up his hands. "Sounds like you're a supertaster, and I want to see what you can do."

Harley scowled. "Like that song by They Might Be Giants? 'John Lee Supertaster'? You *are* making fun of me."

"It's a real thing. Swear to God. Supertasters are people who can taste stuff other people can't."

"I thought that was all made up." Harley studied Marco suspiciously.

Marco shrugged. "Look it up online. In the meantime, come in back and try some of my dishes."

"I guess I wouldn't mind seeing the kitchen," Harley said, as if she was merely trying to be polite. However, Emma recognized the gleam of excitement in the girl's eyes as she swiveled to face Emma. "Is that okay?"

"You sure she won't be in the way?" Emma asked Marco.

"Nah. I'll keep her away from the stoves and the cooks."

"Then it's fine with me." It would leave Emma alone out

here, though. She should welcome the opportunity to talk to Nathan. But she wasn't looking forward to groveling.

Harley stood up from the table and followed Marco through the dining room. When they'd disappeared, Emma took a drink of her tea. She rearranged the salt and pepper shakers, centered the small bud vase holding a carnation. Anything to take her mind off what she needed to do.

While she and Harley had been talking with Marco, Nathan had been standing next to the podium, talking to a man wearing a sport coat. She glanced at them, and when the guy shifted, a badge gleamed at his waist. A cop?

Not that she'd been keeping track of Nathan. Her eyes had simply wandered that way once or twice.

Nathan and the cop had their heads close together, as if they didn't want to be overheard. The cop said something, and Nathan leaned closer. He looked excited. She wondered what they were talking about and if it had something to do with Nathan's mysterious problem.

Then they were shaking hands and the cop walked out of the restaurant. Nathan watched him go, his expression hopeful, then turned and headed for her table. He slowed when he saw she was alone.

"Where's Harley?" He dropped into the chair next to Emma.

"She went into the kitchen with Marco." Emma forced herself to look at Nathan. He watched her, expressionless, making it impossible to know what he was thinking. "Something about tasting his food."

"Yeah?" Nathan's gaze drifted toward the doors. "Do I need to go back there and make sure all the knives are out of reach?"

Emma relaxed a little. "Probably not. It sounded as if Marco wants to do some science experiments on Harley's taste buds, and Harley just wants to see the kitchen."

"He's not a bad guy," Nathan said. "He just has some growing up to do. He's the baby of the family. I think we all spoiled him a little."

A shadow filled his eyes for such a brief moment, Emma wondered if she'd imagined it. "He was fine." She smiled cautiously. "Harley told him he was a jerk."

"Ouch." Nathan smiled back and heat fluttered low in her belly. "He must have taken it okay if he invited her into the kitchen."

"He admitted to his jerkiness." Emma swallowed, reminding herself this was a serious conversation. There couldn't be any flirting tonight.

"That's Marco. Gets angry, says something stupid, apologizes. Then he forgets all about it."

"Nice he has a family that understands him," Emma said quietly. Her mother hadn't understood anything about Emma. She'd been too busy "fulfilling" herself to pay much attention to her daughter.

"That's what families are supposed to do, right?" Nathan leaned closer. "Figure out how everyone works."

Another pang of regret swept through Emma. "If they're lucky," she murmured.

Nathan stared at her. Longing swept through Emma and she struggled to push it away. "Sounds like you weren't lucky," he finally said.

She shrugged. "No one has a perfect family."

Nathan didn't say anything. The murmur of voices, the clatter of silverware against plates, the muted clanging noises from the kitchen all faded into the background. In Nathan's gaze, Emma saw understanding.

She smiled, although her face felt as if it would crack. "I bet even you didn't grow up with perfect parents, and siblings who never fought."

For a moment, she thought he'd ignore her attempt to lighten the mood. Then he touched her hand. Slid his palm over her wrist. Emma shivered.

With one last caress, he straightened. Took his hand away. "Pretty damn close," he murmured. "Until…"

Until his parents died. "That was an insensitive thing for me to say," she murmured.

"No. You're right. We fought just like any other kids. And our parents yelled at us plenty." He stared toward the kitchen. "That first night, when Harley showed up here, I couldn't see a resemblance to anyone in our family." He switched his gaze back to Emma. "Other than her blue eyes. But I went home and looked through old photo albums. My grandmother had red, curly hair. And Harley's got my mother's palate. It's kind of surreal."

"Yeah, it is." Every once in a while, Emma saw things in herself that came from her mother. It always upset her. She didn't want to be anything like the self-absorbed, selfish woman who'd raised her.

"Our parents never die," he murmured, dragging his gaze away from the kitchen door. "Parts of them show up in us. Our children. Our grandchildren." He smiled. "I think my mom would have loved that her granddaughter got her sensitive taste buds. And my dad would have been crazy about his redheaded granddaughter who looked like his mom."

"You need to tell Harley that." Emma put her hand over Nathan's. "She's been so lost since Sonya died. I love her, but I'm not her family. Show her pictures of your parents, your grandparents, you and your siblings when you were children. Let her see that she's part of a family. That she has a history with you, more than just hair color and weird taste buds. She needs that."

To her surprise, Nathan turned his hand over and linked their fingers. His fingers were strong on hers. Warm. He rubbed his thumb over the back of her hand, and she felt the touch all through her body.

"She has more family than just me and my siblings. She has you, Emma. You *are* part of her family. You stepped up when she had no one else. You're very important to her. I don't know her at all, and I can see that."

He continued to rub her hand, and she couldn't think about

anything besides the slight callus on his finger rasping against her skin. The heat growing in her chest. The memory of the way he'd looked at her at Oscar's.

"And I know you care about her," he added. "It's obvious in everything you do."

"I'm glad you told me about your family last week at Oscar's," she said softly. "It was…amazing of you to raise your siblings. Run the restaurant. I bet it wasn't what you'd been planning on, was it?"

He smiled. "I was going to be a lawyer. Thank God I was saved from myself."

Her heart fluttered again. She had no resistance against a man who could laugh at himself. Now, if she was smart, she'd tug her hand away. Reestablish boundaries between them. Get their relationship focused back where it belonged—on Harley.

She couldn't do it. She'd had no idea that just touching a man's hand could make her want so much. Make it so difficult to concentrate. She closed her eyes and tightened her grip on Nathan, as if that would give her the courage to continue.

"You were right," she said softly. "I *am* her parent right now. I *am* the one who's supposed to make the decisions. I always thought, when I had a child, that I'd do everything perfectly. I've seen so many examples of what not to do, that I assumed I'd get it right." She swallowed. "It was hard to hear that I wasn't perfect."

Nathan leaned closer. "There's no such thing as perfect. You do the best you can. You make the best decisions you can make. And you love your kids. That's all you can do."

She held his gaze. Saw the certainty in his eyes. The understanding. "Thank you."

He squeezed her hand one more time, then let her go. "Why don't we see what's happening in the kitchen? It's been awfully quiet back there." He smiled, and butterflies lurched in her stomach. "I'm getting worried."

CHAPTER ELEVEN

NATHAN RESTED HIS hand lightly on the small of Emma's back as she headed toward the kitchen door. The movement of her muscles beneath his palm made him want to press harder. To run his fingers over her spine and slide his hand around the curve of her waist. For now, though, he'd have to be satisfied with watching the sway of her hips in her snug jeans.

He wanted to know more about Emma, and not just because she was Harley's guardian. They'd talked about families, and he wanted to know why that shadow of sadness had filled her eyes. He wanted to know what she did for fun, whether she enjoyed her job, what she liked to eat.

He wanted to know what she tasted like. How she'd feel in his arms.

He dropped his hand as they reached the kitchen. He had no business even thinking about a potential relationship while he tried to solve the mystery of his anonymous benefactor.

While he tried to connect with his daughter.

Would he still be able to go on his trip? He'd spent a long time researching, then making appointments with potential suppliers. If he canceled, months of work were down the drain.

Couldn't think about that right now.

Just like he couldn't think about moving forward with Emma. Adding a relationship between them to her role as Harley's guardian would make things complicated. Awkward.

He shoved the door open and waited for Emma to walk through ahead of him. The familiar scents of the kitchen calmed him. Centered him. Like it or not, this was his life right now. This, and the girl standing next to Marco, staring down at a plate on the counter.

His daughter.

His hand brushed Emma's, and she tensed. He wanted to do it again. To see how she'd react. Instead, he moved ahead of her. Ahead of temptation.

Focus. Marco and Harley leaned over a plate holding smears of several sauces. Harley was gesturing, Marco was scowling, and Nathan moved in to head off a confrontation.

"That's stupid," he heard Harley say. "It needs more marjoram, not oregano."

"It's pizza sauce." Marco swiped his finger across the plate, then licked it clean. "Oregano should be the dominant note in pizza sauce."

Harley rolled her eyes. "Yeah, if you want it to be like every other pizza out there." She copied Marco's swipe through the sauce, licked her finger exactly as he had done, then snorted. "Why don't you just use a sauce from a can? There are a million of them in the grocery store. They even say 'pizza sauce' on the label so you don't make a mistake."

Nathan stopped. Marco and Harley hadn't even noticed him. He glanced at Emma and saw her biting her lip.

She motioned him back. When they were several feet away from Marco and Harley, who were still fighting over the sauce, Emma grabbed his hand.

"Leave them alone," she said, her eyes laughing. "She does the same thing to me when I cook. It's unnerving, but Marco will get used to it." A gentle laugh escaped. "I mostly let her do the cooking now. We're both happier."

"It's kind of scary, actually," Nathan said, watching them move on to a white sauce. "It's like seeing my parents all over again."

Emma watched Harley and Marco. Nathan watched Emma. She smiled proudly as Harley began to critique Marco's sauce, then turned to him. "She's pretty amazing."

"Yeah. She is." He hadn't taken his eyes off Emma.

He linked his fingers with hers and she went still. Her smile faded and her mouth softened as she tugged her hand away. "I was talking about Harley."

"Yeah, I know." He shoved his hands into his pockets to keep from touching Emma again and forced himself to look at Harley. Her head was close to Marco's, and they appeared to be negotiating. Finally Harley smiled, held out her fist, and Marco bumped it with his own.

Harley looked at him and grinned. "We're gonna do a taste test. Jerk-face and I are both going to make pizza sauce, then we'll let the customers choose."

"Listen, brat, that's Uncle Jerk-face to you." Marco crossed his arms and smirked at Harley. "And I hope you know I'm going to kick your ass."

"Yeah?" Harley narrowed her eyes. "We'll see about that."

"Uh, Marco? Language?" Nathan said. That's what a father was supposed to say. Right?

Harley rolled her eyes. "Like I don't hear worse at school every day."

And she'd hear worse in his kitchen if she spent much time here. Which apparently she was planning on doing.

"Sorry, kid," Marco said. "Gotta watch my mouth." He grinned at Harley, and she grinned back.

Who would have guessed that his prickly brother and his smart-mouthed daughter would form such an instant bond? Especially after what had happened the first time they met. It was good, Nathan told himself. The two of them could talk cooking until the cows came home. But it hurt a little. That should be *him* she was talking to. Joking with. Bumping fists with.

Emma tugged on his arm and drew him back a few steps, until they stood next to the pizza counter. "Uncles and aunts can be the fun ones," she said quietly. "They don't have to make the tough decisions. They don't have to say 'no.' Think of Marco as her gateway to the family."

"More social worker talk, Emma?"

She hugged his arm close for a moment, before letting him go. "Yes, it is. Doesn't mean it's not the truth, though."

"Look at them." He shoved his hands into his pockets. "Less than half an hour and they're buddies? *Uncle Jerk-face?* What the hell is that?"

She took his hand from his pocket and linked it with hers— he held on tightly. "They share a passion," she said quietly. "Harley loves cooking. She doesn't watch TV dramas or sit-coms—she watches cooking shows. And she hasn't had anyone but me to talk to about it. I can manage to put a meal on the table, but I'm not in her league. Not even close. Marco is probably the first person she's ever met who loves cooking as much as she does. Of course they bonded. Of course she's loving it."

"So quit being jealous? Is that what you're saying?"

She smiled then. "No, you can be jealous. Just let it be a positive thing. Make an effort to find something *you* have in common with Harley. You both enjoy baseball."

Now Nathan wanted to roll *his* eyes. "Cubs and Sox. Remember? That's like saying cats and dogs can get along just fine, if everyone respects their differences. In real life? They want to tear each other apart."

"Okay, maybe that wasn't the best choice. Although it was an interesting conversation." She smiled, clearly remembering it.

"Not funny, Emma."

"I thought it was hilarious."

"Yeah, well, she's not your kid. You don't have to find a way to connect with her."

Emma's smile disappeared. She disengaged their hands. "You're right. She's not mine. And on that note, we need to get going. Harley has school tomorrow." She rubbed her hands down her thighs and stepped toward Harley.

He caught her elbow. "You know what I meant," Nathan said

wearily, watching Harley laughing with Marco. "You already have a relationship with her. I don't even know where to begin."

Her shoulders relaxed. "Yeah, I know. The reminder just stung a little. But you're good with kids, Nathan. You'll figure it out." She switched her gaze to Harley. "She's a great kid. You'll adore her once you get to know her."

She tugged her arm away and walked over to Harley and Marco. Harley scowled as Emma said something. Then she turned and spoke to Marco. They both grinned.

Emma steered Harley toward the kitchen door, and Nathan fell into step alongside them. "I'm glad you came in tonight," he said.

"I am, too." She nudged Harley. "Aren't you glad we did?" she asked the girl.

"Yeah. It was awesome to see the kitchen and taste the sauces with Marco. He's cool." She glanced at Nathan. "You are, too," she added hurriedly.

Emma bit her lip again. "No higher praise from a teen," she murmured.

"Yeah, if she meant it," he said under his breath.

Laughing, Emma led Harley out the door. Nathan watched until the outer door closed behind them.

He turned back to Marco. "Danny Kopecki stopped by earlier. He's been asking at some other restaurants in the neighborhood, and Fullerton has been getting money from them, too."

Marco picked up the plates he and Harley had been using and stacked them close to the dishwasher. "Freakin' weird, bro. Who would pay bribes for us?"

"I have no idea. But I'm guessing it's connected to whoever gave the alderman the money for our remodel. It's like we have some kind of twisted guardian angel out there. Committing crimes in order to help us. And why did the bribes stop?"

Marco glanced at him. "I don't like this, Nate."

"Neither do I. The fact that the bribes have stopped feels a little threatening."

"We've gotta figure this out, now that you have a kid hanging around. You don't want her to get mixed up in this." Marco smiled. "For a brat, she's pretty cool."

Nathan remembered his daughter smiling at his brother and a tiny worm of jealousy slithered through him. Marco and Harley had connected so effortlessly, even after a bad start. Whereas *he* still felt awkward and uncomfortable with her.

Harley clearly felt the same way.

He went back to the dining room and greeted a couple who'd walked in. Where was he going to find the time to develop a relationship with his daughter? He worked almost every night. She was in school during the day. And his spare time was devoted to running down leads on his mystery benefactor.

And his trip. Was he supposed to forget about that? Forget all the work he'd done already? Postpone the rest of his life?

Whatever he did, he was going to have to make time for Harley. On his list of responsibilities, his daughter had jumped to the front of the line.

Whether he wanted her there or not.

THE DAY AFTER GOING to Mama's Place, Harley slouched in her chair in math class and scribbled notes in her notebook. While listening with one ear to D-bag Dempster talk about stupid equations, she'd gotten some ideas for her pizza sauce contest with Marco. She needed to write them down before she forgot.

She glanced at the equations D-bag wrote on the board, understood them and went back to her recipe. Math was easy for her. She got it. Some of the other kids didn't, which meant D-bag Dempster had to go really slowly sometimes.

"Ms. Michaels." D-bag's voice.

She straightened in her chair, slammed her notebook closed and tried to look as though she was paying attention.

"Would you like to come to the front of the room and solve this equation?" the teacher said with a smirk. Like he thought she was going to screw up. Not know how to do it.

She slid out of her seat and studied his scribbles as she walked to the board. By the time she got there, she saw what she had to do. She finished it quickly and turned to go back to her seat. And her pizza sauce ideas.

Dempster stepped in front of her. His face was red and his eyes were mean. "What were you writing in your notebook, Ms. Michaels?"

"I was taking notes," she said. "Like we're supposed to do."

His mouth got tighter. "Maybe you could show me your notes."

"Sure." *Ass*. D-bag liked it when the kids in his classes were scared of him. Harley wasn't scared. Not much, anyway. She'd learned there were a lot worse things than a stupid teacher yelling at her.

She held his gaze just long enough for his eyes to get small and piggy, then retrieved her notebook. She showed him the page of notes from the day before. He wouldn't be able to tell the difference.

He studied the page, then flipped to the next one. Her sauce recipes. Harley's chest tightened.

"This doesn't look like math." He looked pleased. Like he'd caught her.

She shrugged. "Something I was working on last night." Which was true. She was talking to Marco about the sauces last night.

He set the notebook on his desk and glanced at the clock. "It's almost time for the bell. Ms. Michaels, I'd like you to stay after class, please."

Whispers began behind her, and Harley's face heated. She walked to her desk and slid into her seat, staring straight ahead.

The bell clanged, and everyone hurried to their next class. Harley stayed in her seat, refusing to meet anyone's eyes. A lot of them would feel sorry for her. She was sick of seeing that look in the kids' eyes, sick of being the freak whose mom had died.

Some of the kids would be glad D-bag was picking on her, because it meant he wasn't picking on them. She didn't mind that so much. Only an asshat like D-bag would pick on a kid who didn't understand a problem. Or an equation.

When the room was empty, the teacher walked down the aisle to her chair. "I'm going to have to write a note for you to take home, Ms. Michaels."

"How come? I got the problem right."

"You were doing homework from another class instead of paying attention to our lesson."

"That wasn't homework," she said scornfully. "That was my own stuff."

"What do you mean, your own stuff?"

"It was a recipe."

"You were copying a recipe?"

"No." He was a complete tool. "I was making one up. That's kind of like math—figuring out the amounts of stuff to use. The right proportions. You should probably give me extra credit."

Dempster's mouth tightened. "You know the rules about respect in my classroom, Ms. Michaels."

Why should she respect this pompous old gasbag? He didn't respect any of the kids. "Instead of writing a note, you should be glad I'm doing math stuff on my own. Taking initiative." A lot of the teachers were very big on initiative.

Mr. Dempster's mouth tightened even more. Uh-oh. It didn't look like D-bag was one of them.

"Have a seat while I write a note to your guardian." He stalked back to his desk, scribbled something on a piece of paper, sealed it into an envelope and handed it to her.

Harley stared down at the envelope. Some teachers did this—wrote a note to your parents, telling them what you'd done. They made you sign it and your parents, too.

She couldn't show this note to Emma. Emma would be mad. She might want to send Harley to live with Nathan.

Harley shoved the note into her backpack and ran out the door. She'd fake Emma's signature. D-bag wouldn't know. Piece of cake.

HARLEY PUSHED A piece of broccoli from one side of her plate to the other. Then she slid it beneath the piece of chicken sitting in a pool of sauce. She wasn't very hungry.

"Harley, what's wrong?" Emma set her fork down and leaned closer. "You've barely said two words since I picked you up. Did something happen at school today? At FreeZone?"

Harley moved her plate away, thinking furiously. She could fake the signature. Emma would never have to know.

D-bag might be able to tell.

Emma came around the table and crouched on the floor beside her. Put her arm around Harley's shoulders. "Tell me what's wrong," she whispered.

To Harley's horror, she burst into tears. Emma scooped her close and rocked her as Harley sobbed, leaving big goobers of snot on Emma's shirt. "I got a note today," she mumbled into Emma's chest.

"Yeah? A note about what?" Emma petted Harley like she was a dog or something, over and over.

More tears leaked out. "I was doing a recipe for pizza sauce," she hiccuped. "In math. Stupid Mr. Dempster said I was doing homework from another class. I told him I wasn't, but he still gave me a note to bring home." She bit her lip to keep it from trembling. "He said I wasn't respectful. So you have to sign the note before I take it back." Her breath hitched. "And he kept my recipe!"

"Can we look at the note?" Emma kept stroking. It felt good. Harley's shoulders didn't ache anymore.

"It's in my backpack." She hiccuped again, but she felt better. Maybe Emma wouldn't be mad, after all.

"You want to get it? Or should I?"

Harley leaned into Emma for another moment, then pushed

away from the table. A minute later, she handed over the slightly crumpled envelope. Her foot tapped on the floor as she watched Emma open it and read the note.

Emma's forehead got all scrunched, the way it did when she was angry. Harley's stomach twisted and she slouched in her chair. Her foot tapped faster.

Finally Emma looked at Harley. She smoothed her hair back, and her fingers were cool on Harley's hot face. She didn't look angry anymore. "Let's sign this and put it back in the envelope."

Emma reached for a pen on the counter, scribbled her name, then turned the paper around so Harley could sign it. She put it in the envelope and stared at it for a long time.

"I'm going to stop at the school tomorrow to talk to Mr. Dempster," she said. Her voice was all quiet. The scary voice she used when she was angry with Harley.

"I'm s-sorry, Emma," Harley said, trying not to cry again.

Emma dropped the envelope on the table and grabbed her. Hugged her hard. "Harley, I'm not upset with you. I just need to have a word with Mr. Dempster."

If Emma talked to D-bag, he'd tell her all the snotty things Harley had said. "He's stupid. It won't do any good."

"Have you had to bring home a note before?" Emma asked.

"No." What did Emma think she was, one of the losers? "The stupid boys are usually the ones who have to take notes home."

Emma rubbed her back one last time and stood up. Smiled. "Sometimes boys can be a pain, can't they?"

That was it? Emma wasn't going to yell at her for getting a note? The knot in her stomach loosened. She stared down at the chicken that Emma had made for dinner. It was pretty lame, but she'd eat it anyway. She didn't want to make Emma feel bad.

CHAPTER TWELVE

EMMA PAUSED AT the door to Harley's school and turned to Nathan. "I'm nervous. Are you?"

"A little." The leather jacket he wore over his work pants and dress shirt was broken in. A little battered. It would be soft beneath her hand. Smooth.

She curled her fingers into her palm. The scent of leather and his woodsy aftershave drifted over her as he reached for the door. "I've talked to plenty of teachers. About stuff a lot worse than getting a note sent home. But he made Harley cry. I want to punch the asshole."

Emma gave in, put her hand on his arm and pressed her fingers into the soft leather. "Don't take this the wrong way, but maybe it would be better if we didn't tell this teacher you're Harley's father."

There was a flash of hurt in his eyes. "Whatever you think is best."

"I don't mean it that way." She shook his arm. "We don't know anything about this guy, but from what Harley told me, he sounds like a real jerk. What if he says something to Harley in class about her father and kids start asking her questions? That would be hard to deal with."

The hurt faded. "Has she told any of her friends?"

"I have no idea. But she shouldn't be forced to share something so personal until she's ready."

"You're right." He put his warm hand over her cold one. "I wouldn't have thought of that. I would have puffed out my chest and asked why the hell he was picking on my angelic child."

Emma laughed. "I want to do the same thing. But I'll put on my social worker hat and be calm and professional."

"That's too bad," he said, his hand tightening on hers. "I'd give a lot to see you do the chest-puffing-out thing."

His gaze dropped for a moment, then returned to hers. She shivered as images flashed in her mind. She and Nathan, twined together. Kissing. Spreading her hands over that muscular chest of his.

"Um, no," she managed to say. "No chest puffing today for either one of us."

"Damn shame," he said as he pulled the door open.

Stale air rushed out, along with the universal school smell—old books, old lunches, old gym socks. "Second floor," she said. "Room 204." She glanced at him, her face hot. "I emailed him and he's expecting us. Well, me, anyway." She'd called Nathan earlier and told him about the note—she needed to connect him with Harley somehow. When he'd shared stories from his own teacher conferences, she'd impulsively asked him to come along.

"Let's go talk to him." He smiled at her, and she swallowed. "And thank you for calling me. For letting me come with you."

"I hoped you'd want to."

"I should be here, right?" he murmured. He reached for her hand, and she let him join his fingers with hers. It made her feel as if they were a team. Her traitorous body wanted to be a team in other ways, as well.

A few minutes later, Nathan let her go as they walked into a room that smelled of chalk dust. The window blinds were closed, as if trying to discourage daydreaming. A short man with neatly combed hair and a small mustache stood up from behind the desk. "You must be Ms. Sloan." He glanced at Nathan and raised his eyebrows. "And you are…?"

"Nathan Devereux," Nathan said, reaching over to shake the man's hand. "You must be Mr. Dempster."

The teacher studied Nathan, his expression assessing and a

little smug. Unease slid through Emma. It almost looked as if the teacher knew Nathan was Harley's father. How could he?

Dempster glanced from her to Nathan. He smiled. He *did* know. And that was odd. "Yes. Well. Have a seat." Dempster waved toward the student desks and perched on the edge of his own desk. Middle-aged, he was…soft, Emma decided. And a little sloppy. His dress shirt strained over his gut, showing little white ovals of undershirt, and his shoes were scuffed.

Emma glanced at the desks. If they sat down, Dempster would loom over them. Emphasizing his authority. She smiled at him and perched on the edge of one of the students' desks so they were eye to eye.

"You had a problem with Harley yesterday," she said calmly. "I'm sure you know about her mother's recent death. Mr. Devereux and I are watching closely for signs of problems. And since this is the first time Harley has had discipline issues, we wanted to ask if you've noticed other things in your class. Is she unruly? Does she cause trouble? Is she paying attention? Are her grades dropping?"

Dempster stood up and pulled a notebook out of a drawer. "This is her math notebook. She was writing in it during class, but not about math."

"May I see what she was doing?" Emma asked, holding out her hand.

Dempster hesitated a second too long, then passed her the blue notebook. A power play. Trying to show them he was in charge. Emma held his gaze for a moment, then thumbed through pages of Harley's still-childish handwriting, sprinkled with numerous math equations. The margins of the pages were filled with doodling.

The most recent page held a recipe for a tomato sauce, just as Harley had said. There were several versions of it, each with different amounts of various ingredients. Emma stared at it, fiercely proud of Harley. She doubted there were many thirteen-year-olds making up recipes.

She handed the book to Nathan, who studied the page. Then he narrowed his gaze at the math teacher. "*This* is why you sent a note home?"

"She wasn't paying attention. She was doing homework for another class. That's against the rules, and she knows it." The teacher's tone was defensive, his mouth a thin, hard line.

"Did you ask her which class it was homework for?" Nathan pressed.

Dempster waved his hand. "She gave me some story about it being a recipe she was making up, but kids will say anything when they're caught."

Nathan leaned forward, his eyes narrowed. "Did you even look at it?"

"It wasn't math, Mr. Devereux. That was all I cared about."

Nathan closed the notebook. "How is Harley doing in your class?"

The teacher's mouth tightened even more. "She's doing very well."

"By very well you mean...?"

Dempster cleared his throat. "She's getting an A."

"A low A?" Emma asked. "A solid one? Off the charts high?"

Dempster slid off the desk and walked stiffly to the other side of his desk, and Nathan gave her an almost imperceptible nod. *Your turn to play bad cop,* his gaze said.

The teacher opened the laptop sitting on his desk and punched a couple of keys. He stared at the screen, but Emma saw his hands tremble.

Knowing he was having a conference with Harley's guardian, he would have already checked her grades. He was just giving himself time to think.

Dempster cleared his throat. "Her average is ninety-eight percent."

"She's a good math student," Nathan said without looking at Emma.

"Not just good," Emma said. "I'd say that falls into 'off the chart' territory."

Dempster's flush darkened. "It's a very high average."

"How did you check to see if she was paying attention yesterday?" Nathan asked.

Emma could feel Nathan's impatience, his rising temper. But his voice was steady. Polite, as he asked all the right questions while maintaining his composure. Thank goodness he was here. Emma would have already lost it with this idiot.

"I asked her to do a problem on the board," Dempster said impatiently. "She did it just fine. But I couldn't let her get away with working on other material in class, in front of the other kids." He lifted his chin. "And she was disrespectful to me, on top of it."

"Really?" Emma crossed her arms. "Harley isn't a perfect kid, but she's not disrespectful." Dempster flushed again. "What did she say to you?"

"She said I should give her extra credit because it involved math."

Nathan flipped open the notebook. Took his time studying it. Dust motes danced in the harsh glare of the fluorescent lights as Dempster fidgeted on the other side of the desk.

"She was right," Nathan finally said. He stepped to the teacher's side and showed him the recipe. "She was making up a recipe, just as she told you. See how she's changing the amounts of ingredients? Adjusting them as she went? That looks like math to me. Doesn't it look like math to you?"

"It wasn't the math I was teaching," Dempster said in a curt voice.

"She shouldn't have been working on her recipe in class," Emma said. "Harley knows that was wrong. But if she was able to put together her recipe while she was following what was happening in your class, perhaps she needs a more challenging class," Emma said, standing up. Dempster looked from her to Nathan.

"I agree." Nathan watched the teacher steadily. "Don't you think that a student who's getting an almost perfect grade and doing math projects on her own should be in a higher level class?"

"The advanced class is for freshmen. Harley's not ready for it."

Nathan glanced at Emma, and she nodded. She could read his mind perfectly. "Thanks for your opinion, but we'll discuss that with the principal," she said, keeping her voice pleasant.

Nathan switched his gaze back to the teacher. "Thank you for your time, Mr. Dempster. Ms. Sloan and I appreciate it."

Emma pulled the envelope out of her purse and set it on the desk, in front of the teacher. "Here's the signed note," she said.

"We'll check in with you from time to time," Nathan said. "To make sure there aren't any further problems."

Thank you, Nathan. He'd just put the teacher on notice.

"It's always helpful when…parents and guardians take an interest in our students," he said. "I'll look forward to speaking with you again."

Emma stood up. "I doubt that will be necessary. Since we've discussed Harley's situation, I'm sure we've solved the problem." She and Nathan would be speaking to the principal about that advanced math class before they left today. "Thank you, Mr. Dempster."

Dempster nodded and focused his attention on his computer. Nathan narrowed his gaze at the teacher, but Emma hooked her arm through his and tugged him out the door. Neither of them spoke until they were in the stairwell.

"I wanted to kick that guy's ass," Nathan growled.

"Yes, I know you did." She let go of his arm. "I did, too, and it would have been really satisfying. But if we can't get Harley into that advanced math class, she'll have to deal with that idiot for the rest of the year."

A muscle twitched in Nathan's jaw. "We're going to talk to

the principal right now. I don't want Harley in that class even one more day."

"Nathan. Wait." At the landing, she stepped in front of him. The stairwell was colder than the classrooms, and she shivered. "You were great in there. You were calm and you got your points across. But you have to do that with the principal, too. I'm sure she knows Dempster isn't a good teacher—we can't be the first to complain about him. We'll tell her that Harley isn't being challenged and needs higher level math. She'll get it."

A muscle twitched in Nathan's jaw, but as he stared at her, his eyes softened. "You're right. Thank goodness for your cool head."

She was unable to tear her gaze away from him. "And your steadiness."

"We'll be just as good with the principal," Nathan said, edging closer. "You'll charm her and I'll be the logical one. The woman won't know what hit her."

"I think you're the one who'll charm her," Emma said softly. The evening they'd met, his smile had made her toes curl. "Just like you charmed me."

His eyes darkened as he stared back at her. "When was that, Emma? I haven't exactly been Mr. Suave lately."

In the quiet of the stairwell, his low voice echoed off the walls and felt like a caress. "The night we met," she said. "Before Harley came to live with me."

"What would have happened, Emma?" She didn't see him move, but somehow he was closer to her. "If Sonya hadn't died? If Harley hadn't come to live with you?"

The weak winter sun streaming in through the windows turned his eyes to silvery-blue pools, deep and mysterious. "I think…" She took a deep breath, trying to draw air into her suddenly tight chest. "I would have called you," she whispered. She wanted to lean closer. To test the fragile connection they'd woven between them.

"Only if I didn't call you first," he murmured. His hand

cupped her cheek. He was so close she saw the tiny gold flecks in the blue of his eyes.

He leaned closer and brushed his lips over hers before drawing back a little. Her eyes had fluttered closed, and she opened them to see him hesitating, as if waiting for a signal.

She closed her fists in the leather of his jacket and pulled him in. It was as if a dam broke. He took her face in his hands and pressed his mouth to hers.

He slid his lips over hers slowly, as if memorizing her taste. Emma swayed closer. Let go of his jacket and wrapped her arms around him. His chest was hard against hers as he kissed her more deeply. Nibbled on her lower lip, drawing it between his teeth.

A tiny moan echoed in the silence of the stairwell. Hers? His? She wasn't sure. She slid her hands up his jacket and threaded her fingers into his hair. Opened her mouth to him.

He tasted of coffee and peppermint. Heat rose between them, and she moved against him. She wanted to rip off his jacket. She wanted to run her hands over his skin.

A door above them banged open, and they sprang apart. Panting, they stared at each other. Nathan touched her lips with his fingertips. Then let his hand drop.

Unable to look away, Emma fumbled for the railing behind her. His face was all hard planes and angles, and his eyes were dark. Aroused. She knew she looked the same way.

Footsteps descended above them. Nathan grabbed her hand and led her down the stairs. They waited at the next landing, and the doors above them opened.

He didn't let her go. His thumb caressed small circles on the back of her hand. Each brush of his skin against hers made her want to take up where they'd left off.

"Bad timing," he finally said.

"The worst." She swallowed. Tried to compose herself.

He lifted his other hand, stroked her cheek. "To be continued?"

"Yes," she whispered instinctively. Closed her eyes. "No. This would be a huge complication."

"You're right," he said. "It would. But…"

"Yeah." She swallowed. He'd barely kissed her, and her body was humming with desire. Begging for far more than a kiss. "But."

She tugged her hand away from his and immediately wanted to give it back. But they needed to lighten this up. "Harley would be horrified to know her…that you and I were kissing on the stairs at her school."

He stepped away. "The ultimate in teenage embarrassment."

His smile made her sway toward him again. She gripped the railing, curling her fingers tightly around the worn varnished wood. "We should go find the principal."

"Yes, we should." His mouth curled into a grin. "Before *we* get a note sent home for inappropriate behavior."

He stepped beside her and put his hand on her back. Even through her winter coat, she felt the heat of his hand. The press of his fingers into her spine.

"No," she managed to say. "No more notes."

Arousal still quivered in the air between them, making her legs weak. Trying to distract herself, she said, "We were a good tag team with Dempster. Let's go in and continue our teamwork with the principal." Her voice echoed in the open space, bouncing off the cold, pea-green walls. "Before she leaves for the day."

"Right." When they reached the bottom of the stairs, he pushed the door open for her and his hand fell away from her back.

"Mrs. Simon's office is at the other end of the hall," Emma said, knowing if she looked at him, she would see the same desire in his eyes that coursed through her body.

"You've been here before," Nathan said quietly.

"Yeah. I have." The memories of that first week after Sonya died were painful. Harley's grief had broken her heart.

"Thank you," Nathan said, shoving his hands into his pockets. "For taking care of Harley so well."

"I love her."

He glanced at her, then stared straight ahead. "Yeah, I know you do."

As they reached the hall that held the administrative offices, a man with a fringe of close-cropped white hair stepped into the hall and headed their way. He smoothed one hand down his overcoat, and Nathan stopped abruptly. Stared at him. "Mr. Kopecki," he said.

The older man froze. He dropped his hand to his side. "Nathan. What on earth are you doing here?"

Nathan hesitated. "This is Emma Sloan," he finally said. "She's the guardian for the daughter of a friend of hers, and she needed to talk to one of Harley's teachers. I tagged along. Emma, this is Mitch Kopecki. He's a big deal in the state's attorney's office. His son Danny went to school with Patrick."

"Nice to meet you." Emma shook his hand.

Kopecki smiled. "Nathan exaggerates. I'm a very small cog in the wheels of justice. But he was right about one thing—I've known his family forever." Kopecki glanced at Nathan's leg. "Didn't see you walking the other night. Looks like you're recovering well from your accident."

"I'm coming along. Still have some rehab to do."

Tilting his head, Kopecki asked, "Are you sure you don't want to prosecute Bridie Sullivan? She shouldn't have been driving when she hit you that night."

"I'm good," Nathan said. "And I'm impressed that you know her name."

"Danny told me about the accident," Kopecki said easily. "Cops like those kinds of cases—the ones where all's well that ends well. Don't see that too often."

"I guess not. Is there a problem at the school?" Nathan asked politely.

"Nah. Just had to drop something off. About a case," Kopecki clarified. He held out his hand and Nathan shook it. "Good to see you, Nate. And nice to meet you, Ms. Sloan."

The older man tugged at his collar and loosened his tie as he walked out the door. "He's got a good memory," Nathan finally murmured. He glanced at Emma. "He used to be a cop—I guess that's where he picked up the knack."

"For someone he hasn't seen in a while, he seems to know a lot about you," Emma said.

"Neighborhood guy. He was at Mama's not too long ago. And everyone from Wildwood remembers my parents. Remembers how they died."

"I guess they would," Emma said quietly. She gestured toward the door to the office complex. "Let's go talk to Mrs. Simon. I know you have to get back to the restaurant."

"I, ah…yeah. Actually, our new manager started this week, so I don't technically need to be there. But I want to check in and see how she's doing."

Fifteen minutes later, they were back in the corridor. "That was easy," Emma said. "Mrs. Simon didn't seem to have any reservations about putting Harley in the advanced math class. I wonder why Dempster did."

"The guy has a big ego," Nathan said, opening the door for her. Emma wrapped her coat around herself against the rush of cold air. "Bastard didn't want to admit Harley was too smart for his class."

"I hope Harley's okay with the move," she said as she hurried toward her car. The wind was blowing off the lake, bringing the taste of snow.

"Why wouldn't she be?" He tucked Emma's scarf more tightly around her throat, then let his hand linger on her shoulder. "I'm guessing she'll be glad to get away from Dempster. She's probably bored as hell in his class."

"Were you good in math?" she asked.

His hand fell away. "Yeah. I always liked it."

"Harley gets that from you. Sonya hated anything that involved numbers."

He shoved his hands into his pockets. "That still freaks me out—seeing parts of myself in a kid."

"Really? I think it would be pretty cool. A little bit of immortality."

Nathan rolled his shoulders. "Assuming you're used to the idea of having a kid."

"And you're not?"

"Come on, Emma. I've known about her for how long? A couple of weeks? Of course I'm not used to the idea."

"Plus you have other things in your life," she murmured.

"Yes. I do. My spare time is consumed by the investigation we're involved in."

"You need to tell me about that. Soon. In fact, why don't we do it now? I still have a little time before I pick Harley up." Emma knew her voice had cooled. But she wasn't going to take a chance with Harley. "I need to know what to watch for."

"Not tonight. I have to get back to the restaurant."

"You said you have a manager starting tonight."

"Who shouldn't be alone her first night on the job."

"Harley's important, too."

They stared at one another, and all the warmth from their kiss on the stairwell was gone. Now Nathan looked uncomfortable. Tense. As if it had finally struck him—this was real. He was a parent, with responsibilities to his child. And he wasn't ready to be.

"It looks like it's going to snow," he finally said. "You'd better get going, in case traffic gets bad."

"Right. Have a good evening, Nathan."

She slid into the car, started the engine and pulled away. As she glanced in her rearview mirror, Nathan stood alone in the middle of the almost-empty parking lot, watching her leave.

Everyone had fears about being a parent. She guessed no

one embraced it unreservedly, especially at first. She'd been terrified about being responsible for Harley.

Nathan had been alone for a long time. Ever since his parents died. He'd already raised three siblings. Did he not want to be a parent again? Was that why he was holding back?

She eased her foot off the accelerator. She should turn the car around and invite him to dinner with her and Harley. Maybe he just needed more time to be comfortable with the idea of being a father.

That could only happen if he got to know Harley.

She pressed the accelerator down. The more time he spent with Harley, the more likely he was to bond with her. To want his daughter with him.

The more likely Emma would have to give Harley up.

But Emma wanted to spend time with Nathan, too.

Before she could make up her mind what to do, she saw Nathan get into his own vehicle. She hesitated for a moment, then kept going. She and Nathan were all about missed possibilities.

She owed it to Harley to try to foster a connection between child and father. So she'd call Nathan soon. Try to figure out an activity they could all enjoy together.

The first few snowflakes hit her windshield, melted and disappeared. Just like those fleeting moments inside the school when she'd thought everything would work out so easily.

Just like those moments that had her thinking of happily every after.

CHAPTER THIRTEEN

NATHAN SLAMMED ON the brakes as the light turned yellow, then smacked his palm on the steering wheel. He should have asked Emma and Harley to have dinner with him. He should have gotten them all away from the distractions at Mama's. Away from the emotional land mines that lurked in every memory-soaked corner of the restaurant. He needed to know Harley better—it was his responsibility to take the initiative on that.

And Emma? He *wanted* to know her better.

The truth was, he'd freaked out. Emma had referred to him as Harley's father so easily. So naturally. As if he was supposed to feel all parental toward Harley already.

In reality, the kid was a stranger to him. It wasn't admirable, and it wasn't right, but with everything else going on, he hadn't been in a hurry to change that.

Instead of stepping up to the plate, he'd ignored the reality of having a daughter. That made him feel like a slimeball. *Dad Jerk-face.*

That kiss he'd shared with Emma had freaked him out, too, once he'd gotten his libido under control. The strings binding them together had gotten stronger this afternoon. But those strings were entwined with Harley. He couldn't ignore the fact that Emma was his daughter's guardian. Even though he wanted to.

Emma was a beautiful woman. The chemistry between them had been smoking hot from the minute they'd laid eyes on each other.

But now Harley stood between them. And going to a parent-teacher conference together wasn't the connection with Emma he was looking for. It was like being Mom and Dad. Hell, he wasn't sure he was ready to be a father. Let alone one of a set of parents.

After their kiss in that dreary stairwell, he'd wanted more. In that brief moment of barely kissing her, he'd been ready to drag her somewhere private and make love with her for hours. And based on the way she'd looked at him, she felt the same way.

But…

He and Emma were far more complicated than that. And he wasn't sure if he was ready to go there.

Finally, after battling stop-and-go traffic, with the snow flurries skidding across the street in front of him, he pulled into Mama's parking lot, which was almost empty. With the forecast calling for a few inches of snow, people were staying home.

So what was he doing here? Phoebe didn't need his help. He should have gone to dinner with Emma and Harley.

He was here now, though, so he might as well go in.

The kitchen was as loud as usual, and the familiar scents of tomato sauce and roasting meat filled the air. The combination settled him as he closed the door.

"Hey, Nate, what are you doing here?" Marco called from his position in front of the stove. "I thought Phoebe was on tonight."

"She is. Just stopped by to, ah, get something to eat."

Marco scowled, and pointed his wooden spoon at Nathan. "You're here to check on Phoebe. The point of hiring her was to give you some time away. Of course, none of us thought you'd go easily. Paddy and Darcy are here, too. In your office." Marco smirked at him.

Nathan pushed the office door open. Patrick was sitting in his chair with Darcy on his lap.

When the door opened, they both smiled at him. Darcy slid off Patrick's lap, and Patrick shifted in the chair. "Figured we'd find you here," he said. "We've come to save you from yourself."

"What's that supposed to mean?"

"We need to talk, and we're going to check out our competition at the same time. So let's go."

"Wait." Nathan glanced from Darcy to Patrick. They looked pleased with themselves. "What? What competition?"

"That new Mexican restaurant on Central. We've been meaning to stop in, but we've been busy. But you're free, we're free and tonight's the night."

"Okay," he said slowly. "Mexican it is. But let's go out the front door so I can make sure Phoebe doesn't need anything."

Grinning, Darcy elbowed her fiancé. "You owe me ten bucks, buddy."

Nathan shrugged his coat back on. "Very funny. Let's go."

Phoebe was in the bar, talking to a customer. She looked up as he walked over.

"Hey, Nathan. What are you doing here?"

Her dressy black slacks and dark blue blouse fit her slender body perfectly. Heels and small gold rings in her ears completed the elegant look. She looked good, he admitted. Professional. Put together. "Just on our way out." He gestured to Darcy and Patrick behind him. "Everything okay so far?"

"Absolutely." Small lines formed between her eyes. "Are you checking on me?"

"Why would I do that?" he asked, but he was afraid she saw right through him. "You're doing a great job. Patrick and Darcy and I are heading to the new Mexican restaurant."

His new manager nodded. "Have fun. Don't worry about Mama's. We'll be fine."

Patrick nudged him in the back, and Nathan headed for the door.

Twenty minutes later, as they ate salsa and chips, Nathan looked around the mostly empty restaurant. Multicolored fabric art decorated the walls, and the floor was terra-cotta tiles.

The heavily varnished wood tables all held fresh flowers. It was a completely different look than Mama's. Hipper. More contemporary. It would attract a younger crowd. "It's a nice place, Paddy. I'll grant you that, but it's not our competition. So why are we here?"

"I've got some news, and I didn't think Mama's was the best place to talk about it." Patrick scooped up more salsa, dripping a blob on the table. "That thing Danny Kopecki told you about Alderman O'Fallon's kid? How he mysteriously disappeared several years ago? Well, he was right. Sean O'Fallon got busted for selling weed at his high school. Then the case disappeared, along with the kid. He was in some fancy rehab place out in the suburbs for a couple of months. I talked to the judge, and he said the deal was they'd drop the charges if he finished rehab and stayed clean. Some new A.S.A., a wet-behind-the-ears recent law school grad, set it up."

"You think someone pulled some strings." Nathan leaned toward his brother. "That whoever brokered it is the guy behind the money."

Patrick shrugged. "It's a possibility." He hesitated. "Thing is, that's a pretty common deal for first offenders. Go to rehab, stay clean, charges get dropped. So it could mean nothing."

"And we're back where we started." Nathan clenched his hand into a fist, stopped himself from punching the table. "Damn it."

"Not necessarily. This was a good tip," Patrick said. "I know a couple of people in the D.A.'s office and I'm having them ask around to find out who okayed the deal. Every bit of information helps."

"What about the health inspector?" Nathan's foot was jiggling. This investigation wasn't moving fast enough. "The one who thought I was bribing him?"

"His financial records should be on my desk tomorrow. Won't take long to see if there's a regular pattern of deposits. Then we can start following the trail."

"It was cash in his mail slot. How do you trace that?" Nathan pushed his empty beer bottle to the center of the table. "I want this over, Paddy. *Now.*"

"We're getting there." Patrick's eyes were sympathetic. "We all want this to be over."

"None of you is the one who started the whole thing. And none of you has a kid to worry about. What if this guy starts to feel cornered and tries to use Harley against me?"

"There's been nothing to suggest that this guy's dangerous or means you any harm. Why would he threaten Harley?"

"He stopped paying a bribe," Nathan said. "That's a little threatening."

Patrick leaned forward. "Maybe, but why? What changed to make the bribe stop? Our snooping?" He snorted. "If so, I have no idea what he thinks we've found. The O'Fallon kid? Possible, but so far, it leads nowhere. I don't think you need to worry about Harley."

"How would this guy find out about her, anyway?" Darcy asked. "You haven't told anyone but us. Right?" She took a drink of beer. "So how would he know?"

"Half the neighborhood probably knows," Nathan said. "Harley was pretty loud the night she showed up at Mama's."

Patrick smiled at the waitress as she delivered their food. "Can I get another beer? Darce? Nate?"

"Yeah, I guess. Thanks," Nathan said to the waitress. He shuffled his feet. Relaxing at dinner was foreign to him. Made him antsy. At Mama's, he ate in a hurry, standing up, whenever he could grab a minute.

To change the subject, he said, "Hey, Paddy, you find out anything about Shaughnessy?" The topic of the man who killed their parents was no more relaxing, but at least it was different.

"As a matter of fact, I did. He's working at a place called Urban Table. Far south side. Some kind of farming operation. The owner hires a lot of ex-cons."

Nathan pushed his plate away. "Good. More progress. Think I'll pay him a visit there, since I can't go to his halfway house."

Patrick frowned at him. "Be careful. If you scare him off, we'll never know what 'other stuff' he was talking about."

"Don't worry. I'm just going to talk to him."

THE MORNING AFTER his dinner with Patrick and Darcy, Nathan pulled up outside a beige pole barn that had several green-houses behind it. Urban Table grew herbs and sold them to local restaurants. The owner made a point of hiring ex-cons and giving them a chance at a fresh start. According to Shaugh-nessy's parole officer, he was a model employee.

Nathan got out of the car beneath a gray sky. With any luck, he could talk to Shaughnessy and get back on the main road before it started to snow again. The road to the farm was two dirt ruts that would turn into an ice rink in a storm.

When he walked into the pole barn, several men and a few women were packing small plastic containers into cartons. They all looked at him, but no one said anything. Finally a guy with long gray hair tied at the nape of his neck, wearing motorcycle boots and a Harley-Davidson T-shirt, walked over.

"Can I help you?"

Nathan held out his hand. "I'm Nathan Devereux. I'm look-ing for Peter Shaughnessy, and I was told he works here."

The man studied him. "What do you want him for?"

"I just want to talk to him for a few minutes. Ask him a couple of questions."

"I'm Bryce Crockett. The owner." He narrowed his eyes. "You're the second guy to come looking for Pete in the last couple of weeks. What's going on? I don't allow anyone to ha-rass my employees."

"I have no intention of harassing him. I saw him a few weeks ago and he told me he had something he needed to tell me. That's why I came out here."

Nathan felt as though Crockett could peer into his soul and

uncover all his secrets. But he held the guy's gaze, and finally Crockett nodded.

"I'll get him. But I'll be watching. I don't like it when people show up, looking for one of my guys."

"I understand."

A few minutes later, Shaughnessy walked through the door that must lead to the greenhouses. He stopped dead when he saw Nathan.

"He's over there," Crockett said, laying a hand on Shaughnessy's shoulder and nodding at Nathan.

"What are you doing here?" Shaughnessy's mouth was a hard line. "What do you want? I've done my time. You got no right to come here and bother me."

"You said you had something to tell me," Nathan said in a low voice. Crockett and all the people packing the boxes were watching him. "I need to know what it is."

"Stay away from me," Shaughnessy yelled, backing up. He sounded angry, but his expression was terrified. His hands shook.

"But you said…"

"I said I was sorry. I was following the steps. That don't give you the right to come to the place I work."

Nathan frowned. The guy's voice was too loud, as if he wanted all his coworkers and his boss to hear him. Crockett was hurrying toward them. "Please," Nathan said softly. "I need to know what you wanted to tell me."

"Don't come back here." Shaughnessy kept backing away. "Ever again."

Crockett stepped between them. "You need to leave, Devereux. And I don't want to see you here again."

Shaughnessy disappeared through the door to the greenhouses. Nathan pulled the exit door open and let it close with a bang behind him.

The first fat snowflake hit the windshield as Nathan slid

into his car. He stuck his Bluetooth device in his ear, dialed Patrick and started the engine.

"You talk to Shaughnessy?" Patrick asked as he answered the phone.

"Yeah. He wouldn't tell me a thing. Yelled at me to leave him alone. He put on a good show, but he was terrified."

"Of what?"

"Got no idea. But someone came to see him a couple of weeks ago. Maybe you should look into Shaughnessy a little more."

"I'll do that. Call you back when I can."

CHAPTER FOURTEEN

EMMA'S HAND SLIPPED on her phone as she waited for Nathan to answer. In spite of the cold in her car, her palms were sweaty and she wiped them on her jeans. It had only been two days since the visit to Harley's school. It was too soon to call him. When he didn't answer after a few rings, she cleared her throat to leave a message with equal parts relief and disappointment.

"Hello?" Nathan sounded frazzled, and in the background metal clanged and voices yelled. He was at the restaurant.

This was a bad idea. But he'd answered the phone. She had to say something. "Hey, Nathan, it's Emma."

"Emma." The background noises on his end faded, then she heard the click of a door. He must have gone into his office. "How's it going?"

He sounded so impersonal. So carefully polite. "Everything's fine. I thought you'd like to know that Harley loves her new math class." *Not the most original excuse to call you, but you play the hand you're dealt.* "She has a lot more homework, though. She doesn't like that part."

"No, I guess she wouldn't."

He sounded distracted. She should have realized there was a lot of work to be done before restaurants opened, and that she'd be interrupting. Her face hot, she said, "You're busy. I'll call some other time."

"No, wait." Something creaked. "I was in the middle of an argument with a deliveryman. Can you hold on a second so I can make sure he's giving us what we need?"

"Sure." She heard footsteps walking away, then Nathan's voice again, loud. A muttered reply. Then silence.

A few minutes later, Nathan came back to the phone. "Sorry. He was unloading bad mushrooms on us. I needed to make sure he switched them out." He cleared his throat. "Actually, I was going to call you. Phoebe is managing again tonight, and I was wondering if you and Harley wanted to go out to eat together. Someplace besides Mama's. Or…or do something else. Spend some time together."

"Harley has a makeup soccer game tonight," she said, more disappointed than she should be. "In fact, I have to pick her up early from FreeZone." She hesitated. "You could come, if you'd like. If you wanted to see her play."

"Where is it?"

She gave him the location of the dome and told him what time the game started. "This is a no-pressure deal. All you have to do is watch. Maybe get ice cream or something afterward."

"Okay, meet you there."

He didn't sound very excited. But at least he was willing to try. "Good. I'll see you then."

"Ah, Emma, you called me. Was there something you wanted?"

"Oh, right." She swallowed. The sound of his voice, which triggered memories of that kiss at the school, turned her brain to mush. "I called because Harley wants to learn how to ski. Since we got fresh snow, I thought I'd take her to a ski hill this Saturday. Want to come along?"

His pause stretched out uncomfortably long. "I can't ski."

"That's okay. Neither can Harley, but the ski hill gives lessons."

An even longer pause. "That's not what I mean, Emma." His voice was tight and hard. "I mean I *can't* ski. My leg isn't strong enough or healed enough to put that kind of stress on it."

"Oh, God." She'd forgotten about his injury. Probably because he didn't make a big deal out of it, or ever talk about it.

And because all she'd been able to think about was that kiss two days ago. "I'm sorry, Nathan. I didn't think." She hesitated. Was she digging herself a deeper hole? "I mean, yeah, I knew you were hurt. You limp a little, but I don't notice it anymore. I don't think about your cane. You know?"

"No, I don't." His voice was expressionless. She had no idea what he was thinking. This wasn't the kind of conversation to have over the phone.

"I mean that when I look at you, I don't see a guy who's been injured. I don't see the cane or the limp. I just see you. A guy who can do anything he wants."

"Well, I can't ski. Sorry."

Her breath had fogged the car windows, and she couldn't see outside. "No, *I'm* sorry. That was…insensitive of me. And it sounds as though you're busy at the restaurant. If you have time for the game, I'll see you there. If not, I get it. We'll do something another time." She gripped the phone so tightly that her cold hand ached. "Take care, Nathan."

Her hand shook as she pushed the red end call icon, then she threw her phone on the passenger seat. Squeezed her eyes shut against the tears that wanted to fall. Had Nathan thought she was mocking him?

Thinking about Nathan, about that kiss on the stairway, made her stupid. All she'd focused on was seeing him again. Spending a day with him and Harley. *God.* He must think she was an idiot.

She'd embarrassed herself. He hadn't been very excited about seeing her again.

Let alone Harley.

Emma should have figured that out at the school on Tuesday. Nathan had been great in the conference with Dempster, and he'd been great with the principal.

But when Emma had talked about Harley's relationship with Nathan, he'd shut down.

Her phone rang and she glanced at it. Nathan. She touched the icon for refuse call.

She should have paid more attention when she'd told him about Harley in the first place. He'd said he didn't want to be a parent. She should have believed him.

She shouldn't have pressed. It would have been better if Harley had never known about him at all.

If Emma hadn't left that DVD in her desk, none of this would have happened. Now Harley was going to be hurt, and it was Emma's fault.

In her hubris, Emma had thought she'd be a perfect parent. In reality, she was as far from perfect as it was possible to be.

FOUR HOURS LATER, sitting on the cold, hard metal of the bleacher seats, Emma blew into her hands to warm them. During the winter, Harley played soccer in an inflatable dome, and although there were heaters near the concession stand, the rest of the space was frigid. As the kids ran up and down the artificial turf, she wiggled her toes and tugged her gloves out of her pockets.

On the field, one of Harley's teammates passed her the ball. Harley dribbled it toward the goal. Without looking to the side, she passed it across the field, and one of her teammates shot it at the net. The goalie caught it, but Harley and the other girl high-fived each other.

Emma yelled, "Nice pass, Harley."

The girl glanced toward the bleachers, and even from a distance, Emma could see the blush. And the smile that accompanied it.

Emma leaned forward, watching Harley, as someone climbed the bleachers. Sat down beside her. The hairs at her nape lifted, and she didn't have to look to know who it was.

"Hello, Emma."

Her face flamed, and she couldn't look at him. "Nathan. I didn't expect you."

"I said I would be here."

She'd been hoping he wouldn't be. But she knew his sense of responsibility wouldn't let him skip it. "You're a man of your word."

"I try to be," he said quietly.

Yeah, he'd kept to the letter of his word. Not the spirit, though. At least not with Harley.

He'd said he was responsible for Harley. Responsibility was a cold word. It was all about basic needs—food, clothing, shelter. It had nothing to do with the emotional turmoil of a grieving child.

She focused on the girls running up and down the field. "You know anything about soccer?"

"Yeah. Marco played."

Good. She wouldn't have to explain everything to him. Wouldn't need to interact with him. "Harley's a midfielder."

Emma's hands and feet had already turned to blocks of ice before Nathan sat down. Now the ice had spread to the rest of her body.

"Emma, I'm sorry."

His voice was low enough that none of the other parents could hear, but she turned on him. "Not now, Nathan. Okay? I want to watch Harley."

Harley should have Nathan's attention, too, but experience had taught her that, where some parents were concerned, what kids needed and wanted was irrelevant.

"Fine. I can wait."

The heat from Nathan's body warmed her right side, but she slid farther away from him. She wasn't going to get sucked in by his warmth. It wouldn't last. Before long, he'd be just as cold as she was.

Over the next twenty minutes, Nathan proved that he did, indeed, know soccer. He cheered Harley's good plays, even when they were subtle. The first time, Harley had whipped her head around. Froze for a moment when she spotted him. She turned away, but not before Emma saw her tiny smile.

Harley was glad Nathan was here. Emma hoped he didn't end up breaking his daughter's heart.

The game was scoreless one minute before the end of the first half when Harley dribbled toward the goal again. A different girl took her pass, dribbled a little more, then shot the ball back to Harley. While the goalie was adjusting, Harley kicked the ball into the net.

Emma leaped to her feet with the rest of the parents, cheering loudly. Nathan stood, too, clapping. He cupped his hands around his mouth and yelled, "Way to go, Harley! Nice give-and-go."

Harley gave a double high-five to the girl who'd passed her the ball. But Nathan's words made her study him for a moment. Then the referee got both teams lined up for the kickoff.

Seconds later, the ref blew her whistle for the end of the half. The girls trotted toward the sidelines and both teams gathered around their coaches. Harley was a smart, funny kid who, in spite of her grief, was pretty self-confident. But right now she looked defenseless. Her socks were falling down her skinny legs, revealing the tops of her shin guards. Her too-large jersey swallowed her up. Her baggy red-and-white uniform shorts were rolled at the waistband.

What did Nathan see when he looked at his daughter? The mouthy kid, or the vulnerable one who needed her father?

The parents in the bleachers began to move. Most of them headed for the concession stand and the heaters mounted above it. The smokers pushed through the air-lock door to the outside.

In minutes, only three women, Nathan and Emma were left on their team's bleachers. The women huddled close, murmuring together. Glancing toward the girls clustered around the coach.

Emma felt Nathan's gaze on her. "I need to warm up. I'm going to stand by the heat lamps."

Without waiting to see if he followed, she slid off the cold bench and walked toward the concession stand. The smell of popcorn and hot oil hung in the air, along with the acrid tang of burned coffee.

Heat from the overhead lamps beat down on her as she stood in line. Nathan stood behind her, but he didn't say a word. By the time she reached the counter, her stomach was jumping. What was she supposed to say to Nathan?

"Hot chocolate, please," she said to the clerk, a high school–aged boy with long brown hair and a desperate attempt at a beard.

"Make that two," Nathan said beside her. As she fumbled in her purse for her wallet, he pushed a ten across the cracked Formica counter.

She should tell him it was her turn to pay. That he'd paid last time, at Oscar's. But she didn't want to bring up that afternoon. Stir memories of the sparks that had charged the air between them. So she merely said, "Thank you."

Nathan waited for her to take her cup, then grabbed his and put his hand on the small of her back. Her muscles tensed and he let her go. But his hand hovered, inches from her skin, and herded her toward an empty corner.

She stood staring at the girls, still gathered around the coach. It wasn't hard to spot Harley—her bright red hair was a beacon. Nathan hadn't moved his hand, and it curved around her waist for a moment before falling away.

"Emma." Nathan stepped in front of her. "Will you listen to me? Please?"

She put on her social worker mask—impassive, polite, attentive. "I'm always willing to listen."

A flicker of irritation passed over his face, but he smoothed it away. "Look, I'm sorry about the way I acted on the phone this afternoon. It's not an excuse, but I was having a bad day. I'd been arguing with the delivery guy, I couldn't get hold of

Patrick and my…" His jaw muscles clenched. "My leg hurt like a son of a bitch. I had PT this morning."

From the way he'd struggled with the admission, she suspected Nathan didn't admit to many people that his leg still hurt. And she'd invited him skiing. Remorse and embarrassment heated her face. "I shouldn't have asked you to go skiing. That was insensitive of me. I apologize."

"No. After I got my head on straight, I was glad you asked me. Glad you don't see me as the guy who can't walk very well. I realized I should be flattered." He stepped into her personal space, and she swallowed. "But I had to say 'I can't do that,' and it pissed me off. No guy likes to admit that."

"Yeah, I get it," she murmured. She finally focused on him and saw genuine remorse in his expression. "I wasn't looking at it from your perspective." The knot of embarrassment in her chest began to relax. "I had forgotten about the fragile male ego."

"It's a dangerous thing." He took a sip of his hot chocolate, then licked the fleck of whipped cream at the edge of his mouth. "Directly connected to the stupid center in the brain."

Emma wasn't as cold anymore. She edged a bit closer to Nathan. Because it was closer to the heater, she told herself. "Sitting on these metal benches can't be good for your leg. I didn't think about that, either."

"I'll survive." He took another sip of the hot chocolate. "I'll throw a blanket in the car for the next game. Sitting on that will help."

Some of the tension in her shoulders eased. "You…you want to sit in this refrigerator again?"

"Of course I do." He glanced over his shoulder to where the girls were now warming up for the second half. "She smiled when she saw me. I think she likes that I'm here."

Emma did, too. "I was going to bring a blanket, too. But I forgot tonight."

His eyes darkened. "Don't bother. You can share mine."

There were a million reasons why that was a bad idea, but she couldn't remember any of them. As she held his gaze, she found herself swaying closer to him. Close enough to feel the warm air from his breath caress her cheek. Close enough to smell the hot chocolate he'd been drinking. Close enough to see his pupils dilate.

"Hey, Emma, they're ready to kick off," one of the mothers said as she walked past. Her curious gaze lingered on Nathan.

Emma backed away from him. "Ah, thanks, Judy. This…this is Nathan. Judy's daughter is the goalie," she explained to him.

"She does a good job," Nathan said. "Great reflexes."

"Thanks," Judy said with a smile. "Harley's one of our stars."

"Yeah?" His gaze darted toward the girls, who were back on the field. "I had no idea."

Judy hurried toward the stands, and Nathan put his hand on Emma's back as they followed. This time, she didn't shrug it off. When they reached the bleacher, Nathan's hand curled around Emma's to help her onto the cold bench. After she had taken the big step up, there was no reason to hold on to him. But she tightened her grip before leting go.

He slid in next to her. His thigh settled against hers, warm and solid. She wanted to move closer and press herself against him.

But she needed to concentrate on Harley and the game. Harley would want to talk about it later. And if Emma was touching Nathan from shoulder to ankle, she wouldn't notice a thing on the field.

Emma let her arm rest against Nathan's for a moment. Then she shifted to create some space between them. Her first responsibility was to Harley. Right now, she wished it wasn't.

HARLEY STOOD AT the back of the girls clustered around their coach as he talked about what they'd done right in the game and what they'd done wrong. Same old, same old. Blah, blah, blah. She tried to look as if she were paying attention, but she was watching Emma and Nathan.

It still freaked her out that he was her father.

He caught her watching and waved.

A little buzz in her chest made her look away. He was an okay guy, but she was still mad at him for leaving her mom. For not taking care of her.

Emma was standing awfully close to him. Harley narrowed her gaze. Did they have something, like, going on?

Emma rubbed her hands over her arms. Maybe she was just trying to stay warm.

"See you next week," the coach finally said, and Harley bent to pick up her bag and her jacket. "Nice game, guys."

Harley headed over to the sideline with Melly, their goalie. They talked about one of the players on the other team who made dirty hits. She was a tool, they agreed.

Nathan was smiling at her as she ducked beneath the net surrounding the field, and she felt that funny tingle again. For a moment, she wanted to smile back, but then Emma stepped forward.

"You see my goal?" Harley asked.

"Of course I did. It was beautiful. Placed perfectly."

Emma reached for her, then let her hand drop when Harley reared back. Jeez. Didn't she know how uncool that was?

"You should lay off the hugs in public," Nathan said to Emma. "Teenage girl's biggest nightmare."

Harley's face flamed, but Nathan just kept grinning. "Am I right?"

"Hey…Nathan." What was she supposed to call him, anyway? "I didn't know you were coming."

"Emma mentioned you were playing," he said, making it sound like a *duh* moment. "Of course I wanted to see the game."

She frowned. "Don't you, like, have to be at the restaurant all the time?"

"I hope I'm not that boring," he said with a laugh, but his eyes looked sad. "We have a manager now. I don't have to work every day of the week."

"Cool." Harley studied him for another few moments, then turned to Emma. "Can we go home? I'm starving."

Nathan said, "You want to get something to eat together? A pizza, maybe?"

Harley's eyes shifted from Emma to Nathan and back to Emma. She kind of did.

"That sounds great," Emma said. "Where do you want to go?"

"Up to Harley," Nathan said. "We were just freezing our a...butts off on those bleachers. She was actually doing some work."

Harley rolled her eyes. "You think I haven't heard the word *ass* before?"

"I'm sure you have," he said. "I'm just trying to protect Emma's innocent ears. She's new to this teenage kid stuff."

Harley's forehead furrowed. "You have other kids?"

"Nope. You're my first." Even though she tried not to show it, his words sent a funny ping through her heart. "But I raised Frankie, Patrick and Marco after our parents died. Frankie was about your age. Marco was ten."

She swung around to face him, walking backward. "Your mom and dad died, too?"

"Killed in a car crash."

"Both of them? At the same time?"

"Yeah."

"Wow. That's really sad." Her mouth trembled.

"It's awful," he said quietly. "That's why I know how hard this is for you. How sad you are. How much you miss your mom."

His eyes met Harley's and an acknowledgment of shared

pain passed between them. Harley's mouth quivered and she blinked furiously. Then she turned and shouldered her way through the air lock door. "Pizza sounds good."

CHAPTER FIFTEEN

As THEY ATE, Nathan bit his lip to avoid smiling at Harley's eager eyes and hearty appetite.

"How did you know about give-and-goes?" she asked him around a mouthful of artichoke and spinach pizza at Lenzoni's.

"Marco played soccer. I spent a lot of time on the sidelines, watching him. Watched World Cup games with him, too. Learned more about soccer than I ever thought I would."

"Not as much as Emma, I bet." Harley reached for another slice, bringing back memories of his siblings eating like that. Him, too, before their lives changed forever.

Harley swallowed a much-too-large bite. "*She* played soccer in college."

"Wow." He glanced at Emma, grinned to see her blushing.

"It wasn't that big a deal," she muttered. "It was a small college. They'd take pretty much any warm body."

"I doubt that," Nathan said. He propped his chin on his fist and studied her. "Even at small colleges, you have to be pretty good to make the team." He knew that because Marco had wanted to play in college. Until he'd decided to go to culinary school instead. "And I bet you were a…" He studied her, delighted at her discomfort. "You were a defender. Because that's what you do now. You try to protect everyone."

Emma shook her head, a tiny smile playing on her mouth. "You think you know so much about me, Mr. Psychoanalyst? I was a midfielder."

"Just like me," Harley said. She leaned across the table,

bumped fists with Emma. "She gives me lots of tips. And she still plays. In an adult league."

"Really?" His gaze drifted to his cane, then settled on Harley. "Do you go watch her play?"

"She won't let me." Harley took another bite of pizza. "Says it's too late on a school night. My guess?" She pointed her slice at Emma. "She thinks she looks like a dork."

"That is so not true." Emma dropped her own piece of pizza and narrowed her eyes. "I'll have you know that I..." She cleared her throat. Picked up her slice again. "My games start at nine. I don't get home until eleven at the earliest. That's too late for you."

"Tell you what, Harley." Nathan leaned toward his daughter. "Next time you don't have school the next day, we'll both go and watch Emma play. So we can judge her dorkiness for ourselves."

"Yes." She held up her hand, and he gave her a high five. "Let's do it."

"We will." He glanced at Emma. Instead of the irritation he'd expected, she was smiling at him, her eyes misty.

TWO DAYS LATER, Nathan sat in the lodge at the Wilmot ski hill and watched Harley take a snowboarding lesson. She'd fallen a few times at first, but after an hour, she was pretty steady. She gained confidence each time the instructor took them down the bunny hill.

He'd suspected this trip would be boring and that he'd be uncomfortable sitting all day. But at the end of the soccer evening, he'd asked Harley and Emma if he could join them.

In spite of Emma's initial embarrassment at the soccer game and his reluctance to be there, he'd enjoyed himself. He'd liked watching Harley play soccer. And he'd had fun at that pizza restaurant afterward. He'd been surprised by how much.

So here he was, sitting on an uncomfortable wooden bench

at a long, picnic-style table, drinking bad coffee and watching Harley and Emma on their snowboards.

Instead of being on a snowboard himself.

His hand tightened on the grip of his cane. This whole cane thing, the limping, the weakness, was getting old. He wanted to be done with it, just as he wanted to be done with the investigation into the restaurant mess. He wanted his life back. *All* of his life. Which included stepping away from Mama's, taking his trip and figuring out what he wanted to do with the rest of his life.

As Harley and five other kids stood with the instructor at the bottom of the bunny hill, Nathan's gaze wandered to the steepest slope, where Emma was boarding. She was easy to spot in her bright green, yellow and blue jacket. It clashed with the orange, red and yellow flames on her board, but after studying the crowds, Nathan concluded that was the point. The more color, the better.

Emma was good. Her body swayed gracefully as she slid down, her blond curls streaming behind her. Weaving back and forth, flying up into the air, then down again, she'd even gone down the half-pipe, a curved tube of packed-down snow.

She grinned every time her board caught air for a few moments.

She loved soaring above the ground. Loved taking those risks.

His mouth curved as he watched her reach the bottom, skid to a stop, head for the tow rope. Did she think of herself as a risk-taker? He bet she didn't.

She probably thought of herself as solid. Calm. Dependable. Exactly what her job required.

Watching her board was a revelation.

He wanted to be out there with her, speeding down the hill, feeling the cold air slap his face. Feeling as free as Emma looked. As wild.

He had his own ideas about freedom, he reminded himself. He'd find his in Italy. In busy days, lazy evenings, cool nights.

Emma's version was all about snow and speed. Lots of speed. Taking risks.

His gaze switched back to Harley. She was watching Emma, too, instead of listening to her instructor. God, he hoped she didn't try to go down that steep hill, or do the stuff Emma was doing.

What if she was a risk-taker, too? Like Frankie, he thought with dread. People who liked taking risks always got into trouble eventually.

Harley's instructor said something, and Harley whipped her head around to face him. He spoke again, laughed, and Harley's shoulders relaxed. The small group of beginners headed for the tow rope.

Gripping his cane tightly, Nathan stood to get another cup of coffee. His leg still ached from the cold at the soccer game on Thursday. Next time, he vowed, he'd remember that blanket.

Four ragged lines of people waited at the concession stands, all wearing colorful jackets and pants. They shuffled forward slowly, their heavy boots clomping on the wooden floor. Most of them had sunburned faces. Almost all had goggles shoved onto their heads, revealing pale raccoon eyes.

The smell of cooking hot dogs, spicy and fatty, washed over him, reminding him that, up until recently, it had been a long time since he'd eaten anywhere but Mama's.

Italy. He'd eat at a different place for every meal in Italy. And he'd take an hour to eat if he wanted to. But right now he just wanted to fill his stomach.

As he looked up at the menu board to see what else they had, someone stepped up next to him.

"Hey, bummer about your leg. You hurt yourself boarding?" a woman asked.

He glanced over at the woman standing in the next line. Her short, dark hair was messy, as if she'd just pulled off her hat.

At his questioning look, she shrugged. "I saw you staring out the window. Wishing you were out there."

Yeah. "Actually, I was watching my…friend. And my daughter," he said with a smile.

The dark-haired woman smiled back. "Yeah? They boarders?"

"My daughter's just learning."

"Great place for it," the woman said. She turned and studied the menu board, staring at it intently as if there would be a test later. The line shuffled forward, and she glanced toward the door, then stepped out of line and headed for it.

Wondering why she'd walked away before getting her food, Nathan watched the young woman. She stopped at a table close to the door and slid onto the bench. Leaned forward to speak to a man on the other side.

The woman stood and hurried out the door. Nathan glanced casually at the guy she'd been talking to. Froze.

The guy looked a lot like Chuck Notarro, the man who'd been arrested for bringing a gun into Mama's Place. That face was burned into Nathan's brain. Notarro had been the bagman who'd picked up the mortgage payment for Alderman O'Fallon every week. But he was sitting too far away for Nathan to be sure.

Nathan shuffled ahead another few steps, studying the Chuck clone, his hunger forgotten. He needed to get closer. Finally he was at the front of the line. "Coffee, please. Two creams."

Nathan headed back to his table and stirred the creamers into the coffee. They made the beverage muddy and unappetizing, but he pretended to sip it as he studied the guy near the door. He was almost certain it was Chuck.

What the hell was that thug doing here? He sure wasn't a skier. Maybe he'd come with a friend, the dark-haired woman, just like Nathan had. Maybe he was sitting in the lodge, watching her ski.

Except the guy wasn't watching the woman. Instead of staring out the window, he was watching the room, trying to pretend he wasn't looking at Nathan.

If it *was* Chuck, it couldn't be a coincidence that they were here at the same time. He must have followed them here from Chicago. Why the hell would he do that?

He wanted Nathan to notice him, too. He'd sent the woman to start a conversation, figuring Nathan would watch as she walked back to Chuck.

Was Chuck stupid enough to be planning something violent? In public?

Or was it merely intimidation? Letting him see that O'Fallon and whoever controlled him had a long reach. That they could get to him whenever they wanted.

Get to Harley, too.

Rage swept through Nathan, along with fear. With this damn weak arm of his, not to mention the cane and his worthless leg, he couldn't protect her. Or Emma.

Nathan's hand trembled as he set his coffee on the table. Fifteen minutes until Harley's lesson was over.

If the guy was Chuck, he'd probably already seen her. But Nathan didn't want her to come into the lodge and give the guy a closer look.

Nathan's hands were cold as he pulled out his phone to text Emma. Call me ASAP. He hit Send, then realized Emma would think Harley had been hurt. Harley okay, he texted again.

He clutched the phone in his hand as he pretended to watch the skiers. The other guy was holding his own phone, turning it over and over. Chuck had had the same habit when he came into Mama's. Nathan always figured the shithead was waiting for instructions from O'Fallon.

He didn't like anything about this.

His phone rang, and he answered immediately. "Nathan, what's wrong?" Emma sounded breathless, and the wind whistled through the receiver, making it hard to hear her.

"Not sure. Can you meet me in the lodge?" he said, watching Chuck out of the corner of his eye. "Not the main part where the concession stand is. Around the corner, in the ski rental area." He didn't want Harley or Emma anywhere near Chuck.

"Sure. You okay?"

"Yeah. See you in a few."

He glanced at Harley's class again. They were heading up the tow rope. There was an instructor with her. People all around. She was probably safe enough right now.

TEN MINUTES LATER, Emma clomped into the lodge in her boots. Stopped just inside the door and searched for him. He stood up and headed toward her, damning the cane again. What if Chuck walked into the room right now? Nathan was powerless to stop him from getting close to Emma.

When he finally reached her, her cheeks were red and her hair smelled like the outdoors. She grabbed his hand with warm fingers. "What is it? What's wrong?"

Nathan glanced over his shoulder. No sign of Chuck. "Could be nothing. But there's a guy in the other room... Maybe I'm seeing things, but I think he's a guy who's involved with the stuff at the restaurant. He was arrested a few months ago, spent some time in jail, was finally bailed out. Then he disappeared, and no one's seen him since. Until now. If it's him, he must have followed us from Chicago. I have no idea why he would."

Emma swiveled to look for Harley on the ski hill.

"I've been watching her," Nathan said. "She's fine. Still with her class. But it ends in a few minutes."

"What do you want to do, Nathan?" she asked as she watched Harley.

"You're not going to grill me?"

She turned to him, fierce as a mother bear. "Oh, yeah. You're going to tell me everything. But not right now. Right now we need to make sure Harley's safe. Then figure out what we're going to do."

"If it's Chuck, we need to leave." Urgency pumped through his blood, but he tried to stay calm. "Chuck's not a nice guy. I don't want him anywhere near Harley. Or you."

She tugged her hat off and her hand was shaking. "Okay. I'll wait for Harley at the bunny hill. You make sure it's the same guy. If it is, you get the car. Harley and I will walk around the lodge and meet you in the parking lot."

"Emma…" He hesitated. "If it's Chuck, make sure you keep your hat on. And stuff your hair up into it. Do the same for Harley."

Emma's lips compressed. "What the hell is going on, Nathan?"

"I'll tell you everything. I promise." His hand tightened on his cane. "Go get Harley. I'll see if that's Chuck out there."

HER HEART RACING, Emma watched Nathan limp around the corner, leaning heavily on his cane. He'd moved more slowly today. She'd seen him wince a few times, too. But he'd insisted he wanted to come with them.

When Nathan was out of sight, she rushed out the door. The wind slapped her face and the sun bounced off the snow with a blinding glare. She flipped down her goggles, then stopped and shoved her hair into her hat. She grabbed her board from the rack and hurried toward the bunny hill.

Her phone rang as she waited for Harley to finish her lesson. "It's Chuck. I'm heading for the car."

"We'll meet you there."

Harley came down the hill as Emma slipped her phone back into her pocket. She wanted to see if she could pick out the guy watching them, but it was too bright to see a thing inside the building. Instead, she plastered a smile on her face as Harley slid to a stop in front of her.

"Emma! This is the coolest thing ever." Harley's grin was as blinding as the sun on the snow. "I love boarding."

And Emma had to tell her they were leaving. "I thought you might." Emma maneuvered her body so she was between Harley and the lodge and struggled to smile. "We'll do this again really soon, okay?"

Harley's smile faded. "What do you mean? We're staying until they close tonight, right? That's what you said."

"Something's come up, honey. We have to leave." She pushed Harley's heavy curls into her hat, grabbing the girl's wrist when she tried to push Emma away. "Leave your hair in your hat. Let's go turn in your equipment."

Harley scowled. "You're acting weird and stupid, Emma. I was just figuring it out. Did you see me? I even went over a jump."

"Your instructor let you do a jump? Your first time boarding?"

"I wasn't supposed to, but it was a really small one," Harley said sulkily. "Hardly anything. But I got some air."

Oh, God. Harley was going to be one of those kids who raced down the hill, taking chances. Just like Emma had been when she was learning. "Next time, we'll stay all day. I promise."

Harley bent and loosened her bindings, then slung the board under her arm. "This sucks."

"Yeah, it does." Emma had been having fun, too. And she'd been a little flashier than usual, knowing Nathan was watching.

"What came up?"

"Something with Nathan."

Harley scowled again. "Why did he come with us, anyway? He can't ski or board."

"I thought we'd have a fun day together," Emma said. Instead, Nathan had scared her to death. "When his leg is better, he can board with us." He'd said he'd tried it as a teen. Before his parents died. She nudged Harley. "By that time, you'll be pretty good. You'll beat him down the hill."

Harley scowled. "He'll probably fall on his a—" She glanced at Emma. "On his butt. Or say he doesn't want to get cold."

"Maybe not." Emma kept herself between the windows of the lodge and Harley. If that Chuck guy wanted to get a look at Harley, she'd make it as difficult as possible. "I think Nathan's a pretty good sport. He came to your soccer game, even though sitting on those bleachers wasn't good for his leg."

Harley kicked at an icicle that had fallen off the building eaves. "This still sucks."

"Can't disagree." Emma had forgotten how much she loved boarding. She'd learned in California, where the ski resorts were enormous, compared to this puny little hill. "There will be more chances, Harley. Especially since you like it."

"Can I get my own board?" Harley asked, turning to her with a calculating expression.

"Eventually. Not tomorrow, though." Emma pulled the door open and stepped into the equipment room. "Let's return your gear and get our shoes on."

Harley clomped over to the counter, handed her board to the long-haired guy behind it. "So what did you think, kid?" he asked her.

Emma opened the locker she'd rented and listened as she pulled out her shoes and purse and Harley's shoes. "It was amazing," Harley gushed. "The sickest thing ever."

The guy bumped fists with her. "Yeah, it's sweet. How come you're leaving so early?"

"My father has stuff to do," Harley said.

Emma's throat swelled. She could hear the scowl in Harley's voice, but the girl had referred to Nathan as her father without a hint of hesitation. And Nathan had seemed so proud of Harley at the soccer game. So engaged with her at the restaurant afterward.

Maybe it wasn't going to be as hard as Emma had thought to foster a bond between them.

It was the right thing for Harley and Nathan. Absolutely. No question.

But as Emma listened to Harley, she felt an avalanche of pain and loss rumbling toward her, gathering speed.

CHAPTER SIXTEEN

NATHAN GLANCED IN his rearview mirror again. Thank God Wilmot Road was only two lanes. It would be easy to spot anyone following them.

Although there probably wouldn't be. Chuck's message was that he could get to Nathan and his family whenever he wanted.

Message delivered.

He checked the mirror one more time, then twisted for a second to study Harley. She was curled into a ball, her left cheek against the seat, earbuds in place. Scowling.

"She's pissed at me," he said quietly to Emma. "You are, too, aren't you?"

She shifted in the seat to face him. Out of the corner of his eye, he watched her tuck a curl behind her ear. "I'm not angry, Nathan. A little upset, yeah." Her smile was wistful. "I haven't been on a ski hill in a long time. I was having fun."

He remembered her grin as she flew down the half-pipe. "I could tell."

"And this whole thing with Chuck is freaking me out. Why did the guy follow us to Wisconsin, for God's sake? Was he… was he going to hurt you?" She glanced over her shoulder. "Hurt Harley?"

"I'm not going to let anything happen to Harley," he said.

During the whole business with O'Fallon and Chuck last spring, Nathan had never worried about himself. There hadn't been any threats. He'd wondered about the car accident, but it had turned out to be an elderly woman behind the wheel who wasn't supposed to drive at night. He'd paid his mortgage on time. And even if he hadn't, why would anyone hurt him? They wanted money from him.

But now with Harley in the picture, everything was different. Nathan and Patrick were pressuring the mystery man. Digging for answers. And whoever was behind the money now had leverage. His daughter.

Maybe all of Paddy's questions were cutting too close to the bone. Maybe one of the sources his brother had talked about was close to Mystery Man. Had said something about the FBI and their questions.

Maybe he and Paddy were closer to the truth than they realized.

Maybe Harley was in more danger than he knew.

He let out a breath and tried to convince himself he was overreacting. No one would hurt Harley. Chuck was just a message from the alderman. That damn wife-beater O'Fallon liked to bully people.

No. He wasn't overreacting. This was a kid who could be in danger because of who her father was.

And how did Shaughnessy fit into the picture? Because it was no coincidence he'd shown up right now.

Emma was still staring at him. Her smile was gone. "Emma, no one's going to hurt Harley." If he said it enough times, maybe he would actually believe it. "They want me to back off. That's all this was about."

"Really?" Her voice sharpened. "Because if anyone hurts Harley, I'll…"

"How would I get hurt?"

Harley's voice. She wasn't listening to her iPod any longer. Now she was leaning through the space between the bucket seats.

"You're not getting hurt," Emma said. "As long as…as long as you're careful when you're boarding. Okay?"

"Is that why we had to take off so early? Because you were afraid I'd, like, break something?"

Nathan could practically hear her eyes roll.

"Because that's the lamest excuse *ever*. I was good, Emma. I was the best one in my class. Justin said I was a natural."

"And Justin would be…"

"Duh, Emma." Another eye roll. "The instructor. Who do you think?"

As Emma and Harley bickered, Nathan turned onto the larger state road that would lead back to the tollway. He watched behind him for a while, but no one else turned off of Wilmot Road. When he was certain no one had followed them, he relaxed his death grip on the steering wheel, reached over and touched Emma's hand.

"We were going to tell the truth from now on," he said softly. "Remember?"

Harley had slumped back onto the seat and jammed the earbuds in place. Emma glanced at her, then at him. "Really? Now you want the truth? When it's going to freak her out? I don't think so, Nathan."

"I didn't say it had to be a detailed explanation. Just an outline. But a truthful one."

"Fine. Let's see you tell her what's going on without freaking her out. Or scaring her."

He studied Harley in the backseat. She wasn't listening to her iPod. The earbuds were in, but the device wasn't on. He'd figured that ruse out when Frankie was Harley's age.

"Hey, Harley," he said in a low voice.

She ripped the earbuds out immediately. Nathan smiled to himself.

"I want to tell you why we really left the ski area."

"Okay," she said slowly. She was back to her perch between the seats.

"After you put your seat belt back on."

"It is on." She tugged on it to prove it. "I stretched it out."

"Unstretch it, then."

She flopped back against the seat with a huge sigh. He'd heard those before, too. "So? Why did we have to leave?"

"I had some problems with the restaurant last summer," he said, trying to keep his voice calm. "Money problems. While I was watching you and Emma, something related to that came up. I have to deal with it right away. I'm sorry."

"Why didn't you just say that?"

"I was in a hurry to get going," he said easily. "I knew I could explain in the car."

"It sucks that we had to leave before I could do any real boarding."

"Yes, it does. But we'll go back. I promise. Maybe we'll even go to a bigger hill."

"Yeah?" Harley bounced forward again. "Where?"

"I'm not sure. It's been a long time since I was up there, but I know there are a bunch of ski hills farther north in Wisconsin."

"Sweet. I'll do some research," Harley said eagerly. "Maybe we could go next weekend."

"Can't promise that," Nathan said. He could feel Emma's gaze on him. "Soon, though."

"Okay."

She retreated from the spot behind the console, and a few moments later he heard music spilling from her earbuds.

"Harley?" he said in a loud voice.

"Yeah?" The music was louder after she'd pulled out her buds.

"Rule of thumb—if I can hear the music coming from your iPod, it's too loud. Turn it down, please."

"You sound like Emma," Harley muttered. But the volume decreased.

The first traffic light they'd seen turned yellow in front of him, and he slowed down, stopping as it turned red. He glanced at Emma and found her smiling. Instead of being all territorial about Harley, she liked him suggesting outings. Liked him correcting his daughter.

Because she wanted him to get to know Harley. Really be a father. Take responsibility for his daughter. His hands tightened on the steering wheel again.

He wasn't sure he wanted to do that. Hard to be a parent to a kid in Chicago when he was in Italy. This was beginning to feel like a replay of what happened fifteen years ago—follow his own dreams? Or take care of his family? He couldn't do both.

He'd never regretted dropping out of school, taking over the restaurant and raising his siblings. He'd do it again in a heartbeat, because they'd stayed together. Grown up together. Gotten through the pain and heartache and problems together.

He just wasn't sure he was ready to do it all over again.

NATHAN'S SUV HUMMED along on the pavement, and Emma glanced over at him. Since the discussion about why they'd had to leave, and his promise of another trip, he hadn't spoken. From the way he clenched his jaw muscles from time to time, she figured he was thinking about Chuck.

Harley had fallen asleep in the backseat. Emma craned her neck to look at her. Her cheeks were pink and her mouth was half-open. She looked so young. So defenseless.

Instead of making up a story about why they had to leave, Nathan had told Harley the truth. Severely edited, but a better choice than her own lame story. He'd been straightforward with Harley. And the girl had responded to him.

He'd been responsible. And in a good way. Not the way she'd been thinking of him and his approach to Harley—all obligation, no heart. When he'd seen Chuck, he'd done what he needed to do to keep her safe. Removed them all from a potentially dangerous situation. Then promised to take her boarding again.

Maybe she'd read him wrong. Maybe he *did* want to spend time with his daughter.

At the next stoplight, he pulled his phone out of his pocket and sent a text. When he saw her watching, he explained. "Patrick. Asking him to meet us at Mama's."

"To tell him what happened today?"

"Yeah. It's got to mean something that dirtbag was up there. Paddy and I need to figure out what."

"Are you going to drop Harley and me off at our place?" she asked carefully. Was he looking for an excuse to get away from them?

"Wasn't planning on it." He glanced at her, then back at the road. "I thought we could get some takeout from Mama's and go to your place. Have dinner together. Is that okay? Since I cheated you out of your day on the hill?"

A tight fist uncurled in her chest. "I'd like that. I think Harley would, too."

"Good." He flashed that smile that made her chest flutter. "I don't want to cut our day short."

An hour later, they walked through the back door of Mama's. Emma had only been in this area a couple of times, but it already felt familiar. The scents of tomatoes, baking pizza crust and cooking cheese lingered in the air. Pots clanged on the stove, voices yelled in English and Spanish and water splattered into the sink with a hollow echo.

Nathan strode to the office and pushed open his door. "Paddy. Darcy. Glad you're here." He glanced at Emma and smiled. "Come meet Harley and Emma."

The couple emerged smiling. Patrick was a hair taller than Nathan, and he looked harder. More intense. Watchful, like other cops she'd met.

Darcy was...familiar. Emma frowned, wondering where she'd seen Darcy before. She was shorter than Emma by a few inches, and thinner. She had dark red hair and a big smile as she walked over.

"Harley. I'm Darcy," she said, holding out her hand. "I'm so glad to meet you. I'm engaged to your uncle Patrick."

Harley took her hand gingerly. "Hey. Nice to meet you."

"Welcome to the family," Darcy said. "We're all excited about getting to know you."

Darcy lumped herself in with the rest of the family so easily. Emma's gaze drifted from her to the two men, whose dark heads were together as they talked quietly. What was it like to belong to a family like that? A big group of people who accepted one another. Loved one another.

Emma swallowed and watched Harley look between Darcy and Patrick. Darcy must have noticed, because she grabbed Patrick's hand and tugged him away from his conversation with Nathan. "Patrick, this is Harley. Your niece."

Patrick looked grim and serious as he turned away from Nathan.

What had they been talking about? "Hey, Harley. Good to meet you." He studied her for a moment. "You look like our grandmother. Spitting image."

"Uh, hi. Yeah, ah, Nathan said that." Harley wiped her hands down her jeans, and Emma wanted to shake Patrick. Was that his idea of warm and fuzzy to the kid who already felt awkward?

Patrick glanced from Emma to Nathan. "Maybe the three of us should step outside and talk for a moment. Harley, you want to hang with Marco? I heard you criticized his food. And lived. Think you could survive him for a while today?"

"Ah, yeah. I guess." Harley shoved her hands into her pockets. Emma glared at Patrick and slung an arm over Harley's shoulders.

"You two go outside. I'll be there in a minute."

The two men slipped out the kitchen door, and Darcy shook her head. "Don't mind him, Harley. He's concentrating on a case. It's kind of scary sometimes."

Harley shrugged. "Fine. Whatever."

The tension in Harley's shoulders hummed through Emma's hand, and she tugged the girl close for a moment. Harley had connected to two out of Nathan's three siblings. Emma hoped they'd just caught Patrick at a bad time.

As if she could read Emma's thoughts, Darcy held out her hand. "Emma, I'm Darcy. We met once, a while ago, at the Safety Net shelter. I volunteer there, and you'd dropped a family off."

Emma searched her memory. "Sorry. I don't remember."

"Didn't expect you to. You were focused on the woman you dropped off. Afraid she wouldn't stay." Darcy's smile faded. "And she didn't. Kelly told me she left the next day."

Emma remembered now. The woman's face was etched in her memory, along with the bruises on it. "Mary. Yeah. I was pretty upset."

"What happened with her?" Darcy asked.

Emma smiled. "A happy ending, so far. She did go to stay with her sister. Her husband violated Mary's order of protection, and he was arrested. She testified against him, and he'll be in jail for a while. She's getting her life together."

"God, that's good news." A shadow passed through Darcy's eyes. "They don't all turn out so well."

"No. We take our victories where we get them." Emma squeezed Harley's shoulder, turned to study the girl's closed-off face. "You want to hang out with Marco?"

"With that loser?"

But Harley's mouth curved up a little and some of the tension in her shoulders receded. Good. Marco would make her forget her less-than-effusive welcome from Patrick.

As Harley hurried toward the front of the kitchen, Darcy said, "You caught Patrick at a bad time. He's in FBI agent mode. It's not personal."

"It is for Harley." Emma wasn't about to give Patrick a pass. "She lost her mother, then found out she has this whole other family. She's scared. On top of her grief and sadness, she has all this information she has to process. Figure out family dynamics and where she stands."

"I get it, Emma," Darcy said. "I'll kick Patrick's ass later, okay?"

Emma sighed. "Sorry. I don't mean to take it out on you. But this has been a day, you know? Harley's skiing trip cut short, and meeting another aunt and uncle. I know Patrick's focused on whatever's going on. Nathan is, too. But Harley is my first responsibility."

"I know. Thank God she has you."

Nathan stuck his head in the door. "Emma, we need to deal with this. Right now."

"Yeah. Sorry." As she headed for the door, she heard Marco say, "Hey, it's my favorite niece."

"I'm your only niece, jerk-face."

"Does your father know how disrespectful you are?" Emma heard the laughter in Marco's voice.

"He likes that about me."

"Yeah, Nate was always a sucker for your type. You should have seen Frankie when she was your age. Queen of the smart-mouths."

"Really?"

"Yeah. Let me tell you…" His voice lowered, and Emma couldn't hear him anymore.

She glanced at Nathan, standing less than a foot away. He was listening, too. Their eyes met, and he smiled at her slowly. "Marco's right. Smart-asses are my weakness," he said in a voice meant only for her. "Especially when they're tall blondes with an attitude."

Her face heated, but she didn't look away. Neither did Nathan. Unspoken messages passed between them.

You, specifically. His mouth curved a little. His eyes heated.

You're not so bad yourself. Emma swallowed. Felt an answering shiver of arousal, deep inside.

Could she and Nathan do this? Get involved?

Should they?

"Nate." Patrick's voice. Sharp. "Get Emma out here. We need to figure this out."

CHAPTER SEVENTEEN

As EMMA STEPPED out the back door of Mama's, the wind flung sharp needles of air against her face. It howled around the building, bending the bare branches of the bushes that lined the parking area. An old bird's nest wobbled, then tumbled to the ground in a spray of dried leaves and twigs.

Nathan put his hand on her back and kicked a doorstop into place so the door wouldn't lock behind him. A wisp of warmth drifted through the crack in the door, and she wanted to hover close to it. But Patrick moved away from the door, into the open area where only a few cars were parked. Nathan's fingers pressed into her back, urging her to follow.

"Okay, I don't think Harley's a target," Patrick began. "But we're not going to take any chances, so here's what we'll do. We'll move her—"

"No." Emma stepped away from Nathan's hand. "*This* is what we're going to do. First of all, you're going to tell me exactly what's happening. Exactly who this Chuck guy is and why he was at the ski lodge today. Exactly why Harley *might* be a target."

Patrick's lips tightened as he stared at her, then he swung on Nathan. "You haven't told her?"

A muscle in Nathan's jaw tightened. "Not the kind of thing you talk about in front of a kid," Nathan said. But the red slashes on his cheekbones weren't just because of the wind. "When we've been together, we've been with Harley."

Not always, Emma thought. They'd met at Oscar's and at

the school. Talked about a lot of stuff, but Nathan hadn't told her what the situation was at Mama's.

She glanced at Nathan and found him watching her. In spite of the cold and the fear, heat rose inside her.

Patrick's gaze swung from Nathan to her. Assessing. Trying to figure out how little he could say?

"And don't say it's on a need to know basis," she said, recovering from the moment with Nathan. Patrick closed his mouth. "Don't say it's dangerous for me to know. Don't say it's too complicated, or that it's classified, or that it's too ugly. Just tell me what's going on."

To her surprise, Patrick smiled. Shook his head as he gave his brother a look that was hard to interpret. "Yes, ma'am. Got it. Full disclosure." He nodded at Nathan. "You telling her, or should I?"

"I'll do it." Nathan didn't meet Emma's gaze as he shifted slightly away from her. "My screwup. My job to tell."

He was embarrassed, Emma realized with a jolt. He didn't want to tell her about the restaurant problem because he was ashamed. Guilty. Maybe both.

She stepped closer and hooked her arm around his elbow. *It's okay. I won't judge you.*

He hesitated, then nodded. Took a deep breath and unclenched his fist. Fumbled for her hand and twined their fingers together.

"The kitchen here at Mama's needed to be remodeled a year ago. It was either bring it up to code or close the business. I couldn't get financing from a bank—credit was a bitch back then—and ended up getting a loan through my alderman, from a guy he wouldn't name. He had someone who would finance it privately, he said. Chuck was the guy who picked up my loan payment every week."

Emma frowned. "So what's the problem? That sounds pretty straightforward."

"It was probably illegal," Nathan said, his jaw clenched.

"And I knew it at the time, but I was desperate. It was my last chance to save Mama's."

Emma raised her eyebrows, and Patrick said, "Nate was paying usurious interest rates. His payments were in cash, so chances are the mystery man didn't pay taxes on the interest. But until we catch the guy, we've got no proof."

"We got the alderman," Nathan said, "but he won't give up the money man. So we're trying to find him ourselves."

"It's an FBI case now, but Nate's been doing stuff on his own." Patrick scowled. "Against my advice."

Emma shivered as the wind continued its assault. Her jacket was made for cold weather activity, but she was standing still. Patrick stamped his feet. The tips of Nathan's ears were red, and his hand was bluish where it clenched his cane.

Nathan continued the story, telling her about the bribes to the building inspector, the expedited building permits, even the mysterious disappearance of the alderman's son after a drug arrest.

By the time Nathan finished, Emma couldn't feel her toes. She was teeth-chattering, bone-shaking cold. "D-do we have to stand out here to talk about this?" Emma said. "Hush-hush is fine, but I'm freezing."

"Yeah, Paddy, let's go inside." Nathan's jaw was clenched and lines bracketed his mouth. She wondered if the cold was making his leg ache. But she knew he'd rather die than admit it.

"You want the kid to hear this stuff?" Patrick demanded.

"*Harley* is talking to Marco." Emma narrowed her eyes on Patrick. God, what *was* it with these single-minded Devereux men, focused on the problem rather than the child. Nathan had been the same way.

At the beginning, she admitted to herself. Not as much now.

"So?" Patrick said. "Nathan probably scared the shit out of her. If she thinks we're talking about what happened today, she'll want to know."

Nathan spun around, dropped his cane, shoved Patrick back. "Listen, asshole..."

Emma grabbed Nathan's hand, pulled him to her side. Her temper simmered as she glared at Patrick. "Nathan handled it perfectly. He told Harley just enough to satisfy her curiosity, not enough to scare her." She forced herself to hang on to her temper. This was Nathan's brother. Harley's uncle. "And Harley's not going to eavesdrop right now. She's into food and cooking. She and Marco are either talking about food or tasting food. She won't even notice us coming inside."

Patrick held his hands up and kept his gaze on Emma. "Sorry. Didn't mean to imply Nathan doesn't know how to handle kids."

He turned to his brother. "Sorry, Nate. This case has frustrated the hell out of me."

"Yeah, I know," Nathan answered gruffly. "Shouldn't have called you an asshole. Even though you were."

His words made Patrick laugh briefly. "Yeah, I guess I was." He bent and picked up Nathan's cane, wiping it on his jeans before handing it back. "Let's go into the dining room." His gaze flickered to Nathan's leg. "You're right, Emma. It's cold as hell out here."

Nathan yanked the door open and put his hand on her back again. Even through her jacket, she felt him shivering. She glanced over her shoulder and nodded once to Patrick. He hadn't been great with Harley, but Patrick knew his brother's leg was bothering him. He got points for that.

"Want some coffee, Emma?" Nathan muttered as they passed the stoves in the kitchen.

"I'd love some. Thanks."

Nathan detoured to a coffeemaker in a corner of the kitchen, and Emma followed him, watching Harley discreetly.

She was standing over a sauté pan with Marco. Harley was pointing at something in the pan as she talked, and Marco shook his head. "No, no. Not shallots and onions both. Shallots are delicate. The onions will overwhelm them. Got to pick one or the other."

Emma's irritation with Patrick faded away. Harley loved this. Snowboarding and cooking in the same day. Maybe the girl wouldn't be quite so upset about leaving the ski hill early.

She turned to find Nathan trying to juggle two cups of coffee and the cane, and she took the cups from him. "Lead the way," she said.

She followed him into the dimly lit dining room, where she sat at the big table next to the doors. "Our family table," he said as he eased into the chair next to her. "When we were kids, all the family meetings were here."

"Nice tradition," Emma murmured, running her hand over the gleaming wood. The last time she and Harley were here, they were guests, sitting in a far corner. Today, Harley was cooking in the kitchen with her uncle and Emma was at the family table.

Beneath the varnish, there were scratches and gouges in the wood, and she wondered how they'd gotten there. Were some of them from Nathan, bored with a childhood meeting?

Steam from the coffee warmed her face, and she took a sip. The heat flowed through her body, easing her shivers. As she took another sip, Patrick hurried through the door and sat on the other side of Nathan. In a moment, Darcy came in as well and sat next to her fiancé.

"We need Darcy's perspective," Patrick said.

What perspective was that? Emma waited, but Darcy didn't speak. Instead, she took Patrick's hand and interlaced their fingers.

Darcy didn't need to be here, Emma realized. Patrick just wanted her close. Emma found herself leaning toward Nathan. She straightened and took a sip of coffee.

"Okay, here's what we need to do," Patrick began. "Like I started to say earlier, I don't think Harley's a target. But just in case, maybe you guys should take a trip. Get out of town for a while."

Emma narrowed her eyes. "Harley has to go to school, and I have to work. We can't run away."

"Then maybe she should stay with you, Nate." Patrick turned to his brother. "They won't be expecting that. It'll throw them off."

"No." Emma flattened her hands on the table. "That is not going to happen. Harley isn't moving in with Nathan. She's staying with me."

"Emma, be reasonable," Patrick began. "Nathan knows what these guys look like. He's better prepared to protect her than you are."

"No, Patrick, *you* be reasonable. This is a thirteen-year-old girl. She lost her mother less than two months ago. She's just getting used to living with me, and I'm not going to uproot her again. I'm not going to send her to live with someone she barely knows."

She turned to Nathan and put her hand on his arm. "Is that what you want, Nathan?"

A muscle in his jaw twitched, and she saw the faint panic in his expression. "I want Harley safe. That's the bottom line. But you're the one taking care of her. You get to make that call. And if staying with me will protect her, then yes. I won't let her get hurt."

"Mr. FBI Agent said that was unlikely. What do you think?"

"I think we can't guarantee anything," he said quietly. "Since we don't know who's behind the money, we can't predict what they're going to do. Although no one's been hurt yet. No one's even been threatened."

"Except for the bribe not being paid," Patrick said. "You were right, Nate. That was a threat. A subtle one, but still a threat."

Emma pressed her fingers into the table. What should she do? How should she handle this? "No one's taking her away from me." That was nonnegotiable. Whatever the decision, Emma was with Harley all the way. The girl wouldn't be alone again.

Nathan put his hand on hers. Caressed the side of her wrist with his thumb. "You have the final say in this, Emma. Let's get Harley and go back to your place. We'll have dinner and talk some more."

Emma nodded. Yes. Her and Harley and Nathan. At her apartment. Eating dinner, talking about everything that had happened today.

Just like a real family would do.

Now she was building castles in the sky. Family wasn't in the cards for the three of them. Heck, Nathan couldn't even commit to Harley—he'd been very clear about his desire to visit Italy. Alone.

And they wouldn't just be talking about a fun day. They had to figure out how to handle a possible threat. How to keep Harley safe.

This wasn't about Harley meeting her father and getting to know her new family anymore. It was more urgent than that. More dangerous.

Scared for Harley and all too aware of Nathan holding her hand, Emma tugged her fingers out of his grip and pushed her chair back too fast. She barely managed to grab it before it toppled over. She needed Harley.

"I'll get her." She turned, tried to smile at Darcy and Patrick. "Darcy, it was good to see you again. Patrick, thank you for trying to protect Harley. I appreciate it."

"Emma," Patrick began.

She held up her hand. "Not now, okay? There's a lot to process. Nathan and I have to talk about all this."

"Right. Good." He reached for Darcy's hand while still studying Emma. "Whatever you and Nate decide, I'll help. Darcy and the rest of the family, too."

"Thanks." She nodded to the other couple, pretending she

had a clue about the next step, then headed for the kitchen. Marco and Harley had three carryout boxes lined up on the counter, and they were apparently arguing about what to put in them.

"Don't try to tell me what Nate would like," Marco said. "He's my frig...my brother. He eats my food all the time. I know what to give him."

"I'm just saying I want a box of this special, too. It's awesome."

Marco pointed a spatula at her. "Oh, so now I know how to cook? I'm not a jerk anymore?"

Harley grinned at him. "Nah. You're just a jerk who can cook."

Marco clutched his chest. "Right to the heart."

"I doubt that. It's too small a target."

Nathan stepped behind Emma, pressed his fingers into her hip. "She's amazing. Also a little scary," he whispered. His breath stirred the fine hairs at her temple. She wanted to put her hands over his, press his hands more tightly against her hips. She yearned to lean back, feel his solid strength against her. Instead, reminding herself of thugs and mysterious money, of Italy, she gripped the table to keep from moving.

Marco's lips twitched at Harley's words, then he saw Nathan and Emma. "Looks like someone's waiting for you. Come back soon, though. I'll look forward to hearing you point out more of my flaws."

"Hey, someone has to do it."

"And you nominated yourself."

Harley grinned. "Who better? They've all known you for years. Probably just ignore you by now. Me? I'm willing to step up and do my part for the family."

Nathan's fingers tightened on her hips, then he let her go and stepped back. Emma stared at Harley in shock. *The family.* She already considered herself one of them.

This is what Emma wanted, wasn't it? It was what Sonya had hoped she'd do—foster a bond between Harley and Nathan.

Before long, Nathan wouldn't need her to mediate when he spent time with Harley. It would be father and daughter, and Emma would be the outsider.

Suddenly she was cold all over again.

If only Sonya hadn't died. If only Emma had had a chance to get to know Nathan without Harley between them. Things might be so different.

She wanted Nathan. She had from the moment his laughing blue eyes met hers outside FreeZone. Maybe she needed to gather her courage and reach for what she wanted. Maybe they wouldn't have long, but they could have something for a while. Until he took Harley to live with him. Until he went to Italy.

NATHAN EASED HIS SUV into a cramped spot on Emma's street, then climbed slowly out of the vehicle. Everything today had conspired to punish his still-healing bones—the long drive, sitting for several hours on the hard bench, then standing in the cold to humor Paddy's ridiculous need for secrecy.

Now, instead of sitting with his leg up, drinking a beer and watching the football playoffs, he would spend the evening re-hashing problems for which there was no easy solution.

Figuring out how to keep Harley safe without freaking her out.

Emma shoved her hair away from her face and the sun glinted off a silver earring. Her hips shifted as she hoisted her snowboard out of the back of the SUV. On the positive side, Emma would be there.

And so would Harley. This morning, on the way to pick them up, Nathan had thought of a hundred things he'd rather be doing. But to his surprise, he'd liked spending the day with Harley. Her delight at learning to board had made him smile.

And he'd been able to talk her out of her sulk on the way home. He was proud of that. Pleased he'd made her eyes light up when he promised another trip. He'd sit in an uncomfortable, drafty lodge for hours to see that happiness in her eyes again.

Emma unlocked the front door of her apartment building and stood aside for him to enter. "Sorry," she said, glancing at his cane. "There's no elevator."

"Not a problem," he said. "Stairs are good exercise. I do them at rehab all the time."

"Not after a day like today," she murmured. Two stairs up, he glanced back at the lock as it clicked back into place. It didn't seem very secure. Easy to pick.

"You okay?" Emma murmured.

"I'm good." He didn't want to worry Emma, either.

Harley bounded ahead of them, and Emma hooked her arm through his. She acted as if she was just being friendly, but he suspected it was really to help him up the stairs.

A week ago, he'd have been mortified at needing the help. But Emma was different. He'd never seen pity in her eyes, or impatience. Only a steady gaze that focused on his face rather than his cane.

Longing in her expression when she thought he wasn't watching.

Longing was good. Because there was a lot of that going on at his end, too.

By the time they reached Emma's second-floor apartment, the door was ajar and Harley was inside. "I'm getting the food ready," she called when Nathan and Emma walked in.

"Okay. Need any help?" Emma replied.

"Nope. I'm good."

Nathan examined the locks on this door. A little better—a dead bolt as well as a keyed lock.

Emma smiled at him, clearly having no idea what he was thinking about. "Can I hang up your coat? Or are you still cold?"

"Not at all." Emma holding his arm to her side had done wonders in warming him up. He pushed the door closed, engaged the dead bolt and shrugged off the leather jacket. As Emma took it, he looked around her apartment.

Color was the first thing he noticed. The couch was covered in denim, but red, blue, yellow and green pillows were scattered over it. The rug was an oriental that glowed in the sunlight streaming through the windows.

Bookshelves lined two walls, and a small flat-screen television was nestled on the shelf opposite the couch. Artwork was proudly displayed—some of it framed, some of it children's drawings that had been carefully taped to the creamy walls.

Magazines littered the end tables and coffee tables, and a laptop computer sat on a tiny desk in one corner, half-hidden behind an easy chair. The room was lived in. Messy enough to be a real home.

"Have a seat," Emma said, clearing the magazines off the coffee table and piling a couple of the throw pillows on top of it. "You probably need to put your leg up." She waited as he lowered himself to the couch, then helped him settle his ankle on the pillows. Her hands were cool where they slid beneath his jeans to brush against his bare leg, her skin smooth and soft.

She stepped back, her face flushed. "Can I get you something to drink? A glass of wine? A beer?"

"God, you read my mind," he sighed. "I'd love a beer. Thanks."

She returned a minute later with a bottle of Goose Island 312. "I didn't think you'd want a glass."

"Nope. No glasses for manly men." He took a drink of the crisp, lemony beer and relaxed into the cushions. "One of my favorites, too. You're doing everything right."

"You're easy to please," she said with a smile. "A pillow on the table and a bottle of beer? You're a cheap date, Nathan." She stood in a shaft of sunlight that made her hair gleam and her eyes look dark and mysterious. Her face was still pink from the sun and wind.

He settled the bottle on his knee, hoping it would cool his

overheated skin. "Not always," he said quietly. He held her gaze and let her see the desire that had been bubbling beneath the surface all day. "Sometimes I want more than a beer and a place to rest my leg."

"Really." More color bloomed in her cheeks. "We'll have to discuss your...wants one of these days."

The beer bottle nearly slipped out of his grasp. He set it carefully on a coaster on the end table. "Can't wait to do that," he said, his voice like sandpaper.

Emma leaned closer, her lips parting. She swallowed, and he wanted to press his mouth to the muscle in her neck.

"Hey, guys, the food's ready."

Emma jerked upright as Harley appeared in the hall to the kitchen. "You want to eat in here, or the kitchen?"

"Kitchen," he and Emma said at the same time.

CHAPTER EIGHTEEN

A HALF HOUR LATER, Nathan set his fork on his plate. He had no idea what he'd eaten. It had been good—Marco's food was always good. Harley had been chattering away. But Emma had filled his senses. He couldn't recall a word Harley had said.

He'd watched the way Emma's mouth opened for her fork, her eyes closing as she savored the food. The way her lips had kissed the wineglass. The tiny drop of red at the corner of her mouth that she licked off.

She'd shoved her hair away from her face, tucked the windblown curls behind her ears. He wanted his hands in her hair, her curls wrapped around his fingers.

He needed to concentrate on Harley. But lately, Emma was all he could think about.

"So which was your favorite, Nathan?" Harley asked.

"Huh?" His eyes lingered on Emma. "Favorite what?"

Harley snorted. "Duh! Your favorite dish! They were Marco's specials. I liked the rigatoni primavera the best. But the ravioli with the cheese sauce and the linguini with clams were good, too."

Thank you for telling me what I just ate, Harley. "Yeah. Me, too. The rigatoni."

Harley grinned. "Wait till I see Marco again. He said you wouldn't like that one. He said you're not big on vegetables."

Marco was right. He didn't particularly like vegetables in his pasta. "I like them just fine when they're fixed right. And Marco did a good job with that dish."

"Yeah," Harley said with relish, pumping her fist. "I'm gonna make him eat his words."

Nathan watched Emma smile as she looked at Harley. There was a touch of sadness in her eyes. A hint of loss.

He wondered why. This was what she'd wanted—Harley in his life. In his family's life. Comfortable with the Devereux clan.

Emma set her fork on her plate, which still held portions of all three dishes. He touched her hand. "You didn't like the food?"

She shook her head. Smiled. But that shadow was still there. "They were great, but I'm not very hungry," she murmured before turning to Harley. Her eyes softened. "You bring dessert home, too?"

"Cannoli," the girl said with a hum of anticipation. "Should I get them?"

"I'll save mine for later," Emma said. "But you and Nathan go ahead." She tipped the bottle of wine over her glass, poured another mouthful. She glanced at Nathan's empty beer bottle. "And grab another beer for Nathan," she added.

"No, thanks," he said. "I'm good." He'd already had two. He needed to be a good example for Harley. Moderation and all that stuff. "I'll pass on the cannoli, too, Harley." He smiled when her eyes lit up. "You'll have to sacrifice yourself. Eat mine for me."

"I'll save it for tomorrow," she said happily. She looked from him to Emma. "Since you guys don't want dessert, is it okay if I take mine into my room? I want to call Lissy and tell her about snowboarding today."

"Sure." Emma pushed away from the table. "Help me with the dishes first."

She glanced at Nathan, and her eyes darkened as if they'd been thinking about the same things during dinner. "Why don't you rest your leg again? I'll make coffee and bring some in to you."

"Nah," he said. "I'll stay here. This is where the fun is." He meant it, too, he realized with a jolt of surprise. Emma was telling him it was okay to park himself on her couch and turn on her television to check on the football game. But he'd rather be here in the kitchen, watching Emma. Listening to her and Harley talk.

He wanted to hear what his daughter said next. Marco was right. She was clever. A smart-mouth. And he *did* like that about her.

TEN MINUTES LATER, Emma wrung out the dishrag and watched Harley hang the towel next to the sink. She set a cannoli gently on a plate and put the other two back in the refrigerator. As she poured a glass of milk, she asked, "You sure it's okay if I go talk to Lissy? You won't be, like, offended if I don't hang out with you?"

A wave of love moved through Emma, so fierce it almost made her stagger. "We're devastated, but we'll muddle through somehow," Emma said, smiling. Telling Harley without words that she loved her.

"Dork," Harley said with a grin as she slipped into her bedroom and closed the door.

Emma watched Harley disappear. It had been hard to eat, watching Harley and Nathan so easy with one another. So natural.

This was what she wanted, she assured herself. The point of everything she'd done with Nathan.

She glanced at him, found his gaze on her.

Well, maybe not everything.

Breaking the connection with him, she swiped the dishrag across the table, rinsed it and hung it to dry. She blotted her hands on the towel more carefully than usual. This evening wasn't about her and Nathan. It was about how to keep Harley safe.

Not a drop of water remained on her hands by the time she turned to Nathan. "Sure you don't want another beer?"

"I'm good." He glanced at the coffeemaker on the counter. "I wouldn't say no to coffee, though."

"Great. I'll make some." Coffee was good. She'd had less than two glasses of wine with dinner, but she needed a clear head for this. For this discussion of Harley's safety.

When it was ready, they headed for the living room again. She carried both cups of coffee, and she waited while Nathan sat down. In the middle of the couch.

He raised his leg with a groan, and the cups clattered as Emma set the coffee on the table. Her hands gripped his leg carefully as she helped him settle his foot on the pillows.

When she'd done this before dinner, her hand had accidentally slipped beneath the denim of his jeans. His skin had been warm. Crisp hair had tickled her palm, and she'd felt him tense.

She'd taken her hand away a little more slowly than she should have.

Now, after Nathan was settled on the couch, coffee mug in his hand, she hesitated for a moment, not sure where to sit. Next to him? In the easy chair?

Nathan finally solved the problem by tapping the cushion beside him, as if it was the most natural thing in the world.

There had been that moment before dinner, when she'd completely forgotten about Harley in the other room. When she'd leaned closer. Felt her heart slamming against her ribs.

And that moment earlier this afternoon at Mama's, when they'd communicated with just their eyes.

She longed to sit plastered against him, her thigh pressed up against his, her hip touching his hip. But if they were that close, she wouldn't focus on what they needed to talk about. Wouldn't be able to think of anything but Nathan.

And Harley was only a closed door away.

So she sat down, leaving space between them. Nathan studied the gap. "I don't bite," he murmured.

"Not sure about that."

Her hand rested on the cushion next to her, and Nathan picked it up. Held her gaze as he rubbed the back of her hand, drew circles on her palm with his index finger. "Maybe you'd like me to bite." His voice was a rough sweep of darkness, low and intimate.

There were a lot of things she'd like Nathan to do. A lot of things she'd like to do to him. She tugged her hand away, missing his touch as soon as he let go. Curled her fingers into her palm to hold the memory of his caress.

"We need to talk about Harley," she said, her voice more breathless than she liked.

He raised his eyebrows. "And we can't do that while I hold your hand?"

God, no. "You'll make me lose my train of thought. And I need to focus on Harley and keeping her safe."

"Okay." One side of his mouth curled up. "Good to know. We'll focus on Harley first."

First? She cleared her throat, closed her eyes, reached for the calm that had never failed her. The one she'd developed as a child when confronted with her thoughtless drama queen mother. The one she used now when dealing with difficult clients.

Nathan shifted on the couch, sliding his elevated leg as he turned to face her. "Can't reach you from here. So you're safe."

For now. "Yes. No. I don't…" She closed her eyes briefly, cleared her throat. *Calm.* "About Harley."

The teasing smile disappeared from his face. "Yes."

She leaned toward him. "Why would these people you're pursuing want to hurt a thirteen-year-old kid? What would they gain from that?"

"I don't think it's that they want to hurt her," he said slowly. "I think they want me to understand that they *could.* That if I don't drop this and back off, she's vulnerable."

"So why don't you drop it? You have no proof that anything illegal happened. Just a hunch."

"No, I have no proof." His gaze held hers, and she saw shame in his expression. "Maybe everything was legit. Maybe taxes were paid. But I accepted the money without being sure it was legal. I got the money in a cashier's check. Made my payments in cash. Chuck came to my restaurant two or three times a week, watching me. Keeping track of how much business we did. And he had a gun."

Nathan clenched his hands into fists. "That restaurant is my parents' legacy. All that we have left of them. Neither my father nor my mother would have accepted that money. They would have found a bank who'd lend it to them, no matter how long they had to look. They wouldn't have agreed to a shady deal just because they wanted to get it done. Because they wanted to finish the remodeling and…and run away.

"But I did. So I have to make it right. I have to find the person who gave the alderman that money. If he got it legally and paid taxes on the interest, great. But I don't think he did. So it's up to me to take care of the situation."

"I see." And she did. Nathan felt as if he'd tarnished his family legacy by choosing to participate in a shady business deal. So it was his responsibility to make it right.

She leaned toward him. "No one would think less of you if you let it go," she said quietly. "You don't know for sure that it was illegal."

"I would think less of myself." He reached for her hand, then stopped. "I'm sorry you and Harley are entangled in this. I really am. Neither of you asked for this, or deserve it."

"Then I guess we have to figure out how to deal with it," Emma said. "How to keep Harley safe. And how to catch this guy."

Nathan straightened. Swung his leg off the coffee table. "You don't have anything to do with catching this guy," he said sharply. "That's my job. And Patrick's. Your job is watching out for Harley."

"So what do you suggest?"

"Get better locks on your door," he said immediately. His gaze skimmed over the windows, as if he was assessing their security. "Put in an alarm system, maybe."

"Come on, Nathan. We live on the second floor. No one's coming in through the windows." But she glanced out into the darkness uneasily. His words were creeping her out.

"No. Probably not."

Probably? "What? You think there's some kind of supervillain after you? Someone who can jump two stories and climb in my window?"

"No." He rubbed his chin, and in the silence she heard the faint rasp of his whiskers against his fingers. "I don't want to freak you out. But that lock on the downstairs door? That wouldn't keep out a determined eight-year-old. You've got a dead bolt up here, and that's good. But the door is kind of thin."

"You know, you *are* freaking me out." She jumped up from the couch and stared down at the street, her arms wrapped around her waist. It looked like any other winter night out there. Sidewalks deserted. Lights on and shades drawn in the other apartment buildings. Dirty snow piled at the curb, littered with the skeletons of old kitchen chairs, scuffed plastic milk crates, a broken stroller. The markers of "dibs," waiting patiently for the next snowfall, when they'd be used to guard the parking spaces their owners shoveled out.

Was Nathan's heart filled with the debris of his past? The loss of his parents, the choices he'd been forced to make, the mistakes he'd made in his hurry to leave that past behind?

Was he so focused on his past and his future that he couldn't see the present?

She heard the whisper of fabric as Nathan slid off the couch, and a few moments later, his hands settled on her shoulders. "Sorry," he said softly. His breath fluttered against her ear, making her shiver. "You and Harley have gotten caught up in this mess, and it's my fault. I hate that my stupid, selfish decision has to affect so many other people." His hands tightened on her shoulders, then they were gone.

"You know how we paid off the alderman in the end?" he said, his voice tight. "Cal had to lend us the money. My sister's fiancé. God!" She could feel the tension thrumming through his body.

"I know Cal." She'd met him at FreeZone. "I'm sure he was thrilled he could help."

"Yeah. Thrilled. Now you and Harley are involved. And I can't stop thinking about that crappy lock downstairs and the flimsy door into your apartment."

She turned to face him, stared up into his stormy eyes. "What do you want to do? What would make this easier for you?"

He closed his eyes. "The point isn't to make this easier for me. It's to make it easier for you and Harley. Safer."

She was already terrified for Harley's safety. Nothing would take that terror away besides finding out who was responsible for the loan. But she wasn't going to tell Nathan that. He already felt guilty enough. "Do you have any suggestions?" she asked carefully.

He shoved a hand through his hair. "This is President's Day weekend. Harley's off school on Monday, right?"

"Monday and Tuesday." FreeZone would be open both days. Emma knew Harley would be happy to spend the days with her friends while Emma worked. But after Chuck the goon followed them to the ski hill, Emma didn't want Harley out of her sight.

"Then, would you consider…" He cleared his throat. "What do you think about staying with me for the rest of the weekend? Monday and Tuesday, too." He studied her carefully. "You probably have to work on Monday and Tuesday, right?"

"I'm supposed to."

"So if you both stayed with me, you wouldn't have to worry about what to do with Harley. And I wouldn't have to worry about the two of you alone in this apartment."

Maybe Nathan was more focused on the present than she thought. His solution made sense, in an uncomfortable, awkward kind of way. But her staying in the same house as Nathan? Even with Harley there, as well? "I'm not sure how that would work, Nathan," she said slowly.

"Easy. You and Harley pack some stuff and come home with me. There are three extra bedrooms in the house. Plenty of room."

"Why is your place safer? The bad guys know where you live."

He shrugged. "Yeah, but I've got a top-of-the-line security system—no one's getting in. The police do regular drive-bys. And I'll feel better if you're with me." He tucked a curl behind her ear, his finger sliding over her cheek, lingering at her jaw.

She lifted her gaze to him. "Do you really think that would be smart?" she whispered. "Having me stay at your house?"

"What are you afraid of?" His fingers lifted from her jaw, burrowed into her hair. She shivered at his touch, found herself swaying toward him. Aching for his heat, the muscled plane of his chest against hers, the solid strength of his thighs bracing hers.

"This," she murmured. "This is what I'm afraid of."

He cradled her face between his palms. "Nothing to be scared of," he murmured, leaning closer. "We've already gotten the first kiss out of the way." His breath puffed against her face, heating her skin.

"A kiss in a school stairwell is a lot different than living in the same house," she muttered.

"I'll be on my best behavior," he promised, brushing his lips over hers. "Nothing but longing glances." She felt him smile against her mouth. "Maybe a little footsie under the kitchen table at breakfast. Or some necking on the couch after Harley's in bed." He nipped at her lower lip. "Nothing to worry about."

Judging by the way her heart raced and her stomach fluttered at his words, there was a lot to worry about. This wasn't supposed to be about her and Nathan. It was about Nathan and Harley. And keeping Harley safe.

She put her hands on his chest, felt the tension vibrating through him. She should push him away.

Her fingers curled in his shirt, holding on to him. Pulling him closer. "How do you define necking?" she asked, her mouth hovering over his.

"Mmm." He nibbled at the corner of her mouth, touched the spot with his tongue. "Lots of this. I want to memorize how you taste. Everywhere. I want to know where you're ticklish. What your skin feels like. The sounds you make when you…" He pressed his mouth to hers, and her eyes fluttered closed.

He shifted, and his body was glued to hers, thighs to chest. Somehow, her arms ended up around his neck, clutching him closer. And her mouth had opened beneath his. She touched his teeth with her tongue and smiled at his sharp intake of breath.

"You like what you're doing to me," he said as he sucked her lower lip into his mouth. Tasted it. Lingered to stroke his tongue over the slick surface. "So do I." His voice made her legs weak. His arms tightened around her, his mouth suddenly hot and desperate. "I've been thinking about this since the moment I saw you at FreeZone."

"Me…me, too." She inhaled sharply as one of his hands swept down her back and gripped her rear. Drawing her closer, pressing her tighter. Letting her feel exactly what he'd been thinking.

She wanted to close her eyes and fall into him. His touch. His mouth. Instead, her hands moving far too slowly, she cupped his face in her palms. Created space between their bodies, even though it felt as if she tore something inside her as she separated from him. "This is why it would be a bad idea to stay at your house."

"I think it's a very good idea."

"Too complicated, Nathan," she said, leaning in to brush her mouth over his one last time. "Too many traps to step into. Too much emotion."

He let her draw away from him, let his hands drop to his sides. "It's three days, Emma. Three days that I won't worry so much. Three days you don't have to worry, either." He smiled and touched her cheek again. "Please don't make me sleep on your couch. Because I'm not leaving you and Harley alone."

He was right. Alone in this apartment with Harley, Emma would freak out. And that wouldn't be good for Harley.

Harley's door clicked open. By the time she stepped into the living room, Emma and Nathan were two feet apart. "Hey, guys, what's up?"

She looked from Emma to Nathan. Emma felt her face flame. "Nathan thought we might like to spend the rest of the weekend at his place. What do you think?"

Harley looked from her to Nathan again and a smile flickered at the edges of her mouth. "That's cool." Her gaze shifted between them again. Her smile widened. "Guess that means I can go back to the restaurant."

CHAPTER NINETEEN

AN HOUR LATER, Nathan unlocked the back door of his house, punched in the security code, then waited as Emma and Harley stepped inside. The kitchen light shone on the dirty dishes he'd left in the sink this morning. He'd been in a hurry to leave. To see Emma.

And Harley, he realized.

He dropped his cane into its usual spot by the door and limped inside. So he'd left dishes in the sink. Wasn't the first time. Wouldn't be the last, either.

But he rinsed them and shoved them into the dishwasher. When he turned around, Emma smiled at him.

"Don't worry about it," she said. "We leave dishes in the sink all the time." She elbowed Harley. "Right?"

"Yeah," the girl said absently. She was busy scoping out his kitchen, studying the small table, the stainless-steel appliances, the cat clock that had hung above the table for as long as Nathan could remember.

Harley wandered into the dining area, slid her hand over the old table. That table held a lot of memories for Nathan. Watching his daughter touch it, watching her in the house where he'd grown up, made his throat tighten a little.

His parents should have been here to see this. If it hadn't been for Peter Shaughnessy, they would have been. His dad would have scooped his granddaughter into a huge hug, twirled her around the room, tried to give her a glass of watered wine at dinner.

His mom would have slapped his father's hand away from

the wine bottle and poured Harley a glass of milk. Pointed out the cookie jar after dinner and told Harley to help herself.

He shoved his hands into his pockets. So many memories in this house. But to Harley and Emma, it probably just looked old and shabby.

The scratches in the leather couch seemed bigger, deeper in the bright lights. The cushions saggier. He and Patrick and Marco had spent hours on that couch, playing video games, blasting the Nazis and their dogs in Wolfenstein.

The stain on the arm of one of the chairs by the window looked huge. His dad had been gesturing while he spoke, holding a glass of red wine, and the dregs had spilled onto the fabric. The coffee table was messy with magazines waiting to be read, and the sports section of today's paper was open on the floor.

Nathan looked around the living room, seeing the shabbiness for the first time. The memories. He'd been living in the tomb of his family. Chained to the past. Unable to move on.

It was time to focus on the future. On his trip. On getting his life back.

"I like your house, Nathan," Emma said behind him.

He glanced over his shoulder. "Wasn't expecting guests."

"It looks lived-in. Comfortable. The way a home should be."

"That's the polite way of saying it's a mess."

She hooked her arm through his. "Did I apologize for the books all over the tables in my apartment? The shoes by the door? No. So shut your pie hole."

The knot in his chest loosened a little, and he hugged her arm close for a moment. "You do have a way with words, Emma."

"What are these?" Harley asked. She was on her knees in front of a bookcase, pulling an old photograph album off the shelf.

"Pictures of the family. When we were growing up."

"Can I look at them?" she asked, tilting her head at him.

"Sure. There's a bunch of different albums, but my mom—" he swallowed another rush of sadness "—your grandmother, labeled them with the dates."

"Sweet," Harley said, already paging through the album. She stopped leafing, stared at a page of pictures. "Ms. Devereux is so busted," she crowed. "She was a complete dork!"

Harley was looking for pictures of Frankie. Not him. Throat tight, he leaned over Harley's shoulder. "Cut her some slack," he managed to say, although his voice sounded rough. "She was ten years old."

Harley flipped a page. "My mom babied me, but even *I* didn't have *pigtails* when I was ten."

She stopped again. Laughed. "Hello Kitty? Seriously? Wow."

Why would Harley have looked for pictures of him? She already had a relationship with his sister. Him? Not so much.

He straightened and stepped back. "Want me to show you the spare rooms?" he said to Emma.

"In a minute." She sat beside Harley, crossing her legs. "Can I look, too?"

"Sure." Harley shoved the album closer to Emma. "These pictures are hilarious."

Emma glanced over her shoulder at him, and he shifted his feet. Sank onto the couch. Damn leg. She studied him for a moment longer, then turned back to Harley.

"Here's a picture of the whole family," she said to Harley, tapping the page. "Looks like maybe your father's high school graduation?" She glanced at him again. Took the album and held it up.

"Yeah. Day I graduated from St. Pat's." His parents stood on either side of him, flanked by fourteen-year-old Patrick, ten-year-old Frankie and eight-year-old Marco.

If they'd known they'd only had a few more years with their children, would his parents have done things any differently? Spent more time with them? Been more patient?

No. They'd been great parents. Yeah, there had been a lot of yelling, because both his mom and his dad had been emotional. He and his siblings had had an unorthodox childhood, spending so much time at the restaurant. But that didn't take anything away from what his parents had accomplished.

They'd given each of their children individual attention—and they'd always known when it was needed. Made them feel secure and loved. Nathan had taken his parents for granted, never thought about what they'd done for their kids.

Nathan had had no idea how hard it was to be a parent. How much sacrifice it took. What parents gave up for their kids.

He studied Harley's bright red hair as she bent over the photo album. Hair just like his grandmother's. Was he up to the job? He had no idea.

"You have all weekend to look at the photo albums, Harley," he said, struggling to his feet. "Why don't you come upstairs and pick out a bedroom? You have your choice of Frankie's old room, or Patrick's and Marco's."

Harley shoved the album back onto the shelf. Her fingers trailed over it after she tapped it into place, and she stared at the spines of the leather albums for a long moment. Then she stood up. "Didn't you have a room?"

Did she want to stay in his old bedroom? The flash of pleasure surprised him. "Yeah, but it was in the basement. I moved down there after Marco got too old to share with Frankie."

Harley frowned. "You didn't all have your own rooms?"

Harley always had. She was an only child. "Nah. Not enough bedrooms." He smiled, although it was an effort. "Now I get the biggest bedroom upstairs, so it's all good."

His bedroom was his parents' old room. Ghosts of the past, even while he slept.

Too much to think about. He reached for their two suitcases, even though he wasn't sure how he'd manage to get both of them up the stairs. "Plenty of room for you and Emma, though."

Before he could take the suitcases, Emma grabbed them.

Shook her head when he reached for them. "No way," she said quietly.

"One of them, then." Harley had already bounded up the stairs. He held out his hand, and Emma hesitated. Finally she nodded and shifted one of the bags to his right hand.

"Go ahead," he murmured, waving toward the stairs.

She took two steps and glanced over her shoulder, then continued. He'd wanted her to go ahead of him so she didn't see him struggle. But his slow, awkward climb had one benefit—he got to watch her ass, all the way up the stairs.

EMMA STEPPED OUT of the bathroom, the sharp scent of soap-tinged steam following her into the hall. She'd put on her pajamas—boxer shorts and an old T-shirt, but she wasn't ready to sleep. She was restless. Edgy. Wide-awake.

She opened the door of the bedroom Harley had chosen and saw her sprawled on the bed, sound asleep. She pulled the door closed quietly.

She glanced toward the end of the hall. Toward Nathan's room. He'd carefully avoided her eyes when telling her and Harley that it was the only one off-limits.

She'd been right—staying in his house was beyond awkward. But she'd get through it. This was to keep Harley safe. For that, Emma could deal with awkward.

She opened the door to Patrick and Marco's old room—Harley had chosen Frankie's across the hall, snickering at all the old posters and books—but hesitated. There was a light on downstairs. Nathan was still up.

Without taking time to think, she grabbed her thin robe and threw it on. She found Nathan seated at the kitchen table, beer bottle in front of him, paging through a photo album.

"Hey," she said softly.

He glanced over at her, and the sadness in his gaze surprised her. She slid into the seat across from him. "What's wrong?"

"Nothing's wrong. Just remembering." He turned the album

around to show her a page of pictures of the entire Devereux family. At the restaurant. At Montrose Avenue Beach, with the boathouse in the background. At Lincoln Park Zoo.

Every picture showed a happy family, parents smiling, the kids mugging for the camera. Pictures of Nathan's dad, building sand castles with Frankie and Marco. Watching the gorillas at the zoo, his arms over Patrick's and Nathan's shoulders.

Pictures of Nathan's mom, baking at the restaurant with Frankie. Cooking with Marco.

"Looks like you had a great childhood," she said quietly. Emma had a single photo album, and it didn't hold very many pictures of her and her mother. The ones she had were mostly stiff and posed. She remembered one of the few candid shots vividly—one of her mom's friends had caught a young Emma sitting on a folding chair at a party, wistfully watching her mother laugh with her friends.

"We did. Until our parents died." He closed the album. "Seeing Harley looking at those pictures tonight reminded me of all we lost. All my parents lost." He swallowed. "All Harley won't have."

"You're starting late, but you can still have a relationship with her. You have a daughter. She has a father. You can build on that."

"Yeah." He nudged the photo album away. "The guy who hit my parents—the guy who was driving drunk and killed them—showed up here a few weeks ago. Said he was in A.A. and needed to apologize for what he'd done."

Emma sucked in a breath and reached for his hand. "That must have been hard."

"I've hated the guy for fourteen years." He turned her hand over, linked their fingers. Did he find it comforting? Did it make him feel less alone? "I haven't looked at these pictures for a long time. Tonight, with Harley, I realized again what he'd done to us. Taken from us. From Harley."

Did Nathan regret the choices he'd made? Regret dropping

out of school to raise his siblings? If so, it would explain his insistence that he didn't want to be a father.

Did he still feel that way?

"I need to put the past behind me so I can move on."

Emma knew what "moving on" meant to Nathan. It meant going to Italy. Reclaiming his life. Where did that leave Harley?

Emma didn't want to think about where it left *her.* If she did, she'd have to admit that she wanted more from him than just his acceptance of Harley.

"That sounds like a good idea," she said slowly. "Confront the past, deal with it."

"Is that your social worker mantra? Deal with your past?"

"It's a good one to have," she said lightly. His hands were warm. A little callused as they gripped hers. She held on tightly as she studied his face. She couldn't lecture Nathan about how to deal with his past. *She* still had issues with her past. With her mother.

Emma hadn't had the happy, secure childhood of Nathan's pictures. Her mother had been focused on herself, not her daughter. And, according to her mother, her father had disappeared right after Emma was born.

Nathan kissed one of her palms, then the other, dragging her away from the memories. "You're ready for bed." His gaze trailed down the short robe, lingered on her bare legs. "You must be exhausted," he said roughly. "It's been a long day."

"Yes, it has," she said. Did she want to make it a little longer? Spend some time with Nathan? "You're working tomorrow, right?"

"Yeah. I thought maybe I'd take Harley to Mama's with me. She can hang out with Marco. I'll know she's safe."

"That sounds like a good idea." He *was* thinking about Harley. He'd meant what he said about protecting her.

"You can come, too, if you like," he said.

She shook her head. "I'll have a quiet night by myself." Nathan and Harley needed some time alone together, without her buffering them. Time to bond. Father and daughter. The kitchen lights glittered in her suddenly blurry eyes. "I should go to bed. Like you said, it's been a long day."

"Hey, Emma. What's wrong?"

He reached for her, but she moved out of reach. "Nothing." Her voice was too bright. "'Night, Nathan. See you in the morning."

LATE SUNDAY EVENING, Nathan glanced at Harley as he drove down the deserted streets. Her head rested against the back of the seat and her eyes were closed—he'd kept her up way past her bedtime.

But she'd been bouncing-on-her-toes excited to come to Mama's with him. She'd given Emma a hug and rushed out the door without looking back. Emma had smiled, but Nathan hadn't missed the sadness in her eyes.

"You sure you don't want to come with us?" he'd asked Emma.

"No. You need an evening with Harley by yourself."

He hadn't pointed out that he'd be working, because he understood what Emma was telling him—get to know your daughter. Spend some time with her.

Harley had spent almost the entire evening with Marco. Marco hadn't seemed to mind at all.

Harley stirred and opened her eyes. "We almost there?" she asked.

"Couple more minutes. You have fun with Marco?"

"Yeah." She smiled and shifted to face him. "He let me help him make one of his specials. That was awesome."

"Kind of nice having uncles?" he asked casually. *How about having a father?*

"Yeah. And Ms. Devereux…ah, Frankie, too." She shifted more so she was sideways in the seat. "And you," she said quietly. "I always wanted to know who my father was. But my mom would never tell me."

Sonya should have told him, too. He gripped the steering wheel. She should have let him watch his daughter grow up.

"How come she didn't tell you about me?" Harley asked, her voice tentative and too quiet. "Was she afraid you wouldn't like me?"

Oh, God. He reached blindly for Harley's hand. Felt her fingers curl loosely around his, as if she was unsure of her welcome. "Of course not. Your mother was very proud of you. She loved you more than anything. You're an amazing kid, and she knew it." He tried to smile. "Maybe she was afraid *you* wouldn't like *me*."

"Nah," his daughter replied. "You're pretty cool. And she knew that, right? She knew you were cool?"

He had no idea what Sonya had thought about him. Not much, clearly, since she hadn't told him he had a daughter. "I hope she thought so," he said, trying to keep his tone light.

"I wish she had told you," Harley said suddenly. "I loved my mom, but it was always just the two of us. You know? In those pictures in your photo albums, it looked like your family had fun. You did fun things."

"Yeah, we did." Even though running a restaurant was a tiring job, their parents had spent time with them.

He couldn't make up for not being there for Harley in the first thirteen years of her life. But he could try to give her some answers. Help her figure out what had been going on in her mother's head.

"How about we go on a road trip tomorrow?" he asked impulsively. "We'll drive down to Champaign, where your mom and I met. I know she had some friends she worked with. We'll find them and ask them about her. So you can know what she was like before you were born."

"You'd do that?" Harley asked, awe in her voice. "Take me to find out about her?"

"Of course I would." He hoped he could find some people in his department who remembered Sonya. He needed some answers himself. He'd finally figured out that Harley had been conceived shortly after his parents died—probably on his trip down to Champaign to withdraw from college. But the details were still a blank. "So that's a yes?"

"That would be amazing." Harley sat up straight, eyes shining. "It's not that far away. I've looked at the map."

Of course Harley had thought about how her parents met. In most families, that was one of the first stories the kids heard. "It's a few hours. Little less, maybe. Easy day trip."

"And the restaurant is closed tomorrow, right?"

"Yeah. So we have as much time as you want."

He stopped in the alley and punched the garage door opener. "I'm going to go tell Emma," Harley said, reaching for the door before he could pull into the garage.

"Wait," he said, too sharply. He didn't want her running through the backyard alone this time of night. Or dashing into the house by herself. "Let's get the car put away."

The moment he turned off the engine, Harley was out of the car. He swung down from the seat and grabbed his cane, once again cursing his weak leg. But he managed to get out of the garage in time to see Harley yanking at the back door.

"Hold on," he said. "Emma might be asleep."

He could practically hear her eyes roll. "Duh. Emma's not going to go to sleep until I'm home."

The back door opened and a triangle of light spilled onto the porch. "Guess what, Emma," Harley said as she hurried into the house. "Nathan said…"

By the time he got in the door and reset the security system, Emma and Harley were in the living room. He set his cane by the door and followed the sound of their voices.

He was disappointed to see that Emma wasn't wearing that short robe again. Instead, she wore stretchy black pants that ended midcalf and a sweatshirt. She smiled at him as he walked into the living room. "So. Road trip tomorrow."

CHAPTER TWENTY

EMMA TUCKED HERSELF into the corner of the couch, her legs curled beneath her. Two beer bottles clinked together, then Nathan's footsteps headed out of the kitchen.

A few minutes earlier, Harley had floated up the stairs on a cloud of excitement and anticipation. Quiet settled on the house.

Nathan handed her one of the beers, then sat on the couch beside her. "So. Champaign tomorrow," she said, taking a sip of the cold, yeasty beer.

"Is that all right? I should have asked you first, but the idea just kind of popped out. Oh, hell." He closed his eyes. "You have to work. You already told me that."

"I'll take a personal day. This is more important." For both Harley and Nathan. "It was a good idea. Harley's excited to see the place where you and her mom, ah, met. And maybe you can find some answers, too."

"Yeah, some answers would be good." He took a long drink of beer and his hand gripped the bottle. "Harley asked why Sonya hadn't told me about her. I couldn't answer her. I wanted to be able to." Another gulp of beer. "She wondered if it was because Sonya thought I wouldn't like Harley."

Emma shot upright. "Oh, God, Nathan. Why would she think that?"

"Kids think all kinds of stuff in the middle of the night," he said roughly. "Especially after a parent dies."

He'd been there, she realized. Probably had been taken by the darkness himself some nights. Almost certainly comforted his siblings when they woke up crying.

"We need to get some answers for Harley." He rolled the bottle between his hands and didn't look at her. "She needs to know."

"We might not find any," she warned. She hoped they would, for everyone's sake. Nathan had made it clear he wasn't ready for fatherhood, but he was making an effort. Doing what he thought was right. It must be killing him that he couldn't remember anything about his affair with Sonya.

"Sonya must have moved shortly after Harley was born," Nathan said.

"I'm not sure when, exactly, but Harley grew up in Milwaukee. They moved to Chicago after Sonya found out about the aneurysm." She shifted on the couch to face him. "But there might be people still working in the liberal arts office who remember her."

"I'm counting on it," Nathan said. He edged closer to Emma, set his beer down as if the subject of his relationship with Sonya was done for now. "What did you do all evening?"

Missed you and Harley. "Nothing. And it was lovely."

"You stared at the wall all night?"

She elbowed him. "I took a bath. Read a book." She took a drink and smiled at him. "Drank some of the wine that was open in the refrigerator. Hope you don't mind."

"Not at all." He curled one arm around her shoulder, and its heavy weight warmed her skin and made her heart race. His fingers caressed her shoulder, leaving sparks in their wake, even through the heavy sweatshirt. "Messy house, old wine, leaving you alone for a whole evening? Not a very good host."

"The house is fine. The wine was good. And the being alone?" She cocked her head, listened to make sure Harley wasn't stirring. "It was heaven. I adore Harley. Love having her live with me. But sometimes, I need a little time to myself. She goes to bed before I do, but it's not the same. I don't want to watch television because I'm afraid it will disturb her. And…and I haven't taken any long baths in the evening, because when she was first with me, she had nightmares a lot. I listen for her."

"Does she still have them?" he asked. His touch on her shoulder made it hard to concentrate on what he was asking.

Desire built inside her, and all she could think about were Nathan's hands. What they were doing to her. "Have what?" she breathed.

Nathan leaned closer. "Does she still have nightmares?" His breath stirred her hair, and she tried to hide a tiny gasp.

"Not as...not as much as before."

"You're taking good care of her," he murmured. He put his mouth on her neck, and everything inside her tightened. He tugged her toward him. "Enough about Harley. Let's move on."

"To what?" she gasped as he sucked lightly on her skin. "Is this the necking portion of the program?"

"Hmm. Could be." He licked the spot he'd been sucking. "If you want it to be."

She shouldn't do this. It would lead to nothing but heartache. She was supposed to be thinking about Harley.

She needed to go upstairs. Alone.

But her limbs were too heavy to move. Her heart was beating too fast. Nathan was a magnet, drawing her body closer.

"This isn't smart," she whispered. Nathan short-circuited her brain. Made her want. Turned her into a needy woman.

And that was scary.

She never turned off her brain and let emotion take over. Never stopped thinking. She always stood off to the side, analyzing. Assessing. Thinking.

Maybe that was why none of her relationships lasted. Because she dissected them until nothing was left.

She hadn't been able to do that with Nathan. Huge warning bells clanged in her head. And still she wanted him. Wanted his hands and mouth on her. Her hands and mouth on him.

Her fingers itched to burrow beneath that blue dress shirt. She wanted to skim her hands over his chest. Touch his nipples, see if it made him shudder. Taste his skin, feel his muscles tense beneath her mouth.

She was dangerously close to shutting off her brain and letting go.

"Define *smart*," he said, his mouth gliding over her collar bone. "I want you, Emma. Have since the moment I saw you at FreeZone." He nuzzled the collar of her sweatshirt, tugged it with his teeth. "I think you want me, too. Do you want me to stop?"

"Yes." He froze. Lifted his head, and her whole body shuddered with the loss. "No," she groaned. She couldn't bear it if he stopped.

"You sure?" His trembling hand rested on her shoulder, and he lifted it as if it weighed a hundred pounds. "I need to hear you say it, Emma."

"Yes, I'm sure. Don't stop." She closed her eyes. Felt Nathan's hand on the hem of her sweatshirt and arched toward him. Pushed the warning voice out of her head.

"Me, too," he whispered. "I can't focus on anything besides how much I need to touch you. Taste you."

She ached for that, too, for his hands on her skin. Needed to touch him, as well. "Please, Nathan."

His fist tightened around her sweatshirt. "I'm begging, too, Emma." His hand slipped beneath the shirt, splayed against her belly. Hot. His mouth was on her neck again, leaving a trail of kisses to her ear. She shifted restlessly.

"More, Emma?" His breath tickled her ear, lifted strands of hair.

"Yes!" She barely recognized the harsh cry as her own voice. Her hands were on his chest and she didn't remember putting them there. His dress shirt was warm from his skin, still smelled faintly of starch. She tugged it out of his slacks, and he froze.

Desire burned away the haze of caution, the voice of reason. She touched his skin, felt his muscles tense. Felt them quiver as she explored, letting her hands creep higher until the soft hair on his chest tickled her palms.

"More?" Nathan's voice was hoarse. Barely controlled. His breath rasped in and out too quickly.

"Yes," she said, and her voice sounded like a moan.

He touched her ribs, one at a time, tracing their contours, and his fingers trembled when she gasped. He skimmed his palms up her sides, over her skin. Brushed the backs of his hands beneath her breasts, barely touching them.

"Emma." He curled his hand around her side as his mouth covered hers. "You're not wearing a bra." His words vibrated against her lips.

"Took a bath," she managed to say. "Didn't think…" How could she have known she'd need a barrier to slow down her desire, keep it from burning out of control?

"You're going to kill me," he groaned into her mouth.

He cupped her breasts in his hand, brushing his thumbs over her nipples. She inhaled sharply, then held his head and kissed him, holding nothing back. Their tongues tangled and retreated as he stroked her, until she was trembling and they were both panting.

Her clothes felt too tight, her skin too sensitive. She wanted to rip off the sweatshirt, the yoga pants, then strip Nathan's shirt and pants from his body. Feel his skin against hers.

A door creaked open above them, and they froze. Footsteps padded into the bathroom; the door closed.

She jerked away from him, shocked. "Harley's awake. What were we thinking?"

He smoothed the sweatshirt down over her hips. "No thinking involved."

Her heart galloped in a hard rhythm and her body yearned for his. She slid her hands beneath her thighs to stop their shaking. "I always think, Nathan," she whispered. "Never leap. You're…this…it's a little scary."

"For me, too." He looked at her hands, tucked beneath her legs. "I didn't plan on feeling this way, either."

The toilet flushed in the bathroom and the door opened again. Footsteps going the other way. Harley closed her bedroom door.

"I need to go upstairs." She swallowed. "Alone." She looked at him again and…yearned. "I don't want to, though."

"Me, either," he murmured. Before she could stand up, he kissed her again. "I'll see you in my dreams."

As she headed up the stairs, she paused and looked over her shoulder. Nathan was still watching her, his eyes dark, his mouth red.

She'd be seeing him in her dreams, as well.

NATHAN'S PALMS WERE sweaty as they parked in a garage near the Illini Union the next morning. He hadn't been back to the University of Illinois since that disastrous May fifteen years earlier, and a lot had changed.

A lot was still the same, though. Same buildings surrounding the quad. The Union stood at the north end, stately and serene. The Alma Mater statue welcomed everyone to the campus. He felt as if he'd time-traveled, going back to a place that was eerily familiar yet totally different.

The last time he'd been here, he'd been part of the community. He'd taken classes in most of these buildings. He'd known all the campus stores, too many of the bars.

Now? He was an outsider. A visitor, looking for information instead of an education. The students hurrying past them were so young. So full of hope. They had their whole futures in front of them.

Him? All he had were the memories of his years as a student, the regret that he'd needed to leave. When he'd been a student here, he'd been free. Had the whole world in front of him.

The loss of that boy, of his innocence, hit him without warning, leaving a hollowed-out spot in his chest. It had all started here, with a frantic, sobbing phone call one evening.

Since he'd left, his life hadn't been his own. It had been a sacrifice for his family. He glanced at Harley out of the corner of his eye. Did he want to make that sacrifice again?

Ghosts from the past swirled through the wind as he, Emma and Harley crossed Green Street and started down the sidewalk. The cold, fierce wind he remembered hit their faces.

"So you went to college here, huh?" Harley's voice yanked him back to the present. Her head swiveled back and forth, taking in the buildings, the students with their backpacks hurrying to class, the rare cyclist in the bike lane on Wright Street.

"Yeah. Spent four years here."

"I like it." She grinned happily. "I've never been to a college before."

"Maybe someday you can follow in your father's footsteps," Emma said. "You can come here yourself."

He glanced at his daughter. Maybe Harley could finish what he couldn't. Maybe she'd have control of her life. Her destiny.

He hoped so.

Harley studied him, and he couldn't read her expression. "That would be awesome."

The idea of his daughter attending the same school he had made his chest tighten. "I'll start a college savings account," he said.

"Sonya had one," Emma said quietly.

"Then I'll add to it." He didn't want his kid graduating with a mountain of debt.

Emma smiled. "That sounds good."

She'd been quiet on the ride down. He had been, too. Every time he looked at her, he remembered the way she'd kissed him last night, as if she had to have her hands on him. The way she'd gripped his shirt so tightly. The tiny sounds she'd made when he touched her.

Last night, he'd thought of nothing but Emma. Not the restaurant mess. Not Harley. Not his trip to Italy.

Soon beat like a drum in his head. Soon they'd have the time to explore each other. The time to discover what drove the other crazy. The way they liked to be touched. Kissed. Last night had been merely a taste. A beginning.

His need for Emma burned in his blood. He had to stop himself from taking her hand and pulling her closer. Maybe next weekend he'd see if Harley could spend the evening with Marco at the restaurant. She'd had a good time last night. She probably wanted to do it again.

They'd passed Lincoln Hall by the time he realized where they were. "It's that building." He pointed behind them.

"You forget where you went to school?" Harley said.

"Just thinking about stuff, I guess." He couldn't stop himself from glancing at Emma. Her face was pink and she wouldn't meet his gaze. She was thinking about stuff, too.

He pushed open the door to Lincoln Hall, where the Liberal Arts office was located, and followed Harley and Emma into a memory—the drafty coolness, the smell of dust and old varnish and the flicker of overhead lights. "We want the second floor."

When they reached the administrative office, he approached the receptionist. She looked up from the history textbook she'd been reading.

"May I help you?"

"I'd like to talk to the person who's been working here for the longest," he said easily. "I'm looking for an old friend who used to work here, and I'm hoping someone will remember her."

The young woman frowned for a moment, thinking, then she nodded. "That would probably be Mrs. Montgomery. I'll see if she's available."

Emma and Harley were looking at the framed certificates on the wall. Emma must have felt his gaze, because she stepped closer. "Do you want us to wait out here?"

"Maybe I should talk to her first," he said. "I don't want Harley to hear anything that might upset her."

"That's a good idea," Emma said in a low voice. "Come and get Harley after."

"And you," he said without hesitating. "I want you in there, too. You're part of Harley's life, you were Sonya's friend, and you should hear it, too."

Emma looked startled, as if she hadn't expected that, then nodded. Smiled. "Thank you, Nathan. I'd like to be there."

The receptionist came out and said, "Mrs. Montgomery said to bring you back."

Nathan's heart began racing. She might not even remember Sonya.

But she did. Nathan introduced himself and told the older woman he was looking for information about Sonya Michaels.

"Sonya," she said, as she studied him. "I haven't heard from her in years."

"She…she passed away suddenly a couple of months ago," Nathan said. "And it's complicated. I'm her daughter's father."

The woman narrowed her eyes at that. "I thought you looked familiar. Sonya talked about you all the time." The woman's mouth was a thin, tight line. "She had no family. And the guy who got her pregnant had disappeared. Wasn't around for her pregnancy. Or when her daughter was born."

"Not by choice. She never told me she was pregnant."

"You never asked, either."

"No. I didn't." If he'd remembered having sex with Sonya, he would have. He hoped. "I can't change that now. All I can do is find answers for Harley."

"I told Sonya…" Mrs. Montgomery pressed her lips together. "I told her you had a right to know she was pregnant, but she was adamant. She refused to tell you."

Had Sonya had that much contempt for him? Had she recognized what a screwup he was? Nathan swallowed. "Here's the thing. Harley is here with me. She wants to know why her mother never told me about her. And I have no answers. I was hoping someone who knew her might have an idea."

Mrs. Montgomery nodded slowly. "I can tell her that."

But she wouldn't have told him? "Is it…will it be easy for Harley to hear? I don't want you to lie to her, but if it's something that will hurt my daughter, you can tell me and I'll figure out a way to tell Harley."

Some of the tightness around the woman's mouth eased "You care about your daughter."

"Of course I do." No matter what happened with Harley and Emma, Harley was part of him. Part of his family.

"What I'll tell your daughter won't upset her. Go ahead and bring her in."

A few moments later, Nathan stood back and allowed Harley and Emma to enter the office. Emma hung back, as if she thought she was intruding, so Nathan took her hand and drew her inside.

"This is Harley," he said. He put his hand on his daughter's shoulder, squeezed when he felt her tension. Then he drew Emma forward. "And Emma Sloan. She's Harley's guardian Sonya's best friend."

"Ellen Montgomery. Nice to meet both of you." She gestured to chairs in front of the desk. "Have a seat."

She smiled at Harley. "I remember when you were born. All of us who worked with your mom were so excited. And you were a beautiful baby with your red frizzy hair."

Harley touched her hair self-consciously and studied the woman. "You worked with my mom?"

"Yes. This is a small office. Everyone knows everyone else."

Nathan cleared his throat. "Harley wonders why her mother never said anything to me about being pregnant. Do you have any idea?" he asked.

"I know exactly why." Mrs. Montgomery leaned toward Harley. "Your mother loved your father very much. She'd been in love with him for years. Talked about him all the time." She glanced at Nathan. "We all knew that when you came into the office, we had to let Sonya help you."

From the expression on Mrs. Montgomery's face, she hadn't approved of Sonya's crush on him. Embarrassment, regret and sorrow twisted together inside him. How could he not have known that Sonya was...attracted to him? How blind and unfeeling had he been?

Ellen Montgomery studied him. "Sonya knew what had happened with your parents. She knew you'd dropped out of school and were responsible for your younger brothers and sister. That you were running the family restaurant. I guess you must have told her."

Nathan nodded, although he had no idea. The idea that Sonya had been infatuated with him shamed him. He'd never seen it. Even now, he didn't really remember her.

Harley leaned forward in her chair, hanging on every word. It was sad that she had to hear this story from a stranger.

"Anyway, when Sonya found out she was pregnant, she decided not to tell you. She said you had enough to cope with, and she didn't want to add another burden."

"Harley wouldn't have been a burden," he said fiercely.

"Of course not. But Sonya was convinced she was doing you a favor. She said that after your life got straightened out, she'd get in touch with you. I guess she never did."

"No. She didn't."

Harley shifted in her chair and looked at her lap. Her hair fell across her face, but Nathan saw her lip quivering. Without thinking, he reached over and took her hand.

Her startled gaze jumped to his. She swallowed. Then she gripped his hand so hard his bones hurt. He edged his chair closer to hers and held on.

"Your mother was several years older than your father, Harley. More...settled in her life. She knew what she wanted, and she wanted you. She was certain she could raise you on your own, without worrying your father."

Mrs. Montgomery's eyes shifted from him to Harley. The ice in them had begun to thaw. "I suspect that the older you got, the harder it became for your mother to tell your father about you. It would be so difficult to tell a man that he had a child he'd never known about."

What if Sonya had contacted him and he couldn't remember sleeping with her? He wouldn't have believed her. How would he have reacted? Honorably, he hoped. But he wasn't sure.

He turned to Harley. "Do you have any questions for Mrs. Montgomery?"

She clung to his hand. "Was my mom...was she happy she was going to have me?"

The woman smiled. "Honey, she was ecstatic. She was so careful while she was pregnant—no coffee, no alcohol. She paid attention to what she ate, took her vitamins. She couldn't wait until you were born—she said you were a part of your father that she'd always have."

"What did she do here? For work, I mean."

"She was one of the department secretaries, just like I was. We made copies of tests, helped the students when they had problems, assisted the professors. Different stuff on different days."

"Thank you," Harley said, standing abruptly. "For telling me about my mom." Harley's voice was thick, as if she was trying not to cry. She squeezed his hand hard, then let go and rushed to Emma.

Emma folded Harley into her arms. "We'll go for a walk while you finish talking to Mrs. Montgomery," Emma said softly.

With Harley's face buried in Emma's shoulder, the two of them walked out of the office. Emma was so good with Harley. Patient. Loving. Tender. Nathan watched until they were out of sight, then turned back to Mrs. Montgomery. "I have a few more questions."

CHAPTER TWENTY-ONE

NATHAN TOOK A DEEP BREATH.

"I need to know what happened that night," he said. "I don't remember a thing."

The frost came back to Ellen Montgomery's expression. "I suspected as much. Sonya said you were very drunk when she ran into you at Kam's Bar. She was concerned, so she sat down with you, and your story poured out."

"I was drunk?" So drunk he couldn't remember sleeping with her?

"Yes. And she thought she was in love with you." The woman's tone hardened. "She knew you weren't coming back. But she had to have one night."

It was so much worse than he'd suspected. Harley could never, ever know.

He didn't want Emma to know, either. He didn't want to see her scorn, the contempt she would try to hide.

He closed his eyes. He'd come back to Champaign to get his stuff and withdraw from school. He'd gone to Kam's and gotten drunk. Had sex he couldn't remember. Made a baby he hadn't known about for thirteen years.

One more disastrous consequence of his parents' death.

Not disastrous, he corrected himself. Harley wasn't a disaster. Just one more thing that changed his life. Took away options.

One more impulsive decision come home to roost.

"Was her...did she have a hard pregnancy?"

"No, what I told your daughter was the truth. After her initial shock, she was thrilled."

"I would have helped her," he said quietly. "With money, if she wouldn't accept anything else." Would he? He wanted to think so. But he'd been so grief-stricken, so terrified, so overwhelmed, that he might not have. And even now he didn't have a record of good decision-making.

"Sonya thought you would have helped her. Me? I had my doubts." Mrs. Montgomery's voice hardened again. "I don't know how you could have looked at Sonya and not seen that she was desperately in love with you. You had sex when you were drunk, and you should have known better."

"Yes. I did. And there are no excuses." He stood up, debated holding out his hand and decided against it. She wouldn't shake it. "Thank you for talking to Harley."

"I'd do anything for Sonya's daughter." *But not for the loser who got her pregnant.*

As HARLEY POKED at the whipped cream on her hot chocolate, she glanced around at the college kids sitting in the cafeteria of the Union and tried to act cool. Like she came here all the time. Like maybe she was one of them.

She wondered if her dad and mom had come here, when they were dating.

Emma was watching with that worried look on her face, so Harley hunched her shoulders. "Thank you for bringing me here," she muttered. "It was sweet to hear about my mom and…my dad."

"It was your father's idea," Emma said. "You should thank him."

"He wouldn't have suggested it if he didn't think it would be okay with you."

Emma's face got red and she choked a little on her hot chocolate. "We never talked about this, Harley. It was Nathan's idea."

Harley got that funny tingle in her stomach, the same one she'd gotten in the office when her da…Nathan held her hand. "I'm glad my mom was so careful when she was pregnant. I guess she really did want me, even if she didn't tell Nathan about me."

Harley was angry at her mom for that, and it made her feel guilty. But her mom should have told him. Maybe things would have been different. Maybe they would have gotten married. Been a family.

"Of course she wanted you." Emma put her hand over Harley's. Held on when Harley's began to tremble. "I could tell that as soon as I met you."

Harley shrugged. "She could have had an abortion. Since she didn't, I always figured she did. Want me. But it was nice…" *Nice to hear it.*

Harley crumbled a piece of the blueberry muffin sitting untouched on her tray. "I liked it when Mrs. Montgomery said she loved my dad, and that's why she didn't tell him. She should have, though." She rubbed her finger through the tiny purple crumbs.

"So what do I do now?" Harley brushed the crumbs away and took a deep breath. "Am I supposed to, like, live with him?" The idea was both scary and kind of cool. She could go to the restaurant and cook with Marco. But she didn't want to leave Emma.

Emma set her hot chocolate on the tray, and a little splashed down the side of the cup. "Do you want to live with Nathan?" she asked.

"I don't know." Harley's eyes stung and she stared at her cup. Maybe her dad and Emma would, like, get together. That would be awesome. "He's nice and I like him, but I hardly know him. I like living with you. But maybe my mom wanted me to live with him."

"Harley, listen to me." Emma tightened her grip on her hand, and Harley clung to her. "Your mom didn't make Nathan your guardian. She could have done that, but she didn't. So I think this is exactly what she wanted. For you and Nathan to get to know each other. To get used to each other. Figure out together what you want.

"It's okay not to make a decision," she continued softly. "Okay to take your time. The three of us will figure it out together."

Harley didn't want to choose. "Yeah?"

"Yes," Emma said firmly. "You won't have to do anything you don't want to do. I promise you. Except maybe do your homework and clean your room."

Harley sat up straight and rolled her eyes. "That's so lame." But the pain in her chest eased a little. She pressed her finger into the muffin crumbs on the tray and licked them off. Broke off a bigger piece of the muffin and stuffed it in her mouth. "I'm starving."

Emma's phone buzzed with a text, and she smiled as she glanced at the screen. "It's your dad." She texted him back, then set the phone on the table. "He's on his way."

NATHAN CLUTCHED HIS cup of coffee too tightly, even though its heat burned through the paper cup, and made his way toward Emma and Harley. Harley's shoulders weren't hunched and tense anymore. She was actually smiling a little. Emma touched her hand, said something, and Harley rolled her eyes.

Some of the tension drained from Nathan's shoulders, as well. He'd screwed up, done a horrible thing, but something good had come out of the mess. He had a great kid.

Something good had come out of the mess he'd made at the restaurant, as well. His family was closer than ever. Patrick had found the love of his life and moved back to Chicago. And Marco…his baby brother had grown up a little.

Maybe if Nathan could fix things with Harley, he could fix things at the restaurant, as well.

"Hey," he said, forcing a smile as he sat down between

Emma and Harley. "I see you found the best hot chocolate on campus."

Harley took another sip, which left a faint mustache on her lip. He wanted to lean forward and wipe it off, but he kept his hands wrapped around his coffee. He was still hesitant to touch her. Unsure if she would welcome it, or flinch away.

"Yeah, it's good," she said, licking off the mustache. "But I bet you never drank any when you went to school here. I know what college kids drink."

Nathan leaned forward. "Yeah? What's that?"

"Beer." Harley shot him a knowing look. "Denise, in my algebra class, has a brother who goes here. He's a freshman, and he drinks beer."

"He's pretty stupid, then," Nathan said, a little more forcefully than he might have before his conversation with Ellen Montgomery. "First of all, it's illegal. And second, getting drunk can get you into all kinds of trouble."

Harley reared back. "Hey, don't yell at me about it. I don't even like beer."

"How would you know?" Out of the corner of his eye, he saw Emma lean forward, watching him. As if she could see his shame.

As if realizing she'd said too much, Harley gave him a typical teenage shrug. "I tried some of Mom's once. It was disgusting."

"Good. That's good." He frowned. Leaned closer to her. "Do kids at parties ever offer you beer? Or wine? Or…other stuff?"

Harley scowled at him. "My mom wouldn't let me go to those kinds of parties. God! It was so embarrassing! If I was invited to a party, she'd call the kid's parents and give them the third degree. Then when she dropped me off, *she'd come into the house!* To talk to the parents."

"She was being a good mother," Emma said quietly. "She met the parents because she loved you." A shadow filled Emma's eyes. "Some parents don't care enough to check on what their kids are doing."

Nathan wanted to know what put that darkness in Emma's expression.

"I didn't get invited to any of the good parties after she did that a few times," Harley said, her voice sullen.

Thank God. "I think 'good parties' is a matter of opinion," Nathan said. "Kids can get into a lot of trouble before they realize it."

"Yeah, whatever."

Nathan's gaze met Emma's, and he saw the same resolve that resonated through him. Harley wouldn't be going to any of "those" kinds of parties. Not on her watch.

Or his.

His watch? Coffee sloshed out of the tiny hole in the lid and a few drops stung his hand. What was that supposed to mean? Was he actually thinking that Harley would live with him?

Maybe. Sometime in the future. After he got to the bottom of the money thing at the restaurant. After his trip to Italy. After he figured out what he wanted to do with the rest of his life. Maybe, once all that was settled, he could focus on his daughter.

In the meantime, she had Emma. Emma, who loved Harley and wanted to adopt her.

A tiny voice whispered in his ear. Asked him if he was making another hasty decision. Another wrong choice. He ignored it.

"How about some lunch?" he asked Emma and Harley. "Before we head back to Chicago?"

"That sounds good." Emma smiled and set her hot chocolate on the tray. It was covered with purple crumbs, and he wondered what Harley had eaten.

"I guess," Harley said. She grabbed the tray and took it to the trash bin. When she returned, she fiddled with the zipper of her jacket. "Did you and my mom have, like, a favorite place to eat?" she asked without looking at him.

Only the bar where he and Sonya had met that night. "There were a bunch of places we all liked to eat on campus," he said. "I'll show you some of them, and you can pick."

"Cool." Harley smiled and zipped her jacket.

As they left the cafeteria, they passed the bookstore. It was filled with Illini-themed clothing and merchandise. Harley slowed as she looked at the sea of orange-and-blue clothing.

"Can I look in here?" she asked.

"Sure," Nathan said, with a glance at Emma.

She was watching Harley. "Do you want a sweatshirt or a T-shirt or something?"

The girl shrugged again as she stared at the merchandise in the store. "Some of the kids wear college stuff. From, like, where their older brother or sister goes. Maybe...maybe I could get something from where my mom and dad went."

A lump grew in Nathan's throat, making it hard to speak. Harley had never referred to him as her dad before. Emma set a hand on his arm.

"I think that's a great idea, Harley," she said. "Why don't you go pick something out?"

"Okay." The girl dashed into the store, and he stood watching as she walked slowly through the displays. She touched sweatshirts, held T-shirts up to her body, picked up ball caps.

Emma still held his arm.

"This was such a good idea," she said quietly. "You helped get her some answers."

"Yeah." He slid his hand up to where she gripped his arm and twined his fingers with hers. "I got some, too."

"I'm glad."

"You're not going to ask me what they were?"

She squeezed his hand. "Those are pretty personal. You don't have to tell me."

He should tell her. She was part of this, too. She'd been

Sonya's friend. She was Harley's guardian. But he couldn't bear to reveal the dark places inside him. Wouldn't be able to bear seeing her affection turn to disgust.

"Maybe later. When I've had time to process it." That was an excuse. He was too ashamed to tell her the truth.

"It's part of the past. You don't owe me an explanation." She put her hand on his arm and squeezed. "You don't have to answer to me."

He *wanted* to answer to her. Emma already knew some crappy stuff about him. And if they…if they took this connection where he wanted it to go, she had a right to know the worst.

"I should tell you. But not now."

"It's been a hard day," she said softly. "For you. For Harley. But you're doing exactly what she needs—getting to know her. Bringing her down here to find out more about her mother. Giving her the time to get to know you." Her shoulder touched his.

"And you're forgetting one thing," she said, leaning closer. "If Sonya had come to you and told you about Harley, you would have done the right thing. You would have supported her and tried to be a father to Harley. But she never gave you that chance."

"God, Emma." He pulled her close and held her tightly, inhaling the fragrance of her hair. Her soft curls tickled his nose, and he buried his face in them.

One of her hands tangled in his hair, and she smoothed the other over his back in soothing circles. Her curves pressed into him, soft and womanly, sparking awareness.

Footsteps approached, then he heard Harley's voice. "Emma? Nathan? What's going on?"

CHAPTER TWENTY-TWO

NATHAN FELT EMMA tense when she heard Harley's voice and he held her more tightly. Inhaled her scent one more time. He didn't want to let her go.

But he eased away and smiled easily at his daughter. "Yep. You caught us in the act. Making out in the Union."

Harley rolled her eyes. "That's so lame. You were sad. Just like me," she said.

"Yeah." His smile disappeared. "It's been a tough day."

Emma's fingers touched his before she turned to Harley. "Looks like you found some stuff." Her voice was too bright. But Harley nodded as she held out the armful of sweatshirts and T-shirts. She hadn't noticed the shadows in Emma's eyes. Or his.

Nathan reached for the clothing Harley held. "You want to brag about your old man's alma mater, huh?" He struggled to smile, to act like everything was fine. "Let's see what you found."

AN HOUR LATER, Nathan glanced into the rearview mirror as they pulled out of the parking garage. Harley was already sticking her earbuds into place and fiddling with the control of her iPod. He turned onto Green Street and headed toward the expressway, passing the Deluxe, the seedy pool hall and diner where they'd had lunch.

There were better places on campus, but after hearing his stories about missing his one o'clock class on Friday afternoons for almost an entire semester because he had to have the De-luxe's fish sandwiches, Harley had insisted on eating there.

He'd told more stories about his days as a student, making both Harley and Emma laugh. By the end of their lunch, the shadows were gone from Harley's eyes.

His would be sticking around for a while.

By the time they hit Interstate 57, Harley was slumped in the corner of the backseat, her eyes closed. She clutched the bag containing the navy blue sweatshirt and the orange T-shirt to her chest. A wave of tenderness swept over him as he watched Harley in the rearview mirror.

"You okay?" Emma asked softly.

"I'm fine." He wasn't. But Harley was. That's what mattered.

The wheels of the SUV hummed against the pavement as they flew past muddy fields.

"You don't look fine," she said.

Her soft words reopened the wound that Ellen Montgomery had inflicted that morning. "Knock off the social worker crap, Emma," he said, his voice too sharp.

"'Social worker crap'? Because I asked a friend how he was?"

Her voice rose, and Nathan glanced toward the backseat. Harley's eyes were still closed. "Drop it, Emma. Don't wake Harley up." If his daughter woke up, he'd have to pretend everything was okay. All his pretending skills had been used up for the day.

"Fine. Sorry I intruded." Her voice was stiff, her back ram-rod straight.

He clenched the steering wheel more tightly. "You want me to spill my guts when Harley might overhear us?"

Her silence stretched a moment too long. "You have no reason to spill your guts to me. Clearly, we don't have that kind of relationship. I just asked if you were okay."

Oh, hell. "Fine. I'm not okay. Is that what you wanted to hear?"

"You think I want to hear that you're in pain? That you're beating yourself up?" She spoke quietly, but couldn't hide the anger in her voice. "I was just trying to comfort you."

"Well, you can't. I screwed up, and I have to deal with it."

"Fine. Good. Glad to hear you've got things under control."

She shoved her hands under her thighs and stared straight ahead. A muscle in her jaw tightened and she blinked several times.

Damn it. "Sorry," he muttered, staring at the road in front of him. "I shouldn't have snapped at you."

"Don't worry about it."

He reached across the console and fumbled for her hand. She resisted when he tried to tug it out from beneath her thigh. When he tugged harder, she finally relented. Let him twine his fingers with hers.

"Can we not talk right now?" he asked. Not in front of Harley, even if she was sleeping. And not until he got himself under control.

She shrugged, looking eerily like Harley. "Fine."

"Lots of 'fines' going on here."

She turned to look at him then. Her eyes were bruised, her mouth trembling. "What do you expect me to say? That you're being a jerk? Is that going to make you feel better?"

"Yes. Because it's the truth."

Her mouth softened for a moment, then she slid her hand out of his and stared through the side window. Conversation over.

Afraid she'd slap him away, he hesitated before reaching for Emma's hand again. But he finally curled his fingers around hers. He'd hurt her, and he didn't know how to make it right. At least, not right now.

After a few moments, her hand relaxed. He moved his thumb in small circles over the back of her hand, hoping she understood he hadn't meant to hurt her. She wasn't the bad guy in this.

He was.

She leaned her head against the seat, and he saw her eyes flutter closed.

After fifty miles, Emma's hand slipped out of his. He kept his hand over hers until his arm fell asleep, then reluctantly returned it to the steering wheel.

He liked watching her fall asleep, holding his hand.

Harley's phone chimed with an incoming text. He heard her stir in the backseat, then she shot upright. "I just got a text from Lissy," she said. "She wants me to have a sleepover with her tonight. Can I?" She leaned forward. "You could drop me off on my way home, so you wouldn't have to go out again. I could borrow some of Lissy's clothes in the morning."

He'd be alone with Emma. With no excuse to avoid sharing what Mrs. Montgomery told him. He scrambled for an answer.

Then, with a rush of relief, he remembered Chuck. The ski hill. The reason Emma and Harley were staying with him.

Nathan glanced at Emma, who watched him with still-sleepy eyes. Both of them shook their heads at the same time. Emma turned to Harley. "This isn't a good time for sleepovers," she said.

"How come?" Harley stretched the seat belt and plopped her arms on the console. Frowned. "Tomorrow isn't a school night. I go to Lissy's house all the time."

"Emma and I want you to stick close to home until I settle this situation at the restaurant," Nathan said. *So we can keep you safe.*

"That is so bogus." Harley leaned forward even more, try-ing to see his face. "Why do *I* get grounded because *you've* got something stupid going on?"

"We're not grounding you," Emma said. "Just no sleepovers."

Harley begged and pleaded for another five miles. When she realized he and Emma weren't going to give in, she flopped against the seat and jammed in her earbuds. "I hate both of you." She typed furiously on her phone, and Nathan glanced at Emma. She looked stricken.

"Teenage girl's best weapon," he said quietly. "The 'I hate you.' It hurts, but you know she doesn't mean it."

"I…" She swallowed. "Yeah. Tough to hear, though."

"It is, but we should celebrate. She feels comfortable enough to bring out the big guns. Major milestone for all of us. We'll get a cake."

She made a sound that was either a laugh or a sob. Reached across the console for his hand. "Thanks," she said quietly. She glanced at Harley, who was scowling as she texted. "Maybe she could have a sleepover with Frankie and Cal. They have all kinds of security at their apartment. And I trust Cal to protect her."

He wanted to say no. Wanted an excuse to put off the conversation he knew they should have. But he'd already been enough of a coward for one day. "Sure. Give them a call."

Watching him, Emma dialed and explained the situation to Frankie. Smiled. "We'll drop her off at FreeZone on the way home."

MUCH LATER THAT evening, Emma stepped into Nathan's house with a sigh. When they'd arrived at FreeZone, Frankie had suggested they go out to dinner. She'd called Patrick and Darcy and Marco, and they'd all met at a pizza place not far from the teen center.

Marco and Harley had dissected the failings of the pizza sauce and resumed their trash-talking about their own contest. Frankie and Cal had teased Harley, and Patrick and Darcy had chimed in.

When all the Devereuxs were together, it certainly got… loud. Teasing, stories, laughter.

Emma liked the laughter the best.

Harley would eventually want to live with Nathan. Who wouldn't, when he came with a family like his?

It had been just Emma and her mother when she was a kid. Except for the year they'd lived in the commune. Then there had been lots of people. Not a lot of laughter, though. Those people had been serious. Intense. Earnest about everything.

Nathan dropped his cane near the door, then came into the kitchen. "You want another beer?"

"Sure. Why not?" She wasn't going to go quietly to bed without talking to Nathan. Tonight, she wasn't going to check for a safety net before she leaped.

As Nathan got the beer out of the refrigerator, her phone buzzed. Harley. Smiling, she pressed the green icon.

"Hey, Harley."

"I'm going to bed now," Harley announced with a giggle. "Cal said I had to call you. So you don't come hunt me down."

"Just getting ready to do that," she said. Nathan was watching, so she stood and moved closer and put the phone between them to let him hear. "Nathan's listening, too."

"I kicked Cal's butt at Guitar Hero," Harley crowed.

"He's an amateur," Nathan said. "Next time we're at their place, I'll show you how it's done."

The snort came through loud and clear. "Yeah, you and what teenager?"

The tension that had tightened Emma's shoulders most of the day began to relax as Nathan laughed beside her. His breath washed over her cheek. She told herself to put the phone on speaker and move away, but she stayed where she was. She'd been so cold most of the day. Now, standing close to him, her skin warmed. Her heart thawed.

"I'll call you when I get up in the morning," Harley said. "Bright and early," she added with a sly chuckle.

"Bring it on," Emma managed to say. "I know what bright and early is for you. Ten is practically the crack of dawn."

"No. I have to get up early for real. I'm going to FreeZone with Cal and Frankie." Emma heard voices in the background, and Harley added quickly, "If that's all right with you. And Nathan."

Emma met Nathan's gaze. *What do you think?*

She goes there every day after school.
Cal and Frankie will be there

"I think that would be okay," she said slowly, still watching Nathan. He nodded, as if he'd heard their silent conversation, too. "I'll pick you up afterward."

"Can I go to Mama's with Nathan tomorrow night?" Harley asked eagerly.

Emma was about to say that they had to go home after FreeZone. Harley had school the next day. They couldn't impose on Nathan.

But before she could get the words out, Nathan said, "Maybe. I'll see what's going on. What Marco's doing."

"Okay. G'night."

"'Night, Harley," Emma said.

"Start planning your Guitar Hero strategy," Nathan added. "You know, you can learn stuff in your sleep. You should put the disc beneath your pillow tonight."

"Ha-ha," Harley snorted, but Emma heard the grin in her voice. "You're the one who better sleep with the disc."

They said their goodbyes and Emma pressed the end call button, sliding the phone into her pocket. Moved away from Nathan, far enough that her skin chilled again. "Wow," she said lightly. "I've never gotten the full force of the teen girl mood swings before. It's impressive."

"Fortunately, Frankie and Cal have to deal with it tonight." He met her gaze briefly. Long enough for her to see the shame at the back of his eyes. Okay. They were going to talk about this.

She opened her beer, took a drink. Kept her gaze on Nathan.

He picked at the label on his bottle. Tore off a long strip, then twisted the cap off and tossed it on the counter. It rolled in smaller and smaller circles, before falling flat.

"I don't want to tell you this." He took a long drink. "But I need to. You have a right to know. You were Sonya's best friend. You're Harley's guardian."

She wanted him to tell her because of what she was to him. Her hand trembled as she lifted the beer to her mouth. The bottle clinked against her teeth.

He swallowed again, as if he needed to remind himself of what he'd done. She reached for his hand, slowly, and twined their fingers.

He glanced at her, and she saw the desperation in his eyes. The need to hold on, because she might not want to touch him after he confessed his sins.

Her hand tightened around his.

"Sonya ran into me in a bar." He stared out the darkened window, and Emma saw the flush of humiliation sweep over his face. "I'd come back to campus to pick up the rest of my stuff and officially withdraw from the university. Sonya had a crush on me." He swallowed. "Mrs. Montgomery called it love, but that makes it worse." He set his beer on the counter. Pushed it away. "I was so drunk that I didn't remember what happened the night Sonya and I…the night Harley was conceived."

No wonder he was upset. She touched his face. This was bad. Nathan wasn't going to forgive himself.

"When she saw me at the bar, she sat down and started talking."

He tightened his lips and let go of Emma's hand. "Apparently I was a sloppy drunk. I told her all about my parents, about having to raise my siblings, run the restaurant, leave college. Real pity party."

"So, being in love with you, she took you home. Tried to ease your pain." Emma's voice was soft. Full of regret for Nathan. For Sonya. And for Harley, who hadn't had a chance to know her father.

"I guess so. Harley was the result." He swung around to face her. "She can't find out. Ever. I don't want her to…to think badly of her mother."

Or her father. Emma didn't want Harley to know this about Nathan. It wouldn't do any good, and it could change their relationship forever. "She knows her mother loved you," Emma said quietly. "That's all she needs to know. Harley came from a kind impulse, from a loving gesture."

"She was born because I screwed up." His voice was raw. Full of self-loathing. "I was so drunk I didn't remember Sonya. Don't remember the night my daughter was conceived."

She wrapped her arms around him and held on, even when he tried to pull away.

"Don't you understand, Emma?" His hands were on her shoulders, but she refused to let go. "This is about as ugly as it gets. And you want to hug me?"

Emma lifted her head and studied his face as she held him. "Yes, it was wrong. Horrible. Drunk or not, you should have known better."

She rose to her toes and pressed a kiss to his mouth, holding his head as he tensed. "But I feel so bad for that young man," she said quietly. "He lost both his parents so suddenly. He went from being a kid in college to being a parent to his three younger siblings. He went from having almost infinite choices about what to do with his life to having no choices at all. He must have been overwhelmed. So you got drunk. So you went home with a woman who offered a few hours of comfort. I can't condemn you, Nathan. I don't think less of you for what happened."

He pulled her close and held her tightly, burying his face in her hair. "How can you forgive me so easily?"

"It's not my business to absolve you," she said quietly. "That would be Sonya, and she's gone. But since she finally told you about Harley, I think you can assume she'd forgiven you. Or maybe she was never angry at you in the first place."

He lifted his head and stared down at her. "That night— the night after I packed up my apartment in Champaign—has always been missing. I think I knew something bad had happened. I haven't been drunk since."

She held him against her. Had Nathan ever had anyone to

hold him when he made a mistake, to tell him they would fix it together?

Anyone to share his burdens?

She didn't think so. "You need to forgive yourself, Nathan. Yeah, you made a mistake, but you got an amazing daughter out of it."

"Not sure it's that easy," he murmured into her neck. His breath tickled her ear, his mouth brushed against her skin, and heat bloomed inside her. Spread through her veins like wildfire.

She closed her eyes and leaped.

Turning her face to meet his lips, she whispered against his mouth, "The comfort part of the evening is over. Okay? You clear on that?"

"Right." He sighed against her lips. "Comfort over."

She nipped at his lower lip. "Come to bed with me. I want to make love with you."

CHAPTER TWENTY-THREE

HIS SHARPLY INDRAWN breath made her quiver with need. Need that was echoed in the tension of his body, the sudden tightening of his hands on her back. "Emma." His voice was ragged. "After all this?"

"Yes," she said fiercely. "You're not that man anymore."

"You sure?"

"I'm positive." She'd been so busy trying to figure out what kind of future they had, how they would handle this complicated situation that she had forgotten to live in the moment. She didn't always have to know every step before she took the next one. Sometimes, it was okay to play it by ear.

Scary to begin living that way with something this important. Something that mattered so much.

But she wanted Nathan enough to overcome the fear.

Then his mouth was on hers, his arms iron bands around her. He kissed her desperately, as if he'd die if he didn't.

She cupped the back of his head, felt the soft strands of his hair slide through her fingers as she kissed him back. She was in the air, falling. She wasn't going to look down now. If there wasn't a net, it was too late.

"Emma," he murmured. He eased away from her mouth, nibbled at her ear. Kissed her neck. He stroked his hand down her back slowly. Rhythmically. As if he was soothing a skittish animal. "You're thinking very loudly."

She drew back far enough to see his face. "I...I don't do this."

"You don't have sex? Ever?" He pressed his lips against the corner of her mouth, but she could tell he was smiling.

"Not spontaneously. Not without planning. Without talking about it."

"I'd love to talk about it." He kissed his way down her neck. "Tell me what you like. What you want me to do."

The gentle teasing in his voice, the careful way he held her, made some of the tension drain from her shoulders. "That's not what I meant." Her arms were wrapped around his neck, holding him against her.

"You want to talk about what *I* like? What I want *you* to do?" He nuzzled the neck of her sweater away from her skin, pressed a kiss against her chest. "When it comes to you, Emma, I'm easy. You do it, I'll like it."

"I can't think straight," she murmured, pressing her lips to his. "I want you, Nathan."

"You've got me," he whispered against her lips, holding her gaze. "After tonight? After telling me you understand, that you don't condemn me?" He kissed her again, this time with tenderness. "Whatever you want, I'll give it to you."

Forever. That's what she wanted.

She closed her eyes against the thought. *Don't be silly, Emma.* This was about tonight. Nothing more. There was no forever with Nathan. He wanted freedom. Space. A new life.

So she'd settle for this stolen moment. For whatever time they had. "I want you to take me to bed," she whispered.

Instead of taking her hand and leading her up the stairs, he kissed her again. Nibbled at her lower lip, biting gently, soothing with his tongue. Rubbed his lips against hers, until she opened her mouth and moaned.

He accepted her invitation, sweeping inside. He tasted of the sharp hops of the beer, the decadent chocolate of the brownies Frankie had given them. And desperate need, barely held in check.

He continued to kiss her, seducing her even though she'd already told him she was his for the taking.

"Nathan." Her voice was breathy. Weak. Needy.

"What, Emma?" He slid his tongue along her lower lip, making her shiver. "What do you want?"

"More." She tugged his shirt out of his jeans and ran her hands up his chest. His skin was hot against her palms, his muscles tense. "I need more. I want to touch you. I want you to touch me."

"I've dreamed about touching you," he murmured. He trailed his mouth over her cheek, pressed kisses down her neck. "Dreamed of my hands on you. Of your hands on me."

He tugged the neck of her sweater down, kissed the swell of her breast. Then his hands slid down her sides, grabbed the hem. Drew it slowly higher, until he revealed her black bra.

"Emma," he breathed. He cupped her breasts, tested their weight in his palms. Brushed his thumb over their tips. She sucked in a breath as lightning shot through her.

She reached for his shirt, tore at the buttons. Shoved it open and pressed her mouth to his skin. Felt him tremble, then tense.

Panting, he fumbled to open her bra and threw it on the floor with her sweater. Then they were chest to breast, bare skin to bare skin. He stroked his hands over her back, and she felt him shaking. His mouth found hers again, and this time there was nothing gentle about their kiss. Nothing seductive. It was all urgency and heat and possession.

Without breaking the kiss, he backed her up. She bumped into the wall and didn't care. She couldn't let him go long enough to walk upstairs. Didn't want any space between them.

When they reached the stairs, he pressed her against the wall and surged against her. She wrapped one leg around his hip and moaned when the hard length of his erection burned into her. She felt the vibration of his answering moan in her mouth.

"Upstairs," he said, without taking his mouth from hers. "Now."

They staggered up the stairs one step at a time, mouths fused together, hands exploring.

She stumbled on a stair, and he caught her. He tripped as he leaned toward her, and she held him up. Finally they stepped into a darkened room, but she saw nothing but Nathan. Nothing but his eyes on hers, pupils dilated to black, his face taut with need.

He eased her onto his bed and followed her down, legs tangled, his hands on her face, holding her against him. He kissed his way down her throat, over her collarbone, down to her breasts. He sucked at her skin, making her lift into his mouth.

"Please, Nathan," she moaned. "More. I need...I need..."

He licked gently at one of her nipples, and she arched into him as her desire spiked higher. When he suckled her, she couldn't hold back a sharp cry.

When she was moving against him, desperate to feel him everywhere, he slid down her chest, down her belly, and unbuttoned her jeans. She felt his hands shaking on her skin, their heat burning into her. Then he tugged the jeans down along with her underwear and she was naked beneath him.

He kissed her belly, began to move lower, and she grabbed his hair to stop him. "Your clothes. Off. Now."

He pressed his mouth into the crease between her thigh and her abdomen, then stood up to send his shirt flying, shove his jeans and boxers to the floor. She reached for his penis, smoothing her thumb over the broad head, grasping the thick shaft, loving the way his hips twitched.

He turned and fumbled in the drawer of his nightstand and pulled out a foil packet. He tore it open, sheathed himself, then bent and kissed her abdomen.

"Should we talk now, Emma?" he asked between kisses. "About what I'm going to do to you?" He moved lower. "How I'm going to taste you?" Lower, until his breath washed over her. "How I'm going to make you come?"

"Nathan," she moaned, lifting her hips. Holding her breath.

Then he put his mouth on her. Licked her once. Suckled gently, and she exploded, waves of pleasure crashing through her, over and over. Her cries echoed in the darkness, and she reached for him.

She pulled his mouth to hers, wrapped her legs around his waist and cried out again as he slid into her. As he moved, she felt the tension build again. She searched for his mouth, kissed him deeply. And when he cried out her name and shuddered, she went over the edge again. This time, with him.

As their breathing slowed and her heart stopped thundering against her chest, she curled into Nathan. Her head was pressed to his chest and their arms and legs were tangled together. He smoothed his hand down her back, over and over. She inhaled his scent and held him tightly. She didn't want to let him go. Ever.

Finally, he turned and kissed her cheek. "I think I like your talking idea. I'd like to do a whole lot more of it."

She tucked herself into his side until they were touching everywhere, then tightened her thighs around his leg. He tensed and his breath hitched.

"What's wrong?" She lifted her head, swallowed when she saw his clenched teeth. "Did I hurt you?"

He struggled to untangle their legs, then pulled her against his side. "No. Maybe. Just a little. Damn leg." He eased her across his body until she was pressed against his right side. "Haven't done this since…"

"Since you were injured?" She pressed a kiss to his neck. "I'm sorry. I didn't even think about your leg."

"Didn't want you to."

She felt him flexing his leg and she propped herself on her elbow. Saw too many pale scars on his left thigh. One was jagged, one straight and surgical. The others were small white dots up and down his thigh.

She put her hand on his thigh and caressed him. Let her fingers linger over each mark, each reminder of his ordeal.

Finally he took her hand and kissed her palm. "No one's seen my leg besides the doctors and nurses. I'd forgotten how shocking all the scars are."

"Not shocking." She leaned over his body and kissed the jagged scar. "Just a reminder of what you went through. That you survived." She bent and kissed the surgical scar. "How glad I am that you did."

"Emma." He sighed as he gathered her close. "You make me feel whole. Like there's nothing wrong with me."

"There isn't." She lay back down, left her hand on his left thigh, her fingers touching the hard, smooth scars. "There's not a thing wrong with you, Nathan."

NATHAN PUT HIS hand over Emma's, pressed her palm against his scars. She was wrong. There was plenty wrong with him. But starting tomorrow, he was going to make it right. Fix it for her. For Harley.

He didn't want to be that man anymore. The guy who'd screwed up the restaurant. Who'd gotten a woman pregnant while he was drunk. Who'd been afraid to change his life, afraid to take a chance. Afraid to follow his dreams.

He wanted to be better than that. Better for her. For Harley.

He'd start with Shaughnessy. Talk to him again. Maybe then he could leave the past where it belonged and move on.

Then he'd talk to Paddy about the restaurant case. No one had been able to find anything solid. Maybe he *was* reacting out of guilt instead of logic. Maybe Emma was right. Maybe he'd only wanted there to be a crime to take away some of his culpability.

But tonight…tonight he had Emma in his arms and in his bed. He wasn't going to waste a minute of it. "Emma," he murmured, pulling her against him and tracing his tongue along the curve of her ear. "I think it's time we talked again."

Hours later, the shrill ringing of the phone beside his bed

startled him out of a deep sleep. He rolled over to reach it and found a warm body curled into him. Holding him.

Her blond curls were tousled and wild on the pillow. Her eyes were closed and her breathing was regular. She must sleep like the dead if the phone didn't wake her.

It rang again and he reached across her. "'Lo?"

"Nathan?" Harley's voice. "I tried to call your cell. Emma's, too. No one answered."

"We must have left them downstairs," he managed to say. "We were both pretty tired last night." Not too tired to stay up half the night making love.

"Frankie gave me this number and made me call. We're going to FreeZone now."

"Okay. Thanks. I'll let Emma know. She…we…will pick you up this afternoon. Okay?"

"Yeah. See you then. Bye."

The phone clicked and he leaned over Emma again to replace it in the charger. As he slumped back to the bed beside her, her arms came around him. She snuggled her head into his shoulder. "Think she bought the story about forgetting our phones because we were soooo tired?" Her voice was a little raspy. Sexy.

"We did forget them."

"Being tired had nothing to do with it." She grinned up at him, her brown eyes twinkling. His heart was suddenly too big for his chest.

"No. I couldn't think of anything but you last night." He kissed her and she wound her arms around his neck and pulled him close.

"Make love to me, Nathan."

CHAPTER TWENTY-FOUR

EMMA ROLLED OVER in bed, squinting as the light hit her eyelids. As she struggled to sit up, the muscles in her thighs protested, and she remembered. Nathan.

She opened her eyes and reached for him, but he wasn't there. The sheets were rumpled, the other pillow crushed, but the bed was empty. She sat up, shoved her tangled hair out of her eyes and looked around.

Light poured in through sheer curtains—clearly, Nathan liked waking up with the sun. Last night she hadn't cared about anything but Nathan. She hadn't looked at his room, hadn't even seen the bed. She'd seen only him.

The morning sun illuminated the old-fashioned walnut dresser and chest of drawers. A watch, loose change, his wallet, a couple of pens and a corkscrew were scattered on top of the chest. A second flat wallet, with papers sticking out, sat there, too. Framed pictures stood on the dresser. One was of four children—a teenage Nathan, his two brothers and Frankie. They were at a beach, and they had their arms draped over each others' shoulders. Another was the same four children, a little older, and their parents. Everyone was smiling. Happy. A loving family.

Work and family defined Nathan.

The bed frame matched the dresser and chest. She touched the dark, smooth wood, wondering if it had been his parents' furniture. Wondered if there was anything of Nathan in the room. Then she saw the map secured to the wall with pushpins.

Italy. She climbed out of bed to look at it. Three small towns near Milan were circled in red—Bornato. Rovato. Passirano. Different color pushpins marked a number of other towns. Florence, Venice and Siena. Turin. Milan. And a host of smaller towns. She wondered if the colors meant anything.

Nathan's plans, laid out in stark simplicity. The flat wallet on the dresser, beneath the map, was a passport wallet. She opened it and her heart shriveled.

A brand-new passport sat inside. Beneath it was an Air Italia ticket. The departure date was in three weeks. Open-ended. And changeable.

Clearly, as soon as the restaurant situation was resolved, he was leaving. When had he planned on telling her and Harley?

She stared at the blue booklet and the white paper and her stomach twisted. *That* was his future. Not her. Not Harley.

Nathan was leaving. And from the number of pins on that map, he was planning on being gone for a long time.

She'd made love with him last night as if it was the beginning of forever. But, in reality, it was only three weeks at the most. Possibly less.

He'd come back eventually, but she had no idea what he'd want.

What have I done?

She'd leaped off the cliff, and he wasn't going to catch her. She'd end up bruised and broken at the bottom. She'd fallen in love with a guy who wasn't interested in the long term. A guy who was dancing away from her and everything else in his life. Who wasn't going to stick around. She closed her eyes as the realization hit. All this time, she'd tried so hard to be different than her mother, but really she was just the same. Emma had chosen a man who didn't want to be chosen.

Emma closed the passport wallet. She had to get her head on straight. Right now there was only one priority. Harley. She was going to need Emma when Nathan took off for Italy and left her behind.

Left Emma behind, too.

That's what happened when you led with your heart instead of your head.

She gathered her scattered clothes. They'd torn each other's clothes off, tossed them away. Paid no attention to where they'd landed. She'd thought her sweater had been left downstairs, but Nathan must have brought it up for her.

The fire, the heat and passion from last night, coalesced into a cold, hard ball in her stomach.

Last night had been magical. Amazing. A memory she'd hold in her heart forever. But it was morning now. Night and magic were done. He'd told her, right from the beginning, this couldn't be permanent. Nathan had been upfront about what he wanted, and it wasn't more family. Wasn't a daughter and a clingy girlfriend.

So she wouldn't burden him with her feelings. Wouldn't try to guilt him into staying. Her feelings were not his fault. He'd never promised forever.

Her hand tightened on her jeans. He hadn't promised Harley forever, either. She glanced at the brown leather passport wallet. The passport and ticket were merely a reminder of what he'd said all along.

She hooked her bra with hands that shook, then tried to smooth out the wrinkles in her sweater. She could do this. She could smile, kiss him good morning. Have a quick breakfast, then go to work. Pick up Harley from FreeZone that afternoon, go back to their apartment that evening.

She'd do it by focusing on Harley, who needed her. Harley, who'd lost her mother and now was going to lose her father.

And Emma's feelings for Nathan?

She'd bury them. She'd deal with her loss the way she'd dealt with the other losses in her life. She'd protect her heart and tell herself she'd survive this, too.

NATHAN TURNED TOWARD the stairs when he heard Emma moving around in his bedroom. He'd been lingering in the living room, torn between letting her sleep in, since they hadn't gotten much rest the night before, and waking her up with a kiss.

His heart fluttering, he hurried into the kitchen and searched the refrigerator for something he could feed her for breakfast. Nothing.

Nathan yanked a loaf of bread out of the freezer and tossed it on the counter, then opened the fridge again. Butter. He set that on the counter. But he didn't have any jam.

He checked the coffeepot to make sure it had finished brewing. Smoothed the place mats Frankie had left behind, then headed for the living room to intercept Emma.

She stood at the bottom of the stairs, watching him cautiously. He hurried toward her with a smile, and wrapped his arms around her, lifting her into the air. Kissing her.

Her arms circled his neck and she kissed him back, her mouth opening beneath his, her hands tightening around him.

When he raised his head, they were both breathing heavily. "Good morning," he whispered, brushing his lips along hers. He knew he had a stupid grin on his face, but he couldn't help himself. Emma made him feel as if anything was possible. As if he could climb out of the old Nathan's skin, like a butterfly emerging from a chrysalis, and become someone worthy of her.

"Good morning to you, too." She leaned away from him, studying his face. Smiled back at him, although there was a shadow in her eyes. "Is this going to be one of those awkward morning-afters?"

"God, no." He kissed her again, then slung an arm around her shoulders and steered her toward the kitchen. "Unless you insist on more than coffee and toast. My refrigerator isn't equipped for morning-after breakfasts."

Some of the smile leached into her eyes. "That's good. I think."

He turned to her, cupped her face in his hands. Her skin was soft beneath his fingers, and he couldn't stop touching her.

"No one but you here in the morning, Emma." He kissed the corner of her mouth. "And Harley, I guess."

Her mouth trembled beneath his before she eased away. "Coffee made? I'd kill for a cup. Then I need to go to work."

He reached for her hands, brought them to his mouth. "Back to the real world." He kissed one palm, then the other. Watched her fingers curl into a fist, as if she wanted to hold his kisses there. "Let me fill you up with toast and coffee before you leave me. You're coming back tonight, aren't you?"

She tugged her hands away from him. "Harley has school tomorrow. I think we need to let her get back into a routine. And nothing's happened this weekend that seems threatening." She smiled, but it was shaky. "How about if I bring her to Mama's for dinner?"

"Yeah, do that." She seemed nervous. Unsettled. Probably that morning-after awkwardness she'd been worried about. He bent and kissed her again, more slowly this time, and all his desire for her came rushing back. He broke away before he could lead her up to the bedroom again, and poured her a cup of coffee. "I'll look forward to seeing you and Harley tonight."

"Okay. It's a date." She took a sip of coffee. "Now bring on the toast."

TWO DAYS LATER Nathan was in his office at Mama's, comparing this month's receipts to the previous month, when his cell rang. He picked it up and smiled when he saw it was Harley. She and Emma hadn't stayed with him Tuesday night or last night, but they'd come to the restaurant both evenings. Harley had done her homework at the same table where he and his siblings had done theirs.

Emma had been a little distracted. Maybe a little distant. He'd bent to kiss her, and she'd slid away. When he'd asked her what was wrong, she'd said she had a difficult case.

Harley, on the other hand, seemed delighted to be at Mama's. After she'd finished her homework, she'd hung out with Marco. Teased Nathan. Practiced her Spanish with the cooks.

He hadn't been expecting a phone call. Maybe she wanted to make sure he'd be at Mama's tonight. Grinning like an idiot, he pushed the answer icon.

"Hey, Harley. How are you?"

"You need to come here. To FreeZone." Her voice was shaking, and she sniffled, as if she'd been crying. "I need you."

"What's wrong?" He jumped up from his desk and the chair banged into the wall behind him. Shoved his hand into his pocket for his car keys. "Where's Emma? Is she with you?"

"She's not answering her phone." Harley sobbed. "I'm scared, Dad."

Dad. She'd never called him that before. In spite of the fear crushing his chest, warmth flowed over him. "What happened, Harley? Are you hurt?"

"I got a note." Her voice wobbled. "In my backpack."

"A note from school?" he asked, bewildered.

"No," she sobbed.

Someone took the phone from her. "Nate, get over here. Now." Cal's voice. He could still hear Harley's muffled sobs.

"On my way." He ran to his car, jammed the key in the ignition. "Be there in fifteen."

"We've got the doors locked and the police are on their way. Your kid needs you."

"Police? Doors locked?" he said sharply. His tires screeched as he pulled out of the parking lot and headed east on Devon. "What the hell's going on?"

Cal had already hung up the phone.

Twelve minutes later, after breaking about a hundred traffic laws, he parked illegally in front of FreeZone and pounded on the locked door.

"Where is she?" Nathan demanded when Cal let him in.

"In the office with Frankie and a couple of cops. They're…"

Nathan didn't wait to hear what Cal said. He ran toward the

office and yanked open the door. Two uniformed cops stood to the side, one writing in a small notebook. With Frankie plastered to her side, Harley was saying something. Her face was sheet white and her freckles stood out like dots of ink. Tears streaked her cheeks, and as she talked, she swiped her sleeve across her nose. When she saw him, she let go of Frankie and threw herself at him.

He wrapped his arms around her, holding her tightly. She clutched at his shirt, sobbing into his chest.

"It's okay, Harley. I'm here. You're okay." He pressed a kiss to her head, smoothed her tangled hair. Without letting his daughter go, he looked at Frankie. "What happened?"

The cop who wasn't taking notes held out a plastic bag with a piece of white paper inside. "When she got to Free-Zone, she found this in her backpack." Harley's hands tightened on his shirt.

Keeping one arm firmly around his daughter, he took the bag with the other. Printed at the top of the paper was a short message.

Tell your old man to stay away from Shaughnessy. Or he won't like what happens. And neither will you.

CHAPTER TWENTY-FIVE

THIS WAS REAL. They'd threatened Harley. His arms tightened around her until she struggled a little. He loosened his hold, but he wouldn't let her go.

They'd threatened his daughter.

Had they threatened Emma, too? Or worse?

"Have you called Emma?" he asked Frankie.

She nodded. *Not answering*, she mouthed.

"You try her office?"

"Was just about to when the police showed up."

"Do it now. Please," he added. *God.* If Emma was hurt, or worse, because of him? He'd never forgive himself.

He might not, anyway. His daughter and the woman he lo…the woman he really cared about were in danger because of him.

He kissed Harley's head again, inhaling the familiar fragrance of her shampoo. The same shampoo Emma used. His throat tightened, and he closed his eyes. Emma was okay. She had to be. He couldn't bear to think of any other possibilities.

Frankie had her back to him, and she was murmuring on the phone. "Thanks," she finally said. "No, I'll leave her a message. Appreciate it."

When Frankie turned around, she squeezed Harley's shoulder and watched Nathan. "Emma's in court today. You can't bring camera phones into the courthouse, so she probably left her phone in her car. That's why she's not answering."

Thank God. "Would you leave her a message to…"

"Already done." Frankie grimaced. "She's going to freak

out. She'll have about a jillion missed calls from Harley, Cal and me."

Harley lifted her face from Nathan's shirt. "Emma's okay?"

"She's fine." He stroked Harley's hair away from her face. "As soon as she's done in court, she'll call."

Harley's face crumpled again. "When she didn't answer, I thought… I was afraid…"

He cupped her face in his hands. "I know. Me, too." He used his thumbs to wipe away Harley's tears. "But she's okay."

Harley nodded. Gulped. Wiped her nose again, then let go of his shirt. But when he put an arm across her shoulders, she huddled close.

"We need to talk to you before we leave, Mr. Devereux," the younger officer said.

Frankie held out her hand to Harley. "You want to get a cupcake while your dad talks to them?" she asked.

"Maybe."

"Okay." She waited for a moment, and Harley finally moved away from Nathan and took Frankie's hand.

"I'll be out in a few minutes, Harley," he said. Forcing himself to smile, he said, "Make sure they save one of Frankie's cupcakes for me."

As the door closed behind Harley and his sister, he turned to the police officers. "What the hell is going on?"

EMMA SLID INTO her car and sat for a moment, staring over the steering wheel, not seeing the concrete walls and pillars of the parking structure, the slice of downtown Chicago over the half wall of the garage.

All she saw were the two women on opposite sides of the aisle—the determined foster parent and the mother who'd come to court, rail-thin, seemingly sober, but missing several teeth and her face bearing the unmistakable scars of methamphetamine addiction.

That, and the photos of her abused child Emma couldn't bear to remember.

Sometimes, her job really sucked. Yes, she'd saved a child today. But a family was broken. It hadn't been much of a family to begin with, but still. Taking a child away from a parent was always heart-wrenching. Unbearably sad.

Harley was going to lose her parent soon, as well. Not from drug addiction, not from abuse, but Nathan would be just as lost. Thousands of miles away in Italy.

He'd return eventually, but the damage would be done. After being abandoned by her father, would Harley ever completely trust him again?

Emma bit back tears. During the four days she and Harley had spent with Nathan, Harley had been so easy with him. So comfortable. As if she'd finally accepted that he was her father.

Although it meant Harley would eventually leave her to live with Nathan, Emma had been happy. Harley needed her father—and even if he didn't realize it, Nathan needed his daughter.

Now? How was she going to help Harley deal with this new loss? Especially since Emma was having a hard time dealing with it herself.

Swallowing the hard lump in her throat, she opened the console and fished out her phone. Seventeen missed calls.

Heart thundering in her chest, she pulled up the call log. Harley. Frankie. Cal. Nathan. All had called more than once. Oh, God.

Her hand shook as she punched in Nathan's number. "Emma," he said immediately. "Thank God."

"What's wrong? Is Harley okay? What happened?"

"Harley's fine. But you need to come to FreeZone."

She closed her eyes, gulped for air. "Why…what's wrong?"

"There was a threatening note in Harley's backpack when she got here." Emma gasped and Nathan said quickly, "She's fine. Having a cupcake. The police are here. No one's going to hurt her."

All Emma heard was *police. Hurt her.* A fist tightened around her chest, squeezing. She couldn't breathe. Couldn't think.

She must have made a sound, though, because Nathan said, "Where are you, Emma? I'll come get you."

"No," she managed to say. That would take too long. "I'm okay. Stay with Harley. I'll get there."

She ended the call and dropped the phone on the seat. Took a breath, another one. Put the car in gear and drove.

Fifteen minutes later, she was running toward the door at FreeZone. Frankie was waiting at the door and Cal was playing some kind of game with the rest of the kids. As soon as Emma was inside, she said, "Where is she?" She scanned the room, looking for Harley's bright red hair.

Frankie put her hand on Emma's arm. "The office. Nathan's with her." Frankie kept talking, but Emma ran across the room and threw open the door. Harley sat in the desk chair, and Nathan stood behind her, his hands on her shoulders.

Tears had dried on Harley's face, but her eyes were still red and puffy. When she saw Emma, Harley leaped from her chair and ran to her.

"Oh, baby," Emma whispered, clutching her too tightly. "Are you okay?" She leaned away from Harley, smoothed her hair away from her face.

"I'm…I'm okay now," Harley said. She glanced over her shoulder at Nathan. "Dad came. He came really fast."

Dad. The vise around Emma's chest tightened for a moment, then the ache eased. She looked at Nathan, saw his soft smile as he watched Harley. But when his gaze rose to hers, the smile disappeared. He moved around the chair to wrap his arms around both of them, squashing Harley between them.

His face in her hair, his fingers curling into her as if he was holding on to a life preserver, he murmured, "I was so scared when we couldn't get hold of you."

"Court," she managed to say. She needed to pull away. Needed to put some distance between them. Her arms tightened around him. She could wait a few moments for that distance. Right now she needed to hold on to Nathan.

"Yeah." He dropped a kiss on her hair, then let her go. Pulled Harley to his side. He handed Emma a plastic bag holding a piece of paper. "This was in Harley's backpack. The police have questions for you."

THREE HOURS LATER, Emma and Harley sat at Nathan's kitchen table, finishing a pizza from Mama's. When they'd ordered the pizzas, Emma's stomach had twisted into a knot at the thought of food. But she'd managed to pick at two small pieces.

Patrick had come by a few minutes ago, and now he and Nathan were talking in the living room. Their voices were low murmurs, too faint to hear. Whatever they were saying was intense, because Nathan's voice rose. "Tonight, Paddy. No excuses. I don't care if every freaking FBI agent in Chicago has to spend all night looking at the security tapes from that school."

Patrick's voice again, saying something soothing. Finally the front door opened and closed, and Nathan walked into the kitchen.

He sat down, took a piece of pizza. "Patrick says they haven't found anything. No strangers in the school. No one near Harley's backpack. None of the kids she walked with to FreeZone remember seeing anything." He tossed the pizza slice back into the box. "It's as if a ghost stuck that note in her backpack. It had to have happened at the school. Paddy's going to go over all the footage from the security cameras there."

Harley hunched her shoulders, and Emma dropped the piece she was eating to put one hand on Harley's. "They'll figure this out, baby. Sooner or later, they'll see something on the tapes. Or someone will come forward."

"In the meantime, I want you to stay here," Nathan said. He reached for Emma's hand and curled his fingers around hers. She should tug away, but she left her hand where it was. For Harley's sake, they had to be a united front. Protecting her together.

He must have felt her hesitation, because he squeezed her hand. "Please. A police officer is going to sit in his cruiser in front of the house tonight. Maybe tomorrow, too. I won't worry as much if you're here."

Emma glanced at Harley, who'd been quiet since they got to Nathan's house. "That okay with you, Harley?"

She nodded as she picked a piece of mushroom off her pizza. "Can I still go to school tomorrow? And FreeZone?"

"Do you want to do that?" Emma asked. Harley nodded as she picked off another mushroom.

Emma wanted Harley close until the person who'd given her the note was caught. She saw the same desire in Nathan's gaze. She wanted to shout at him. To ask who was going to protect Harley when he was in Italy. But this wasn't the time for that.

"What do you think?" she asked Nathan carefully. "I can drive her to school, then drive her to FreeZone."

He nodded slowly. "Yeah, I guess so." His expression said it was the last thing he wanted, but he reached for his daughter's hand. "It's really brave of you to want to go to school tomorrow."

Harley rolled her eyes, but it was a halfhearted effort. "It's not brave, Dad. I have tests tomorrow."

"I'm still proud of you. Lots of kids would use it as an excuse to stay home."

Harley ducked her head, but Emma saw her cheeks redden.

"I need to study," Harley said as she pushed away from the table." She looked at the dishes and leftover pizza on the table. "Do you want me to help clean up first?"

Emma's throat tightened. "We'll get it, baby. Go ahead and study."

Harley scowled. "I'm not a baby."

"Of course you're not. It's just…" Her throat tightened. How much longer would she have Harley with her? "Just a silly nickname."

Harley retreated into the living room, and moments later Emma heard her footsteps heading up the stairs.

She looked at Nathan, and the forced cheerfulness he'd worn all evening was gone, leaving nothing but worry, fear and remorse.

"Emma, I am so sorry that you and Harley got dragged into my mess." He shoved his hands into his hair. "When she called this afternoon…" He closed his eyes. When he opened them, she saw desolation. "It brought back all those memories of when Frankie ran away. The helplessness. The terror. The sickening feeling of knowing your kid was in danger and there was nothing you could do about it.

"And then when we couldn't get hold of you…" He reached over and dragged her onto his lap. Wrapped his arms around her and pressed his face to her neck.

In spite of her determination to protect herself by keeping her distance from Nathan, despite her knowledge that he'd be leaving soon, she couldn't help relaxing into him. It had been an awful day.

Finally she rested her forehead against his. "You didn't do this, Nathan," she murmured. He needed comfort, too. And because she loved him and she didn't want to see him suffering, she wanted to give him that comfort. "Maybe this was good. Maybe it was the breakthrough you needed. Maybe Patrick will find something on those tapes."

"And maybe it just means my kid and my…my lover will live in fear."

Was that what she was? His lover? He couldn't even say *girlfriend? Lover* sounded cold. Sterile.

And *girlfriend* sounded so seventh grade. *Cut it out, Emma.*

"You'll find this guy. He's getting scared. Desperate. Taking stupid chances. And nothing is going to happen to Harley. She'll never be alone. Okay?"

"What about you?" he murmured. "Can I keep you close? Keep you safe?"

Yes. Please. But she knew that wasn't in the cards. "I'm a big girl, Nathan. I can take care of myself."

He stroked his hand up and down her back. "It wouldn't be a hardship, you know," he murmured, brushing his lips against hers. "Keeping you close."

She leaned into him, slid her arms around his neck. She'd been careful not to be alone with Nathan the past few days, but she missed this. Missed kissing him, missed feeling his body against hers.

She couldn't afford to get used to this—Nathan kissing her in the kitchen. Holding her on his lap, teasing her. It would be too painful after he left.

So she slid off his lap even though she wanted nothing more than to stay there for the rest of the night. Swallowing the stupid tears that gathered in her throat, she began to clear the table.

They were sitting on the couch two hours later, watching television. It was an excuse to sit close together, thighs and shoulders touching.

She should go upstairs, shut herself in her bedroom. Alone. Take that first step.

Before she could move, someone knocked softly at the back door. Nathan stood and pulled her off the couch. "Go upstairs," he whispered. "Don't come down until I get you."

Emma nodded. As she began walking up the stairs, she watched Nathan square his shoulders, then head toward the back door.

NATHAN PEERED OUT the back door. At first he saw no one. Then something moved in the shadows along the side of the house, and Peter Shaughnessy appeared in front of him.

Shocked, he simply stared for a moment. Then he opened the door. "What are you doing here?" he asked, his voice low.

"There's a squad car at your front door. Don't want no trigger-happy cop getting excited."

"No. I mean here. At my house."

"You wanted to know what I had to say. I want to tell you. But first, get that FBI brother of yours over here. I need protection."

Staring at Shaughnessy, Nathan pulled his phone out of his pocket as he let the man in. Dialed Patrick, told him he needed to be here. Now. Hung up while Patrick was asking a question.

This was the man who'd killed his parents, and he was standing in Nathan's kitchen.

"Have a seat," Nathan muttered, then dropped into a chair himself. Shaughnessy pulled one out carefully. Perched on the edge.

"Why couldn't you tell me whatever it is the day I went to Urban Table? Why did you make that scene?"

The other man made a scoffing sound. "You think he don't know you were there? Of course he does. And he knows I didn't say nothing to you. That I told you to get lost."

"Who's *he*?" Nathan's heart jerked against his ribs and began to pound. Hard. Fast, as if it might leap out of his chest. Was he finally going to get some answers?

"I ain't saying nothing until the FBI guy gets here."

"He'll be here in a few minutes. You, ah, want something to drink? Iced tea or something?" He couldn't wrap his mind around offering his parents' killer hospitality. Nathan shifted on the chair.

"I'm good."

Nathan jumped up and poured himself a glass of tea, even though he hated the stuff. He wanted a beer, but the thought turned his stomach. Shaughnessy had been drinking shots and beers the night he'd killed Nathan's parents. It was a detail burned onto his brain.

Finally, after the longest five minutes in history, Patrick pounded at the front door. Nathan jumped up to let him in.

"Shaughnessy's here," he said in a low voice. "Wants to tell us something, but he wants protection first."

Patrick's jaw worked and he clenched his fists. Then, as Nathan watched, he shook off all emotion. Checked his gun in its shoulder holster. Straightened.

He was no longer the son who'd lost his parents because of the man in the other room. Now he was the FBI agent. Professional. Detached.

Squaring his shoulders, he walked into the kitchen. Dropped into the chair opposite Shaughnessy. "What do you need?"

"I need protection. That witness protection thing. Because he'll kill me if I tell you the truth."

"If you have information that can help us, we can put you in protective custody," Patrick said. "Get you into a safe house. After you give us the information you have, we'll call in the marshals and make a determination about the witness protection program."

"Your word on that? Because I don't trust no one."

"You have my word," Patrick said.

Shaughnessy wiped at the stubble on his face. Slicked back his hair. Glanced from Nathan to Patrick and back again. "I'm not the guy who killed your parents."

CHAPTER TWENTY-SIX

"WHAT THE HELL?" Nathan shot to his feet. "You were driving the car. You were drunk. How can you say it wasn't you?"

"I'd like some of that tea now, please." Shaughnessy licked his lips. Nathan stared at him, but went to the fridge anyway. When Nathan set the glass in front of him, the ex-con took a long drink. "I wasn't the only one in the car," he said after he put the glass down. "I was the passenger. The other guy was behind the wheel because I was too drunk to drive. Then he blew through a red light and hit your car."

Shaughnessy stared at the table. Swallowed. Then curled his hand around the glass, as if he needed something to hold on to. "But he'd been drinking, too. He knew he'd blow more than the limit, and he'd lose his job because of it. And the job he was hoping to get, too. So he made me a deal. I take the rap, and he'd take care of my family. Make sure my wife and kid had enough money. Put my kid through college. I was broke. I'd already been fired because of my drinking. So I agreed."

"You're making this up," Patrick said. He leaned closer. "Trying to blame someone else."

Nathan wanted to grab Shaughnessy and shake the truth out of him.

But the guy didn't look as if he was lying. Shaughnessy was calm. Sitting up straight. Meeting Patrick's eyes. Nathan's heart began to race.

The older man took another drink. "I kept my part of the deal. Kept my mouth shut, did my time. But he's turned into a scary shit, and I'm afraid he's going to kill me. He's desperate to keep his secret safe."

He looked down at the table. "Been on my conscience, too. You got a right to know who killed your folks. At A.A., we got to be accountable."

Shaughnessy met Nathan's eyes. Nathan's stomach twisted and his nerves tingled. Patrick leaned across the table. "Okay, moment of truth," he said to Shaughnessy. "Who is this mystery guy who was really driving the car that night?"

"Mitch Kopecki."

Stunned, Nathan stared at the guy calmly drinking iced tea at his kitchen table. "Mitch Kopecki? That's not…we know him. He's a family friend. His son went to school with Patrick."

Mitch had eaten in their restaurant. Had shared a drink with Nathan, more than once.

"Maybe he's your friend. But he was the one who killed your folks." Shaughnessy glanced at Patrick out of the corner of his eye. "Hurt you."

"You have any proof of this?" Patrick asked. "If you don't, it's your word against his."

A small smile curved Shaughnessy's mouth. "He thought he was being so smart. Paying me to take the blame. But I wasn't too drunk to cover my ass. So before I agreed, while we were sitting in the smashed-up car, I made him write down what he'd done and what he was going to give me for taking the rap. He probably doesn't even remember. He was real scared. He'd been going to law school while he worked as a cop, and he knew he'd never be a lawyer if he was arrested."

"And you still have this paper?" Nathan asked.

"Yeah. It's in a safe place."

"Okay," Patrick said.

His brother glanced at Nathan, and he shook his head. His mind was trying to wrap itself around the revelation. He shook his head again, trying to clear it. Trying to adjust everything he'd thought about his parents' death.

Trying to change the way he thought about a friend.

His mouth tightening, Patrick pulled out his phone. "I'm going to call my colleagues and have you taken to a safe house," he told Shaughnessy. "You'll stay there while we get the evidence together, make sure it's solid. You don't tell anyone about this. None of the other FBI agents, no cops, not your family. No one. You hear me? Kopecki is a powerful guy, and he has lots of connections. I don't want anyone else to hear about this until our case is solid."

Shaughnessy just looked at him. "I haven't told anyone in fifteen years. I'm not starting now."

Patrick held his gaze. Nodded. Then he walked into the living room and began speaking in a low voice. Nathan looked at Shaughnessy, but the other man wouldn't meet his eyes.

It was too much to process. Peter Shaughnessy, the guy he'd hated for years, wasn't the one who'd killed his parents. He'd lied about it and allowed the real killer to walk free, though. And all this time, Mitch Kopecki had been the one. The guy who'd eaten at his restaurant, socialized with him, had been the one who'd killed his parents. The guy who'd changed Nathan's life forever.

"If you're telling the truth," Nathan managed to say, "thank you for coming to us."

After the accident, Nathan had hated Shaughnessy with a fierce, all-consuming passion. And when Mitch Kopecki extended his hand in friendship, Nathan had grasped it.

He'd never guessed the secret Kopecki was hiding. Never questioned why he'd help Nathan's family when he had a family of his own. He'd assumed the guy was being a good neighbor.

Nathan had gone with the easy, obvious answer. And when O'Fallon offered the money for the kitchen renovation, Nathan had made another impulsive decision.

When would he learn to think before he leaped?

As soon as more FBI agents arrived, Nathan left Patrick

to deal with them and Shaughnessy. Leaving the quiet intensity of their voices behind, he hurried up the stairs to Emma.

Frankie's old room was dark. Harley was asleep, thank God.

But a welcoming beacon of light gleamed beneath the door of Patrick's old room. He'd known Emma would be awake. She wouldn't have gone to sleep without seeing him. When he knocked, she opened the door immediately, as if she'd been listening for his footsteps on the stairs.

"What happened?" she whispered, searching his gaze. "Is everything okay?"

No. He wasn't sure if it would ever be okay. The magnitude of Mitch Kopecki's betrayal was overwhelming. As was Nathan's inability to see past the guy's facade.

But he took Emma's hands in his. Pressed his lips to her palm. "It was the guy who was in prison for killing my parents. He had things to tell us." Nathan swallowed. "I want to tell you what he said, but the most important thing is, Harley's going to be safe. You, too."

"You don't look happy," Emma said, gripping his hands tightly.

"I'm relieved that you and Harley are safe. But the rest of it?" He shook his head. "No. I'm not happy."

IT WAS DAWN when Emma woke up the next morning. Alone. Again. Nathan was gone, leaving behind only the ghost of his scent and an indented pillow next to hers. They hadn't made love—he'd just told her what had happened, then curled his fully clothed body around hers and held her.

She'd thought he needed her, and she'd relaxed against him. But now she wondered if maybe he'd just needed the comfort of a warm body. Maybe anyone's would have done the job.

The echoes of his pained words shimmered in the morning light. The man who'd confessed to killing his parents wasn't guilty. Mitch Kopecki, the charming man she'd met at Harley's school, had been behind the wheel. A man Nathan had liked. Had trusted.

As he'd talked, he'd kept her pressed to his side. She couldn't see his face, couldn't gauge how he felt. Had no idea what his steady voice was hiding.

When she'd tried to look at him, he'd tightened his arm around her. Her tender lover from two nights ago was gone, replaced by this man who didn't want her to see him.

Finally he'd eased her down beside him, spooning her back into his chest. "Just for a minute, Emma. I need to hold you."

He'd kissed her hair, cocooned her with his warmth. It had been a long, emotional day, and in spite of her determination to stay awake, she'd soon fallen asleep in his arms.

Emma stumbled down the stairs, still half-asleep. She needed coffee to wake her up, to help her focus her thoughts. Harley would need her today.

When she reached the ground floor, she saw a light in the kitchen. Heard the faint murmur of agitated voices. She hesitated, wondering if she should go back upstairs. But she was tired of waiting. Tired of being cautious and careful.

Nathan and Patrick looked at her as she appeared in the kitchen door. Neither of them seemed to have slept. The skin beneath Nathan's eyes was purple and shadowed, his face drawn and tired. But he smiled when he saw her.

"Emma." He stumbled to his feet, bent and kissed her cheek. "Coffee?"

"Yes. Please."

He waved her to a chair, poured a cup of coffee for her. Then he dropped heavily onto his chair.

"Paddy and I are waiting for the bank to open so we can get the proof Shaughnessy stashed in a safe-deposit box. The FBI's going to expedite identifying any fingerprints we find and comparing the handwriting to Kopecki's. Then we're going to pay him a visit."

Patrick scowled. "There shouldn't be any 'we' about this.

It's a police case, and Nate doesn't belong there. But he's insisting." Patrick rubbed at the bristles on his face and glanced at Nathan out of the corner of his eye. "Hard to refuse. Mom and Dad's death changed his life more than anyone else's. Maybe he deserves to be there when we take Kopecki down."

"What can I do?" she asked.

Nathan reached for her hand. "Take Harley to school and then go to work. Keep everything normal. I'll call you as soon as I have any information."

"I'm going to worry," she said quietly.

"I know. But I'll be fine. So will Paddy. Kopecki's not going to try anything at his office."

Emma looked from Nathan's determined face to Patrick's stone-cold demeanor. She hoped he was right, but her stomach twisted and she pushed the coffee away.

NATHAN ROLLED HIS shoulders as he stood beside Patrick outside the door of Kopecki's office at the Daley Center. His brother reached beneath his jacket, checking the gun tucked into a holster. Then he rapped on the door.

"Come in," Kopecki called.

He smiled when he saw Nathan and Patrick, but there was a cautious shadow in his eyes. Had it always been there or had Nathan just failed to see it?

"Paddy. Nate. Good to see you." He stood up and shook their hands, motioned to the chairs in front of his desk. "What can I do for you?"

As soon as he was seated, Nathan leaned forward. "You..."

Patrick shoved him back in his chair, shot him a warning look. "Mr. Kopecki, I have a warrant for your arrest. For vehicular homicide, driving under the influence and fleeing the scene. You going to let me search you, or do I have to cuff you and walk you out in front of your colleagues?"

Kopecki's gaze shifted from Patrick to Nathan, and he

tugged at his collar. "What the hell are you talking about, Paddy? I don't even drink."

"You were drinking fifteen years ago. The night you ran a red light and killed my parents. Injured me." Patrick stared at the older man, his gaze unwavering.

"That's bullshit. They caught the guy who did that." A bead of sweat rolled down Kopecki's temple. "Sent him to prison. That's over."

"I guess you don't remember that Peter Shaughnessy made you write out a statement before he agreed to take the rap for you." Patrick laid a piece of paper on the desk in front of Kopecki. It was a copy of the paper they'd found in the safe-deposit box. "The writing matches yours, and your fingerprints are on it."

The older man's gaze skittered from the paper to Patrick to Nathan and back to the paper. Then he seemed to shrink into his chair, collapsing like a sand castle swallowed by a wave.

Nathan leaned forward, the taste of the betrayal bitter in his mouth. "You were a friend of ours. Your son is Paddy's friend. You came into our restaurant. Ate with us. How could you do this?"

"It was an accident." Kopecki's Adam's apple bobbed. "I was scared, and I acted impulsively. But I tried to make it right. I watched out for you all these years. Where do you think you got the money for that work you did on the restaurant?"

"So that *was* you," Nathan murmured. "Were you the one behind the expedited building permits? The bribes to the inspectors?"

"I took care of all of it. I tried to help you out when I could." He smiled, but it was more of a grimace. "You were just a kid. You were in over your head, so I did what I could. Protected you."

"Why did you go through O'Fallon with the money? Why not give it to me yourself?"

"I figured you wouldn't take it. Or if you did, it would make things awkward when I came into Mama's. I didn't want to embarrass you."

"So you let O'Fallon's thug do your dirty work."

"I had nothing to do with that. I just wanted to get you the money." He leaned toward Nathan. "Didn't you ever do something you shouldn't? Make a bad decision?"

"Yeah," Nathan said slowly. The realization hit him, his similarities to Mitch Kopecki. And his differences. "I've made a bunch of bad decisions. Taking that money for the renovation was just one of them." His head spun as he stared at Kopecki. "But the stuff you did was to protect yourself. To keep your job. To keep your reputation."

"It's so long ago, Nathan. Patrick. Can't you forgive me for what I did?" Kopecki's face was gray, his eyes haunted.

"Not now." Nathan leaned forward. "I can understand being scared after the accident. Running away and bribing someone else to take the blame. I know how people can make a bad decision on the spur of the moment. And I can see you thought you were doing something good when you helped me out with the restaurant. But you came after my kid. You threatened my daughter. Terrified her." Nathan would never forgive Mitch for what he'd done to his daughter. "Who put the note in Harley's backpack?"

"Chet Dempster. A math teacher at the school. I've done him a few favors, and he owed me one. I only wanted you to stay away from Shaughnessy, but you wouldn't stop. You kept digging. I wouldn't have hurt the kid."

"She didn't know that. And neither did I."

Nathan stared at Mitch Kopecki. Nathan had considered him a friend. He'd *liked* Mitch. But the man had built his life on a lie, and it was all dissolving in front of him.

Nathan slumped in his own chair. Looking at Mitch was almost like looking in a mirror. Nathan had made bad decisions, too. He'd acted without thinking. Accepting the money from O'Fallon had been the latest example.

Nathan took a deep breath. Mitch looked years older than he had fifteen minutes ago. All the bad decisions the older man had made were rolling over him and tearing his family apart.

How was Nathan any different?

CHAPTER TWENTY-SEVEN

EMMA WANDERED AROUND her empty apartment. It was the first time she'd been alone here since Harley came to live with her. There were a million things she could do—take a long bath, read, catch up on the television shows she'd missed.

Instead, she wondered if Harley was having a good time with Nathan and Marco at Mama's. Wondered what Harley and Marco were cooking. Wondered why Nathan had wanted to take Harley to Mama's. Without her.

Did he simply want to spend time with his daughter? Or was he going to tell Harley he was leaving?

He wouldn't do that without discussing it with Emma first. Would he?

She had no idea. The man she'd thought she'd known had turned into a stranger after his brother had arrested Kopecki almost a week ago. She'd seen him once, the evening he'd come to their apartment to tell them Kopecki had made a full confession, that he was in jail and Harley was no longer in danger. Holding his daughter tightly, soothing her tears, he'd added that Chet Dempster, Harley's former math teacher and apparently a friend of Kopecki's, had put the note in her backpack, and he wouldn't be back at her school.

Then he'd kissed Emma, murmured that he had a million things to take care of at the restaurant, but that he'd be in touch.

Emma was happy that Nathan's questions had been answered, happy his burden had been lifted. But she'd ached for the way he blamed himself for not seeing the truth earlier. For his doubts about his judgment.

She hadn't seen him since. She'd begged him to come over. She wanted to comfort him. But he'd had to concentrate on business, he'd told her.

He called her every night. Talked to Harley, made her smile. Laugh. But when Harley passed the phone to Emma, there was no laughter in Nathan's voice. He sounded sad. Tired. Worn down.

And he didn't want to see them.

Finally Emma had taken Harley to Mama's for dinner a few nights ago. She was pretty sure Nathan had been glad to see them—he'd hugged Harley, kissed Emma's cheek, but he'd been busy. He'd stopped by their table once, but hadn't lingered.

She threw herself on the couch, turned on the television. But after scrolling through the channels, she switched it off again. She was in no mood for *The Bachelor*. Or a fluffy romantic comedy. Or an angsty drama.

She wasn't in the mood for anything. She'd thought she'd been so smart to be cautious with Nathan, to guard her heart against his leaving. But his absence this week had been an unbearable taste of what it would be like when he left. If it was bad now, it would be hell when he actually walked away.

When her buzzer rang, she didn't even bother to get off the couch. She wasn't expecting anyone. When it rang again, longer this time, she dragged herself to her feet and pressed the intercom. "Yes?"

"Emma, it's Nathan. Can I come up?"

Her fingers trembled as she pushed the button to unlock the vestibule door. She opened her own door and listened to his footsteps on the stairs. He wasn't using his cane—she'd gotten used to the thump of it as he walked.

When he reached her floor, she threw herself at him, forgetting that she'd been hurt by his distance. He was here now, and somehow that made things better. "Nathan." Her arms tightened around him, and she pressed her mouth to his. "I've missed you."

His arms engulfed her as he kissed her back. "I've missed you, too," he murmured into her mouth.

She let herself cling to him for a moment, then eased away. "Where's Harley?"

"With Marco." He brushed his mouth over hers again. "Working their magic together. I wanted to see you, and I figured she wouldn't miss me."

"I'm sure she will, *Dad*."

His eyes lit up and he smiled. "Not when she's cooking."

She drew him into her apartment and closed the door. "Want a beer?"

"No." He drew her close. "I just want you, Emma."

Closing her eyes, she rested her forehead against his. This was what she'd missed this week. Nathan's arms around her. His mouth on hers. Inhaling his scent, feeling his muscles against her. "Me, too," she murmured. "I want you, too, Nathan."

"Then you'll love my idea."

He stood back, grinning. "I've been thinking about my trip all week. I've wanted this trip for so long, and although I have a lot of work to do while I'm in Italy, I can't bear to leave you and Harley behind. And I realized the solution is simple."

Was he going to stay home? She grabbed his hands, twined their fingers. "Tell me."

"I want you and Harley to come with me. I bought two more tickets, so we can discover Italy together. All three of us."

Her heart soared. He was as serious about them as she was. They were solid. Together.

"That sounds wonderful, Nathan." She rose on her toes and kissed him. "Harley will be out of school in three months. The timing will be perfect."

He eased away from her, puzzled. "I wasn't talking about three months from now, Emma. We're leaving next week."

"Next week? You want us to go with you in a week?" She swallowed, but held his gaze. "Why so soon?"

"Why not?"

"Is there a reason we have to leave so quickly?" *Tell me you love me. That this isn't just an impulse. That this is forever.*

"I have a bunch of appointments with potential suppliers. Marco and I have talked about this, about using authentic Italian pastas, about buying our cheese in Italy, our canned tomatoes. Our sausage. It took me months to set it all up. I could cancel them, I suppose, but why would I do that? The problems at the restaurant are behind me. Kopecki's in jail. We have another manager who can take over. I've planned this for a long time."

"Harley...Harley has school. I have to work. Summer would be better." She stared at him, hoping he could see what she needed. That she needed to know this wasn't another impulse for him. That he had a reason for wanting them with him.

"School? Work?" He frowned. "This will be the best education possible. We'll be gone three weeks, but we can get Harley a tutor when we get back, to help her catch up. And you get vacation time, don't you?"

"Yeah, but...but I can't just announce I'm leaving. There are forms to fill out. Paperwork. Someone has to take over my cases."

"Those are just details, Emma. Small details."

"*Important* details." She couldn't leap again. She needed to know why he wanted her to go with him. *Tell me you love me. That you can't live without me.*

"Emma, you're being unreasonable." He stepped away from her, shoved his hands through his hair. "These are excuses. I thought you cared about me. That you'd want to go with me. Was I wrong?"

"I do care about you, Nathan. But I can't just...just turn my whole life upside down on a moment's notice." Nathan was her mom all over again—jumping in without looking. Doing things without thinking of the consequences.

And she was protecting herself, just as she'd always done with her mother.

"It's only three months," she said, and she heard the desperation in her voice. "Why can't you wait?"

"Because it doesn't make any sense to wait. When I first planned this trip, I needed to get away. Figure out what I wanted to do. Now I know what I want, but I have all these potential suppliers to meet. But I don't want to leave you and Harley behind. I want you with me, Emma. Both of you."

"You can't make arrangements with these suppliers from here?"

He shook his head slowly. "Face-to-face. That's how they do business. I have to go." He closed his eyes and took a deep breath. "The rest of it is personal. My mother's family came from there. They opened Mama's Place. It all started with Italy and the restaurant and their accident. I…I need to go to the source. Figure out how not to screw up again."

Her heart contracted into a hard lump of pain. "If you can't wait, you'll have to go without us."

He turned to face her. "Is it really that black-and-white, Emma? Can't we figure out a way to make this work?"

"How? Even if I could get the time off, Harley can't miss three weeks of school." She was digging in her heels. Being unreasonable. She knew it, and she couldn't stop herself. She blinked, trying to clear her vision. "How long are you going to be gone?"

"My ticket's open-ended."

"So it could be more than three weeks. You expect us to drop everything and run away with you?" Her voice thickened. She clenched her teeth to keep the tears from falling.

"I have to go, Emma. I want you with me. You and Harley." His low voice was anguished. "I learned a lot about myself in the past year, and I don't like much of what I learned. I have to figure out who I really am."

"If you leave now, you'll be abandoning Harley." Just as

Emma had been abandoned by her father. And her mother, as well. "How can you do that to her?" Emma welcomed the anger that was stirring. It was better than this jagged pain in her chest.

He clenched his jaw and his eyes darkened. "I'm not abandoning her. And if you won't come with me, I'll make sure she understands that."

"Why can't you stay, Nathan?" she whispered. "Figure stuff out here. With me. And Harley. I don't want you to go." The pain was so sharp that she looked down, expecting to see blood on her chest.

"Why can't you both come with me?" he retorted.

Once before, she'd leaped before she looked with Nathan, and she'd fallen off the cliff and into love with him. She wasn't sure she could do it again. "I can't," she said, tears clogging her throat, blurring her vision. "I can't run away with you."

"Emma, sometimes you have to take chances. Sometimes, you just have to jump."

"The way you've always done? You just said you didn't like the way that turned out."

His face tightened. "It's not the same thing."

"It's exactly the same."

"You're scared, Emma. But sometimes you have to take chances. Sometimes you just have to let go."

But the last time she'd tried that, Nathan hadn't caught her. "I can't. I'm sorry."

"Damn it, Emma! I…I care about you. I want you with me."

"I want to be with you, too. But I can't run away."

A muscle in his jaw twitched. "You could come if you wanted to. I'm going to miss you, Emma. But I'm going. With you or without you."

He waited. When she didn't move, he yanked the door open. "Goodbye, Emma."

"I hope you find what you're looking for," she said, but the door closed behind him.

TWO HOURS LATER Emma heard Harley's boots clomping up the stairs. She took one last look in the mirror to make sure she'd erased all signs of tears, then opened the door and forced a smile onto her face. Harley's hair bounced as she flew up the stairs, and when she reached the door, she threw her arms around Emma.

"Emma! Did you know? Dad's going to Italy. Isn't that amazing?"

"Yes, I knew," Emma said carefully. "You're okay with him going away?"

"He won't be there long." Harley's tone was confident. "He told me he's meeting with a bunch of people about stuff for the restaurant. And that he needs to get his head on straight after all the sh...stuff that happened. He said maybe we'd go back in the summer. Wouldn't that be *awesome?* Did you know my grandmother was born there?"

"I did know that," Emma murmured. Nathan hadn't told his daughter that Emma had refused to go with him. He hadn't put Emma in the middle.

Nathan was a good man. Why did he have to go to Italy to figure that out? Why didn't he just ask *her?*

Tears clogging her throat again, she closed the door behind Harley. "So, tell me what you did at Mama's tonight."

A WEEK LATER, the day after Nathan had left for Italy, Emma sat at her desk at work, unable to concentrate on the files in front of her. She missed him with an all-consuming ache. He'd been gone for less than twenty-four hours, and she couldn't bear it.

Her mother had flitted from one relationship to the next when Emma was growing up. Periwinkle had never seemed to miss the men she left behind, or the ones who'd left her behind. She'd always just said it wasn't meant to be.

How had her mother managed to keep her heart intact all those times?

Emma thumbed through her cell phone contact list. Her

finger hovered over the listing for Mom, and it took her a long time to press it. Three rings later, her mother answered.

"Emma! How are you?"

"I'm good, Mom. How's it going out in California?"

"Oh, well, things have been better. But I'll survive." Emma heard the slight catch in her voice. "I always do."

"What's wrong?"

"The man I told you about?" Periwinkle tried to sound airy, but she just sounded sad. "The one who owns the organic farm? Jason? We've broken up. He's a little too stodgy for me. Too set in his ways. You know me. I'm a…a butterfly."

"Yeah, Mom, I know." She tightened her hand around the phone. "I know." Emma swallowed. "It sounded as if you were good together. Do you miss him?"

A long pause. "Some." Periwinkle cleared her throat. "But it wasn't meant to be."

Oh, Mom. "Didn't you ever fall in love with one of the guys you dated? Miss them when they left?"

"Once," Periwinkle said softly. "Your father. But he wasn't ready to settle down. I tried to force him to. So he ran away."

And her mother had avoided love ever since.

"You never told me that," Emma said quietly.

"What was the point? It was over a long time ago." Periwinkle's moment of introspection was over. She wrapped her butterfly persona around herself again. "Enough of this depressing stuff. How's my granddaughter?"

"She's really good." Emma swallowed. "A great kid."

"I'll have to come to Chicago to meet her."

"I'd like that, Mom." Emma wasn't going to hold her breath. Her mom would get distracted by something and be off on another adventure. She'd forget about Harley. Forget about Emma.

Periwinkle Sloan had always been that way. Maybe that's why Emma was so organized. So steady.

So stuck in the mud.

She chatted with her mother for a while longer, before saying goodbye. Emma's mother had always lived her life in the mo ment. She never looked before she leaped. In reaction, Emma had made herself the complete opposite. Unwilling to take chances.

Afraid to take chances.

She froze. Stared out the window for a long time, then slipped the phone into her pocket and started to pace her office. Was she really afraid to take chances? Was she clinging to her routine to keep from ending up like her mother?

Maybe she needed to take a few chances. Maybe she needed to do some things completely out of character.

CHAPTER TWENTY-EIGHT

HOPE YOU find what you're looking for.

Sitting at an outside table in a small café in Bornato, enjoying his *aperitivo,* Nathan ate a lemon-marinated anchovy and washed it down with a sip of chianti.

He swirled the wine, watched the red liquid gleam in the sun. He'd been here for three days and hadn't figured anything out.

The heat of the sun had baked his skin, burned into the muscles of his left leg. Soothed them. Eased the tightness.

He'd met with two potential suppliers, and arranged to try a brand of pasta and another of canned tomatoes. But it didn't feel as good as he'd thought it would.

The suppliers were shipping their products to Mama's. He should be happy he'd made progress.

But the hollowness hadn't disappeared. He'd been so determined to come here, so certain he'd find some answers. Magically discover who he was. Instead, he was the same confused man he'd been when he arrived.

He was staying in the town where his grandparents had been born. It was a beautiful town, surrounded by vineyards and full of friendly, welcoming people. But all he could think about was the reaction he knew Emma would have had if they'd walked into Bornato's town square, seen it washed in golden sunlight that turned the ancient stone buildings a soft rose. How she would have loved being here.

He missed her. He missed Harley.

With an intensity that all the sunlight and Chianti in Ital
couldn't soothe.

Emma had been right. He didn't need to travel thousands c
miles to figure out who he was and what he wanted. He coul
have conducted his business with suppliers online. He wante
Emma. And Harley. So why, exactly, had he come here?

He'd needed time and space to think. To figure out wha
he wanted his life to be. But all he'd been able to think abou
was Emma. The scent of her skin, the silk of her hair, the wa
she'd wrapped her arms around him as though she would neve
let go. The soft murmur of her voice in his ear, telling him sh
wanted him to stay with her.

And Harley. His daughter, who looked so much like he
Irish great-grandmother with her red hair and her Devereu
eyes. Who'd called him when she was scared. Who had emaile
every day so far, telling him what she was doing. Which friend
she'd sat with at lunch. What had happened at FreeZone tha
day.

Nathan set his wineglass carefully on the café table. Wh
had he come all the way to Italy to figure out who he was? H
already knew.

He was the man who'd just discovered he had an amazin
daughter. Who'd fallen in love with her faster and harder tha
he'd thought possible.

The man who'd fallen in love with Emma, as well. Th
man who wanted Emma in his life, every day and every nigh

He'd been so afraid that he was just like Mitch Kopecki—
impulsive. Reckless. Making bad decisions and worse choices

But he was very different from Mitch, and it had take
coming all the way over here, away from the people he loved
to make him see it.

Yeah, he'd done some stupid things, but he'd done then
out of love. He'd been trying to take care of his family. Pro
tect them. None of his decisions had been to protect himself

Maybe Emma and Harley would be safe with him after al

HARLEY LEANED AGAINST the counter in the lobby of the hotel in the small Italian town of Bornato, weariness tugging at her. She hadn't slept much on the plane last night—she'd been too excited about coming to Italy. Now they were here in this cool Italian town, where her dad was supposed to be, and she could barely stay awake. How lame was that?

Emma wrapped one arm around Harley's shoulder as she handed the clerk her credit card. As the man made a copy, Harley said, "Are you sure this is where Dad is?"

"Positive, Harley." Emma's arm tightened, then she dropped a kiss on Harley's head and let her go. "I've already asked Alessandro. Your dad is here."

Harley heard footsteps on the stairs, then a voice called, "Ciao, Alessandro."

"Dad?"

"Nathan?"

She and Emma spoke at the same time, and they both hurried toward the staircase. Nathan stood on the bottom step, looking stunned.

"Emma? Harley? What are you doing here?"

Emma threw herself at him. "Looking for you," she said.

Harley's dad gave Emma a huge hug, then he kissed her. And it looked like there was tongue. "Ewww. Gross, guys." It was actually kind of cool. Although she'd never admit that.

Her dad lifted his head, grinned and reached for Harley. Crushed her to his side. "Better get used to it, kid. You're gonna be seeing a lot more of that."

Emma was staring at her dad as if he was a rock star or something.

Wow. Her dad and Emma. That was…awesome.

Harley bent her head so her hair covered her face and smiled. She'd seen her dad look at Emma. Seen Emma look at her dad. Their hands touched all the time. At the soccer game, they'd looked as if they were glued together on the bleachers.

And the evening after the ski trip? When she'd walked into the living room? They'd jumped apart like she'd caught them doing something dirty.

Maybe she had.

"So. What's going on?" she asked.

"I was just heading out for some breakfast," Nathan said with a straight face. "You hungry?"

"Daaad."

He smiled, keeping his arm around Emma, and took Harley's hand. "Need to talk to Emma. You, too. But first, tell me how this happened. How did you get here?"

"Duh, Dad." She rolled her eyes. "We walked." He was such a dork. Just like Emma. "Emma took me out of school! Can you believe that? She said it was more important to be here with you. This is the sickest thing *ever*."

"Yeah," he said, staring at Emma. Who was blushing. "The best surprise I've ever had. You must have heard me wishing last night."

"Wishing what?" Harley asked.

"That you were both here with me."

Harley was bouncing on her toes. It wasn't cool, but no one here knew her. "And we came! That's so awesome!"

"More than awesome." Nathan looked from Harley to Emma. "A miracle."

"That's what Emma said! She said it was a miracle she found seats on a plane."

"You were right," Emma said. "Being here with you is so much more important than going to school or working. I was a fool for not realizing that."

Emma stared at her dad as if nothing but him existed. And her dad was staring back. The lump that had lived in Harley's chest for a long time slowly started to dissolve. Maybe this was going to be okay, after all. Maybe she wouldn't have to choose between Emma and her dad.

But she was going to have to do something about it. They were standing there like the complete dweebs they were, not saying anything. "Can I, uh, take a nap or something? I'm, like, really tired."

Emma jerked her gaze away from Nathan. "Of course, honey." She glanced at Dad. "I don't think she slept at all on the plane."

"Then let's get your bags upstairs." He reached for her bag, but Harley snatched it away from him. No way was he carrying her bag. He was still limping.

She climbed the stairs, surprised to realize that she was legitimately tired. When she got to the top, she looked down to see her dad and Emma halfway up the stairs. Emma had her arm wrapped around Dad, and his was wrapped around her. "You are so gross," Harley said. "You better not do this stuff at home." But inside, she was smiling.

Her dad looked up and grinned. "Never letting her go. You, either."

"What? You're going to college with me?"

"Maybe."

She rolled her eyes because, jeez, what if he said stuff like that in public? But inside, she got all mushy.

When they found their room, Emma unlocked the door and waited for Harley to go inside. There were two twin beds, a tall closetlike thing and a dresser and desk. Sunlight poured through the window.

Harley sank onto one of the beds, her eyelids heavy. She lay down and curled on her side, and Emma bent and kissed her head. "How about a short nap, then we'll get something to eat?" she said.

"Uh-huh." Harley smiled to herself. Maybe her dad and Emma could have that talk now.

"We'll be back soon, honey."

The door clicked shut behind them, and Harley finally let her eyes close. She liked the sound of that. *We.*

EMMA WAS A disorienting combination of exhausted and wired. She stood in the narrow hallway, staring at Nathan, suddenly uncertain. She'd been sure this was the right thing to do, and Nathan seemed happy to see them, but she was too tired to think logically. Had he really wanted them here? He'd chosen to come to Italy instead of staying with her and Harley. Maybe he'd decided he needed time away from them.

Then he drew her into his arms. "My room," he whispered into her ear. He held her tightly to his side as they walked two doors down the hall. As soon as they were inside, he backed her against the door and claimed her mouth.

His kiss was hungry, almost desperate. "Emma," he groaned when he took a breath. "God, Emma, I missed you so much. I was stupid to leave you and Harley."

No," she said fiercely. "You needed this trip. You kept your family together after your parents died. You gave up every-thing to run the restaurant and raise them. I was selfish to try and keep you from leaving. Stupid not to grab the chance to go with you. Selfish, stupid and scared."

"Why were you scared, Emma?" he murmured against her throat.

"Because I was afraid to take a chance. Afraid to trust you. Afraid you'd let me fall if I leaped." She laid her cheek against his. "I don't take chances. I plan everything. I need to be in control."

"And now?"

She kissed his throat, nibbled his earlobe, began to unbut-ton his shirt. "You make me lose control."

He took her hands away from his chest, held them between their bodies as he nuzzled her neck, pressed a kiss to the sen-sitive skin beneath her ear. "Everything here was gray with-out you. Everything I saw, every place I went, all I could think about was how much you'd like it. How much Harley would enjoy being here."

"I missed you, too, Nathan." She kissed his cheek, the corer of his mouth. "You'd been gone less than a day and I realized I'd made a mistake. We needed to be here. With you. For you." She pressed her lips against his. "You're more important han school or my job."

"You're more important than a stupid trip I planned before I even met you."

"It's not stupid," she said, her hands bracketing his face. 'Not coming with you was stupid. Being afraid was stupid." She closed her eyes and kissed him again. "Nothing was right until I turned around downstairs and saw you."

He smoothed a hand along her neck, down her arm, touching her as if he still couldn't believe she was in front of him. 'God, I missed you, Emma. I tried to book a flight home, but they told me they didn't have anything for five days. I didn't care about anything except having my family with me."

The last of Emma's fears fell away. "I'm not your family."

"I want you to be. I love you, Emma." He brushed her hair to the side and kissed her. "These days without you were horrible. Italy is wonderful, but I couldn't enjoy it. I just wanted you."

He kissed her again, her mouth, her nose, her eyes, her neck. "Marry me, Emma. Please. *Be* my family. Make a family with me. I love you."

Her heart grew and grew until she was afraid it would explode out of her chest. "I love you, too, Nathan." She slid her mouth along his, pressed closer when he shuddered against her. "I missed you so much and I love you and of course I'll marry you."

His mouth covered hers before she could say any more, and he backed her toward the bed. "We have an hour," he whispered against her lips. "Not nearly enough time to show you how much I love you. But I'll do the best I can until we wake our daughter up and discover Italy together.

"Before we tell her we're going to be a family forever."

EPILOGUE

NATHAN STOOD IN the kitchen at Mama's Place, his arm draped over Emma's shoulder, and watched Marco and Harley making pizza sauce. Frankie and Cal, Darcy and Patrick stood next to them. Harley had a Coke, everyone else had glasses of red wine and they were all talking and gesturing at once.

It was loud. Boisterous. And the most fun he'd had since... he tugged Emma closer. Since last night.

They'd returned from Italy two weeks ago, but he hadn't really felt as if he was home until he'd walked into Mama's. The scent of garlic, baking pizza crust and pungent cheese, the sound of raised voices yelling in Spanish and English, the scarred table in the corner of the dining room—this was home. It always would be.

Nathan was going back to school part-time to finish his degree. After that? He wasn't sure. But he'd never leave Mama's completely. It was in his blood.

Tonight was the big pizza sauce contest, and Harley had talked about nothing else for the past several days. Before the contest started, Marco had given Harley a chef's toque and a white jacket with her name embroidered on it. Harley had stared at her uncle, swallowing hard, for a long moment. Then, her eyes glittering, she'd thrown herself into his arms.

Emma's mouth had quivered as she watched, and Nathan had a hard time swallowing. Then Marco stepped away with a huge grin. He smirked at Patrick and Cal. "Guess we all know who the favorite uncle is."

Now, as Marco and Harley worked, Nathan sipped his wine

and looked at his siblings. Fifteen years ago, he'd thought his family had been destroyed. But they were all here, stronger than ever. Happy. In love. His parents would be proud of the way their kids had grown up.

Harley lifted her pot of sauce and carried it to the pizza counter. "One ladle, Pedro," she told their pizza maker. "Not all the way to the edge," she added. She leaned over the counter to examine the crust Pedro had already prepared. "That looks good. Sauce it!"

Nathan bit his lip as he watched her. The expression on her face was so familiar. His mom had looked exactly like that when she was preparing a dish. Finally satisfied with the pizza, Harley backed away. Grinned at Marco. "You're roadkill, chef-boy."

"Yeah?" Marco set his own pot of sauce on the counter, and Pedro took it with a grin. "We'll see. You're gonna eat your words."

"Ha. The only thing I'll be eating is a pizza. My pizza. The winning one."

Nathan tried and failed to hide his grin. And twenty minutes later, after everyone sampled both pizzas and voted, they waited for Francisco to tally up the votes.

He and Emma would vote for Harley. He was pretty sure Patrick and Darcy would vote for Marco. Frankie had told him that she and Cal had fought about it, and neither of them would budge—she was voting for Harley. Cal had Marco. Harley and Marco would vote for themselves.

It was going to be a tie, but that was okay. It would give Harley and Marco something to bicker about. Because that seemed to be their favorite way of communicating.

Francisco looked up from the scraps of paper ballots and grinned. "Harley won!"

"Harley won?" Emma looked around and frowned, and Nathan knew she'd counted up the votes in her head, too. Someone had changed the script.

He saw Marco watching Harley, a tiny smile on his face. And he knew.

Taking Emma's hand, he drew his brother to the side. As Harley high-fived the rest of the family, Nathan said, "You voted for Harley, didn't you?" in a voice too quiet to be heard by his siblings.

"Yeah." Marco watched Harley, who was explaining her recipe to her aunts and uncles. She was practically dancing with excitement, and she left tomato-sauce-stained fingerprints on her toque as she grabbed it to keep it from slipping off her head.

Marco smiled at Nathan and Emma. "Need to motivate the next great Devereux chef." His eyes softened as he watched his niece. "She's as good as Mom was. She'll be better than me, eventually."

As Nathan watched his daughter, he could have sworn he felt two pairs of hands settle on his shoulders. He was tempted to look behind him, but he knew no one was there.

He felt their presence, though. His parents were watching. In his head, Nathan could see the smiles on their faces.

Mom and Dad would always be with them. They'd always be part of the family. Here at Mama's Place.

* * * * *